BLACK SEQUINNED BOWS AND CHAMPAGNE NIGHTS

Jude E. McNamara

**Black Sequinned Bows
And Champagne Nights**

Author Contact
Website: www.judeemcnamara.com
Email: jude@judeemcnamara.com
Facebook: Jude E. McNamara
Twitter: @judeemcnamara
Instagram: iamtwojudes

Two Judes Publishing
668 Stony Hill Road Suite 339
Yardley, Pennsylvania, 19067

TABLE OF CONTENTS

ACKNOWLEDGEMENTS

I am beyond grateful to everyone who was part of the process of creating *Black Sequinned Bows And Champagne Nights.* Thank you to:

My loyal and diligent beta readers: Nicole Arnold, Jeanine Hillesland, Donna Harden Nelson, Erica McCarty; all of who read multiple versions of the story, providing me helpful feedback until I felt it was right.

A.D. Cooper at ADCooperBooks for designing the beautiful cover capturing the essence of my vision for Black Sequinned Bows and Champagne Nights.

My editor: Michelle Phinney-Smith for all her work, without which there would be rambling and other grammatical offenses.

Donna Sebastian: the inspiration for the name Two Judes Publishing.

Britter, whose "bright green smiley-faced" note that's been on my door four years now and reads "Keep Writing," reminds me not to quit and to keep doing what I'm doing.

Candy Cane for helping me sort through tons of imagery for all things graphic. Your talents are never lost on me. I see you.

Tymoney, Diva, and Tootsie Pop: You're the best fan club ever.

A special thanks to Lani Diane Rich and Alastair Stephens at StoryWonk.com You guys are my first and my last word on all things story.

To my readers: To all those who purchased my novel and those who have shared my stories on your book blogs and with your book clubs, thank you for your unfailing love and support. You rock, and I am eternally grateful.

And last, but not least: To my mother for your undying love, motivation, and support throughout my entire writing life. To my father who is with me always in spirit.

DEDICATION

In memory of my sister, who taught me early on how to recognize an asshole heartbreaker. Thank you. It took me a minute, but I finally did learn the art of how to spot them a mile away and to gracefully get out the way. For broken hearts set you free. And to all the asshole heartbreakers—your loss.

Riley Cook has been busy building her empire while barely escaping a marriage to a lying, cheating, womanizing man that has broken both her heart and spirit. Having endured the death of her husband, heartbreak, and loss, Riley has lost all hope of finding love and believing "Mr. Right" exists. Only the "idea of him" lingers in the recesses of her heart and mind.

Captain Noah Dunham is a man on a mission. He's the keeper of promises and the holder of secrets. So what's Riley to do when this certain sexy Navy Captain steps into her life? She certainly hadn't counted on falling in love. But, just when things heat up between Riley and Noah, tragedy strikes and a secret is revealed. Can Riley and Noah's new found love survive the discovery?

CHAPTER 1

RILEY

"I told you I don't mix business with pleasure."

"C'mon, Riley. It's time to get out from under your rock and find a date to escort you to the Memorial Gala."

Damn. Madison's persistence was getting on my last freaking nerve. The mere mention of my taking a date to the Memorial Gala was causing me to get dizzy. I could feel the sweat building on my palms as I right clicked my mouse, surfing the net for images for my new food and wine book.

"I'm not under a rock, Madison. Don't forget, my company is doing the event planning for this gala. I have no intentions of turning my most significant business event of the year into 'date night'."

"All you think about is business. I'm starting to worry about you."

"Madison, if this gala goes well, I'll be able to springboard my business to new heights. I can leverage this event by pitching my five-year growth plans to some angel investors. This will catapult my business to the next level."

"That's what you always say, Riley."

"I say that because it's going to be a very important night. One in which I need to be focused. Business is the only hat I plan to wear."

"Well there's no reason you can't focus on business and a man too."

Madison's mind was in overdrive. The fact that she was browsing intently through my choices of graphic covers didn't mean she was giving up on this subject. I had no doubts she was not backing down on this business of my dating.

"Riley, you of all people know how to multi-task."

Yep I called that one right. Madison was pulling out her big guns. A look of determination flashed on her face. It was hard to argue against a crazy person settled on her ideas. Madison wasn't going to let this discussion go without a win. She was on a roll. She was going for the gold medal this time.

"Attending the Memorial Gala without a plus one doesn't bother me one bit. It will be hard enough sitting through the reading of the names of the 'Fallen.' Lucas is posthumously receiving the Navy Cross Medal commendation for heroism and meritorious service. The night will be difficult enough as it is," I sighed.

"You can do this, Riley. I have complete confidence in you. Having a date will make it all that much easier."

"Have you gone loony tunes? Easier how?"

"Umm. Emotional support for one. Eye candy to stare at for two," she said, trying to appear thoughtful, but failing. She was holding back a laugh, big time.

"Madison, I've spent the first half of my life as Lucas's wife, never having to deal with this business of having to date. Dating feels like taking on some new challenge that I don't have a lot of experience in, frankly. It means work."

"It's not meant to be work, Riley."

"So you say," I grunted.

"Dating is intended to be fun. You haven't had fun in so long you've forgotten what it's like to have a man fawn over you. A little male attention can be a good ego booster, girlfriend."

"Easy for you to say, Ms. I always have a man."

"Riley, you've gotten way too serious these last few years."

"Since Lucas's death, I've managed to have a pretty funky track record in picking the right guys."

"Only because you haven't picked *the one,* Riley," Madison said, motioning her fingers in imaginary quotation marks. "You're too young to be alone sweetie."

"In case you've forgotten, we're middle age."

"I know how old we are, Riley. But that doesn't mean we both aren't beautiful, young at heart, young in spirit, and can still knock 'em dead. Woman, we could be trophy wives ten years from now," Madison laughed with a wink.

"Well I might be young, beautiful, and alone, but I'm not lonely," I blabbered.

"Says who?"

"Says me."

"Woman, you haven't been out with a man since the dark ages. Would you even recognize loneliness if it stared you in the face? Look at you. You're held up in your own private world like some suburban princess on lock down, dedicating your entire existence to these kids and work."

Madison waved her hands out in front of her, pointing wildly at my laptop, multiple computer screens, graphic images, and a desk full of paperwork. She pointed her index finger at my paper trail of work spread out across the floor leading to my chair. The room did look like a workaholic lived here. She was playing hardball now, determined to take complete advantage of my surroundings, using my work area as props to make her point.

"I've been busy building an empire, Madison."

"Doesn't mean you're not a full-fledged, bona-fide, certifiable, Type A workaholic. It's high time you played the get out of jail free card now honey. Have some fun for Christ sakes. It's been eleven years since Lucas's death, three years since you broke off your engagement with Warren."

"Oh please Madison, don't remind me."

"Life is too short, woman. You need to inject some testosterone into the mix. Stir things up," Madison said, tossing a couple of the graphic covers aside. "Besides, most of the time you lace up your track shoes and go running for the hills any time a man shows you the slightest bit of interest."

"That's because I attract the crazy guys," I said nonchalantly, stacking the graphic covers up neatly that Madison was tossing aside.

"It's because you're so lovable Riley, and everybody knows that crazy people need love too," she giggled. "They do seem to find you sweetie. But honey, you need to weed through that haystack in order to find that needle. It's like playing the lottery. You can't win if you don't play the game," Madison demanded.

Madison was right. She knew me better than anyone. We'd been best friends since seventh grade, roommates in college, and now lived on the same cul-de-sac two houses apart. When we were teenagers, we pricked our fingers, meshed the redness together, and promised to remain loyal to each other forever. There wasn't anything that we each didn't know about the other. Madison was my whenever, wherever, whatever friend.

"Madison, I've resigned myself to the fact that I may not ever find another life partner as wonderful as Lucas. Those days are

13

long gone. Frankly, if my broken engagement with Warren is any clue, I'm not so good at picking them now either. Besides, where is it written that I have to have a man?"

"Warren doesn't count. He came along when you were grieving the loss of Lucas. You were on the rebound. Who knew he was going to turn out to be dog shit," Madison snorted.

"Obviously I didn't."

"He was a rebound relationship. Everybody knows rebound relationships don't count."

"Yeah right," I said sarcastically, rolling my eyes up in my head.

"Every woman has had at least one rebound relationship in her lifetime where we fail to hit the 'eject the loser' button. We all get that one relationship that doesn't count," Madison said, smiling to make me feel better.

"Well it sure as hell counts to me. Sadly, it took me far too long to realize I was on a sinking ship."

I tried to re-focus my attention back on my Internet image search. My own emotional state of disgust was rising internally from thinking about my failed engagement with Warren Shaw. I was in too decent of a mood to want to be reminded of that disaster.

None of this talk was new to Madison. She was use to listening to my rants about my failed engagement. Nonetheless, she patiently allowed me to vent no matter what, when, or where. She thought my venting was a good stress reliever. The truth was, there wasn't a day that hadn't gone by that I hadn't given thanks to God that I did not marry Warren. The mere thought of him brought me to the brink of nausea.

"I know, girlfriend," Madison said with a look of contemplation.

"At the end of the day, I only have myself to blame for such a poor choice of a man," I sighed, exhaling heavily. "Eight years ago I was totally unaware that I didn't need to couple up with a man in order to feel good about myself. I never considered it might be okay to just do me and the kids," I said in deep reflection.

"You were a widow, alone and afraid with three kids. What woman could imagine herself that young as a widow? And with three kids to raise," Madison sighed. "It was to be expected that you'd lose your footing. If we knew better, we'd do better. You should give yourself a break sometime Riley."

"Looking back I realize Warren took advantage of my vulnerability. It almost cost me my business," I sighed deeply, trying to mask my own disgust with myself.

Madison raised her head, staring at me sympathetically.

"Look Riley, I know it's been hard all these years without Lucas. But you've healed from the pain, the loss of Lucas and that lower than dirt piece of shit Warren. With the exception of Claire, your children are grown. It's time to do you now babe."

"Have you finally lost your senses? In case you haven't noticed, that is exactly what I've been doing these past three years. I have been doing me."

"Well, fine then Riley. So now that you're done doing you, a bit of male attention in your life won't kill you," she nodded, arching her eyebrows up. "All work and no play makes you a dull gal," she smirked.

It was clear I wasn't going to win this battle. She wasn't going to let up on this business of my need to start dating. Madison worried that I might be single forever, as if that were a crime. Why the hell was it so important that I be attached to a man? Who the hell cares in the millennium? Not me.

"Well I'm pretty much over this whole business of coupledom. Okay, so, I could have done things differently these past several years. I could have played the field. But I've long since realized that if I were going to be successful in my business, I had to do that without a man at my side to muck it all up."

"There you go again Riley, preaching that nonsense. No woman is an island. You feel me?"

"Look here Madison, I don't believe that there will be another Lucas or a "Mr. Right for Riley" to come along and build a future with me," I said, positioning my fingers in air quotes. "I would have needed to have made different choices a hell of a long time ago."

"Would of, could of, should of," Madison pounced back. "The good news is, baby look at you now," she said excited, getting a bit hyper. "You are a New York Times best-selling author, Who's Who of Pennsylvania's Fast Company Entrepreneurs, and you rank number eight on Bucks County's Top 100 Most Creative Women in Business."

"So you're going to try to convince me to date by blowing my head up now?"

"Girl, you're a celebrity in your own right. Not to mention

that you're well known nationally for your passion, prestige, and philanthropy, last I read. Hell Riley, the way I see it, you got the last laugh, babe."

We both couldn't help but grin like two Cheshire cats that had swallowed the mouse. We looked at each other in amusement, laughing heartily, slapping each other a high five and bumping our hips together doing our own little happy dance.

I was hopeful that once we stopped giggling like two school girls, and regained our sense of calm, Madison would re-focus her attention back on my book layout, forget this whole business of my relationship status, and drop the subject of my need to take a plus one to the gala. I shoved my book layout back in her hands.

"I need you to tell me what you think of this new layout, Madison," I said, forcing a change in the subject.

Madison began turning the pages of the food and wine book layout slowly, analyzing each page with a discerning eye.

I quieted down so as to give her a moment to concentrate and focus. I re-directed my attention, glancing out the back bay window, watching as my oldest daughter Samantha came hurriedly through the back yard gate.

I kept my gaze on her as she walked around the covered pool, crossing the cedar deck, thumbs moving rapidly on her cell phone. Samantha pranced towards the back door of the house pausing only to pat our family Labrador retriever, "Stogie" on top of his head. "Cleo," our miniature white poodle belonging to my youngest daughter Claire, was barking up a storm. Cleo began running around in excitement, jumping up and down on Samantha hoping to be picked up and brought inside out of the cold. Predictably, Samantha scooped Cleo up in her arms, tucking her close to her side. Samantha moved towards the back door of the house, leaving Stogie whining and begging to get inside.

Wearing a North Face jacket and her black Swarovski-studded "Spoiled Rotten" baseball cap, Samantha's facial expression was one of irritation.

"Hey Mama Dukes what's up? Hey Godmother," she said directing her attention to Madison.

"Hey Sammi," we both acknowledged in unison.

"Mom, have you seen X? I've been blowing up his phone all day. He's ignoring me. He gets on my last nerve. I could yank every one of those dirty reddish blond dreads out his head one by one."

Samantha hated to be ignored despite the fact that she failed to accept that she herself was the "ignore your phone call queen."

"No dear, I haven't spoken to your brother today."

Xavier, known as "X" to close friends and family, was my twenty-five year old son. Samantha, born two years after Xavier, had trouble pronouncing the name Xavier as a little girl, so we nicknamed him X.

"I expect I'll hear from him later today. He promised to help me convert my "How To Guide for Easy Entertaining" into the E-Pub format today."

"E what?" Samantha responded, looking puzzled. "Never mind," she said, heading off to the kitchen, grabbing a chocolate chip cookie from the plate sitting on my desk.

Xavier's new found sense of independence was irritating Samantha. Samantha's rebellion toward Xavier's self-imposed role as father figure was trying on him. This was a hard concept for both Xavier and Samantha to grasp. Despite their pushback with each other, Xavier and Samantha were close. They were known to talk tough with each other, but they wouldn't under any circumstances let anyone else outside the family speak poorly about the other.

"I could dog walk X right about now," Samantha fumed, headed back our direction with a Greek yogurt in hand, cookie crumbs on her chin. "He's too busy to answer me yet he has time to swoon over those bimbo bobble-heads at the gym."

Like Samantha, I too was pretty convinced that Xavier was morphing into a big flirt these days. He was hard not to adore. He'd grown to be as tall as Lucas, towering over the girls like a professional basketball player, and often being mistaken for one. His muscular build was similar to his father's. But unlike his clean cut father, Xavier had grown a mustache, goatee, and sported a single diamond in his ear. He wore long kinky dreadlocks that drove Samantha bonkers. She disliked anything and everything that was close to giving the appearance of

Reggae.

"When I see him I'd be happy to let him know you're on the scout for him. Would you like for me to pass along a message or something?"

Irritation brewed on Samantha's face. I was glad Xavier was nowhere to be found right about now. Samantha had that look on her face that she gets when she's ready to make like a panther and pounce. She could readily go from pussycat to bitch in 3.5 seconds.

"He promised to front me some dinero's tonight," Samantha barked. "I don't get paid for my freelance work until tomorrow," she grumbled, rolling her eyes up in her head in frustration. "There's a poetry slam tonight in Philly. He promised to help me out with gas money."

"I'm sure he hasn't forgotten, sweetie," I said hoping to reassure her.

"It's so like him to make a commitment and then get lost. He was kicking it with that girl Nena at the gym when I spoke to him last. But these days all he can seem to focus on is boobs and booty."

None of this was a surprise. Xavier was popular, clever, charismatic, and like Lucas, totally irresistible. He was becoming more handsome every day. I suspected much of his new found attention was starting to go to his head.

"That Nena girl was eye fucking him non- stop while he flexed his bi-ceps in her face, showing off his tattoo," Samantha ranted on. "I knew I should have taken the money right then and there," Samantha said, her face scowling.

My heart warmed thinking about Xavier's tattoo. Xavier had a tattoo on his upper left arm with two naval swords crisscrossed with the words "Rock-in Wingman" emblazon across the middle. Lucas had the same tattoo. "Rock-in Wingman" was the nickname bestowed on Lucas by his classmates at the Naval Academy. When Xavier was growing up, Lucas use to say to Xavier, "X, You're my Rock-in Wingman," reinforcing with Xavier that he too would one day be a Navy pilot following in his father's footsteps. Unfortunately, Xavier had other plans for his life. Those plans didn't include military school or airplanes.

"Sammi, here's forty dollars for gas for your jeep," Madison interrupted. "Take it, and have a good time on Godmother," she said, kissing Samantha on the cheek.

I shook my head at Madison, giving her my best "you're spoiling her" look, but held my peace. I was fighting a losing battle with Madison when it came to the kids. While I wanted them to be self-sufficient, Madison didn't give a hoot, spoiling all three of them as if they were her own.

"Thanks Godmother. I appreciate it," Samantha said, giving her a big hug. "And Mom," she said, looking back over her shoulder, "The next time you see X, tell him I said to kick rocks!"

"What?" I questioned.

"Never mind. I'm going upstairs to find Claire to practice tonight's poetry on her," she said, tucking the money inside her bra.

"Riley, what does that mean exactly; kick rocks?" Madison said, lifting her head up and taking notice of a new stack of magazines lying near the new book layout.

"Girl, I don't know. The objective is to let all that gobbledy-gook go in one ear and out the other while giving the appearance that you know exactly what language they're speaking, which obviously isn't English."

"You think?" Madison asked.

"Just shake your head and pretend like you understand. Girl, they don't know that you don't know."

I grinned at Madison, watching as Samantha leaped up the steps of the spiral staircase by two's, and headed to Claire's room. Madison shrugged her shoulders. She went back to analyzing the book layout.

"Yeah, let Claire deal with that foreign language," Madison said.

"Honey, she speaks it too."

Claire was Lucas and my youngest child. She hardly knew him well, being only three at the time of his passing. Xavier and Samantha were fourteen and twelve at the time of their dad's death. My older children had a genuine closeness with Lucas that death had robbed from Claire.

Claire was Lucas and my mid-life baby. After Xavier and Samantha were born, Lucas knew I wanted to have another child. We were having trouble getting pregnant and our attempts to conceive were hindered by the fact that Lucas was going to be leaving on another tour of duty in the Persian Gulf. It took a while for Lucas to get on board with the idea, but I pleaded with him to freeze his sperm. Lucas didn't like the idea of my potentially having to raise three kids alone if he didn't make it back.

But after much persuasion, Lucas decided no matter what, if he were dead I was going to do what I wanted to do anyway, and that he wanted to give me the baby I wanted. He was beyond shocked when he came home from his tour of duty to find me seven months pregnant and waddling, having used his frozen sperm to impregnate myself as part of my welcome home gift to him. Claire was born two months later.

Lucas was beyond happy when Claire arrived. He would beam when we cuddled together while looking at Claire in her bassinet. Lucas often murmured that Claire was a very special baby. He use to whisper to Claire while rocking her in his arms, telling her that they were tied together by their love for me.

"Riley are you listening to me?" Madison shouted out while gesturing her hand in the air, snapping me out of my thoughts.

"Yes I'm listening to you Madison," I said with the most patient look I could muster. "I always listen to you."

Madison was shaking her head in frustration.

"You need a date for the memorial. And, if worse comes to worst, you can ask Reese to escort you," she grinned wickedly.

I felt the scowl forming on my face, watching as Madison set down the book layout. She began rifling nervously through a stack of European fashion magazines I had lying on the corner coffee table, not pausing on any particular page long.

"And if that doesn't appeal to you," she went on, "I'm sure Lily knows a ton of available men who'd be happy to accompany you to the gala. It would make the evening so much more fun if we all could hang out together again," Madison replied, faking a starry-eyed look.

Now I had to count to ten to keep from losing my temper. We were back to this again.

"Reese, Madison? Reese? Really?" I paused looking at her as if she had two heads. "Reese Nelson does not equal to a fun night," I insisted, trying to refrain myself from splitting a gut.

"Sure he does," Madison said.

"Reese, who would dare not let any man get within fifty feet too close to me?" I said sarcastically. "I love my younger brother dearly, but you know how he gets," I said with narrowed eyes.

"Yeah," Madison said casually. "I realize Reese has that

whole macho, overprotective "I'm gonna kill whatever man gets anywhere near my sister" vibe going on."

The expression on Madison's face momentarily changed to one of possible acceptance. Perhaps she was beginning to re-think her suggestion through a bit more. Otherwise, I was sure her temporary lapse in judgment was an indicator of how desperate things were getting for me on this matter of my taking a plus one to the gala. What was I missing here?

"C'mon Riley. After what Warren put you through, Reese is not going to sit back and watch any man mistreat you," she said, scrunching her brow. "But taking your own brother to the gala can't be all that earth shattering. You'll be free to be on the hunt as I see it."

"You know and I know that Reese has been overprotective all his life. Warren sent him into overdrive, Madison."

"Well I get that whole over-protective brother thing he's got going on," Madison said, flipping the magazine pages. "This is me you're talking to, sista'. I know how many black eyes he doled out in high school to your admirers. Now that we are grown, he feels he has to keep his eye on your best interests since Lucas is gone. Nothing's changed," she said, shaking her head. "Same story, different day."

"Yes, except now I'd have to deal with keeping his overprotective butt in check with a room full of deliciously overfed, uncontrolled drunken male testosterone on the loose. There's way too much opportunity for a male pissing match when Reese is around," I said, shaking my head and waving my hands up to the ceiling. "Tell me again Madison," I said, cupping my right hand to my ear, "how is that supposed to equate to my having a fun night at a Memorial Gala that I'm already on pins and needles about anyway?"

By now I had decided that this conversation was starting to get stressful, which meant it was time for me to bake some bread. Thank God bread making had a calming effect on me whenever I had to endure stressful conversations such as these.

My head was spinning as I searched for more food and wine images, passively listening to Madison's babbling about how it was time to for me to find a man. As far as I was concerned, any conversations about dating and men all lead back to me missing my beloved Lucas. Yep, it was definitely time for me to bake some bread.

I headed to the kitchen searching for the bread flour and my marble pastry board.

"Oh hell no, Riley," Madison said, heading into the kitchen, watching me flour the marble bread board and warming my baking stone. "I know you are not going to bake bread in the middle of the afternoon," she snapped. "Really Riley? You're kidding me right?"

"So what if I am," I said.

"This is not a stressful moment Riley," she insisted, sounding exasperated. "It's merely a conversation about a date with a freaking man! And, if all else fails, we both know for sure Reese would love to have an excuse to hop the train and spend time with you and the kids and be your plus one at the gala."

"Who wants to go to a gala with Reese?" I moaned.

"It's his type of event. Reese loves Washington's Crossing. And, we both have known since we were kids, that he considers himself the great protector of your well-being," Madison laughed.

"Which by the way, is why I don't need Reese around if a single man is to be found," I sighed. "A new man for Riley equates to family drama moments with Reese."

"Try not to be too hard on Reese. He wants what's best for you."

"I love my brother dearly. I would love to see him. But if he comes to Washington's Crossing and there's a man in play, you and I both know that I may get rid of him. He will be ordering the both of us around, telling us what to do."

"Ya think?" Madison said sarcastically.

"Reese loves being here playing boss. He loves the Big Apple right up until the point that he gets here, and then he falls in love all over again with the sereneness of Washington's Crossing and being around family," I protested. "Reese needs to stay in New York and tend to his financial forensics business locating everyone's money," I scowled.

My younger Brother Reese owned RJN Forensics, LLC., a New York firm specializing in forensic technology and investigative accounting worldwide.

After Lucas passed, he routinely shuttled back and forth between New York and Washington's Crossing in the name of keeping a watch over the kids and me.

"It's one night Riley."

"Reese can do a lot of damage in one night. Every time Reese comes to town, he puts in so many new patches, updates and additional layers of security into my business systems, I end up having to call him up just to access my own systems to run my own company," I sputtered.

"He loves you Riley. He only wants the best for you and your business after everything that happened with Warren."

"I know, but that doesn't mean that Reese can't be a real pain in the butt. I love my brother, but damn."

Reese loved Washington's Crossing as much as Lucas and I did. Our home was located along the Delaware Towpath Canal which was ideal for peaceful walks.

Our six bedroom brick Georgian style home was nestled on several acres on a cul-de-sac on River Road. Built around the turn of the last century our home was perfect for both living and entertaining. Almost every room had its own fireplace, and bay window. Each room was finished with beautiful molding, contemporary lighting and hard wood flooring. The bedrooms had their own gorgeous marble baths, skylights, and access to the screened-in porch that wrapped around the entire second floor, overlooking the garden, half court basketball, heated pool, and Jacuzzi.

Shortly before Lucas's death, we re-designed the entire kitchen in marble, granite, and cherry. We added top of the line Viking stainless appliances, turning it into our own vision of a gourmet eating area with seating for six. Together Lucas and I had built our dream home, but our dream life was not to last.

"Look Riley, I'm sure Reese only wants to protect you from heartache and heartbreak," Madison said. "His heart's in the right place. And don't forget, Riley Cook, you're a serious force to be reckoned with in the world."

"Yeah, Madison, but my life is different now. I've gone through major life changes and significant emotional events. Heartache and heartbreak has become the very thing I've needed to find my newfound purpose in life and peace in my heart. I've grown over the years as a woman," I smiled.

I could tell by the look on Madison's face that she wasn't the least bit moved by my words.

"I am not one of those women whose life needs to pivot around a man in order to feel complete," I said. "I like the fact that I live a content drama-free life. Besides, this business of engaging in a few meaningless flings has long since convinced me that singleness suits me."

"Since when, Riley?"

"If there is a Mr. Right out there for Riley, he only exists in my dreams. I have finally gotten my priorities in life straight. Namely my children, my business, and me. I'm happy that I have a wonderful circle of girlfriends that are the icing on my cake."

Sentimental as she was, Madison started to get a bit teary eyed, moving to hug me. Hell, I was getting teary-eyed eyed too listening to myself talk out loud. I needed to shut this conversation down before the flood of tears building behind my eyes start to gush.

I admitted to myself that there were days when I indeed thought I wanted a companion. I had my moments when I could imagine that it would be nice to share my joys and life with someone. Perhaps down the road once I became an empty nester. But I wasn't yet convinced that picture would ever happen for me now. It wasn't like I wanted my self-identity to reflect that I was incapable of relationship either. I didn't see myself that way. But of course I knew full well that from the outside looking in, it could appear to others that way.

I began kneading dough, marveling at how well things had progressed for me despite my life's tragedies. Yes indeed. I was now very successful. I had launched my very own e-commerce epicurean food and wine business, "Black Sequinned Bows and Champagne Nights." Showcasing artisanal specialty foods that celebrate all things wine, cooking, and entertaining, my latest book, "Wining and Dining with Riley," a definitive guide to food and wine was a huge hit, centering around what to drink with what to eat. With a focus on easy entertaining, the book focused on what foods would complement a wine in the same way a sauce could complement a meat. I was now working on my second book, seamlessly mating specific wines with the flavor and style of the dish, highlighting seasonal and sustainable living.

I had confidence that my next book would also be a hit. I was hoping to draw a new segment of millennials to the business, offering uniquely designed products suitable for everyday living.

My life was full. I couldn't ask for more, I told myself, or could I? I suppose a piece of me longed to be attracted to man that could cause my heart to tremble, my knees to weaken, butterflies in my stomach, and sleepless nights. But, then again that could just be wishful thinking on my part. Jesus, I need to gather my wits.

Samantha entered the kitchen, interrupting my thoughts, and clicking the play button on the answering machine. Listening passively while pulling out my French rolling pin, I heard, "Riley girlfriend, this is Lily. My plane is landing at Philadelphia Airport in three hours. Pick me up at the baggage claim area. I'll be waiting there with bells on, dear."

It was the voice of my dear friend Lily DeLuca.

"Oh, and Riley, I can't wait to talk to you about the Captain," she squealed through the machine. "You're going to thank me, girlfriend. This gala is going to be so much fun. I'm tickled pink."

What Captain? What the hell was Lily talking about?

"There will be paparazzi there from Philadelphia Magazine, the Philadelphia Inquirer, and the Daily News," her voice rang out through the machine. "So you know we have to get our sparkle on, girlfriend."

I shook my head wondering what new scheme Lily had hatched this time. Lily loved playing Cupid. I used to swear she walked around with a hot pink Ricky bag full of arrows. Always the matchmaker.

The answering machine clicked to the off position. I closed my eyes. I yelled out loud to Samantha, "Erase please."

I turned to Madison with dough on my hands and flour on my cheeks, wiping my hands on my "Wines For A Living" apron. I stared at Madison as sternly as I could manage without breaking a smile.

"I know you and Lily are up to your old tricks again, Madison Jo Keyes."

"I have zippers on, Riley," Madison said motioning a closed sign to her lips and staring at me with a very telling silly grin on her face. "Riley if you keep stressing yourself like this over the sweating the small stuff, I'm going to have to change dress sizes sweetie or be held captive to the likes of Xavier for months just to get the pounds off me. There are only so many bread loaves I can consume when you get like this."

"Who said this was small?" I pouted.

"I hate it when you get like this," Madison spewed. "You've never been any good at having your boat rocked, Riley. It's not like there's a man around here to eat all this bread when you get stressed."

I opened one of the loaves of bread I'd made yesterday when I was stressing over which publisher would publish my book. Madison grabbed the serrated bread knife out the butcher block. She pulled the Herbs de Provence flavored dipping oil down from my cabinet. We both fell out laughing as I grabbed us both bread dishes and napkins.

CHAPTER 2

NOAH

"Fasten your seatbelts please as we prepare for our arrival to Philadelphia International Airport," a sultry female voice echoed over the intercom.

I opened my eyes and downed what was left of my second vodka martini. My mood had slowly turned crappy. I was brooding over the flight delays, totally behind schedule now. I was scheduled to attend the Navy's regional annual fundraiser this weekend sponsored by the Navy wives. The wives hosted a Memorial Gala every holiday season in honor of the fallen comrades, raising money each year to purchase Christmas toys for the families of the Fallen.

Fatigued was starting to feel like my middle name. My need for sleep was catching up with me as a result of having changed so many time zones the last few weeks.

Unlike my travel plans the last several weeks, this trip was a command performance. There were only a handful of African American Senior Naval Officers to even attend. I happened to be one of them. Each year, the African American wives insisted that the Memorial Gala event be diverse in leadership. I was the senior-most officer in the region. Yet again, I had been asked to be the Master of Ceremonies for the gala. Predictably, the wives would insist every year that Captain Noah Dunham host the event. It was almost starting to become a tradition. I was beginning to feel like Billy Crystal at the Oscars.

"Captain Dunham sir, may I ask that you put your seat in the upright position as we prepare for landing," she said.

I watched as the pretty black-haired flight attendant grabbed what was left of my vodka martini and peanuts, pulling my tray table upright. Her well-manicured hands brushed slightly against mine.

"Sure thing," I said, knowing this one was trouble with a capital T.

I pondered whether the flight attendants in the Coach section were as pretty as the ones in Business Class. She was one of those sexy-as-sin beauties capable of competing in one of those Ms. Universe Pageants. The way she worked her luscious rear up and down the aisle was disruptive to every man's concentration and libido. Her signature strut was a reminder that I needed to steer clear, lest she'd be a complication waiting to happen.

"Thank you sir. By the way, I'm Leah Chen," she smiled, running her finger across her gold plated nametag, bending over to adjust the pillow behind my head. "It's been a pleasure to serve you this evening Captain Dunham."

"Leah Chen, it's nice to meet you. And thank you very much."

I closed my eyes, meditating momentarily on Ms. Leah Chen, noting her beauty, pegging her in my mind as one of those fast hotties that signaled nothing but trouble. Intuitively, I knew she was lecherous. I had plenty of experience with her brand of wildcat. She was the type of woman that would lock a man's balls tight in her grip and never let go. When it came to fast women I had built-in internal radar. Hell, I knew myself. Typically my taste leaned toward a love of fast planes, fast boats, fast cars, and fast women. While I had an innate pension for all things fast, I was working diligently now on moving beyond my past desires of life and lust in the fast lane, which was often inextricably linked with a slew of fast women.

Nowadays, I was no longer permitted to pilot any planes due to my having had Lasik eye surgery. Even the younger pilots were no longer allowed to let us older heads fly side saddle as the naval moms complained that too many planes went down due to our typical air shenanigans. Too many of their sons were being lost unnecessarily. Besides, these days my work schedule was too busy to even keep up with the fast women. Thus I was pretty much resigned to driving fast cars. I couldn't help but think that this trip schedule-wise always came at the most inopportune times. This year the trip had interfered with my weekend plans to take delivery of my latest automobile acquisition, a brand new White Porsche Carrera 911S. I reminded myself to stop brooding over my change in plans and to get over it.

While I valued my service to the fallen and the philanthropic mission of the event, it was getting to be increasingly more difficult. Each year, I found it harder to attend. This year was worse because my best friend Lucas Cook's name would be called amongst the fallen. He would be receiving the long overdue Navy Cross Medal. His widow Riley Cook would be there to accept his award. Thus, my interest in continued participation in this event was starting to get convoluted. My nervousness around the gala this year was increasing rapidly. Not to mention that last year the gala moved far too slow for my taste.

With my eyes still closed, I could hear Leah's sultry voice saying, "We'll be landing at the Philadelphia International Airport shortly, arriving at Gate Five, Terminal Three. We thank you again for flying American Airlines."

I opened my eyes slowly at the sound of her sultry voice. The two young, well-suited corporate guys seated across from me were giving each other fist-bumps, whispering, "Hell yeah baby, we'd love to fly with you again." God, they were like two inexperienced frat boys in heat.

Leah passed them again in her navy and red accented uniform. She wiggled her ass in a way that took one's breath away, making you forget there was such a thing as self control. Who could forget?

My body stiffened at the mere thought of having to fly this route again with Ms. Leah Chen on board. She had to know her effect on the male psyche. I seriously needed to re-think this business of flying to Philadelphia out of D.C. again.

Working in Washington D.C., commanding several reserve units, and pin-balling around the world to some very exotic places had taken its toll. I'd been globetrotting so much that I had stopped unpacking my home all together. There had been no time or desire. Perhaps I unconsciously wasn't ready to commit to the area.

I had lived outside D.C. in Alexandria, Va. for seven years now. That felt longer than anywhere else I had lived lately. My furniture was still under tarps, and the boxes were still unpacked. Whenever I brought a woman home, she'd either wanted to play house and unpack me herself, or she'd looked half askance wondering what day I'd be leaving town for good.

Hearing the wheels of the plane go into lock position brought me back to my present moment, reminding me of how much my body was starting to feel achy and stiff. I hoped I wasn't catching a cold.

I'd would solve that concern and have another vodka martini upon my arrival at the Four Seasons Hotel. That was going to be my best plan of attack to knock out any cold or flu bug that might be coming on.

A familiar husky voice rang out saying "Flight attendants prepare for landing."

I wondered whether my American Airline friend and pilot Jason Taggert was going to let this baby down easy or not tonight. Jason was ex-Navy. I was glad he was piloting this trip, because I could do without a rough landing. I'd flown many times with him on other routes so it was pretty natural for me to take note of his piloting skills and the flight crew. Tonight I had made a mental note to myself that Leah was new to his crew this trip. The fact that she was such a huge distraction didn't hurt any.

I was returning to the States a couple of days early from Monte Carlo, Monaco, and from a few days in Pamplona, Spain, where I spent time participating in the Running of the Bulls Fiesta. Running with the bulls was one of those personal monumental bucket list experiences requiring cool nerves, quick reflexes, and a good level of physical fitness. It was an experience where I really missed and felt the loss of Lucas. Lucas would have loved running with the bulls, the bullfights, and the mass gathering of folks coming from all corners of the world celebrating the Patron Saint San Fermin. We both loved living life on the edge.

Lucas and I were each other's wingman in the air and on the ground. He would see me and say "Rock-in Wingman" and I would say "Rock-out Wingman" and we'd both high five, fist bump, and fall out laughing, memorializing our mantra with matching tattoos one night during our Academy days when we were partying hard and wilding out.

I moved down the aisle to de-board.

"Good Job Jason. You put her down nicely tonight."

Jason shook my hand saying, "Hey Mico, I've seen the time you could put her down a whole lot better man so it's a compliment coming from you," he grinned.

I noticed out the corner of my eye that the curvaceous Leah Chen was looking curiously at Jason, begging for an introduction, all the while coaxing me with her eyes as all kinds of pheromones passed between us.

"It's a Navy Academy nickname," I said, responding to her look of curiosity, and wondering to myself how in the hell did the very married Jason keep it together with that firecracker on board. She was the kind of woman that any man in his right mind would want to back that ass up against the cockpit doors and tame that tiger once and for all.

"Again, it's Noah. Noah Dunham," I said extending my hand to Leah. She held onto my hand longer than necessary. I pulled away, moving to shake Jason's hand, patting him on his shoulder.

I smiled and kept it moving. Seeing Jason again reminded me of Lucas and how much I missed how we rocked the world together during our days in the Navy. I needed to keep it together. I could hear Lucas's voice ringing in my head saying "Man, stand down on this woman."

The way I figured it, Ms. Leah, the beautiful Asian angel that she appeared to be, was the poster gal for the "I want to fuck you senseless club." That was the last thing I needed right now.

I was on a mission Lucas had assigned to me a long time ago. It was time now for me to be about the business we had discussed so many years ago. I silently spoke to Lucas in a prayerful way telling him that I would not drop the ball this time distracted by a fast 'I want to fuck your brains out' flight attendant. It was my mantra now, no matter how many times I'd have to lecture to the torpedo that we were on an important mission and were beyond that lifestyle now. I could not afford to agree to be prey to Ms. Leah Chen and whatever hottie antics she might have in her mind tonight. This was a bullet I intended to dodge.

It was moments like these that I felt Lucas's absence. He and I had come into the United States Naval Academy together as presidential appointees and had remained friends for life. His life, at least. But now he was gone and I missed him. We always had each other's back. We maintained each other's confidences. We kicked it hard together at the academy. When we had down time together we threw back vodkas, partying for days on end. We worked hard. We played hard.

Lucas had been instrumental in introducing me to my ex-wife Casey. I remember him saying, "Just date the girl, Mico. Don't get stupid, because she doesn't strike me as the wifey type."

But I, on the other hand, jumped blindly into those waters like an imbecile and married Casey. I had that bad boy persona that she found attractive, but she didn't even come close to possessing the wholesome wifely mother characteristics that I wanted in a wife. She was just fast, and I had a pension for fast. But I'd also made the mistake of marrying her.

Lucas was less reckless and more grounded. He was deeply rooted in his Italian heritage with strong family values. His loyalty to his Italian heritage came through a lot, as I would oftentimes catch him speaking in Italian when he was either studying, thinking out loud, cursing, or interacting with his grandparents at family gatherings. He was loved by everyone he met. Lucas was charismatic, anal retentive, highly educated, and the devoted friend.

One weekend Lucas and I decided to run down to Baltimore to attend the annual Army Navy Game. We hit the concession area to get beers. The most beautiful woman appeared with chili dogs in her hand. She'd taken a sudden spill right at our feet. Drop dead damn gorgeous. I was speechless as that exotic body smelling of fresh lavender with dark brown shoulder length hair and big brown almond eyes tumbled at our feet. That lean frame with great legs was sprawled out before us as if she were being served up on platter. As far as I was concerned it was divine order. Carmel colored with a wholesome Brazilian kind of look about her, she was "Hello Gorgeous" personified.

Shit. Shit. Shit. I couldn't decide if she was the girl next door or a figment of my imagination. The eyes. The lips. The everything. And, to make matters worse, she had on a pair of those cute fuck-me heels, that broke as she landed at our feet.

Lucas was immediately mesmerized by her beauty, as was I. She was stunning. You knew instantly that she was a beauty from childhood and would still be beautiful in her old age. Those big brown eyes looked up at him and Lucas was done. Stung by Cupid's arrow. I whispered in his ear insisting, "Man. do. not. let. her. get. away."

He took my advice to heart too and married her two years later. Her name was Riley Nelson. She proved to be the love of his life. From the stories he told she loved him dearly as well. Hell, I could see why she loved him because I loved him too.

I was miserable and pissed off the day they wed, because I couldn't be there. I couldn't stand by his side as best man at their wedding, having been called away at the last minute to the other side of the world on a special ops intelligence mission for the Navy. Lucas understood, knowing the nature of how life in the Navy was full of unforeseen moments. His new brother-in-law Reese stood up for him instead.

Walking briskly to the baggage claim area, I reflected on how Lucas was loyal to anyone he called his friend or lover. He and I were more than friends. We held each other's confidences. We were closer than most brothers. Lucas had come to my rescue once when one of our units came under deadly attack taking down another enemy plane that had me in its path. I was minutes from being shot down.

The Navy had invested a million dollars in Lucas's and my training. I was glad for it because he had saved my life. We both were well trained pilots in the air and black belts on the ground. We were lean mean killing machines. We would give our lives for each other.

While my own marriage with Casey had failed, Lucas and Riley really had it together. Lucas always reminded me on days I had an inkling to feel bad about Casey, that Casey really wasn't for me, and that one day I too would have the kind of life with someone like he had.

Every now and then when we'd get ripped, downing vodka shots, Lucas would hold me hostage to a promise. Over and over and over, Lucas would make me swear on my life that if anything ever happened to him, that I would step in for him and watch over his kids and Riley. We were as close as blood brothers, so I had every intention of keeping my promise.

My career circumstances kept me so occupied that Riley and I had never gotten a real chance to get to know each other. I'd only been in her company briefly, meeting her the same day that Lucas met her. We'd have the occasional hello and good-bye by telephone a couple of times later in the months that followed their marriage, with Lucas shouting "Mico say hi to Riley," then he'd quickly grab the phone back so he and I could catch up. Riley hardly knew me, but I on the other hand very much knew her. I knew every inch of her. Now and then when we were on tour, Lucas would get homesick. Sentimental. He'd start talking about Riley and go on non-stop about her. Perhaps he knew deep down that he would be leaving us. In his own way I surmised that he wanted me to know as much about her as he did. Lucas insisted that I know every little detail. I wanted to know everything about her too. And, I was very attentive. I paid careful attention to him. Listening to his stories, I had learned to love her as well. I knew in my heart of hearts that women like Riley Cook only came around once in a lifetime.

I dreaded this Memorial Gala. As much as my interest in this event had waned, this year was going to be different. This year Riley would be at the gala. And, this year I was coming to get her. I would not fail this time, but succeed. This would be the year she would come to know how special she was to me. This would be the year I would turn in my player card and fulfill my promise to Lucas. For like Lucas, I too have always loved her.

Exiting the baggage claim area, moving swiftly past the late night passengers, I waved my hand high. "Taxi!" I yelled.

CHAPTER 3

RILEY

"Hey Mommy. What's happening, Sammi?" Claire said, moving down the hallway through the kitchen headed into my home office area.

I was still camped out with Madison, who had a mouthful of bread, still thumbing through the European fashion magazines. Claire planted a warm kiss on my cheek.

"Hi baby," I said, giving Claire a once over, making a mental note that while Samantha had grown to be the spitting image of Lucas, Claire was growing up to be more like me in every way.

"How was your day?" I redirected my thoughts, giving Claire my full attention.

Claire grunted.

"Ahhh, it was okay. My class is working on a new play at school to present at parents' night. I think I may be getting the lead role."

"That's wonderful, Claire."

I glanced at her lovingly, thinking about how Lucas knew Claire would have lots of talent.

"I'm glad when you were born your dad and I agreed to enroll you in The George School. The advanced placement classes, the photography, and the performing arts curriculum has been a good return on our investment. You are so talented, dear."

"I enjoy the photography, but not so much the acting," Claire grunted.

"You are your daddy's child. Lucas knew you had creative skills that could be developed there, even though his belief was based solely on the fact that as a baby you were drawn to anything bright in color," I laughed. "Your dad used to throw disposable cameras around the house, letting you take tons of pictures, most of which ended up crooked and sideways. But I must admit, they were colorful."

"Yeah, well my drama teacher, Mr. Davies must disagree with my dad," Claire snorted. "Because he's pushing me to take on the lead roles every semester whenever it's time to do a new play. I don't feel like being Juliet to that pest of a boy who's playing Romeo this semester," Claire snarled. turning her attention away from me before I could answer.

"Sammi, I see you're back on a money mission again today." Claire said, noticing Samantha's money laid on the kitchen counter top. "I've got something for you to hear." She grinned a mischievous smirk.

"Yeah, what?"

Before Sammi could put her money away, Claire headed to dock her iPod in the sound system. My phone rang at the same moment the microwave timer went off, letting me know it was time to pull my bread loaves out of the oven.

"Mamma Dukes, it's Uncle Reese," Samantha shouted, having answered the phone.

Damn, I could almost bet that Madison and Lily were conspiring against me. This was no coincidence that my brother Reese was calling me right now. "Hey Riley baby. You know your posse has been begging me to head up your way," Reese said huskily.

Now my suspicions were officially confirmed.

"I hear you need a plus one for the Memorial Gala. It won't bother me one bit to come this weekend to bat all those Navy fly boys off my big sis."

"Hey baby brother," I said sweetly. I can't talk about it now Reese. I'm late picking up Lily from the airport. She's flying in this afternoon. She and I are knee deep in managing the planning committee's activities for the Gala."

"You've got your hands full, huh?

"Yes, considering my company is managing the food, wine, decor, and other catering activities. I'm guessing you know this already," I said, hoping he was aware I had peeped all of their little hold cards.

"Yeah I got the word, Riley."

"Since Lucas is getting the Navy Cross Award, it's going to be a big night for me. The press will be there. My staff is on high alert. I'm hoping to leverage all this gala buzz for my company in order to pursue a few angel investors for the business.

"Good you're thinking ahead."

"I know. It's high time I take *Black Sequinned Bows and Champagne Nights* to the next level, Reese."

"You're doing a bang up job with the business. I have no doubt the gala will go off without a hitch with you at the helm. I'm proud of you."

"Thanks Reese. Having you in my corner means more to me than you can imagine."

"I will always be in your corner Riley."

One thing's for sure, Reese was the most loyal brother any sister could have. He was like that growing up. Time and age hadn't changed a thing between us.

"I should be back from the airport in a couple of hours. I can call you back when Lily gets here. Madison is here too."

"Ahhhh, my three favorite lovelies."

"You can talk to them on the speakerphone when I get back since I know you guys have already planned out my gala night," I sneered. "The gals and I will be here opening up some wine, test driving some of my new desserts, and having our own girls night out catching up."

"Cool. Don't worry about calling me back. I'm leaving New York's Penn Station now. I'll be there in under three hours."

Damn. Things were seriously starting to get out of control if Reese was coming to town. Did my brother not hear me say "Girls Night Out?" He was truly a piece of work. A freaking control freak.

I used to maintain greater control over the clandestine tactics of my own posse. There used to be a time when I had a little bit of control over Madison and Lily, but Reese was an entirely different matter. Nobody, but nobody, controlled Reese. He was his own man. If anything, he controlled everyone else, that manipulating little sneak. He surely was his daddy's child, always in freaking command. It's true, the apple does not fall far from the tree.

Suddenly, the audio on my compact disc player started spewing out fart sounds. Claire and Sammi were laughing and rolling all over the floor. I looked at them both with unabashed disdain. Jesus. I had two clowns on my floor.

"I've got to go now Reese. As you can probably hear, Claire's got jokes today."

Reese starting laughing in my ear, hearing the fart sounds in the background.

"Lighten up Riley. Life is short. Tell my nieces Uncle Reese is headed their way and a new sheriff is coming to town," he chuckled.

"Whatever," I groaned. "You are just as bad as these girls. I don't know which of you is worse."

"I do. Those girls of yours are worse. Anyway, I'm hoping I can shoot some hoops with X and win the money he took off me the last time I was there."

"Aren't you getting a bit old for basketball, brother?"

"Are you kidding me? I'm a decade younger than Barack Obama and he still plays. The day Obama quits, I know I've still got ten more years to play. I'll see you soon Riley," he chuckled as he hung up.

"Claire. Samantha. Must you guys constantly clown around? I don't have time for the shenanigans today," I said grabbing my bag. "You guys are too old for this silliness."

I was working hard to keep a straight face. Samantha and Claire loved getting my goat. Claire definitely had Lucas's sense of humor. Samantha lived for the day to encourage her. And with their Uncle Reese coming to town, the girls were surely going to be on cut up mode. I needed to brace myself. I hung up the phone, turning my attention to Madison who was headed toward the front door.

"Riley, I'm on my way to my final seminar for the day with the newbie teachers. Then I'm going home to change. I can't be caught looking this rough for girls night out with Lily and company."

"Correction, you mean girls night out and Reese, don't you Madison? I'm officially putting you in the dog house along with your partner in crime Cupid Lily. You two are always up to some mess," I said, raising my voice loud enough for Madison to hear me as she headed to the door.

We both jumped as my doorbell rang.
"I'll get it," Madison yelled out.

Who could be at the door this time of day? I wasn't expecting company.

"It's a certified letter," Madison said, signing my name, casually dismissing the postal person. "Looks pretty important," she glared, waiting on me to open the letter. Madison and I weren't one to keep secrets so I knew she wasn't going anywhere until she got the 411 on what was in the letter. I ripped the letter open trying to read it. Madison was already reading over my shoulder, screaming to the girls, snatching the letter out of my hand, showing off the fast reader that she was.

"Oh my God, your Mom's been nominated for the James E. Beard top ten finalists for the Food Writer's Book Award!" Madison shrilled at the top of her lungs. She grabbed me, pulling me in a tight hug. We started jumping up and down, turning in our own circle of joy. We looked much like we did when we were in seventh grade bouncing up and down on my bed when her high school love Steve Harvey asked her out on a date for the first time. Samantha snatched the letter out of Madison's hand insisting that she read it for herself. Claire joined the group hug with me and Madison.

"Party over here, people," Samantha said, while simultaneously doing some old school MC Hammer dance move, rocking her fisted forearms in a circle and brushing her fingers across the tops of her shoulder like she was flicking dust off herself.

"You go Mamasita," she said to me with joy and excitement.

"Thank you grasshopper," I said slapping her a high five.

"Oh my God," Samantha exclaimed, running to the computer. "I wonder if this news has hit the internet yet? Claire, our mom's a big deal sister."

Samantha shuffled rapidly towards my Macbook Pro while Claire moved in lockstep with her looking over her shoulder.

I could hear Samantha's fingers tapping the keyboard quickly as she mentioned in passing how much she loved the speed of the thunderbolt technology on my laptop.

"Yep. It's on the Beard Foundation's website already. There is buzz of the nominations trending already on Twitter," she squealed.

I was in a state of shock. I couldn't believe this was happening to me. Samantha kept thumbing through the tweets that were trending.

"It says right here that the James Beard Foundation Book Award is presented each year to the nation's most outstanding Wine and Spirit Professional from the food and beverage industry. The award honors the best and the brightest talents in the industry, celebrating outstanding achievement in order to elevate the appreciation of our culinary excellence."

"I guess there's no keeping this news a secret. Tell the internet, tell the world," I said, a bit overcome by my nomination.

"Oh Riley, this is such wonderful news. I'm thrilled," Madison said, glancing down at her watch.

"Woman, we better hit the pause button on this celebratory news or else you're going to be late getting Lily. You know how much she hates to wait. This information is probably streaming across Lily and Reese's cellphones right about now anyway."

"Lily's still in the air, otherwise I'm sure she'd be blowing up my phone right now. I doubt I'm going to be able to keep this a secret."

"And Reese, he's going to be overjoyed," Madison giggled. "Make my day, Riley Cook, but I'm late for my seminar, girlfriend."

Madison kissed me on the cheek and ran out the door. I grabbed my navy quilted Burberry jacket.

"Samantha, Claire. I'm off to pick up Lily," I yelled, following Madison out the door and waving good-bye.

I jumped in my black BMW X5, plugging my iPhone into the charger, moving it to hands-free. I was in a whirlwind of glee having been nominated for the Food Writer's Book Award. All my years of hard work pulling myself out of the bowels of the turmoil Warren left me in was starting to pay off. Things were looking up, but I knew more than ever that my work at the gala was starting to take on a new significance.

All eyes would be watching me now. I had to get every single detail right. It was bad enough that Lily mentioned that the press was going to be there. That knowledge alone had amped up my anxiety. But now this? I needed this event to go well. Between the James Beard Foundation Award, and the good buzz that I could leverage from my company's work at the gala, this could mean that all the stars were aligning at the right time. This would help me set the stage to gain an angel investor to take my business to the next level. The Memorial Gala had to go smoothly for more reasons than I could count.

Thank God Lily was coming to town. She would anchor me. I was starting to feel like a bundle of nerves.

A professor of law, teaching Legal Writing at Georgetown Law in D.C., Lily and I met as classmates at the Wharton Business School shortly after my tumultuous relationship with Warren Shaw had ended. *It seems every time I come to this airport I-95 is always backed up.* Lily was bright, loyal, and totally informed on how my life had evolved after Lucas's death.

A fire engine redhead with a beautiful smile and a knock out body, Lily and I hit it off from the first day we met. She prided herself on being an active member of the Sons of Italy, a national organization of men and women of Italian heritage. The Sons of Italy were a major contributor to the military wives' Memorial Gala. Lily and Madison were friends now too, each from having met the other through me. The three of us were a trio now, relishing the times we could share events and activities that brought us all together.

"Siri how many minutes away am I from the Philadelphia International Airport?" I asked, glancing briefly at my iPhone.

"You are 15 minutes away."

Damn, I'm still fifteen minutes away.

I waited for traffic to proceed. How I hated making trips to the airport. It always brought back unpleasant memories. Better yet, ugly thoughts of the old days of picking Warren up at the airport. I could never quite put my finger on why my mind continued to re-hash those anxious moments. A late night freezing in the cold at Philadelphia International Airport baggage claim area waiting on Warren's late planes from his routine trips to Puerto Rico could be a solemn drag. Unless you needed to be there, I could always think of better places to be.

Once when I had to pick up Warren, I was sure I was having heart palpitations. My heart raced in anticipation hoping that his brief trip and our time apart had done our strained relationship some good. The digital clock on my dashboard revealed it was well past midnight. He was late yet again.

As I tried to calm myself, I eyeballed Warren. He had a look of relief walking towards me; I suppose because I was on time. For a brief delusional moment I felt like maybe we were in fact a loving couple. My eyes momentarily strayed from Warren's. I noticed another arriving male passenger walking slightly behind him. Warren reached my car, embracing me with a hug and a kiss, directing me to the passenger's seat. The arriving male passenger's eyes locked in with mine. He hesitated briefly, but smiled warmly. The hour was late, the night dark. Yet still, I felt his penetrating gaze, his eyes expressing something I couldn't define. He peered right through me, piercing my soul.

My eyes followed his fading silhouette like a tracker hunting deer. I couldn't control myself. In that exact moment I realized my relationship with Warren was over. The man's essence called to something deep within me, igniting a kind of appeal, a kind of attraction over and beyond what the man I had been waiting on curbside for hours could ever achieve. I felt a deep sense of longing. Part of my soul was missing and it sure as hell wasn't to be found with Warren. I was having an epiphany.

In that moment of clarity, I realized with a great sense of knowing that Warren and I were done. We only looked the part of a loving couple. We were pretending. WE were a lie. The man fading in the distance was the man I wanted to know, silently calling to some deep longing for love inside of me.

For the first time in my relationship, I admitted to myself that I was miserable and hurting on the inside. I supposed that in my grief, rebounding from the loss of Lucas, it had gotten too hard for me to separate the fantasy from the reality. The fantasy couple Warren and I had created sufficed right up until the moments Warren would predictably morph himself into Mr. Hyde.

In retrospect, it was amazing how much I failed to admit to myself. Whatever I thought about what the mystery passenger may have seen in us, it never quite lined up to my own truths of my relationship with Warren. The outer appearance of our relationship never lived up to the fact of it. We were comfortable at faking it. And my mystery man represented everything I wished, imagined, and hoped for in a man.

I maneuvered the wheels of the X5 into the airport's arriving passenger lane looking for Lily. I eased towards the baggage claim area for American Airlines hoping to catch a glimpse of her.

Lily would be on Cupid mission mode. I was determined to

stay on my nice comfortable rock with me, myself, and I. Lily didn't take no for an answer so I was going to have to gird my loins for everything Ms. Cupid was going to throw at me with respect to this Captain Dunham fellow, arrows and all. If I lost the battle with Lily, I at least hoped the Captain wasn't going to be some hard to ditch, flash in the pan, overzealous military type. Or worst yet, some old moneybag geezer that I'd find repugnant, batting off like a gnat most of the night.

"Over here, Lily," I said, just as I heard a deep male voice of someone behind me say "Taxi."

Lily was wearing a black Armani pantsuit, trench coat, carrying large black hobo bag slung over her shoulder. She had a Louis Vuitton weekender at her side. Lily was my resident fashionista. She had a great wardrobe. We both had similar fashion sense, both loving to shop until we dropped.

Lily knew all the right outlet shops and hot spots to find great bargains for vintage clothing in every major city. She was an avid reader of good literature, rarely ever seen without her Kindle.

Today, Lily was adorned with a single Tiffany bangle, diamond post earrings, and rocking a pair of Burberry checked framed sunglasses on top of those curly red locks. Her hair was slightly parted to the side with a bang. As usual, she was remarkably put together.

"Oh my God Riley. Congratulations love on the news of the James Beard Foundation nomination. The nominees are trending on Twitter."

"I was hoping I'd get to break the news to you first," I said. "So much for the speed of social media. Nothing is private anymore. What happened to surprises?"

"Surprises went by the wayside along with the mainstream media. I got a notification alert on my screen as soon as I took my cellphone off airplane mode. I'm so ecstatic, I'm about to bust. This is wonderful news," Lily said, squeezing me in her arms tightly. "I've missed you so much."

"Me too," I said, hugging her back. "I received a certified letter notifying me a little over two hours ago. I'm still in a state of shock. This is just the kind of thing I need to propel my business and raise investment capital. But there are other nominees in my category, so I've got lots of competition."

"Who cares about the competition Riley. It's a high honor to be nominated. I have no doubt you'll rise straight to the top of that flock and win," Lily beamed.

"I'm so glad you're here," I said kissing her on the cheek. "You can help me think straight throughout all this excitement. Between the gala, the paparazzi, and this award nomination, I feel like my head is spinning."

"Well, I've arrived at the right time then. Everything happens for a reason, Riley, and this is the kind of good press your company can take advantage of at the gala. I'll be right there to fan the flames," Lily giggled.

"It's been too long between our visits," I said fondly, as we both jumped into the car. "What's new in your world?"

I honked impatiently at the car to my left, pulling out the baggage claim standing area, hating to be at this airport.

"Gabriel's in love," Lily said solemnly.

Gabriel was Lily's son and only child. This was not good news. Lily was like the mother bear protecting her cub against all enemies when it came to her son Gabriel. I waited with baited breath to hear the news. This was not good. Somebody could die. Lily's son Gabriel was everything to her.

"He's found a woman overseas that he wants to marry. It's been difficult because he's back in the country from his stint with Doctors Without Borders. He found a new love overseas in Columbia. It's all too much for me to have to deal with right now."

"Wow. Gabriel's in love," I sighed, contemplating internally as to how I would feel if that were Xavier. Gabriel and Xavier were the same age.

"He hardly knows her. I hardly know her. I feel like they should take their time to make sure this is real, not about her wanting to hitch herself to a walking ATM or something. You know the deal, Riley."

"Please don't remind me Lily. It's hard to tell that age group anything."

"He feels like he knows what he's doing. And, she in fact

does knows what she's doing, inflating that ego and libido." Lily momentarily gritted her teeth and made a growling sound. "Gabriel can be like an unguided missile sometimes. It's hard for him to hear me. Nathan is too unplugged with anything other than work to engage our son," she said, looking concerned.

"And how are things with Dr. Nate?" I asked rapidly changing the subject, hoping to re-direct Lily's obvious frustration with Gabriel.

Lily's husband Dr. Nathan DeLuca was a Cardiologist. "Mending hearts and breaking hearts," she said.

We both busted out laughing at our inside joke. But a look of pain flashed across Lily's face that I hadn't seen before.

I knew Lily well and this was not a good sign. I recalled the day when Lily and I were in business school. I came sprinting out of Professor Osman's class on Marketing one day in a pair of my favorite Louboutin stilettos. I was rushing. I fell straight on my butt, breaking my ankle. Falling seemed to be in my nature now that I think about it. Lily drove me straight to the hospital.

I knew Dr. Nate because he had been my dad's cardiologist. He was fine as hell and a real head turner.

Dr. Nate saw me arrive and stopped in the emergency room to see how I was doing. I was in immense pain. He proceeded to write me a prescription for Percocet saying "My dearest Riley, I don't want you to be in pain, dear," all while he couldn't take his eyes off Lily.

I nudged Lily, saying, "Geez, did you notice he didn't ask me what other medications I was taking? He must really be smitten with you to miss that fact. Aren't I the patient here? What has modern medicine come to?" I said with a bit of sarcasm. "Earth to Dr. Nate," I whispered at Lily when he momentarily left the room.

Lily and I both spoke at the same time, grinning, saying, "mending hearts and breaking hearts."

We starting cracking up and howling, knowing Dr. Nathan was smitten with Lily.

From that day forward, the saying "mending hearts and breaking hearts" became our favorite mantra, our inside joke whenever we spoke on Nathan.

Sometime thereafter, Nathan and Lily starting dating. It was a difficult start to a relationship. Nathan broke numerous dates. His patient's hearts were always going down on date night. When Lily threatened to give up on the relationship, Nathan popped the question of marriage. He swore he couldn't imagine his life without her. Lily and Nathan married, but it was no denying to anyone with eyes that Nathan always appeared to be more married to his profession.

"Nathan's having an affair, Riley."

"Oh my God woman, how do you know?" I gasped loudly.

"The signs are there. Things have gotten so bad, I'm not sure he's even working hard to hide the affair now. Not to mention, I can see it in his eyes. He's getting careless. Sometime, I think he actually wants me to know. You know, get himself caught and put us both out of our misery," she sighed with a tone of disbelief.

"Lily, are you sure?"

"Yeah. Some young blonde wall street hottie that works for CNBC."

"Jesus Lily, you know we can always go snatch little Ms. CNBC, and let her know that you know and put a stop to this. What about your marriage?"

"What about it?"

"Nathan is sacrificing your marriage for this woman? What are you gonna do? Are you going to work to save your marriage?"

I was talking a million miles an hour now. I couldn't even begin to fathom the idea that Lily's marriage was on the rocks. How could she be working so hard playing Cupid for me all while her own marriage was hitting the skids?

"That boat sailed years ago, Riley. I'm going to turn on a dime, call it quits. Then I'm going to go to Italy, drink a ton of wine, purchase a flat in Tuscany, and move a hot young Italian stallion in with me to make love and feed me grapes all day. That's exactly what I'm going to do, Riley."

Lily gave me her best "read my lips" look of determination. That was the look she often gave folks when she demanded that they stand down on the discussion.

"But enough about me. I've made some changes this year for the gala," Lily said speaking rapidly and changing the subject. "Since I'm a major contributor, I took the liberty of getting myself on the planning committee so as to liven the event up this year. I want to kick things up a notch."

"Oh God, what have you got planned up your sleeve this year?" I said, with suspicion.

"Riley, I can't thank you enough for donating your company's expertise for the event. I'm beyond overjoyed that you've been able to arrange for each table to have its own wine tasting flights. The fact you're flying in Chefs Eric Ripert and Bobby Flay to do the food is more than I could have ever expected for this event."

"This is what my company does best Lily. We make magic happen."

I sensed Lily was ignoring the matter at hand with respect to her failing marriage with Nathan and was throwing herself into her work to escape.

"Riley, I arranged with the Admiral that we'd like Captain Noah Dunham to be the Master of Ceremonies again. I plan to introduce him to you."

"Introduce me Lily, or set me up?"

"I think the two of you will really hit it off. It won't hurt you to get back in the saddle again, Riley. You've thrown every man that has come along back into the pond," she said firmly.

"I don't need setting up," I insisted.

"Oh look, there's the Franklin Mills Outlet Mall exit," Lily said with a look on her face that she wasn't taking no for an answer.

We both turned, looked at each other and said "Detour," as the wheels to my BMW X5 made a sharp right turn.

"Oh, Riley you're going to love the Captain," Lily coaxed as we entered Saks Off Fifth. "It'll be a great way for you to get your sea legs again. There's tons of fish in the pond. So what if you wasted a few years loving that jackass Warren. Captain Dunham is really very charming," she swooned.

"Lily, you say every guy is charming," I said dryly, unimpressed.

"No, he's beyond charming Riley. He's the kind of man you say "drop and give me ten, baby," while underneath him," Lily laughed.

That was the one thing I loved about Lily. The world could be falling apart at the seams and Lily DeLuca was focused on the good times like a laser beam, never getting lost in the depths of negativity.

"Riley he's Idris Albas, Denzel Washington, Barack Obama charming honey."

"Jesus Lily, it's bad enough that you and Madison are conspiring to set me up with a man at this gala, but on top of everything else, Reese has gotten into the mix too. I spoke to him on my way out the door to pick you up. He's leaving New York today, talking about he's coming in town to be my plus one? I can believe it."

Lily appeared completely unfazed about Reese coming to town. She was wading through tons of scarves on a discount table as if I had merely said the sky were blue.

"We both know he's coming to town to try to control outcomes now that he knows I may be introduced to a new man. You know the deal with Reese, Lily."

"Honey, I've got this whole thing under control. Trust me. This is what I do best. You just relax and let me handle Reese."

"As if anybody handles Reese."

"I have no intention of letting this year's gala go by without you meeting the Captain, Riley. He's beyond McDreamy McSteamy," Lily crooned like a dreamy-eyed school girl.

"Oh please, Lily."

"You're gonna thank me one day for the introduction, girlfriend. I'll lay bets on the fact that this man is for you."

"There you go again, Lily. How many times do I have to tell you guys, that I'm fine without a man. Really, I am."

Lily ignored me, honing in on a beautiful Pucci scarf. She was drooling with a look of glee in her eyes. I might as well have been talking to the hand.

"You're a huge romantic, Lily DeLuca."

Lily, held her palm up in the air for me to be quiet. She turned her attention to the salesperson.

"Miss, I'd like to purchase this handbag please. My friend here is gonna take this scarf."

We both reached in our purses, simultaneously pulling out our Platinum American Express cards. We grinned wildly at each other.

"Don't leave home without it," we both said at the same time.

Lily and I often spoke and thought in unison.

An hour later, shopping bags in hand we jumped back into the Beemer, headed north to Washington's Crossing.

"Siri, call Madison Keyes."

"Calling."

CHAPTER 4

RILEY

An hour later, we turned onto River Road, pulling into my home's circular drive. Xavier appeared before my eyes, throttling his hot red Multistrada 1200S Sport Ducati as Lily and I were exiting my car.

"Heeeeey Ms. Lily, You're looking mmm mmm good today," Xavier said, kissing Lily on the check.

"Hello, Mother."

"Xavier," I replied.

"You're looking more scrumptious than Ms. Robinson today Ms. Lily."

"Oh Lord, make my day, Xavier."

"Are you up for a run today before playtime with the gals? I'd love to be the one to help you keep those beautiful gluts of yours in shape," Xavier grinned mischievously.

"Boy, you need to keep it moving," Samantha snapped as she came out the front door to greet us. Samantha gave Xavier a full eye roll, tossing her head, pulling her shoulder length reddish brown hair behind her ear.

Xavier was a personal trainer degreed in physiology. He was always up for anyone he could find to run through the neighborhood with him. We called him the exercise junkie.

"Xavier you will not have me passing out on the street this trip calling for an EMT."

"You know I'm trained in CPR Ms. Lily. I know how to administer mouth to mouth resuscitation," Xavier smiled seductively.

Xavier was looking like the sly fox giving Lily his infamous hang dog look. I wondered where he got those moves. Surely it was encoded in his DNA. He was Lucas's son.

"Xavier, mind your manners, dear," I said, deciding that I

needed to rein him in a bit.

"Yeah X , mind your damn manners boy," Samantha said as she grabbed Lily's weekender bag out of the back seat.

"You stay in your lane, Sammi. You know Ms. Lily is the only woman for me," Xavier responded with delight. Lily grinned ear to ear taking the whole conversation in stride all while I was mulling the fact that Xavier was starting to rock that same irresistible demeanor that Lucas possessed. I finally concluded those attributes did in fact run in the gene pool. Fighting the gene pool was a losing battle.

Xavier grabbed Lily's weekender from Sammi's hand. He headed through the door, tucking his iPod in his back pocket, simultaneously putting earbuds in his ears, taking Lily's luggage to the guest room.

"You know Mom, since he's been dating that jazz head girl Nena, X thinks he's God's gift to mankind. He thinks his shit don't stink. Most of the time he spends his time either lifting weights, looking in the mirror, talking to Nena, riding that bike, or feeding his vegan face."

"Try to give him a break Samantha. He's trying to figure out who he is right now. That can be hard at his age. And you should work at curbing your language."

"I'm over him, Nena, and Miles Davis. I've been texting him for days for the money he promised. He committed to help me throw up my hip hop blog site. He's constantly dragging his feet," Samantha growled.

Samantha was getting to a place where she was on the verge of losing her noodle, yet working hard to maintain her cool in front of company.

"Samantha, I'm an avid believer in the philosophy that if you want something done darling, do it yourself. Don't be dependent on others. I'll give Xavier a nudge, but dear try to have a plan B. How many times do I have to tell you this?"

"Yeah I got X's plan B all right, she blurted out, heading quickly up the staircase. Samantha turned back briefly.

"Claire's out back snapping pictures with Cleo and Stogie."

My doorbell rang.

"Come on in," I sang out loudly.

I heard a familiar voice call out. "It's me, Madison."

"Come in Madison. We're in the den."

"Honey you look like a million dollars." Lily said as she stood up to hug Madison.

Madison had freshened up. She was sporting a glen plaid Kango Hat, a crisp white shirt, and skinny jeans that accentuated her bow-legs. Her feet were adorned with blue leather Minnetonka moccasins, and a cross-body messenger bag that had a copy of Jude E. McNamara's new book "The Heart of A Helmsman" peeking out of the back pocket.

"Thanks Lily. You're looking state of the art yourself," Madison exclaimed. "Here Riley, I bought a half case of your favorite Pinot Noir."

"Perfect," I said, reaching to unpack the bright green bags embossed with the Wegman's logo that were filled with wine.

"I am serving wild salmon tournedos with caramelized turnips with a pinot noir sauce. A new world Pinot Noir in lieu of a burgundy is a good choice. The rich salmon and the sweetness of the turnips make sense with the Pinot Noir."

"Good choice, Maddy."

"Yeah. I've actually been reading these books you write. Trying to keep up, girlfriend," Madison exclaimed.

I opened my refrigerator to grab a Godiva chocolate cheesecake, a strawberry cream-filled shortcake, and some new rum-filled miniature cupcakes my company was sampling. I sat the desserts on the coffee table and sauntered across the room to put on some music. I grabbed Samantha's Beyonce, Keisha Cole, and Jay-Z compact discs out of the Bang and Olufsen player, replacing the trays with Sade, Gino Vanelli, Diana Krall, and Kem. I grabbed four tumblers, hoping not to drop any of them and set them on the table in front of us. Lily kicked off her shoes. She flopped down on the white overstuffed love seat and began telling Madison about our shopping detour at Franklin Mills Mall. I loved these moments when my girlfriends were around enjoying good food, good wine, and life.

"Oh yeah Riley, Zoe is five minutes right behind me," Madison said. "I told her you had gone to get Lily. She's headed this way."

No sooner had Madison gotten the words off her lips than Zoe walked through the door.

"Holla, people."

"Come on back Zoe. We're here in the den."

Zoe Cook Gardner was my sister-in-law. My husband Lucas and Zoe were fraternal twins born only two minutes apart. Lucas prided himself on the fact that he was born first. He chided Zoe about being the oldest, and the one in charge. He often bantered that Zoe was taking up too much room in the womb.

Zoe was tall, blonde, and described by most men as a "brick house." Between all of us gals, Zoe was the one that could stop traffic.

Wearing a camel turtleneck cashmere poncho, blue jeggings, a leopard bag, calf skinned ballet flats, and oversized Audrey Hepburn-esque sunglasses, Zoe was beautiful as ever.

"Hey Zoe. Come on in baby, Ms. Philadelphia's most popular jazz singer," Madison screamed.

"Hey ladies. Happy to see you guys. Congratulations, Riley."

"Thanks Zoe."

"Samantha and Claire sent me texts about your James Beard Foundation nomination. That's awesome news. Lucas would be so proud of you."

"Yes he would," I said, feeling a bit remorseful about the fact that Lucas wasn't here to celebrate with me.

"I'm excited for you. We need to celebrate. I'm long overdue for this girls night out," Zoe squealed.

Zoe was happily married to Julian Gardner, a renowned local pianist. A member of Mensa, musically talented, and recognized nationally, Zoe Cook Gardner was one of Philadelphia Magazine's most sought after personalities. Whenever Zoe made an album, her followers were known to create a huge siege on the iTunes store as soon as her albums dropped. Zoe could sing any music genre. Contemporary, jazz, R&B, pop and country. She loved contemporary jazz the most, so her signature albums were in the contemporary jazz genre.

Zoe's love of jazz had rubbed off on Xavier. Xavier's interest in jazz was first seeded by Zoe. Who knew when I married Lucas that I was also be marrying into a celebrity family that centered around Jazzist Zoe Cook Gardner.

When Lucas was killed, Zoe immediately stepped in, acting as a surrogate parent to help with the kids as they grew up. Zoe helped me cart the kids to their schools, sports activities, dancing schools, and soccer games.

Zoe and her husband Julian didn't have children of their own. Their career and lifestyle choices didn't allow much room for kids. Despite that fact, Zoe was great with her nephew and nieces. She had a natural knack for relating to them. When the kids were growing up, Zoe often sat at our white baby grand piano in the living area, singing soulfully in front of the fireplace, lulling the girls to sleep. Xavier would remain awake at her feet, forcing his eyelids to stay open, saying "play it again Aunt Zoe."

By the time Xavier was 12, Zoe gave him a saxophone that he played very well. When Lucas died, Xavier stopped playing.

Now that Nena had come into his life, I'd noticed Xavier beginning to pick up the saxophone again. I would hear him playing more often these days, impressing Nena with his own rendition of "Fallen" from the movie Pretty Woman. Xavier's renewed interests in music made me wonder if my son was falling in love or had he just finally gotten over his grief.

"Madison said she was bringing Pinot Noir tonight Riley, so I grabbed a couple bottles of Syrah. I don't do wimpy wines," Zoe said, motioning her fingers in air quotes. "I like my wines bold and in my face just like I like my man," Zoe snickered.

"Well I'm pouring mine now," Madison replied. "These new teachers have pressed my nerves all week. It is time for me to wind down and relax. They spend more time whining about the kids driving them crazy then they do to intellectually stimulate them."

Madison was director of the Bucks County Community College's Early Childhood Development Program. She ran an outstanding program that was often modeled by most of the surrounding universities in the State. Madison was divorced from her husband Alonzo Keyes, an engineer and self-proclaimed "entrepreneur."

Alonzo was always starting a new company every time you turned around, none of which were particularly prosperous. Unable to deal with Alonzo's fast changing unprofitable business escapades, Madison divorced him. She was currently dating Quentin Stoll, a wealthy architect, and son of the Stoll Brothers family, a Pennsylvania family owned land development magnate.

"Speaking of crazy," Madison said, "You'll never believe this one. Riley, I think one of my crazy new teacher's sister is dating your ex, Warren Shaw. She came to one of my guidance and counseling seminars today with a book Warren supposedly had authored. I asked her where she got the book and she said the author was her sister's new boyfriend and that she had purchased it off Amazon."

"Are you kidding me?" Zoe said.

"All I thought was "Oh my God. Wait until I tell Riley,""" Madison continued uncomfortably. "And speaking of God, the book was about some religious transformation Warren experienced."

"This is joke right?" Lily said.

"Nope. The synopsis said Warren defined himself as a man "saved by God." Claims he was shaped by the predominant women in his life as a young male, helping him to be a successful adult male. Word is he's doing speaking tours to young male audiences. Can you believe this fool? He's really concocted a new scheme this time."

"That's just dog shit, Madison," I said, standing up with my hands on my hips.

"Yeah Madison," Zoe stuttered. "That's . . . just . . . just . . . just . . . doggie shit," she said, looking as shocked and exasperated as I was feeling, but still working overtime to have my back.

Lily was working her fingers quickly on her iPhone, linking to the Amazon website.

"How many times could a lie be told not only in life, but on Amazon for Christ sakes?" I spurted out. "Jesus, Madison, now he's trying to grab his five minutes of fame with his lying narcissistic self?"

"Yep," Lily said. "Because here's his page on Amazon. That loser!" Lily exclaimed in exasperation.

I could feel myself turning red. I was disgusted.

"Forget about it, Riley. That was just a bad time in your life," Lily nodded.

"Bad time? That's an understatement," I offered, bending slightly forward. "It was just ugly all the way around. He was such a huge prick. I can never believe how much of my life I wasted loving him," I said.

"Love doesn't often arrive at the right time or in the right person. It wasn't the right time in your life and he definitely wasn't the right person," Lily said.

I sat down a few dessert plates, looking at the Pinot Noir label and feeling like I needed something stronger. I debated which wine I was gonna pour for myself.

"Who the hell was I then Madison?"

"You were just who you were then Riley," she said compassionately. "You're not that woman anymore. You've come a long way babe." She poured more of the Pinot Noir, grabbing a strawberry to have with her chocolate cheesecake.

"Yeah," Zoe said. "You're not that woman any more, Riley. Because now you would cut his balls off," Zoe laughed.

We all fell out laughing as Zoe stood up and sang "to the left to the left, all you shit-heads and assholes to the left" while throwing a toss pillow at my head.

I knew then this party had officially gotten out of hand.

I turned briefly, noticing Stogie strolling in and sniffing the cake.

"Sit, Stogie," I said, patting him on his head. Stogie momentarily whined knowing I was not giving him any cake. He looked at Zoe for a bit of sympathy.

"Riley, you know your father always says, "If you run around with dogs you're gonna get fleas" and "Riley, I wouldn't want a man that doesn't want me,"" Zoe responded nonchalantly.

Daddy is so wise, I thought. "I find that was good advice that applies to women as well as men," I responded politely.

"Changing the subject, Zoe, since we're all going to the holiday Memorial Gala together this weekend, you can help me with this one," Lily said warmly. "I've told Riley that I'd like to introduce her to Captain Noah Dunham. It's about time Riley get out from behind that laptop and meet a man," Lily said.

"I don't need a man," I blushed.

"Who said you need a man. We said "meet a man,"" Madison interjected.

"That's right," Lily said. "He's perfect for Riley. Isn't that right Zoe?" Lily nudged.

Zoe shrugged her shoulders shifting uncomfortably. "I suppose," she said with very little enthusiasm.

"Zoe, tell her," Lily went on.

I took note of the fact that Zoe was silent.

"Do tell her Zoe," Lily begged, a bit more persuasive, eyes narrowed.

"Am I missing something here?" asked Madison.

"Not at all," said Lily. "Right Zoe?"

"Fine," Zoe huffed. "Riley, Captain Dunham was a close friend of my brother Lucas." She paused, slowly articulating each of her words as if I was missing something.

"Yeah, then why don't I know him?" I argued, fidgeting with the strawberries. "What's the big deal? Who is he anyway?" I went on. "And, it's not like I give a damn anyway." I stuffed a huge strawberry in my mouth.

"You met at the Army-Navy game," Zoe said sternly.

"Army-Navy game? The only thing I met that day was my ass getting introduced to the concrete and chili dogs," I laughed. "Who else was there to meet that day besides Lucas?" I snickered.

I was starting to feel my head getting buzzed from the wine. Zoe walked out of the room, headed for the kitchen. Madison shot me a look that spoke volumes. I decided I wasn't in the mood to go down that path and get my panties in a bunch over whatever was obviously ailing Zoe. I murmured to myself that I had baked my bread, and to calm myself down and that I was in a good mood. I was a teeny weeny bit buzzed, but still having a good time. I had no doubt that we'd be certain to re-visit the subject before the night was over because Lily was extremely persistent. She had no intention of being denied. Zoe entered back into the den, happy to have had a reason to change the subject.

"Look who I found."

My handsome brother Reese entered the room. I thought he was almost a carbon copy of Vin Diesel.

Reese sauntered across the floor stealthily, wearing his aviator Ray Bans on top of his head. His chest bulged from the tight fitting grey tee embossed with ARMY on the front. He sported faded denim washed blue jeans with a hole ripped at the knee. He was carrying a Tumi backpack over his shoulder. He had grown a mustache since the last time I had seen him, his face revealing a hint of a five o'clock shadow. His hair was cut so close it appeared practically bald. He was handsome as ever. I watched him setting Cleo down, tossing her a ball across the floor.

Reese whisked me into his arms, spun me around, kissed me on the cheek sweetly, whispering in a husky voice.

"Hello sis; your plus one has arrived, baby."

Madison, Zoe, and Lily all crowded around Reese joining into what became a group hug, giggling endlessly about how happy they were to see him. Reese hugged and kissed each of them individually grabbing me by my hand, taking a seat and landing on the oversized stuffed ottoman while sitting me on his lap.

It wasn't long before I heard Xavier, Samantha, and Claire's footsteps entering the room from hearing all of the commotion. They were shouting "Uncle Reese. Uncle Reese!"

Cleo and Stogie began to bark loudly again from the girls' commotion. Cleo was now running around in circles vying for attention. Leave it to Reese to manage a huge entrance with my girlfriends, kids, and the dogs.

"The celebration is on, ladies. I've already heard the good news, Riley. My secretary called me on the train, forwarding the Beard Foundation's news release to my email," Reese said, moving me off his lap. He reached in his bag pulling out a couple of bottles of Verve Cliquot Champagne.

"Congratulations Riley. Where can I find the flutes, Sis?"

I kissed Reese on the cheek, squeezed his hand hard and whispered in his ear how happy I was to see him. I grabbed champagne flutes off the nearby wet bar. Reese popped the champagne while the kids huddled, managing to catch up with their Uncle Reese. After exchanging congratulatory toasts, as I expected, Lily picked the ball up again. The elephant was still in the room.

"Well Reese, were all glad you're here to be Riley's plus one for the Gala. But for the record, I want you to know in advance that I plan to introduce her to Captain Dunham, the Master of Ceremonies for the Gala. There will be plenty of beautiful single women for you to meet. I'll be happy to play Cupid for you if you'd like, but this is definitely the man I plan to introduce to Riley. So, don't go getting all overprotective and in the way of a good thing," she said sweetly.

"Yeah," Madison laughed. "We know how we have to keep you from personally killing any male that gets near your sister. Despite what you think, Reese, there are a few good men left in the world suitable for Riley. As a matter of fact I'll be bringing a good man myself," Madison replied, rendering much needed support to Lily's pleas.

A hush fell over the room as all eyes turned to Reese.

"Ladies, ladies, my sister can date anybody she pleases, as long as they meet my standards," he chuckled.

Everyone had a look of disbelief on their face. We each knew better.

"No really, Riley doesn't need my permission to date. She can date whoever she wants to date. But that doesn't mean I am not going to have a third eye on those asshats. I'm not having my sister hurt again," he said downing his champagne in one big gulp.

"Jesus, you people act like I'm not even in this room," I said, a bit giggly, pouring myself another glass of the Bin 23.

Looking out the corner of my eye I could see Zoe was hitting the champagne pretty hard.

"You can introduce me to a whole room full of eligible men if you like Lily, but like I said, I'm perfectly content with my life as it is. I will not unravel because of some big shot Navy Captain Masters of Ceremonies what's his name," I said now getting indignant. "Honestly you people need to get some lives so you guys can stop worrying about mine."

I knew full well they each had their own agendas and had all put their heads together, but my job was to my maintain status quo. Life would be a whole lot less complicated.

"Reese, speaking of guys, before you came, Madison was sharing a story about Warren Shaw," Zoe said.

Now I knew for sure this conversation was headed to a road of shaky ground. Reese hated Warren. Why would Zoe bring his name up?

"Don't mention that motherfucker's name to me," Reese growled. "You'll ruin my day. And so far it's going pretty well," he said, swallowing hard.

"You're a tad bit over-protective, brother man," Lily said.

"That's my job," Reese snapped back at her. "I guess you didn't get the memo. I'm protecting my sister from these opportunistic shit heads trying to take advantage of my sister now that she's renowned in her field. My antennas are up and I will deal with any guy that doesn't treat her like the princess that she is," Reese said with a loving smile. "God, I love Washington's Crossing," Reese said, walking across the room gazing out the back picture window looking at the gazebo.

My turned my attention immediately to Madison, Lily, and Zoe, glaring hard. I shook my head at each of them, lip mouthing that I was going to personally kill them, moving my index finger and thumb like a gun trigger shooting at each of them, despite the fact my heart was warmed by their presence.

CHAPTER 5

NOAH

"Ladies and Gentlemen, our next guest is very special. When she's not performing, she spends her time off raising money overseas for our Toys for Navy Tots Program, all around the world. No one has offered more energy, commitment, and dedication to the cause than she. Ladies and gentlemen, please join me in welcoming our very special guest this evening, Broadway Tony Award Winner, Ms. Anika Noni Rose."

The room filled with thunderous applause. Everyone stood.

"Thank you so much, Captain Dunham," Ms. Rose replied as she put her hand in mine.

I reached out to help her to the podium. As lovely as she was, she was not nearly as beautiful as the woman sitting next to Lily DeLuca.

The wait staff bombarded the room, hurriedly pouring champagne in anticipation of the evening toast. The reading of the names of the Fallen had begun, but my mind was distracted less by the words being spoken, but more focused on the poise and elegance I thought she exuded sitting there next to Lily and Lucas's sister Zoe. Damn, she was gorgeous.

"John Christian Adams," I heard Ms. Rose say in the background as my thoughts of her held my mind hostage, triggering my momentary escape from the reading of the names.

Her dark brown hair was flowing in the air softly as the loose waterfall of curls framing her face were as I remembered them from Lucas's family pictures. She still wore that wispy bang slightly parted to the left.

"Stephen Russell Ballentine."

My memory hadn't failed me. She was as beautiful as ever. She still had that incredibly attractive exotic look that made you question her origins. My mind couldn't comprehend anyone else in the room knowing that I was this close to the captivating woman glittering across the room like a well cut diamond.

What sensible man wouldn't admire the beauty adorned in a black sequinned turtleneck gown that clung to her body in ways that paid homage to her curves? She was even more glamorous now than she was as a young woman. I admired her beauty then, but now she was a breathtaking drop-dead-gorgeous-mom-shell. Damn. How many men in this room was I going have to bat off to keep them at bay? No doubt they too had her in their sights. I recognized predators in waiting when I saw them. I used to be one. What man in their right mind couldn't help but notice her?

"At this time we'd like to present posthumously the Navy Cross Award to Lucas Xavier Cook for his exceptional heroism under enemy combat," Ms. Rose said with a great deal of reverence.

Most of the men in the room had subtly directed their attention to Riley. She revealed very little in her dress, except for the deep slit cut all the way up to her upper thigh, teasing all eyes with a little peak of her lean, toned legs. I suspected with legs like that she must be a runner, or she works out with a personal trainer, but either way I was up damn well up for the chase.

Suddenly my mind snapped back to attention as I noticed Zoe's head turn to watch Riley come to the podium to accept the Navy Cross Award. She walked like a gazelle and looked like an angel. Riley gracefully approached the Dias, practically floating on air to accept the award on Lucas's behalf. There was no mistaking her beauty. The sound of her voice broke through my daze as I listened to her politely accept the award, then giving a heartfelt thanks. The resounding audience applause reverberated across the room.

Who was the man seated next to her? He hovered over her in a protective manner, helping her off the dais and back to her seat. Undoubtedly, he had a close personal relationship with her. I felt the painful beat in my heart as I instinctively caught myself panicking, internally contemplating if she was again in a new relationship. I gave myself a mental shake, scrambling to clear the fog out of my head, recalling that Lily DeLuca said she'd be alone. What was up with Lily's information? She was far from alone.

I warily studied the way she leaned against his broad shoulders, wiping a tear from her eye, moving her lips close to his ear. Was she whispering sweet words of affection? Who in the hell was he? I needed to be him. I yearned for those words to be for me. She lifted her chin slightly higher, nodding as she thanked him as he helped her to her seat, parting her lips with a half smile respecting the moment.

Anika continued down with the remaining awards. My heart felt a deep pang as I shared the loss I too felt for Lucas. So many times I thought about Lucas during my midnight sprints. My nightly runs now were never quite the same without him.

"Captain Dunham. Captain Dunham. Captain Dunham." I heard my name called only after the third time.

I rose quickly from my seat, being careful not to trip over my own feet and darted to the microphone. I thanked Ms. Rose and called for a round of applause, watching as Ms. Rose headed back to the left side of the stage to her handlers in waiting. Thank God this part of the program was over. I was ready to get off this podium. Could we just be over this ceremony so I could focus on the matter at hand? I needed to be front and center with Riley. I'm putting closure on this program.

"I'd like to extend a special thanks to all of you that have joined us this evening to show our gratitude and to pay tribute to those who have given their lives on behalf of this country. President Barack Obama has sent his regards. I've been asked to read his statement."

A soft hush fell across the ballroom. I began the reading of the presidential letter.

"Mindful of each of you who have had to trace your fingers across black granite, and to all the nation's veterans who have served with honor and distinction. We thank you for your service to a call greater than yourselves. In this 9-11 generation, as the tides of the wars in Iraq and Afghanistan are receding, each of the Fallen have earned their place in the minds and hearts of the greatest generation. For those who have felt that tug to tirelessly serve, and to those who have given their life, as a symbol of the nation's gratitude, I'd like to present each Fallen member's family a special thank you note from President Barack Obama."

The ballroom filled again with thunderous applause.

"Now if you'll raise your glasses with me and share in a toast. May you never forget what is worth remembering, or remember what is best forgotten. Cheers."

I peered across the room, gazing directly into her eyes as if the words were only for her, watching her as she raised her glass. The sound of champagne flutes clinking in the room signaled the end of the night's more formal agenda. Now we could get on with the serious business at hand. I was wrapping this puppy up.

"And now ladies and gentlemen," I announced, "feel free to mingle, eat, drink and dance to the music of the Julian Gardner and the Joshua Clayton combo, with special vocals by the incomparable Zoe Cook Gardner."

The air in the room shifted to a more relaxed mood. I couldn't take my eyes off of her, watching as she smiled, sipped her champagne, applauding happily for Zoe. She looked happy. I liked her happy face. I imagined myself holding her hand, kissing her cheek tenderly. Damn, she was beautiful. It was going to be hard for me contain myself being in this close proximity to her. I didn't want any man near her but me, lest I'd have to break him in two.

I silently reminded myself to reign my emotions in quickly. I wasn't in a war zone. I needed to conduct myself in a civilized manner. But it was difficult being in her presence, not wanting to be the center of her attention.

Zoe was belting out *Fly Me To The Moon*, as Lily DeLuca waltzed my way. The noise level had gone up several notches in the Four Seasons. The guests were loosening up considerably. Champagne was flowing freely from the elaborate champagne fountains positioned all around the room. I desperately desired to get to the other side of the room where the bar was located. I thought a manly drink would help to calm me now that my part of the evening was over. It was everything I had to stay focused. My attention kept drifting back to her. I'd always known and loved her in my heart, and in my dreams, but tonight she was within my grasp.

The man next to her continued to hover over her like a drone, as if he had the reins on her every move. She was conversing with the celebrity chefs while several photographers snapped photographs of the three of them together. I growled to myself watching him put his arm around her waist. A couple of local television anchors where interviewing her. There was a lot of buzz and hand shaking going on around her. God I hoped she wasn't in relationship, because I had expected her to be alone. If she was in a relationship, I was going after her anyway. I would walk barefoot over hot coals for her if necessary. There wasn't a man alive that was going to get in between me and her. I had no intention this time of foregoing on my promise to Lucas. Surely, Lucas couldn't have foreseen these circumstances, but I had no doubt he believed I was the man for this mission.

I wanted to smoke an Opus X, unbutton my jacket, and savor a Stoli martini right now. As soon as I made it to the bar, I heard my name called out.

"Noah."

"Yes?" I replied, turning in time to see the charming Lily DeLuca.

Thank God.

"Hello Lily. It's so good to see you again. You're looking lovely as always this evening," I said, reaching out to grab her hand, kissing her on both cheeks. "How'd we do this year?"

"Oh Captain, without fail you did a wonderful job. What would we do without you? We raised thousands of dollars over last year's numbers. It was a great turnout, don't you think?"

"I love helping the kids. May I get you a drink Lily?"

"No. No, not right now. I have to get these checks to the hotel safe first, but thank you anyway. I'll have something later when I'm finished with business and securing these donations. Don't you just love the decorations and table favors?"

"Very much so, Lily," I said as my eyes shifted to look at each table's centerpiece of white candles tied neatly with a black sequinned bow. "Everything was perfect," I added, hoping to assure Lily that her committee's hard work was worthwhile.

"And speaking of perfect, Noah, I have that special someone I mentioned to you earlier that I'd like to introduce you to if I may," Lily smiled a bit too innocently. "Her company is responsible for this evening's chefs, artisans, wine selections, and decor."

"Why sure. How could I ever deny you Lily?" I said with a smile that met hers, knowing we were in cahoots with each other.

"Bartender, I'll have another please." *Hmmm. I loved those black sequins.*

Chapter 6

Riley

"Thank God, Lily had the good sense to put our whole group at the same table," I puffed, taking a long deep breath.

Madison was focused on her date Quentin, whose attention was directed at the black and gold engraved gala brochure, but she managed to quietly nod her head in agreement.

"We're near the program's end," Quentin uttered.

"Good to know. The night has been hard enough as it is," I said, breathing a sigh of relief.

"Not to worry, sis," Reese replied, breaking his momentary silence. "I would have never let you sit alone at a table with this vulturous crowd," he said, surveying the room.

"Yup. Vulture bait," Quentin chuckled. "She's both beautiful and available. Bad enough I'm trying to hold on to mine in this room of Navy elite," he said, smiling at Madison, scooting closer to her and wrapping his arm around her chair.

"Half of the guys in here are asking me who's the woman I'm with tonight. They're acutely aware after the award ceremony that Riley's a widow. It's going to be open season. I'm prepared to swat them off one by one," he growled.

"I love you dearly, Reese, but I can take care of myself," I said, giving his hand a squeeze. "It means a lot to me that I could receive Lucas's award surrounded by the company of those I love."

I was hoping that I had shaken off the brief tremble in my voice from the knot that had welled up in my throat after accepting Lucas's award.

"You got through it just fine," Madison said, fully relaxed. "She really is in a good place," she said, directing her words to Quentin, giving me a wink.

"That's definitely true. You did well Riley," Zoe agreed.

"Besides, you've long since completed your five stages of grief from the loss of Lucas. You're over the broken engagement with Warren. You're rocking it now honey," Zoe said, co-signing with Madison.

"I'm by myself now but I'm good. My world hasn't collapsed because I am alone. I've gotten through accepting this beautiful, prestigious Navy Cross Award. And, God isn't this supposed to be a fun night on some level? I'm ready to let my hair down."

"Indeed it is," Madison said.

"Can we please get the attention off of me then and talk about something else. It's hard enough not to go down memory lane."

"Well, it might be harder than you think to get the attention off you tonight, Riley. You're a bit of a celebrity in your own right," Madison said, lifting her glass, her ruby lips pressing against the rim. "That was so cool watching all the photographers taking your picture, the folks with press badges interviewing you. You're for sure gonna make the ten o'clock news tonight."

I grinned at Madison, watching as Reese loosened his black silk necktie, unbuttoned the top button on his shirt and ordered more champagne. It was nice to sip champagne. Relax. Exhale for the evening.

I needed this chill moment after spending several hours setting up the room, coupled with the long ride to the Four Seasons. Lily had worked my ears off in the limousine over my meeting the captain. Zoe spoke way too little in the limousine ride, nervously pouring herself champagne every time the subject of meeting the captain came up.

"You've done a beautiful job with the room, Riley," Julian said, joining our group table with Zoe, who was taking a music break. Julian pulled a chair out for himself, casually directing Zoe's attention to the centerpiece.

"Thanks Julian," I said, agreeing that my advance staff had done a great job with the decor.

"The room is simply elegant Riley," Zoe added. "I love the white candles tied in black sequinned bows. It's beautiful. Somehow I feel like I sing better in a room that has your stamp on it," Zoe said, smiling, then rubbing her nose against Julian's cheek, both looking very much in love.

"I'm glad you feel that way," Julian said turning to Zoe,

"because this break is gonna be short. We'll have to warm up with the combo soon."

"I try to leave a bit of myself in the room at these events so you know I was here," I laughed back at Julian. "It was a huge undertaking, but I'm glad I got to create an intimate, elegant aura that respects the nature and intent of the gala."

"Many of the guests gasped upon entering the ballroom, commenting on how beautifully the room was decorated," Zoe answered back. "It's simply magical. Very fitting for a black tie affair."

"Thanks Zoe. That means a lot coming from you. You have such great taste yourself."

"It's the perfect touch for a room filled with well adorned women in lovely designer gowns, coupled with this delicious buffet of well styled men in black tuxedos and dress naval attire," she laughed nudging Julian playfully in his side.

I giggled right along with Zoe, joining in with her teasing of Julian.

"This truly must be the place where the wild things come out to play. Just think, a whole entire room full of alpha males all to ourselves," Zoe teased.

"Are you trying to make me jealous, woman?" Julian turned to Zoe, "because you are doing a damn good job of it," he said, kissing her tenderly on the lips.

"Forget the alpha males," Madison said. "I'm still drooling over what you did with the menu Riley. I've died and gone to heaven twice. You've really outdone yourself on the food this time, Momma."

"Flattery will get you guys everywhere," I joked.

"I may not be able to leave," Madison said turning towards Quentin. "After-all, Chefs Eric Ripert and Bobby Flay are in the house," Madison squealed. "I'm tickled pink! The buffet stations are literally to die for. It's borderline obscene. All of the foodies in the house are in awe."

I was pleased to be able to arrange for Chef Ripert's station to serve a seafood buffet featuring oysters Rockefeller, broiled lobster, and poisson en papillote. Bobby Flay's station featured filet mignon and prime rib. The side dishes included roasted eggplant garlic soup, herbed rice, potatoes au gratin, whole tomatoes gratinée, sweet potato puree, asparagus spears, and hot rolls. The dessert bar included crème brûlée ice cream atop caramelized pineapple soaked in crème de cassis.

I gave myself a silent pat on the back. All my hard work had indeed paid off. Everything had turned out picture perfect. I really couldn't complain. So far the gala was turning out to be pretty nice.

With all of Lily's chatter in the limo about meeting the captain, I finally got to lay eyes on the man. Lily was beyond right. Jesus, the man was tall, handsome, and intriguing. As Master of Ceremonies, his charming personality really shone through.

Captain Noah Dunham was well-spoken, carrying the pace of the evening's Memorial Gala flawlessly. From his beginning introduction of Ms. Anika Noni Rose to the reading of the Fallen, the receiving of Lucas's award, and final champagne toast, it was a job well done. We each agreed that Lily's chairmanship of the gala this year was the right dose of fresh input that was believed by many to be long overdue.

Julian and Zoe excused themselves as the jazz combo returned from their interlude and began revving the music up a notch. Zoe was singing angelically in the background of the excitement in the room, accompanied by Julian on the piano. Many of the guests were on the dance floor while others were chatting endlessly, tapping their feet to the beat of the music or scampering to the bar. Madison and I waited patiently for Lily to return from the hotel safe. We could see her across the room, leaving the bar area, striding across the room with the captain. Lily was wearing the most dazzling silver beaded gown that glittered under the ballroom lights. Her curly red locks were adorned on one side with a single strand of silver pop hair tinsel. Lily looked her usual elegant self.

The captain walked next to her dressed in U.S. Navy Dinner Dress whites, black bow tie, and gold cumber-band. My heart skipped a beat as he strolled our direction with graceful ease. I started to have déjà vu. There was something oddly familiar about him, yet I couldn't quite put my finger on the feeling.

"What do you think, Madison?" I whispered, as I leaned into her ear, watching as Lily and the captain made their way through the crowd towards our table. Butterflies were starting to flutter within my stomach.

"I think that ass is fine," Madison cooed. "You could spot that fine thang out of a crowd at a Million Man March that's what I think," she said as she bent my way, grinned, and took another sip of her champagne. Neither of us had taken our eyes off the captain.

"Oh wow," I gasped. "Lily said he was a lady-killer, but I had no idea he was gonna be the 'you can put your shoes under my bed' fine," I whispered under my breath, wide-eyed, grabbing my white cloth napkin to wipe any sweat off my hands.

"Oh Lordy Lordy," Madison shrieked. "He looks good enough to eat. He's the melt-in-your-mouth-not-in-your-hands kind of fine, Riley. Strictly dickly fine," Madison swooned. "Check out the walk. That's all swagger baby. Umph Umph Umph. Girl, he just can't help himself."

"I see."

"That is plain downright unadulterated sexy on a stick. I bet that man can rock a woman's world like a turbulent storm that you need to get out of its path. That's pure *Chocolate Thunder*, baby," Madison said, shaking her head in acquiescence.

"Well God bless the universe for *Chocolate Thunder*," I whispered.

Madison and I slapped each other five under the table. I was desperately trying to wipe the silly school girl grin off my face. Of course, I couldn't deny that on some deep level that there was some part of me that wanted to be able to love and trust again.

"Maybe meeting a new man wasn't such a bad idea after-all, Madison."

"Ya think? Umm. Hmm. I just bet it isn't," Madison said, as if she knew all along I would agree with her.

But then again, my other self—the disciplined part of me—had lost all faith in the hope that someone as wonderful as Lucas would ever come along for me again.

"Hey guys, I'm back," Lily said, as all the men at the table rushed to stand. Lily casually motioned them to sit, acknowledging them, saying, "Don't, I'm not staying. I'd like to introduce you to our Masters of Ceremonies for the evening, Captain Noah Michael Dunham."

"Please, call me Noah," he said, his voice rich, deep, and sensual.

"This is Riley Cook," Lily said, motioning her hand in my direction.

I extended my right hand to shake his. He gently placed my hand in his, planting a soft kiss on the top of my knuckles.

"Hello Riley."

An intense warmth from the touch of his hand raced through my body head to toe, leaving me feeling as if his presence took up the air in the room. Where in the world did that come from? Perhaps I needed to ratchet my intake of champagne down a notch.

"And this is Riley's brother, Reese Nelson," Lily said, looking at Reese sternly. Reese put his arm around the back of my chair and did a half raised stand out of his seat.

"Nice to meet you man," Reese said, an overdose of icy coolness thrown in to ward the man off.

"And, our good friends Madison Keyes, her date Quentin Stoll," Lily continued on with introductions, ignoring Reese.

"Hello, nice to meet you," Madison said, unrestrained curiosity flashing across her face.

Quentin stood, shaking Noah's hand.

"Good evening."

Madison was suffering from the same ailment I was. We were both trying not to stare like two stalkers. Except, Madison had a silly looking grin on her face and I was trying to maintain my composure. Lily, meanwhile, opted out of our group, excusing herself to attend the ladies room, but managing to wink at me as she turned away.

"May I?" Noah said, asking to sit in the open seat next to me.

"Please."

Reese shuffled uncomfortably, pulling his chair closer to mine.

"Quentin, they're playing our song," Madison said, grabbing his hand, suggesting they dance.

Was she kidding? *What You Won't Do For Love* was playing. Quentin looked perplexed but moved on cue, responding to Madison's command like a puppy dog. I didn't doubt for one minute that Madison was giving Noah and me space. Reese, however, was planted to his chair like Elmer's glue to construction paper. I refrained from poking my elbow in his side knowing he was unlikely to go anywhere. Getting Reese to move in this moment would be asking the impossible. Madison and Quentin unequivocally did not have a song. I made a mental note to myself to re-visit that little matter with Madison later. My ears were ringing with Julian riffing on the piano keys in the background, accompanying Zoe who was singing the melody like an angel.

"You're Lucas Cook's widow, correct?"

"Yes, I am."

"I've not seen you at this gala before," Noah said.

"I've normally chosen to forego the gala in years gone by, but this year I wanted to come. I needed to come. Intuitively, it felt like the right thing to do since Lucas was receiving a special award."

"I'm glad you did," Noah responded, his tone gentle.

"It was nice to be able to be at place in my life where I could pause and comfortably honor Lucas, while at the same time help out a worthy cause."

"That's very noble. You've done a wonderful job this evening planning the gala. Lily tells me you've been nominated for the James E. Beard Foundation Award. Congratulations. I couldn't help but noticed you've also gotten a lot of press coverage tonight."

"Thank you. It's a wonderful honor indeed. I'm hoping if I'm lucky, that I can grab the attention of some angel investor for my business once this is over, especially since things are going well."

"Well you certainly have my attention."

My stomach did a backflip. I smiled amicably at Noah, feeling the heat from the blush on my face. Reese was tapping his fingers on the table like they were piano keys. His leg was moving non-stop next to mine, shaking nervously under the table. I placed my hand on his leg to calm him. I suppose the presence of a man on my other side was making him edgy.

"It's nice to finally see you again."

"See me again?" I questioned. "Really? Have we met before? I somehow don't recall," I said, looking deeply into his eyes with a bit of bewilderment.

"Actually, you and I encountered each other briefly a long time ago."

"Really? When?" I asked quizzically.

"Perhaps you know of me by my nickname. Lucas and

people intimately close to me from the Academy refer to me as Mico. Lucas and I were close. Actually he was my best friend."

"Yesssssss, Mico," I said, now speaking more warmly. "Lucas rarely referred to you as Noah, so I guess I failed to connect the dots."

"Mico is my nickname. My middle name is Michael as given to me by grandmother. My grandmother used to send me care packages at the Academy addressed to Mico. The guys in the dorm got wind of it. It was a wrap after that."

"Yes, Mico. I remember well now. Noah Michael Dunham, huh."

"Yes, that's me," he said, his eyes piercing mine.

I paused, waiting for him to speak. Maybe I was holding my breath in awe. It had been a long time since a man had affected me the way he was.

"Lucas and I were in the same class at the Naval Academy. He loved to tease me, routinely chiding me saying, "Mico Mico," in a high shrilled voice. "Something has come for you in the mail from your Nanna, Mico," he would say." Noah's face bared a heartwarming smile, with a sense of reflection. "Besides my grandmother, only a handful of folks, mostly those from the Academy, call me that," he grinned, shaking his head. "You and I met several years ago. I was the guy standing next to Lucas at the Army Navy Game the day the two of you first met. Of course I was several pounds lighter back then," Noah chuckled.

It was hard for me to imagine Noah lighter in weight, because as far as I was concerned he was as tight as a drum in all the right places. There was no middle-aged pot belly or love handles on this man anywhere.

"I believe you were on a chili dog run if I recall," he said, politely being careful not to embarrass me by mentioning my tumble.

"Oh yes, I remember the day well. I remember you now," I said, noticing that Reese, who'd been peering across the room glaring at some Asian woman, was re-directing his attention back to my conversation with Noah.

"Well funny, I don't," Reese said sharply, interjecting himself into our conversation.

"I'm sorry, Noah, my brother Reese here was quarterbacking that day for the Army. Army won the day he was playing which is likely why he doesn't remember you," I said sharply, kicking my foot at his ankle under the table, physically suggesting that he should shut his mouth and behave. "So that was you, huh?" I said softly, my face turning flush again from recalling that moment.

"Yes it was," he smiled. "Of course I already knew your sister-in-law Zoe from our days at the Naval Academy. Zoe and I met prior to your marriage. Back in the day, Lucas used to bust Zoe's chops when Zoe would come up for the family day weekends. All the guys wanted to meet his beautiful twin sister who could hit a softball further than he could. The Navy didn't admit women back then so it was unusual for us guys to actually see a female hit a softball that far. Amazing how well Zoe could crack a bat," he laughed.

"Athleticism is one of Zoe's many attributes," I laughed with him.

"Zoe has many wonderful qualities," he nodded.

I wondered what he meant by that, but dismissed his comment knowing my tendency to over analyze.

"I guess I've known her as long as I've known Lucas. Every time I look at her I miss him. They look so much alike."

"Funny, why hadn't I got to know you better before now," I said with a puzzled look on my face. "Lucas spoke fondly on many occasions about his navy buddy Mico. He considered you his confidante."

"And he mine."

"What? Did you do a disappearing act or something?" I said, feigning teasing but really wanting to know the answer.

"Yeah," Reese said, engaged back in my conversation again. "Man did you do some disappearing act or something, because I don't know you."

"No," Noah said, addressing his response now to both Reese and me. "I was assigned to a navy intelligence team on an assignment for the Secretary of Defense. The assignment took me out of the country for a while," Noah responded, looking past me directly at Reese.

"My mission was highly classified," he said, turning his attention to me. "I wasn't allowed to discuss the mission with anyone. I was allowed contact with only a hand full of people, Lucas being one of them."

"I see," I said, remaining engaged, eager to learn why I had not interacted with my dead husband's best buddy.

"Even though I was half way across the other side of the

world, Lucas knew of my mission and its dangerous nature. He kept my confidences, helped me to avoid getting homesick by writing letters often and staying in touch."

"Are you saying my brother-in-law had a pen pal?" Reese grunted, interrupting our conversation.

"Lucas wrote mostly about you and the kids," Noah said, ignoring Reese's comment. "As a matter of fact, you were *all* he wrote about," Noah acknowledged, his eyes flirtatious, holding me spellbound.

A warm glow shimmered through my body from his look that went through me. I quivered. He was mesmerizing, like some homing beacon that I was being drawn to like a magnet. I figured I might ignite any second now from the heat. My heat however, was nothing compared to the heat radiating off Reese's body, but for entirely different reasons. I couldn't ignore my intuitions that were screaming at me that Reese's mind and body were on high alert. My body was on high alert too, but not because of me.

"I really do feel like I know you, despite the fact Lucas was generally a private person," Noah said smiling, his stare sliding over me, drawing me in like I was the prey.

Jesus, I felt vulnerable. I wondered if my sense of vulnerability was triggering something in Reese. Exactly what had Lucas said about me? I was curious, yet dared not ask the question out loud. I didn't want to push Reese any further into his state of high alert. I had plenty of practice growing up around military men all my life. It didn't take much to trigger their sensibilities. Even when we were kids, Reese was plugged into my emotional energy, as I to him, so I knew where I was emotionally couldn't be good. Reese and I were always vibing each other.

"Lucas and I ended up on the same destroyer together in Yemen, shortly before his plane went down," Noah continued. "I was scheduled to fly out with him that day to bring in a group of Seals, but was grounded due a bad bout of food poisoning. I felt like somebody cut off my left arm the day his plane went down. I thought maybe I could have done something if I had been with him. The funny thing about life, no matter how well you think you have it planned out, it throws curve balls at us all the time."

I could hear Zoe's melodic voice singing the first few lyrics of Etta James's "At Last."

"Riley would you like to dance?" he asked quickly, changing the subject.

I was glad for the change. My mood had lifted earlier and I didn't want to talk about memories that made me sad. Reese was energetically putting his lock and load overprotective guns into place. I could just about hear the wheels turning in his head. His facial expression was a dead giveaway.

"Sure. I'd like that."

Reese snorted in my right ear at the notion of my dancing with Noah. Noah smiled, ignoring Reese but never taking his eye off him. Noah rose, pulling the back of my chair out from under me to help me up. Reese stood too, looking eye ball to eye ball, giving his best death stare to Noah as he helped me out of my chair. Jesus, the testosterone rush that passed between Reese and Noah was scary. I felt as if a pissing match was subject to unfold at any minute.

I smiled gently at Reese, squeezing his hand slightly, looking at him with begging eyes that were starting to narrow. I wanted him to chill the hell out.

Madison was still way across the room with Quentin, but was easy to spot in her red chiffon Chanel gown. Madison, Quentin, and Lily were all grouped together in a tight huddle, laughing and mingling at the bar. Some guy decked out in a black velvet trimmed tuxedo holding two champagne glasses was obviously putting the moves on Lily, because her head was cocked to the side a bit. That was her signature move she does when she's being hit on.

My heart was constricting, skipping beats as Noah led me to the dance floor. Madison glanced my direction from the bar area, lifting her champagne flute slightly, letting me know she was still taking notice of Noah and me.

"It's been awhile since I have been in the arms of man, even for a dance," I said, not realizing I actually had said that out loud.

I bit my lip quickly to force myself to shut up before I put my foot in my mouth even further. Lord, have mercy, I muttered to myself. Be still my heart.

"Well then, I consider myself the envy of every man here knowing that I have the most beautiful woman in the room in my arms."

When we reached the center of the dance floor, Noah gently pulled me towards him. He smelled heavenly. I recognized his scent, a mix of cool, citrus, and crisp. It was the smell of Clinique's Happy fragrance. It was a fragrance Lucas used to wear. My son Xavier wore it now. The familiarity of his smell was having an emotional effect on me, giving me a feeling of closeness, familiarity, and comfort.

Other gala guests were joining us on the dance floor. A few of the partnered women dancing near us were looking at Noah seductively, trying to force his attention. He was having the same effect on them that he was having me. It wouldn't have surprised me if most women didn't react to him that way.

Noah's head towered over mine. He rested his head close, his cheek touching the top of my forehead. I had an uncontrollable urge to run my hand around the back of the nape of his neck, but was shouting at myself in my head to knock it off. I gently placed my hand on his shoulder instead. I put my right hand in his. He grabbed it, tucking it ever so slightly in his own, positioning both our hands behind his back so as to reign me in closer.

My heart was thumping so fast I thought surely he might be able to feel it skipping beats. A part of me felt a deep sense of belonging all while I was reminding myself not to lose my head in the moment. *No more champagne for you tonight Riley.* I was fully aware of his confidence, charisma and charm. I desperately needed to maintain my cool.

Noah began to sing along with the song, humming but then verbalizing the words in the tune when he got to the part *"the night I looked at you."*

Oh God. I hoped I wouldn't melt in a puddle right then and there. I closed my eyes, taking in the fact that he sang really well. Deep. Sexy. Melodic. I was putty in his hands. I was mindful of not singing a single word out loud myself. I never could carry a tune, despite the fact my heart was singing along with him.

I felt the hardness of his six pack through his shirt against my breast as he pulled me even closer to him. Sirens were going off in my head. My imaginary internal antenna and flags were twirling around out the top of my head at high speed. Oh my God. I was out of my league.

Zoe was ending the song. Noah gave me slow twirl, ending our dance on the last note, softly whispering "thank you" in my ear, dropping his arm around my waist and guiding me across the floor.

We began to exit the dance floor through the crowd of other dancers, with him guiding me. I heard a woman's voice call out "Mico! Mico!" right before I saw her arm grab his from behind.

"It's me, Leah."

Startled, I turned around, surprised to face a tall, strikingly beautiful thirty-something Asian woman. She had thick strands of hair as black as night that hung in loose waves nearly to her waist. She was the woman that had Reese's attention earlier. She was wearing an exquisite, yet suggestive, short black dress with the back fully cut out low to her waist, her skin creamy as snow. Her lips were a deeply tinted red.

Noah's forearm tensed as she threw her arms around his neck, suggesting that they were more than friends, kissing him slightly on his cheek. I broke my hand away from his fast. My pulse rate began to speed up. All my emotional guards went to a heightened level of attention, wondering why this woman had her arms wrapped around Noah's body. Noah grabbed her wrists from around his neck, forcing her to break the embrace.

A familiar male voice interrupted the exchange.

"Introduce me to your friend, Leah."

I whipped my head around sharply in surprise. There stood Warren Shaw. What the hell was he doing here? He couldn't have been invited. Definitely not to this affair. He was underdressed, wearing a dark grey sport coat, jeans, a crisp white shirt, and no tie. It had been years since I had seen him. He was much heavier than I remembered. Other than the extra pounds, not much had changed with him these last eight years, except he was now wearing some god-awful red-framed eyeglasses that made him look silly as hell. You couldn't help but notice him. Those stupid cherry red framed glasses were way too bold for a dark skinned African American man. They did nothing for his appearance, but he must have known they would garner attention. Yep, same old Warren. Narcissistic. What in the hell did I ever see in him? I had to have been blind in one eye and couldn't see out the other. It was too embarrassing to actually think I was once engaged to him. My self esteem had to have been in the gutter back then.

Before I could breathe a word, Noah was pushing this Leah woman off his chest, practically lifting her off the floor and setting her feet back on the ground several spaces away from us. Noah grabbed my hand, tightening his grip and pulling me closer to him despite the fact I was physically resisting him.

"Or perhaps I should ask you Riley? Long time no see," Warren said. "Who's the lucky man?" he taunted, cocking his head to the side with a half ass grin on his face.

Immediately, the atmosphere turned arctic. Noah stepped slightly forward in Warren's direction with crackling animosity. Noah's six foot three body towered over Warren, who at five ten looked like the dwarf that he was.

"I'm Noah Dunham to the *both* of you," he said, emphasizing the word *both*, cutting his eyes sharply at Leah. Noah moved even closer to Warren, asking "Who wants to know?"

Julian was now playing his and Zoe's jazzy rendition of *Represent, Cuba* in the background.

Noah and Warren weighed each other with disdain. I was choked up and speechless. Reese had flown like a stealth fighter to my side, grabbing my other hand into his, pulling me towards him, flanking me on my other side. Reese was the first to break the ice.

"You and your little friend don't belong here Warren," Reese snarled with a quiet, but threatening voice. "This is a military only event. Last I checked you weren't military, so that translates into you're looking to get your ass kicked straight out of here," Reese growled.

"Actually my friend Leah and I were here in the hotel for my book signing, Warren said braggadociously. "For the record, you're not the only person allowed to be an author, Riley. We happened to pass by the banquet room, glanced inside, and wouldn't you know it, there was the precious Ms. Riley Cook. Leah and I thought we'd crash this shindig, have a drink, say hello. No harm No foul," Warren laughed wickedly.

Warren was reeking with the smell of alcohol. I suspected he'd long since reached his limit.

"Riley, this room's got your signature all over it baby," Warren said, looking around the room out the corner of his eye but never really dropping his gaze off Reese.

"She's not your baby, asshole," Reese replied, stepping closer to Warren.

"Humph, a bit too uppity for my taste," Leah murmured, barely audible, gazing at me coolly. "Whatever did he see in you?" she mumbled under her breath, turning her nose up and eyeballing me from head to toe with a look of jealousy that spoke volumes.

"I guess you're having a bit of a memory lapse this evening huh Mico . . . Noah . . . whoever . . . whatever," Leah said, simmering as if she were on a back burner on low flame.

Leah was hugely annoyed, clutching Warren's arm a bit more possessively. Turning her eyes away from me, Leah quickly switched gears, beginning to sensually bite the tip of her well-manicured finger, looking slyly at Noah, then at Reese as if they were both something good to eat. Reese shifted uncomfortably under Leah's gaze but Noah remained oblivious to her seductive stare.

"My memory is fine Ms. Chen," Noah replied back sharply.

"I heard about your nomination, Riley, and that little book you're working on," Warren smirked knowingly, agitating the confrontation even more. "I recently formed my own publishing company for aspiring authors. I might even consider taking on the project of pressing out that little book of yours, assuming it's any good."

Jesus, I was starting not to like this picture. I stiffened, realizing he had insulted me, my mood having already plummeted to a new low. I was in a state of shock, and somehow I'd managed not to have found my own voice.

"Motherfucker don't you dare insult my sister. She's a New York Times Bestselling author capable of buying you, your bullshit company, and three more just like them," Reese shouted a bit loudly, freeing his hand from mine, balling his fist.

"You really don't want to go there man," Noah said, stepping next to Reese, peering down on Warren as if he were ready to stomp him in the ground. Noah seemed to be restraining himself. I suppose it was his best effort to calm the situation.

"C'mon Warren, I wanna dance," Leah whined in a huff, tugging on Warren's arm, looking Noah up and down head to toe.

Ignoring the gorgeous woman on his arm, Warren kept his attention on Noah.

"Well I know where you two jokes can go, and while I'm at it, I'd be happy man to teach you how to handle the precious Ms.

Riley Cook," he slurred with a patronizing grin. "You two military blue bloods could use a few lessons in managing the precious Ms. Riley," he said speaking maliciously.

I immediately tightened my grip on Reese's hand, holding it more securely knowing that he would lose it right then and there and knock Warren out cold.

"The only lessons that are going to be taught here, man, are the ones that are going to be given to you," Noah growled back. "I suggest you and Ms. Chen keep it moving." Noah was all in this mix now. "You don't want a piece of me, man. I'm telling you directly, if you come anywhere near Riley or her family, Reese Nelson will be the least of your problems. Not only will you have him to contend with, but you'll have me to deal with as well. This is the only warning I intend to give you."

I was in a state of shock and disbelief. I clutched my arms around myself, my skin feeling hot with fury and embarrassment. This felt like some weird scene out of a bad Stephen King movie. A freaking horror show.

"You and Ms. Chen need to go back to whatever rock you crawled out from under. The next time we have to have this conversation, I won't be so nice," Noah hissed.

Still hearing the music blaring in the background, I glanced around, noticing we were the only ones left on the edge of the dance floor. This untimely scene was attracting the attention of the other guests and some of the paparazzi that were still in attendance.

The warm brown fuzzy feeling I momentarily had on the dance floor in Noah's arms had packed its bags and taken flight. I wanted to go somewhere and truly act on the mental puke that was forming in my head and stomach. To add fuel to the fire, Lily, Madison, and Quentin had quickly appeared, standing around our little group, adding to the tension as they watched the ugly scene that was playing out before their eyes. The fact that I was even in the same room with Warren was beyond disturbing. I figured the universe was responding to all this talk about Warren this week and I had attracted him right into my space. I had to get out of here before Reese flipped the switch and turn the whole entire gala into a brawl, having found his perfect excuse to put Warren's lights out once and for all. God only knows what Noah was capable of at this point. He looked as if he was going to lose it any minute. My mind could only begin to fathom what he was capable of, knowing he was Lucas's confidante and wingman. The odds were high that this would end up being a race between Reese and Noah as to which one might try to kill Warren first.

"Reese," I said sharply, turning towards him cracking my voice like a whip. My shock subsiding, words were actually starting to form out of my mouth. "I believe I've had enough of this gala for one night. I'm ready to leave now, Reese," I said, trying hard to pull him away from this confrontation in the opposite direction.

I hoped Reese hearing my voice would be enough to cut through the anger that was building within him. The sound of clicking and flashing lights of paparazzi cameras pointed at our group caught my attention. I edged myself out from between Noah and Reese, proceeding double time towards the exit doors of the banquet ballroom as the flash of camera lights continued. God, I couldn't believe the months of hard work I had put into this event, was now starting to turn into a potential brawl. And, I was at the center of it. None of this craziness was going to be good for my business or the Beard Foundation nomination.

My eyes were filling with tears. I couldn't believe this magical night of honoring Lucas, winning kudos for my business, and taking a chance moment of meeting someone new, had turned into a shitfest at the hands of Mr. Asshole himself, Warren Shaw.

"I'm coming with you," Madison said, her heels clacking sharply behind me on the marble floor. I watched her roll her eyes at Quentin who hadn't yet moved from behind the men."

"Me too, I'm coming," Lily said.

"Reese!" I shouted again impatiently.

Finally, Reese followed behind me, red faced and steaming, pausing only to pick up Lucas's award and my little black feathered clutch off the table. Quentin managed to extract himself away from the man huddle and was right on top of Madison's heels working to catch up with the rest of us.

"If Warren Shaw thinks for one minute he is going to interject himself into my world and wreak havoc on my life again, he has another thing coming," I said, teary-eyed.

"God damn right," Madison said.

"Fucking right," Lily co-signed.

"He and his little tempestuous bitch better take a hike," I

snarled. "Even I have limits as to how much I'm gonna take. He can't make my life miserable after all these years. I am not that same woman Warren thinks he used to know," I growled angrily through my tears. "I don't need this freaking drama," I huffed, tears streaming down my cheeks.

"No more drama bitches," Madison said, echoing my words.

"Mary J. Bitches," Lily co-signed again.

Madison and I looked at Lily in mutual momentary surprise. Madison nodded her head at Lily, saying "Right, Lily."

I looked back over my shoulder, embarrassed and angry. Noah was in some kind of ferocious stare down with Warren, glaring at him as if he were mentally willing him out of the room so as to avoid a public beat down. He had that same look on his face that Lucas used to get when he thought someone was threatening his family.

I could still feel the heat from the flashing camera lights pointed in my direction. My feet couldn't move fast enough. The last thing I needed was to be bothered with a bunch of men, flexing with each other at the expense of my business's reputation all under the glare of media, journalists, and paparazzi. I knew better than anyone that it was a bad idea from the giddy-up to try to mix business with pleasure. All I needed to do was to get the hell out of here. I headed speedily to the banquet exit doors.

I bolted toward the door. I could hear Zoe at the microphone nervously say,

"We're going to take a brief break now."

CHAPTER 7

WARREN

Staring at the black haired beauty crashed sideways across the bed, and reaching for last night's left-over Jack and Coke, I had to admit she wasn't the sharpest knife in the drawer, but she wasn't the dumbest either. She followed orders pretty well, getting everything I wanted for the gift basket, arranging each Italian delicacy in just the right way. Perhaps that was why American Airlines saw enough talent in her to let her join their organization watching over other people's lives. She managed to get every requested item correct that I asked for from DiBruno Brothers Italian Market. The gift basket was perfect. It was filled with Extra Virgin Olive Oil, Sourdough bread, Mini Flatbread, Canned Olives, Tomato and Basil Sauce, Rustichella d'Abruzzo Stortini Pasta, Rosemary Grissini Sticks, and a large stainless steel colander, big enough for me to tuck my own personal message meant especially for Riley.

I looked back over at her. She was an Asian beauty that gave pretty decent head. It didn't take much, other than for me to tell her I had strong feelings for her and that I could see us having a future together for her to fuck me so hard, you would have thought I had a diamond ring hanging off the end of my dick. I figured Leah was as gullible as Riley, but without the haughty morals. I aimed to use her up, then toss her aside. All I had to do was to throw the L word around some more to string her along.

I'd bet money she'd make the same mistake as Riley. Fall in love with me and then I could manipulate her to get anything, do anything. Commitment was off the table. I had no plans of doing deep and meaningful. But she didn't need to know that.

Jesus, these bitches were beginning to bore me. Each one seemed to be more stupid than the last. Leah flung her best assets around, turning every male head that had eyeballs. I'm gonna miss banging that ass when I'm done with her. She thinks she's the smart one. Actually her ego is so big she hasn't figured out that I don't give a damn about her beyond what she has to offer to me sexually.

I looked at the basket of perishables again. Something was missing. I threw in some special doggie biscuits for those dumb ass dogs, Stogie and Cleo, laughing to myself. Payback is truly a dog.

That bitch Riley always was a big bread freak. This basket is going to be right on time. I wrote very carefully on the ivory stationary. Too bad I didn't have a little something in this basket for that shit-head Reese.

Damn, he is always the thorn in my side that I can never quite anticipate. That motherfucker is a real unknown. I don't know who I despise the most, him or Riley. Both of them carry themselves like they are military pedigree, acting better than everyone else. I resent everything about them including their attitude towards me, always looking down on me.

So what if my own father was dishonorably discharged from the Army. That didn't make those ass-clowns better than me. Their type look down their noses at me like I am a first class reject lacking in their military blue blood pedigree.

And that Riley, she thinks she's so damn smart. But she ain't smart enough to out-fox me. I'll fix her good this time. She will never guess that I've known for months, that the gala was going to be booked at the Four Seasons. That was real smart of me to deliberately schedule my book signing at the same hotel so as to give the appearance of a coincidence. I should pat myself on the back. Damn, I was the surprise of the evening. Yeah I screwed her up good. Who knew Riley would be surrounded by paparazzi as a result of her little James E. Beard nomination. What a fucking bonus.

Now, I will wage a full scale war against her business and bring her down once and for all. It will be sweet revenge and payback for her calling off the engagement, publicly embarrassing me, and acting like she is some prima donna princess put on the military pedestal by her officer father, punk ass army brat brother, and dead pilot husband. And to think she's got some new fuck Naval Captain standing by her side. Yeah, I am not done with the precious Ms. Riley Cook. No way was I done with that bitch. I'll teach her not to treat me like I'm not good enough.

"I have a nice little gift basket for you Ms. Riley. Red bow and all. Tie a red bow around the likes of Ms. Riley. Signed. Sealed. Delivered."

The Asian beauty lying in bed rolled over on her side, her creamy white leg falling out from under the bed covers. It was time for her to wrap her beautiful mouth around me again. I stalked towards the bed, waking her up by pulling a fistful of her hair in my hand, holding my hard bone in the other.

"Kiss me baby."

CHAPTER 8

NOAH

"Room service, how can I help you Captain Dunham?"

"I'd like an order of eggs Benedict, two slices of wheat toast with jelly, butter, bacon on the side, black coffee, and a Bloody Mary please. Oh, and can you please provide me with a copy of this morning's local newspapers, please."

"Yes sir, We'll have that sent right up to your room, sir."

I leaned over the balcony window looking out onto the Ben Franklin Parkway. I prayed that the ugly scene at the end of last night's Memorial Gala would not hit the newspapers. I began my daily regimen of morning push-ups trying to figure out how in the hell I was going to convince Riley that I had nothing to do with that man-eater Leah Chen. The way Leah slung her arms around my neck, coiled around my chest like a snake choking its prey, I knew the appearance of things had left a bad taste in her mouth. I could see it in her eyes. Not to mention Leah called me "Mico," as if she knew me intimately. Riley would never believe I only recently met that piranha on the plane ride into Philadelphia.

The sweat dripped off my chest on my third repetition of pushups. It was clear I had to recover from what was a really funky beginning. Lucas would not be happy about this mess at the Gala. For someone attempting to pursue a relationship with Riley, things were getting off to a really bad start. A real fucking train wreck.

I could only hope that by the time the newspapers arrived, there would be nothing but good press from the earlier part of last night's evening. That ugly scene that had taken place on the dance floor was nothing less than a publicity nightmare.

I did another three repetitions of pushups. I wanted to punish myself for what had happened last night. Riley felt so good tucked in my arms as we danced. I am never ever going to let her go. It wasn't just about my promise to Lucas. I would have kept my word to him no matter what, but the best part is I love her too. There was no way that creep Warren Shaw and that man-eater Leah Chen were going to get in between me and Riley. Riley was special. There were so many things I needed to tell her. I gave my word. I had promised Lucas.

In my heart I knew there was a lot of ground to cover with her. I might as well start laying the groundwork now, I thought, pushing myself through my seventh repetition of pushups.

I finished my exercise regimen, heading towards the bathroom to take a shower, hoping the hot water would help me to clear my head and soothe my tight muscles. I finished quickly, towel drying my body and putting on a fresh pair of briefs.

I slipped on a pair of jeans and a clean t-shirt and a white shirt. My wandering thoughts were interrupted by the knock on my hotel door. I opened it.

"Room service. Your morning papers, sir."

The young male attendant placed the silver tray down on the desk, lifting the dome up to let me see that my order was correct. I quickly reached for the copy of the Philadelphia Inquirer, nodding that everything was okay.

I flipped rapidly through to the back sections to the local style and entertainment sections like an out of control madman, shoving a tip in the hand of the hotel staff, wanting him to leave.

My heart sank reading the headline: *Celebrity Chefs Cover Rich Culinary Ground At Memorial Gala While Bucks County's Own Cook Stirs Up Drama.*

"Fuck."

Below the headline was a picture of Riley, Reese, Warren, Leah, Lily, Madison, Quentin, and a barely recognizable me, captured in an ugly hostile circle looking as if we were seconds from throwing blows.

The text read "Buck's County's own Riley Cook, this year's James E. Beard Nominee, was not to be outdone by celebrity chef's Bobby Flay and Eric Ripert at this year's Memorial Fundraiser for the Fallen. She served up her own plate of spicy drama as she and brother Reese Nelson, New York's most notable financial forensic executive, had their own personal throw-down with an unknown couple. Too many Cooks in the mix?"

I could hardly read any further, getting sick to my stomach knowing how much the night meant to Riley coupled with her desire to use the event as a positive to leverage potential angel investors. I had to fix this. She needed my help. And I knew how to help her.

I picked up the hotel phone, praying Nicholas was still in the States. His phone rang only twice before he picked up.

"Milk Money, God speaking," Nicholas answered in his typically self-indulgent arrogant manner.

"Nicholas, this is Noah. Do you always answer your phone like that, man? Damn."

"Well, if you need money, you're gonna likely see me as God," he chuckled. "I'm only remaining true to my essence man. Whatcha need my brother? I'm on a clock, Mico. What gives?"

"I'm calling in my chip."

"Seriously Mico? You? You're calling in your chip, Captain? Tell me, man. Who is she? Your nose must really be open this time to be calling in your chip," Nicholas laughed heartily. She's must be pret-ty special," he whistled. "Not like you to call in your chips for just anybody."

"She is special, Nicholas. She's Lucas Cook's widow. Remember him?" I snapped back.

"Well, well, well. Now why aren't I surprised. You and Lucas were thick as thieves. Always secrets between you. It wouldn't surprise me if you two guys weren't tapping the same till. Admit it man."

"It's not like that Nicholas. Try to keep your mind focused here for a few minutes. It's not like that," I repeated.

"Tell me what it's like Mico. I'm listening intently. I gotta hear this one."

"I promised Lucas I would look after her and the kids. I gave my word. And for the record, she's beyond special to me."

"Uh huh," Nicholas said. "Is that pony you're gonna ride Mico?" he said, with a great deal of skepticism.

I didn't want to go down this road with him out of fear of

opening Pandora's box. Too much information was dangerous for his brilliant mind.

"I'm fulfilling my promise to Lucas. I gave my word. But I also want this too. That's the truth."

Truth it was. But the entire truth? No. The entire truth was only to be heard from my lips to Riley's ears.

"Yeah, well we know how you are when you give your word, Mico. You're gonna honor it hell or high water until death do you part, my brother."

"Forget the chit chat. Like I said, this is serious business man. I have a vested interest in the outcomes here," I said, trying to be cautious not to reveal too much information to Nicolas Becker lest he turn into my competition for Riley.

Nicholas loved beautiful women. He was smart as a whip. Actually he was a genius. The smartest man I know. It was hard to conceal information from him. I knew better than to underestimate his abilities. He was shrewd. He didn't get wealthy, rather wealthier, from being stupid. Everything he touched turned to gold.

At the Academy, Nicholas was under the tutelage of Lucas and me. A post-graduate of the Columbia Business School, Nicholas knew everything there was to know about money and investment banking. He came from money. He had built in money management skills, but Lucas and I taught him life survival skills and everything we knew about women. He was the geeky think-outside-of-the-box   working-overtime-to-stay-close-to-the-insiders guy.

Lucas and I were upper classmen at the Naval Academy when Nicholas was a freshman. Everyone else at the Academy gave Nicholas little attention, but Lucas and I knew we had spotted a diamond in the rough. We took Nicholas under our wings his freshman year. We protected him, keeping him under our protection as best we could from the ongoing slew of initiation schemes earmarked for the freshman class. Perhaps we taught him too well.

Coming from a privileged Maryland family whose family owned a chicken processing dynasty, Nicholas was sheltered from the ways of the world, particularly how envious people would take advantage of his brain power. We taught him how to survive at the Academy.

Nicholas landed on Wall Street after graduation, working his way up in the investment banking world. Over time, he had morphed himself into an even wealthier person beyond his family's wealth, investing his own independently earned funds into new companies that were looking for cash to finance a fast growth stage. Six hundred million dollars and Forbes' list of top 100 richest men later, Milk Money and Nicholas had arrived, by both Lucas' and my standards. Lucas and I used to joke, calling Nicholas, "Big Willie." We had great respect for his business acumen and took all his advice regarding our own personal investments. We always knew Nicky would excel in the cut throat world of Wall Street. We were proud of his success and how far he had climbed, exceeding even our expectations of him. With his good looks and wealth, women flocked to him like bees to honey and he enjoyed every one of them. Lucas liked his women wholesome. I liked my women fast. And, Nicholas Becker just plain loved them all.

"What do you need man. Spill it. I'm headed out of the country for the holidays. I've got a couple of really knock out Brazilian honeys waiting for me on *The Julianna* out in the Mediterranean man. You want to come kick it with me on the high seas, Mico? We can throw back tons of Stoli, chill on my yacht, deep sea dive, catch some lobster, and fuck beautiful women all holiday. It will be like old times man, love 'em, eat 'em and leave 'em," he laughed wildly. "You can even get your tan on, Mico," he laughed, chiding me hard, working overtime to get my goat.

"Seriously man, listen up. Lucas's widow, her name is Riley Cook. She has a food and wine business that is prime for the right angel investor. Her business is called *Black Sequinned Bows and Champagne Nights.*"

"Whoa, Mico. I'm having a moment. Visions of black bows and champagne nights, huh. I can just see myself all tied up in one of those bows."

"Knock it off Nicky. I'm serious, man. Just because you fucked things up with Harper doesn't mean you get to screw this up for me."

"Okay. Fine Mico. I don't want to go there. I'm in a good mood. What do you need?"

"Do your homework. Google it or fire up that Bloomberg software I know you have there. Her financials are good. She's a sharp business woman, trying to kick her business up the next rung, man. She's been nominated as a James E. Beard Foundation award nominee. This is an opportunity even you don't want to pass up," I stressed, using my best don't-fuck-with-me voice. "I need you to give her a look-see man. This means a lot to me."

"Yeah, man. What does she look like? I love doing business with the young, beautiful, and the restless," he laughed.

"Fuck off, man. This is serious business. She's off limits to you. I'm only going to say that to you once, motherfucker," I said, feeling myself getting jealous. Pissed off.

"Yeah, Yeah, Mico, Rock-out Wingman. Cool your jets."

"Yeah right man," I snorted.

"Ease up man. I'll do it for you. But listen, I only have a small window of opportunity to meet with her. On the serious side, I can tell without even looking at you dude, you are catching feelings. I hear it in your voice. Not a good look, Mico."

"Please do me this favor Nicky," I pleaded.

"Are you trying to turn in your playa card, Mico, leaving me out here with this treasure trove of beautiful women all by myself?"

"What's it to you Nicky?"

Nicholas Becker knew me well. He knew me well enough to know that I was dancing around the important stuff and there was no way he was going to be left out of the 411. He wanted every detail. He was true to who he was during our Academy days. Nicholas thrived on information. As far as he was concerned, the more information he had the better. He was nobody's dummy.

"Do tell Mico, I believe you're on the rails of getting serious and deep," he laughed wildly. "I tell you man, I hear it in your voice," he laughed again. "You're catching feelings, dude."

"None of your business Nicky. Just get with the program, man."

"Well let's see here. Can you get her to come to the Apple? I'm leaving the country, unless you want to catch me in London, next week. I'll be doing my island hopping express for the holidays, like old times."

"I can get her to New York, Nicholas. Just tell me when and where. I'll see to it that she'll be there."

"Frankly, your timing is pretty good, Mico. My partner, Lucia Falco, and I are taking on a small elite group of U.S. companies this month that we hope to groom to go global in the next five years. We've got one slot left out of ten for new businesses that we want to incubate and direct our financing along with some technical assistance. We've got $100 million on the sidelines to toss around for lending, philanthropic support, incubation, and commercialization of technology driven businesses. We could squeeze her on the list of ten if she's got the moxie, Mico."

"Perfect Nicholas. I'll get her to you. I'll see you soon, my man. I appreciate all your help."

"Don't think about hanging me out to dry on this one Mico. God sees all."

"Becker, I guarantee you won't be disappointed."

"Oh I can't wait," he laughed wildly again.

"Thanks Nicky. See you soon."

As soon as I hung up the phone, I knew I had to smooth things over with Riley and use this entry as an opportunity to convince her to go to New York and present her business portfolio to Nicholas. I was setting her on an inside track that was guaranteed to launch her business into the next orbit. The fact that Nicholas was going to be in the mix was an added dimension in the scheme of things. Nicholas loved beautiful women. I was going to have to face up to that that keeping his paws off Riley was going to be an additional layer of work if he so much as sensed I wasn't serious about her. He wouldn't go after her if he thought I was serious because he was respectful like that. But, I had my own poor reputation for dealing with the fast and furious, and then tossing them aside. Nicholas was not beyond making himself available to catch all those broken hearts thrown overboard. He loved competition when it came to beautiful women. And the beautiful women loved Nicholas. On top of everything else, I was going to have to keep an eye on Riley to make sure she stayed out of Nicholas's grasp.

No doubt, Riley was going to be pissed off to the high heavens about Warren, Leah, and the bad press. But this angel investment business would be good news. It would give her something to look forward to for her company's future. I needed her to feel like this was the light at the end of that dark tunnel she was in last night. I needed her to know that I'm here to support her. That she can rely on me to keep everything she holds dear, safe.

I finished my workout, sitting down to eat breakfast and contemplate my next move.

Yes, I would call Riley today. I would give her the good news.

Jude E. McNamara

CHAPTER 9

RILEY

"Wake up Riley, get up sister. Sunday morning brunch is what we do when I come to town," Reese said, barging through the french double doors of my bedroom pulling the covers off me, smacking me on my rear hard like he used to when we were kids.

"God Reese, why must you be the early bird all the time? What time is it anyway?" I asked, rubbing my eyes, throwing my down feathered pillow over the top of my head. "It's too early and it's cold," I grumbled.

"It's nine o'clock. Time for you to get up. I'm cooking blueberry pancakes, mascarpone scrambled eggs, Canadian bacon, garlic toast, and Mimosa's for breakfast, he said, reaching down, throwing a log onto my bedroom fireplace. "Madison and Quentin are on their way over. Lily is already up and downstairs helping me cook. You promised that posse of yours we'd do brunch, remember?"

"God, I hate that I did that to myself. I want to stay in this bed, pull the covers over my head and never come out."

"Xavier spent the night out at Nena's. Samantha and Claire are scrutinizing me as if I can't cook breakfast fast enough, hovering like drones ready to attack," Reese chuckled, momentarily thumbing his Android.

Reese intended to ignore my comment, which meant lying in bed vegging for the rest of the day wasn't going to be an option.

"Lucas's kids are kind of crazy," he mumbled, looking down at me warmly. "How many times have I told you that you should pay closer attention to that damn Cook gene pool, sweetness?"

"I think they love your cooking as much as mine," I shrugged, rubbing my eyes, rolling over, not wanting to get up.

"Those kids have Lucas's stamp all over them. They'll sure as cut your legs off as look at you when it comes to good food. You know that's why Lucas married you, don't you?"

"No. I have other wonderful qualities besides being able to cook well," I grunted.

"I haven't forgotten how as toddlers they threw their bowls and sippy cups at you when you weren't feeding them fast enough," Reese laughed. "Not much has changed with your crew."

"Leave my babies alone, Reese," I snarled, pulling the covers completely over my head.

"Did you forget you agreed to do brunch, Riley? Get your butt in gear woman," he commanded, throwing another toss pillow at the top of my head.

Reese grabbed the fireplace prod, stoking the fireplace a bit more. God he was his father's son. Always running the tight ship.

"I agreed to do brunch long before I knew last night was going to turn into Nightmare on Elm Street," I said, leaning out of my super king sized bed, throwing the soft silver paisley print comforter off me, stopping momentarily to fluff the down-filled pillows.

Grabbing my white satin robe off the lounge chaise ottoman, I passed through the open white shuttered doors to my master bathroom. I honestly wasn't up to starting my day already. I turned my shower heads and massage jets on, grabbed my electric toothbrush and topped it with toothpaste, shoving it in my mouth. I turned back towards Reese, who was following closely on my heels. I paused briefly looking him up and down, my hand resting on my hip.

"Ahhhh, do you think a moment of privacy is in order here?"

"Sorry. I wanted to make sure you weren't going to put the covers over your head, get back into that bed, and not come back up for air for the rest of the day."

"Why ever would you think that?" I said, with a ton of sarcasm.

"Ha. This is me you're talking to; or did you forget? I know who you are," Reese said, turning away from me, heading out my bathroom doors.

"I'm up. Leave me alone," I grumbled.

"Yeah, Yeah, Yeah," he said, leaving the bathroom.

I waited for the door to close behind Reese.

In the silence, the events of last night's gala flooded back into my consciousness. All I wanted to do was to try to forget the whole Noah, Reese, Warren, Leah, nightmare. I hated scenes. And our group had made a huge scene.

Who could predict that Warren Shaw would crash the gala with this year's flavor of the month. I cringed at the thought of her making those googly-eyes at Noah and Reese. And to think, I had the audacity to be starry-eyed over Noah for a minute. No way was I dating that guy. So much for some freaking Chocolate Thunder. More like some' Chocolate Chip off the ole playa block' if you ask me.

I don't care what Lily thinks about the captain or how awesome he is. I have no intention of getting myself involved with a player. The way that Leah Chen woman curled herself around his neck, calling him Mico, surely those two had history. They could be long standing bedfellows for all I knew.

Soaping my body in small circles, pouring shower gel over my breasts, I could only imagine what it might have been like having Noah's body next to mine with his strong fingers running lavender scented shampoo through my hair, massaging my scalp, as he'd kiss my lips softly. Whoa. Where did those thoughts come from?

I replayed the entire night over again in my mind, letting the hot water beat on top of the back of my neck. The water felt invigorating. I needed to stay under these jets a little longer to help get my perspective back. Yep. Man-whores were definitely off my list of things to take on this month. Yessireee. My plate was full enough. Serving myself up a plate of Chocolate Thunder was going to be a recipe for disaster.

I opened the bathroom sliding door, tiptoeing into the cold air, jumping from the shock from being cocooned in the warmth of the hot water massage. What a waste of time I had spent on the dance floor in my moment of fantasy, wondering what life could be like with the infamous Captain Noah Dunham in my world. What was I thinking? Hadn't I had learned the hard way to go it alone with only me and my kids?

I grabbed a fluffy white towel, drying my hair, then wrapping it snug around my body. I surveyed myself in the mirror, my mind drifting again to what it might feel like to be tucked in his strong arms.

No. This was silly thinking. Captain Noah Dunham was off my list of things to occupy my fantasies. I needed to put all thoughts of him to rest. I totally needed to make up my mind to bring my body into submission because it sure as hell betrayed me last night. Might as well have colored me smitten.

I moved out of my bathroom, back into my bedroom, headed to my closet, pulling my favorite ragged edged denim washed blue jeans off the top shelf. I grabbed my old Wharton Business School sweatshirt, and black suede over the knee boots. My comfy clothes would help me to stay focused. I had my company and the Beard Foundation nomination to think about. I would not let this matter of Lily playing Cupid with the Captain occupying my thoughts, getting in the way of business. I would not make that mistake twice in a lifetime. As fine as that man was, I absolutely needed to talk to myself harder so as to tow my own line.

I headed down the spiral staircase into the kitchen. Reese was at the stove flipping pancakes. Stogie and Cleo were sitting at attention below Reese's feet, both hoping he'd drop a few crumbs of garlic toast their way.

"Hey sleepy head," Lily spoke first. "I've already set the table. I'm helping Reese out so you could sleep in this morning. I know last night had a rougher ending than we all expected."

"Rough is putting it mildly."

I grabbed a piece of garlic toast off the silver tray.

"Mornin' Mom," Samantha said. "Glad you're up. Uncle Reese is the slowest cook in the freakin' world."

"Yeah, we could die of starvation by the time Uncle Reese gets this meal on the table," Claire joked.

"My cooking is well worth the wait ladies," Reese shot back. "Good God Riley, even these two dogs are begging. What exactly goes on in this house at mealtime, woman?" Reese kidded.

The doorbell rang. Samantha moved first to answer the door. I could hear her in the foyer.

"Hey Godmother. Hey Mr. Quentin."

Madison and Quentin arrived, Madison heading straight for the kitchen, Quentin on her heels.

"I'm following the smell of food," Madison nodded to Samantha.

Quentin had a folded copy of the Philadelphia Inquirer under his arm. He looked like how I felt. Dragging. I wondered who kept who up last night. Quentin or Madison. It was hard to tell, because Madison walked into the room full of spunk like she was the head person in charge. I gave her a raised eyebrow look, loving how she exuded energy and confidence. Nothing seemed to ever get her down. I doubted that last night's antics were going to be a first.

"Hey everybody," Madison said, looking bright-eyed and bushy-tailed. "Ummm something smells really good. You're doing the cooking Reese?"

"Pretty much."

"Taking lessons from Riley are you?"

Madison poked Reese in his side while grabbing a piece of toast off the tray on the butcher block island.

"Hell no. I've got a few cooking skills of my own in my bag of tricks darlin'. Riley isn't the only one Mother taught how to cook. Mother made sure I wouldn't starve waiting on some woman to come along to cook for me. When push comes to shove, I know how to feed myself," Reese said with pride.

"You really don't expect us to believe those gals in New York that flock to you don't cook for you," Madison answered, fixing Quentin and herself a plate.

"Woman, I'm a single man. I can't be totally dependent upon you females to eat. It's a wonder any of you even know how to cook anymore. Isn't that right, Quentin?"

"I plead the fifth," Quentin responded, grabbing his plate from Madison, totally occupied with his newspaper.

"Jesus, Riley, is there such a thing as a New York Times around here?" Reese asked, changing the subject. "I'll be damn if I'm gonna read that rag of a paper Quentin is reading."

"It's probably still outside on the ground. I'll get it for you Uncle Reese," Samantha said, jumping up hastily, headed for the front door.

"Riley, it was a real bummer last night, Warren showing up and all," Madison said chomping on a piece of toast. "I guess that witch on Warren's arm was my colleague's sister that I heard he was dating."

Madison sighed, her eyes focused on Quentin who was pouring himself a cup of coffee, planting himself in the chair near the bay window, opening the local newspaper.

"It's a small world isn't it?" Madison continued.

"Yeah, Riley, who the hell knew Warren would show up and crash the gala," Lily said, shoving her coffee mug next to Reese, nudging him to pour her a cup.

"And to think, you were getting along so well with Noah. Isn't he totally the most Madison?"

"Yeah, Riley, that 'Chocolate Thunder' was to die for," Madison swooned, co-signing Lily's comment.

Madison wanted to make the point that she too approved of Noah. She reared back against the marble countertop, blowing a kiss at Quentin and stuffing her face at the same time with Canadian bacon. Quentin winked at Madison.

"Well, I finally got to lay eyes on the infamous Warren, and frankly you haven't missed out on a thing with that man out of your life," Lily said, tossing her red locks back like she frequently does when she's dismissing someone. "Warren is a real piece of work," she said, shoving a forkful of eggs in her mouth.

"I'm glad you held it together Reese," I said patting him on his back. "The last thing I needed was for you to end up in brawl in front of all the paparazzi at the gala last night. I don't need the bad press if I expect to cinch the Beard Foundation Nomination."

"I hate to break this to you, Riley, and be the bearer of bad news, but I'm sorry to say all of our pictures are plastered front and center in the Style and Entertainment section of this Inquirer," Quentin said. "I'm so sorry."

"Damn," Reese said, grabbing for the newspaper from Quentin.

"Let me see," Madison said.

Madison looked stunned, rushing to Reese's side, grabbing the newspaper out of his hand before he could read any further.

"Yeah let's see," Lily said, with a look of deep concern, setting her fork down, moving closer to Madison. Reese towered over both their shoulders, all of them doing a group read.

"How bad is it?" Lily asked. "Oh my God."

I rushed over to the table to join them. Madison spread the paper out for all of us it see. It was awful. Seeing the picture of the group of us looking like two opposing teams about to open up a can of whup ass with everyone all up in each other's faces was painful. It was utterly ugly. Plain ugly.

The headline was even worse.

"This is horrible," I shrieked, setting the paper down, watching Reese and Madison continue to read together. Quentin shook his head in disbelief.

The house phone rang. I moved to answer it. Samantha was coming back inside with the New York Times in hand for Reese. She had a huge gift basket wrapped in cellophane tied with an oversized red bow in her hands. I answered the phone.

"Hello?"

Noah's familiar voice was on the other end.

"Good morning Riley."

"Good morning, Noah," I said, surprised. "Are you calling to rub salt in the wound this morning? Perhaps you should be dialing your little friend Leah instead of me," I sneered.

I glanced in Lily's direction. She was shaking her head, lip-mouthing the word, "No." Madison was dragging her index finger across the front of her neck to suggest that I cut the attitude out. I had no idea why I was angry with Noah but I was. I figured he was a player at heart. And I was repeating my same old mistakes again getting my panties in a bunch over a man who in the long run would mean me no good.

I sighed into the phone as Reese placed plates of food in front of Quentin and himself, grabbing the New York Times out of Samantha's hands. Reese mumbled something under his breath that I couldn't quite make out. Claire was ripping the cellophane off the basket, tearing pieces of bread in half, feeding Stogie and Cleo some strange looking doggie biscuits that had a funny smell.

"Actually Riley, I called to see if you were all right. And to explain," Noah said calmly, ignoring my foul mood. "I figured the appearance of things with Leah may have given you the wrong impression. I never got a chance to explain after the confrontation with Warren. You took off so quickly."

Madison and Lily were eavesdropping in on my conversation. I wanted them to get this notion of me and the captain out of their heads

"Excuse, me for one second Noah. Madison, Lily, go see who that basket is from that Claire is toying with please."

I figured if I gave Madison and Lily a job, they would get out of my conversation.

103

"I hope you're not trying to sweet talk me with this gift basket this morning," I snapped.

"I'm sorry. But I have no idea what you're talking about," Noah said puzzled.

"Oh."

I felt a twinge of embarrassment for being overly presumptuous. Now I was really wondering about that gift basket.

"I wanted to call you and let you know that I really loved seeing you last night. I enjoyed your company. I'd like to see you again Riley," he said slowly. Softly.

"You seem to keep a lot of company already, Mico, is it?" I said, trying to recover my composure and regain my pissdom despite the fact I could feel myself losing the battle on maintaining my anger. Damn, he was hard to resist.

"I know things may have appeared a certain way, but I want you to know Ms. Chen is of no importance to me. She's just some flight attendant on the crew of a plane I flew here on from D.C. I'm friends with her crew captain. Prior to my flying here and meeting her on the plane, she and I have never met."

"Well Ms. Chen seemed to be all too familiar, if you ask me, not that it's any of my business."

I knew my voice sounded snide, but I didn't care.

"Well, I hope you'll make me your business, Riley. Leah Chen is nobody to me, now or never. Forget her. Forget Warren Shaw. Don't let those two losers rob you of any of your joy."

"Not to worry. I'm fully capable of taking care of myself," I snarled.

Warren Shaw hardly ever crossed my mind anymore. I had no intentions of giving that woman on the arm of Warren who was drooling over Noah and my brother a second thought. As for Noah, he had consumed too many of my thoughts over the last twenty-four hours. I knew that in my head but apparently my body hadn't gotten the message based on the flutters that were going on in my stomach from hearing his voice.

"Good things are happening for you. You deserve nothing but success," he paused. This is your time right now, Riley."

Why was he calling me really? Wasn't last night's humiliation and insults hurled at me by Warren Shaw enough for one twenty-four hour period? Okay, so I came, I saw, I met him.

"And, speaking of business," Noah continued, "I was calling

this morning to tell you that a close friend of mine has agreed to let you pitch your business to his angel investment company in New York," he stated, ignoring my deliberate rudeness.

"Agreed?"

"I hope you don't mind Riley, but upon learning from our conversation last night how much you're looking to reach out to some angel investors for your company, I put in a call on your behalf. His name is Nicholas Becker. We went to the Naval Academy together. He knew Lucas. The three of us were friends."

"Hmph. With last night's bad press, I doubt anyone is eager to consider me a worthy investment of anything right now," I said, dismissing this conversation, not taking him at all serious.

I pondered whether to engage further in this nonsensical conversation or to hang up. Noah was probably trying to get on my good side from my having seen that woman curled around his neck. This conversation was a waste of my time. I'm not looking for handouts.

"I doubt that scene last night with those two idiots will be hurtful to your brand. Besides, last night's press coverage is limited to a local newspaper. Your company has an excellent reputation nationally. This angel investor could be the perfect opportunity Riley," he said still very serious.

"I guess you got the memo late, or should I say this morning's papers."

I was irritated at the thought of this morning's newspaper photo, headlines. I was feeling incredibly embarrassed.

"Bad press is bad press, Noah."

"Oh hell to the no!" Madison shouted out loud.

"Are you kidding me?" Lily added.

Before I could finish reading Noah the riot act, both Cleo and Stogie started vomiting all over the kitchen floor. Reese was knocking bread out of Claire's hand moments before it reached her mouth. Quentin rushed to Madison's side grabbing a book out of Madison's hand that she had snatched from Reese.

"I can't believe this is happening," Madison squealed in a state of shock.

"Oh my God. Good Lord, Maddy," I said directing my attention away from my conversation with Noah.

Claire was crouched on her knees crying over Cleo who was sprawled out on the floor on her side whining in pain. Samantha was screaming, yelling "Stogie! Stogie!"

Stogie was vomiting and defecating at the same time. I dropped the phone on top of the kitchen counter. Noah's voice was blaring through the receiver.

"Riley. Riley, is everything okay?"

I couldn't think straight. I didn't know who to respond to first. Before I could act, Reese was barreling back into the room carrying Lucas's Glock 38 that was kept locked in the gun cabinet in the den. I was in shock watching Reese as he headed out the front door with Quentin on his heels.

"Reese Nelson," I screamed loudly.

"I'm going to deal with this motherfucker once and for all. Fuck him," Reese shouted.

"Yeah man," Quentin said. "This shit is crazy. Let's deal with this asswipe."

"Call the vet," Samantha shouted.

I picked up the book Quentin dropped when he tore out the front door on the heels of Reese.

"I'm calling the vet now," Madison said grabbing her cell phone out of the back pocket of her jeans.

"I'm calling the police," Lily shrieked.

I looked at the book cover. It was a copy of Warren's new book. I opened it. The title page had the words "A Foolish Woman is clamorous: she is simple and knoweth nothing. Proverbs 9:13" scribbled on it in red ink.

"What the hell does this mean exactly?"

I gasped in confusion trying to figure out what those words meant. Why was this happening? I looked out back kitchen bay window. Reese and Quentin were circling the perimeter of the house and the grounds. Reese was still waving Lucas's gun in his hand. My heart was beating overtime. My legs were getting wobbly so much I thought they would give out on me at any minute. Madison rushed back and forth between the kitchen and the foyer looking out the front door. Claire and Samantha were grabbing Stogie who looked to be walking sideways. Cleo was still whining on the floor in pain.

"We're going to the vet," Samantha yelled, grabbing Claire.

"We're headed to the vet's office," Madison repeated. "We'll call you later."

Claire had tears streaming down her cheeks. My heart broke in half from looking at her.

I grabbed Claire in my arms, hugging her.

"It's going to be okay sweetie," I said, trying to console her.

I needed to gain order amidst this chaos.

"Cleo and Stogie will be okay," I said, kissing the top of Claire's head.

"If anything happened to either of these dogs I am personally going to deal with Warren myself," I said to whoever was listening, talking out loud in my own state of hysteria. "I can't believe Warren would stoop this low ."

Reese stomped back inside the house, picking the phone up off the counter. I'd forgotten about Noah being on the other end in all of the commotion.

"We need to call the police," Reese shouted through the phone at Noah, who had remained on the line.

Reese hung up on him with nothing more said. Quentin grabbed the gift basket, sweeping the basket contents off the counter top, stuffing everything that was in the basket inside a trash bag while Reese dialed 911.

"Warren is a lot of things, but I can't believe he would actually try to physically harm me or my family," I said, a bit flustered. I was scared and panicky hearing Reese on the phone, giving the 911 operator my address and phone number.

"Well this makes no sense at all," Lily said softly in utter disbelief. "Maybe this isn't Warren's doing at all? Maybe it's that wicked woman he had hanging off his arm. She was looking pretty peeved if you asked me."

"Well, whoever is at the bottom of this, did they want to try to harm us? The dogs?" I said, shaking my head.

What little appetite I had for breakfast, had taken flight. I glanced at the pitcher of Bloody Marys Reese made earlier, pondering it for a split of a second. Instead of eating, I grabbed the opened bottle of champagne off the counter, skipped the orange juice and filled a couple of flutes half full for Lily and myself. Lily was besides herself.

"Lily, you've got to stop pacing around in circles. My head is still spinning as it is from my conversation with Noah, the dogs puking their insides up, and Reese running around the house like a crazy person with Lucas's gun."

I gulped the champagne down, pouring myself another glass, but not before Lily emptied hers, setting it in front of me for a refill.

"Lily, things are really starting to spin out of control. I feel like I've been pushed off the side of a boat without a life vest. This can't be happening to me."

"It's called anxiety, Riley. I'm having it too."

Before I could collect my thoughts and gain some momentary sense of sanity, Zoe and Julian barreled through the front door. The Washington Crossing Township Police arrived at the same time. Thank God Reese had returned Lucas's gun back to the gun case.

"Riley are you okay, honey?" Zoe said. "We got a call from Samantha saying there was some kind of emergency going on here," Zoe said looking quizzically. "Samantha was beside herself. We got here as fast as we could. I put in a call to Xavier, but got no answer," she said.

Lily interrupted us.

"Oh my God, Riley. I forgot you were on the phone with Noah when all this commotion broke out. He must be worried sick," Lily said. "You were a bit tough on him on that call. And Mr. Overprotective hung up on him without an explanation."

I knew she was referring to Reese.

"God, Lily, I forgot all about him in the commotion. Noah was babbling something about how he didn't know Leah Chen and that he wanted to introduce me to some angel investment company in New York. I couldn't focus on a word he was saying with all the commotion. I guess I lost sight of him."

By now I was waving my hands in the air like a mad woman. Between last night and this morning, I pronounced myself officially on overload.

"Well that's to be understood," Lily said.

"Before I knew it the dogs were sick, the kids were crying, Reese was going crazy and the police were here. I simply can't take another thing today. Bad enough my picture is spread across the Sunday papers this morning," I said flustered, fighting back the tears.

"Angel investor? That sounds promising," Lily said, putting her arms around me.

Leave it to Lily to distill my rant down to what was important to the business.

"You've been wanting to pursue an Angel investor for your business. If Noah can help you open a door, it doesn't hurt to expand your network. Out of every bad comes some good," she said.

"I'm hardly optimistic at this point, with everything that has happened." I said, scowling.

"Riley, what in God's creation is going on here honey? Spill the beans," Zoe said. I want to know exactly what is going on here and I want to know it now."

Zoe's words reminded me of how much she and Lucas had in common. Lucas would have said the exact same thing, always in control. Authoritative. It was moments like these that made it hard for me to look at Zoe. She looked like Lucas. She sounded like Lucas. She acted like Lucas.

Lily and I took turns telling Zoe what had happened, starting with the local newspaper article, progressing to the gift basket, managing to fill Zoe in on the details of the morning's hysterics. Meanwhile, Reese and Quentin were filing a police report. Julian was soaking in every detail, positioning himself with the men.

By the time Lily and I finished updating Zoe, she was so upset I think she wanted to go after Warren and Leah herself. Soon after, Samantha, Claire, and Madison made it back with the dogs. The vet had sedated both Cleo and Stogie so they could rest. I was worried Cleo was going to have a nervous breakdown. She was excitable by nature. Thank God the dogs were going to be okay. Cleo and Stogie just needed some TLC according to the veterinarian.

"Riley, the police took the trash bag filled with the remains of the gift basket as evidence," Reese barked. "They assured me if this was intended to be a threat, they would get to the bottom of it."

"The police seemed to think those doggie biscuits may have been old or expired. They doubted they were laced with anything bad, but couldn't say for sure since the dogs consumed them," Quentin added. "They want to talk to the veterinarian first."

"Yeah, they promised to check out the rest of the perishables in the basket. They were reluctant to conclude that the verse of scripture written on Warren's book was necessarily a threat since the book was of a religious nature generally," Julian said.

"Unfortunately, Samantha didn't see where the basket came from, only picking it up off the front door stoop just as a female delivery person was driving off."

"This feels like something Warren would do," I complained. "He's a vindictive man."

"Anybody could have sent this," Julian said, trying to tamp down everyone's paranoia. "None of us could say for sure that Warren was the source of the gift basket," he said pouring himself a Bloody Mary, adding more vodka.

All of us were extremely perplexed, except for Reese who insisted he was certain Warren was behind this charade.

"Riley, the police promised to thoroughly investigate the whole matter, but if you ask me they seem far less convinced than the rest of us that the gift basket was intended to be a viable threat," Reese said. "But then again, they hadn't lived through last night's escapades."

"Well, I have had about all I could stand today between last night's gala and this morning's chaos. I think I'm going to go bake some bread."

"Quentin!" Madison shouted, "it's time to go, love. I've got no plans to hit the treadmill all next week from eating Riley's bread just because she's on overload again. Riley, I'm across the street, dear, if you need me." Madison grabbed Quentin by the hand and headed out the door.

"I'm here for you honey," Madison yelled back. "But I damn sure ain't eating any more bread this weekend."

"Oh Lord, Reese I need you to open some more champagne if Riley is gonna get on a bread baking marathon today," Lily added. "I still want to be able to fit on the seat of the plane going home to D.C," she laughed nervously, holding out her champagne flute for a refill.

"Time to go," Zoe said, looking at Julian. "I have to look good on stage. Riley's bread is too damn good for me to sit here and eat it all afternoon commiserating. Samantha and Claire are upstairs on their beds nursing Cleo and Stogie so I think we're all done here. Call us if you need us, Riley."

I walked to the door to show Zoe and Julian out.

"Thank you guys for coming by. I really appreciate the support as always," I said, hugging them both.

Reese stood behind me, resting his hands on my shoulders. He kissed Zoe on the cheek. Reese and Julian gave each other a bear hug.

"Riley, I'm going to hang out, do some work in Lucas's study," Reese said turning me around to face him. "I need to make some return phone calls to New York. Holler if you need anything. I'm here for you sis," he said, kissing me on the top of my head.

I nodded, smiling at my brother, thankful he was in town for me. I was grateful I didn't have to go through this experience alone. I headed back to the kitchen.

"Lily honey, I guess it's just me, you, and bread-making today. You want to help me?" I asked innocently.

"No I do not. I'll watch you work, keep you company, but that's it. This is your thing, not mine. I don't do dough unless is going into my bank account," Lily giggled.

It started to feel like things were calming down a bit. I needed a sense of calm right about now. I needed to punch some dough.

"Riley, Nathan's been blowing up my phone all morning. I've not returned any of his calls since I landed here this weekend. Sooner or later, I guess I'll have to deal with him," Lily exhaled deeply. "My nerves are shot. I really don't want to deal with him right now."

"Well it would serve him right. If he needs some attention he can call Ms. CNBC. Right girlfriend?"

"Yeah, damn right," Lily answered.

"Breaking hearts and mending hearts," we said in unison, reading each other's minds again.

Reese refilled our flutes with champagne, shook his head, and headed into Lucas's study.

"Now what? I stomped, hearing the door-bell ring.

"God I can't catch a break this morning," I said out loud, punching the dough and feeling the flour fly up on my cheek.

I wiped my hands on my black 'This Sista Can Cook' apron wrapped around me.

"Maybe the township police forgot something," I said casually, looking back at Lily.

I yanked the door, brushing my hands down the front of the black apron, then across my cheeks, blowing a heavy sighed that caused my bangs to rise and fall. I looked up into the face towering over me. My breath hitched quickly.

"Riley, sweetheart, I needed to see that you are okay."

Uh, Oh.

Chocolate Thunder!

Tall, dark, handsome, and in-command had landed on my front doorstep. Surely there's a law against being this damn fine.

CHAPTER 10

RILEY

Oh my God, this day couldn't get any more crazy. I was standing in my foyer with flour on my flushed face gawking at Chocolate Thunder. Oh my. Captain Noah Dunham was standing in my home. Jesus he was beautiful. I felt like my brain had stopped communicating with my mouth, but I managed to get out a "Hello, Noah."

Minding my manners I said, "Do come in."

He stepped inside my door. Observing him was like watching my first rise of the perfect soufflé. Anticipation. Loss of breath. Body gone hot. Shit. Shit. Shit. Chocolate Thunder was standing in my foyer and I looked like I'd been dipped in a bath of flour. Caught so unaware. Immobilized yet again. I hated this feeling. After last night's chaos and this morning's drama, I hadn't had time to re-group on any level. Can't I just please have a freaking moment, sighing inwardly, completely hysterical.

"Welcome to my home," I greeted him with both warmth and surprise.

"Riley, dear, I was troubled," he said, cutting the distance between us in half.

Whoa, there was that magnetic pull again occupying my body again carrying me yet again like a moth to the flame.

"I could tell there was an emergency going on here," he said, looking down on me. "I was worried about you. The kids," he sighed, his brow wrinkling. "Reese disconnected our call without explanation. I got here as soon as I could. I was not going to have any peace of mind until I knew you were okay," he said, his eyes staring at me in a way that made me feel like I were prey.

Noah visually scanned my body. I felt a shiver course through me, knowing on some level my attraction to him was real. Those sexy eyes were darkening, flickering over me, then penetrating me to the core. I was overcome with a flood of excitement I hadn't connected with in years. He smelled crisp, fresh, and intoxicating this morning much like he did last night. He was wearing that fragrance Happy again, making me want to totally inhale his essence like the nose of a good wine.

Thank you Jesus, I was baking bread. I seriously needed to calm the hell down. The last thing I wanted to do was to lose my mind in front of Chocolate Thunder. I was already one crisis away from calling this entire day over, declaring a nervous breakdown and taking to my bed. Umm, bed. So not the thing to be thinking about with Chocolate Thunder in my presence.

Noah glanced Lily's direction.

"Good morning Lily," he said, moving over to her, kissing her on the cheek.

"Noah, would you like to join Lily and I for champagne, a Bloody Mary perhaps? Some breakfast?" I asked, pulling up a chair near the bay window, positioning it close to Lily.

"I had breakfast at the Four Seasons very early, sweetheart," he said, still not taking his eyes off me and not yet moving to sit down. "I will have a Bloody Mary though," he said, "hold the blood."

I looked at him puzzled and confused.

Lily immediately scurried across the kitchen to get a cocktail glass saying, "I've got this Riley."

Lily knew on some level my brain had gone out to lunch. Thank God, Noah and Lily already had a working relationship because I stood by kneading dough as Noah stood near me. He was leaning against my butcher block island with his arms folded, legs crossed, listening to Lily explain the morning's events. I hadn't offered a thing to the conversation beyond an 'umm and an 'aha', emotionally stuck on stupid. I had no idea what was wrong with me nor why my mind was all of a sudden paralyzed in Noah's presence. I had forgotten how to both speak and breathe.

Just watching him listening to the events as told by Lily, I intuitively knew he was so not happy. Noah was pissed off. I could feel his anger. Despite my constant kneading of dough, I hadn't calmed down nearly enough. I was starting to get so scattered; I wanted to throw my mound of dough up against the wall, and call the day over. Noah's close proximity to me was having a profound effect on me. Same as last night. His, nearness was my enemy, endangering my sense of control. He sensed my discomfort.

"Riley, I need to know you're okay baby," he said, grabbing me on both sides of my waist, positioning himself behind me, pinning me in between him and the table, cupping his hands over mine. Noah began kneading the dough slowly with me, extending his arms full length on top of mine, careful not to touch the dough directly.

"Tell me you are okay, sweetheart?" he said bending his head down, whispering in my left ear. His voice soft. Husky. His breath warm on the back of my neck.

My mouth fell open, but then I closed it only to speak softly.

"Yes, my brother Reese seems to have things under control this morning," I whispered, letting myself feel the gentle strength of Noah's touch.

Noah was slowing moving his hands up and down with mine, kneading the dough with me. I hardly believed myself that Reese was in control, recalling him running around the outside of the house with Lucas's Glock 38 like an enraged mad man. Hell, I wasn't in control. My heart was racing a thousand beats per minute.

"I know your brother has your best interests at heart. He's family, sweetheart," Noah said, still kneading the dough slowly with me, speaking softly in my ear. "But I want you to know that you're special to me dear, and I'm keeping tabs. I want to support you in any way I can."

"Thank you," I said, trying to glance at Lily out of the corner of my eye.

"Your interests are my interests, sweetness," he said, still talking in my ear, sucking what was left of all the air out of the room. "I need to trust that you are okay," he said, backing away from me, but not before holding me solidly on my waist bracing my body against his as support, realizing my knees must have turned to jello.

Noah turned me around to face him.

"Right now, I can tell you're pretty shook up, and rightfully so. I'm not going to let anything happen to you or the kids," he said looking at me directly. "You should get some rest and relax today, gorgeous," he said, scanning my body up and down.

Gorgeous. Dear. Baby. Sweetheart. It's like that already?

"Thank you Noah. I appreciate your concern and it means a

lot to me . . . us . . . that you've personally checked in to inquire about our well-being," I said, wiping my hands on my apron. "I assure you this whole nonsense with Warren, threat or otherwise, is nothing and is under control," I said, knowing I sounded flustered.

"I'm not sure one can be sure about anything at his point. It's hard to say," he said, grabbing both my hands in his, his eyes never leaving mine.

"The police are investigating. I'm blessed to have the support of family and friends," I said, trying to dismiss this whole Warren business as being nothing serious.

"Good," he said, though I doubted he was convinced by my words. "Just know that your support in this matter includes me. And, I will without a doubt ensure your happiness and the kids' safety. I will see to it myself."

Support includes him? Ensure my happiness? What in the hell is Chocolate Thunder saying? Does he not know who I am? Of course not. He does not know who I am. Riley Cook does not mix business with pleasure. Been there. Done that. Bought the T-shirt. Slept in it. I ensure my own happiness.

"Now then, if things are under control here, then you won't be opposed to my having arranged for you to meet Nicholas Becker in New York to discuss his company becoming an angel investor for your business. We didn't get to finish that conversation over the phone. So let's finish it now," he said.

"New York? Angel investors? I don't know."

"Oh Riley, an angel investor? That's great news," Lily said, looking at us in awe, seizing the moment to chime in and stay supportive. She handed Noah another martini glass of chilled vodka.

"This is such a huge break. An angel investor is such a great opportunity," she said wide-eyed, smiling at Noah. "This is so exciting Noah," Lily said, clapping her hands together.

"Great then, Riley. I will personally see to it that you get to New York to have a face to face sit down with Nicholas. I'll take care of the arrangements. I'll call you with the details sweet-cakes."

"Now wait a minute, Noah. I haven't agreed to any such thing," I said, injecting myself into what was starting to feel like some decision-making that didn't include my input. I was overwhelmed. Sweet-cakes and angel investors. What the hell was going on here?

My voice was betraying me in his presence, not revealing the sound of confidence I wanted to muster.

"Riley," he paused, "you did say you were ready for an angel investor, right?" Noah asked, focusing on me like a laser beam.

"Well yes. I did."

"And you are ready to take your business to the next level aren't you?"

"Well yes," I whimpered.

"You have a business plan, correct?"

"Of course I do," I said rather nonchalantly, working overtime internally to gain control over myself.

"Then this issue is a no brainer babe."

He sounded like the voice of reason.

"There's nothing more to consider. Take a few days to prepare your pitch. Reese can review your financials."

"I have financial statements already," I said searching for my business voice.

"The only thing you need to remember is that angel investors bet on the jockey, not on the horse. It's less about liking the product and more about liking you. Investors want to like you. Trust you."

I nodded, hardly able to form words out of my mouth, as his eyes collided with mine making my heart do backflips again.

"And, Riley sweetheart, who in their right mind wouldn't love you?" he said, staring down on me, his eyes burning a hole into my soul.

There goes that word sweetheart again.

Jesus Christ, what a maddening impact Noah was having on me emotionally, curling around me like a warm blanket. I seriously needed to keep my head, despite the fact my feet and my heart were floating off the ground. And Lily, she was of no help to me, agreeing to everything Noah said, as if she too had lost her right mind. Bad enough I was screwed, but Lily was supposed to have my back. You might as well have stuck a fork in the both of us, because she and I were done in his presence.

"Riley, I have a driver waiting outside and a plane to catch. I don't want to interfere with your Sunday plans with Ms. Lily here," he said, nodding at Lily and giving her his million-dollar smile, downing his vodka. "I know you gals need your private time. I just needed to see that you were okay and safe. Now that I know you're out of harm's way, I can rest easier," he said, kissing me on the top of my forehead then pulling my chin to his lip, giving me a peck. "I'll be in touch," he said with all masculine grace.

And like that Chocolate Thunder was gone.

I looked over at Lily who was now fanning herself with one hand, her lips touching the top of her champagne flute, looking at me with her other hand up in the air as if she had nothing to do with what had just occurred.

"Well you're a big help, Cupid," I said looking at her hard with narrowed eyes.

"Uh uh. I can't do anything to help you out girlfriend. Color me silly putty when Chocolate Thunder is in the house," Lily laughed heartily. "Party over here," Lily said with excitement.

I shook my head in disgust.

"In the words of Madison Keyes, you are strictly dickly on your own Riley."

Lily and I both fell out laughing so hard, tears were flowing from our eyes.

"Tell the truth now Riley. You know you like that man," Lily said gleefully. "I told you he was the one, girlfriend."

"Lily there ought to be a law against letting that BMW loose," I said, feeling my face flushed, my heart pounding.

Reese entered the room, and took one look at the both of us. He shook his head.

"I absolutely cannot leave you two gals alone for one second. Obviously you've both had too much champagne this morning. Riley can't you smell that the bread is burning in here? What's the matter with you?"

"Oh Lily, girl, the bread, why didn't you tell me?"

"Riley can I have a little Chocolate Thunder with my bread and a bit of BMW on the side please?" Lily said, laughing hysterically, tears falling from her eyes.

We both started laughing so hard we were clutching each other trying to hold ourselves up.

"Riley you need to get a grip on yourself here today. I know you guys might be having trouble coping, given all the chaos the last twenty four hours, but in case you forgot, the family has been threatened here," Reese said sternly.

I squinted my eyes at him, deciding that he was looking more like my Dad the Lieutenant Colonel every day. God knows he was for sure acting like him.

Lily and I bust out laughing again completely giddy and out of control this time.

"So no more champagne for you two," Reese said, pouring more champagne in his own flute, grabbing a pot holder, moving to pull the burnt bread out of the oven. "You both look buzzed. And you act buzzed. And what the hell is this BMW and Chocolate Thunder stuff anyway?" Reese asked, walking barefoot with a handful of work related papers in one hand and a pot holder in the other.

"Well Reese," Lily said, attempting to straighten her shoulders a bit more upright, her head held high, "It's like the feeling a man gets when he's driving a really beautiful, racy, hot BMW. Now imagine it's a feeling that only a woman gets."

"Beautiful. Mister. Wonderful," Lily and I said at the same time.

We were smiling with stupid grins on our faces stomping our feet in hysterics, laughing so hard we were falling all over each other again.

"I swear I simply can't comprehend you two this morning," Reese said. He shook his head, deciding it was best to leave Lily and I to ourselves.

And me, I was stuck trying to figure out what in the world was I going to do with half burnt bread loaves, the delicious Noah Dunham, and an angel investment pitch on the horizon.

CHAPTER 11

RILEY

"Samantha, where are my black pearl earrings?" I yelled as she entered the room with Stogie and Cleo under foot.

"I don't know off hand, but I do know I returned them to you the last time I borrowed them."

"I see you decorated Cleo and Stogie this evening," I said, taking a moment to pick up Cleo to kiss her and to stroke Stogie behind the ears.

"I am so glad they both are feeling better from those tainted doggie biscuits they ate a couple of weeks ago."

Stogie and Cleo were adorned for the holidays with their diamond encrusted dog collars that I had made years ago, having sold Warren's engagement ring back to the jewelers. I thought it quite fitting that the carets from Warren's ring ended up chopped into two dog collars for Cleo and Stogie. It was the perfect outcome from one dog to another.

"Well I don't know how much I buy the story that the police didn't turn up anything in their investigation on that gift basket," Samantha said solemnly.

"Yeah I know. I wish there were more to go on. But I'm glad things calmed down a bit so that Reese felt comfortable enough to get back to his business in New York. I was afraid he was going to move in this time. He must have gone over my financials a hundred times for this pitch."

The phone rang. I could see Samantha glancing at the caller ID.

"Pick up the phone Mom, it's Lily," Samantha shouted from across the room.

"Hey Riley, Happy New Year's. Good luck tonight on your pitch. I had lunch with Noah in D.C. right after I got back. He told me all about Nicholas Becker's Company, *Milk Money*. I have a really good feeling about tonight first date and all."

"It's not a date Lily, it's business."

"Okay, so it's a business date. Power women have those all the time. But a date by any other name is still a date, Mommy," Lily chuckled.

"Yeah, well, call it what you want. The fact is, Nicholas Becker is leaving the country tomorrow. He could only meet with me on New Year's Eve. At the end of the day I really appreciate him squeezing me into his schedule. I think this is the right time to take my company to the next level."

"I know you're going to do well with the pitch. I have complete confidence you will land the deal. Noah too. I knew the two of you would be good together," Lily said, sounding pretty proud of herself. "Just think Riley, all while you're pitching to *Milk Money*, the Beautiful Mister Wonderful is going to be pitching to you," Lily chuckled. "Honey, how I wish I could be a bug on the wall."

"Well, I'm as ready as I'm going to be. Reese is joining us to tonight to answer any questions regarding the financials of my business. He has put in as much work on this pitch as I have. And, as far as Noah goes, you know how I simply despise mixing business with pleasure."

"I know Riley, but think of this situation as the exception to the rule. Lots of women have found love while handling their business, if you get my drift."

"I'm breaking my own rules. It makes me anxious. But I must admit, so far as Noah is concerned, he's everything you said he was, Lily. I hope this whole matter of mixing business with pleasure doesn't blow up in my face down the road."

"Oh Riley, think of it as networking. Friends do it all the time. Except in this case, think of it as friends with benefits," Lily laughed.

"Lily, you're the consummate Cupid. You never take that hat off do you?"

"Not when it's as right as this Riley. You two people belong together."

"Anyway, Happy New Year's to you Lily. What are you and the Doc doing?"

"We're in London tonight."

"Whaaaaat? You're not in D.C.?

"No, I insisted we spend New Year's in London. You know,

get out of the country for the holidays," Lily said, sounding a bit more pensive now.

"Wow, and what did Ms. CNBC have to say about that?"

"I don't know and I don't care. I'm done with Nathan for the most part. I think he thinks this holiday will do us good. He's trying to create his own fireworks with me. Frankly, I no longer want Nathan, but she can't have him until I say so. Besides if she's going to end up with him she might as well get used to "mending hearts and breaking hearts" we both said simultaneously.

"Oops he's coming. Gotta go, Riley."

"Okay, enjoy London, Lily. Love you."

"Love you too."

I wondered if Lily was truly done with Nathan. They had been together so long, it was hard for me to think of them as not being a couple anymore. We all grew up together. I knew at some point Lily was going to have to grieve the loss of her marriage much like I once had to grieve the loss of Lucas, and later Warren. It would be no walk in the park. I knew she didn't know that yet. Life had taught me differently. I wasn't convinced that 'done' necessarily looked like what Lily was doing.

I hung up the phone, turning to see Samantha coming back into my bedroom.

"I came to get my New Year's Eve kiss, Mamma Dukes, before you leave. My friends and I are going into Philly for the midnight poetry slam. You're wearing that on your date with the captain?"

Samantha pointed to the vintage inspired black sheer floral lace silk dress laying on the bed.

"I was hoping the high neckline, the below the knee pencil bottom, and cutout back would be the perfect fitted silhouette to give me a festive yet professional look. I was going for that retro 50's Mad Men look."

"I think it's perfect, but you're gonna need a hose to put the fire in out in Mr. Navy himself. This dress is hot."

"Too much?"

"Not at all. It's a perfect holiday night look. Cool. Classy. Sexy. Light a fire," Samantha grinned.

"Done. I'm not trying to over think it with everything else I have on my mind."

"It's a shame I'll be gone before he arrives. But I'll try to stick around as long as I can before my ride comes. I am so looking forward to who this man is that has finally gotten my mother to get her head out of her work and go on a date."

"It's not exactly a date," I mumbled.

"That's not the way I heard it, but whatever."

"So what have you guys planned for the evening? Claire's spending the night at Aunt Zoe's and Uncle Julian's."

"X and Nena have decided to have a quiet New Year's in, listening to "Miles", and streaming movies on Netflix. Last I checked, they were downstairs in the den having a social media moment."

"A social media moment?"

"Nena was on Facebook, and X was exchanging tweets with his posse of motorcycle heads from the sons of the Navy Vets," Samantha said. "So what shoes are you wearing?"

We both heard Madison calling my name out from downstairs. She was heading up the spiral staircase to my bedroom, her voice getting closer. I finished clipping my La Perla black garter belt to the ultra-sheer black hosiery with the thin seam running up the back of my leg. La Perla's Private Show Lace Garter happened to be conveniently playing softly over the intercom.

"Hand me that black cocktail shoe right there Samantha."

Samantha headed into my walk in closet, tripping on a couple pair of shoes along the way, trying to fix her gaze where my finger was pointed.

"The one with the Swarovski crystals that wrap around the ankle, dear."

"All sukki sukki now," Madison said as she entered the bedroom. She moved closer to help me zip the back of my little black dress, as Samantha headed back downstairs.

"Girlfriend you are pulling out all the stops tonight. You're wearing Marchesa Couture this evening? Things really are moving along well with you and Noah. That man is in trouble tonight. You're a real knockout girlfriend."

"Well, we haven't seen each other since our Sunday brunch after the gala, but he's called every day since then. We've had some marathon phone conversations, video chats, and have given our text messengers a workout these last couple of weeks."

"And how's that been going?"

"We decided to use our phone time to learn as much as we

could about each other until we could see each other again. It's worked for me since I've been busy with the pitch, the Beard nomination, and life in general. Noah's been in travel status. He's coming back into the States from a twenty-six hour journey from Washington to Kabul via Dubai. Usually when I talk to him, he's either getting on a plane or getting off one. Somebody famous is always on board. One day it was Al Gore, the next time it was Chief Justice Roberts, another time, Leon Panetta. I was starting to wonder if he was an US Air Marshall or something. So many notable people in his orbit."

"Yeah, but tonight's pitch night and date night all rolled into one. That makes you the one in his orbit." Madison grinned like a school girl. "You better hope you can keep those panties on woman. That man is all the way fine," she said, reaching into the candy jar on my night stand, grabbing a hand full of jelly beans while plopping on my bed.

"You heard from Zoe lately?" Madison asked, changing the subject.

"No I haven't. We haven't spoken much lately, although Claire is spending the night with her and Julian this evening. Ever since Claire started taking those martial arts classes, she's been making Julian pull out all of his old Bruce Lee movies."

"She is so like her Dad," Madison said, separating the black jelly beans from her pile.

"She's been pretty pumped about hanging out with her Aunt and Uncle tonight. Claims she's following in her dad's footsteps hoping to become a black belt like Lucas."

"Like I said . . . ," Madison said.

"Zoe did call earlier to wish me a Happy New Year. She knows I'm seeing Noah this evening."

"I sense this whole business of your dating Noah has un-nerved Zoe a bit for some reason. What's up with that?"

"Not sure. Who knows. I've long since stopped trying to figure other people out. Zoe's known Noah awhile now from Lucas's Naval Academy days. He speaks fondly of her though," I said.

"Maybe she knows something we don't and hasn't come out with it," Madison said.

"Zoe tends to move at her own pace. I'm sure if there was something she felt I needed to know then she would definitely tell me."

"Well you know Riley, it is one of those things that makes me raise an eyebrow."

We headed towards the staircase to go downstairs. I paused to grab my black feathered clutch. I tucked my Swarovski crystal flash drive inside. I loaded my presentation pitch on the flash drive earlier in the day to keep from lugging my laptop all night. I had forwarded my prepared pitch earlier in the week to the staff at *Milk Money*, but I knew it was best that I have my own digital copy in my possession for my own peace of mind. I had been in this business long enough never to take anything for granted. I was fully prepared, ready to nail this puppy down. I was so happy to be bringing in the New Year with a bang.

"It's mad cold out," Madison said. "I practically froze my booty off on the way over. You'd better grab a fur, Riley."

Darn, I was halfway down the staircase. I turned back around, headed to my closet, grabbing my white full-length mink, expecting New York to be even colder.

The doorbell ringer began playing *I Wish You A Merry Christmas.* I sensed my anxiety level momentarily rise. I glanced in the mirror, touching up my lip gloss, hoping I looked all right. My hair was pulled up, and adorned with a black feathered hair clip. My hair was styled differently than when Noah saw me last.

I got halfway down the stairs when I saw Samantha's face. She looked wide-eyed, both eyebrows raised. Madison spoke first.

"Riley, woman, your ride is here."

Madison and Samantha were still looking out the opened door. A huge gust of wind blew at them. The both shivered at the same time.

"Jesus, What is with you two? You both act like you haven't see a man before," I said, moving in front of them to open the door a bit wider. "I take that back," I gasped.

My eyes got two sizes wider as my brain tried to process the white super stretch Rolls Royce Phantom limousine in my circular drive with a young hunky hot sexy chauffeur standing beside it with the door open.

"Let me help you inside, Ms. Cook. My name is Cameron. I'll be your chauffeur this evening. There's champagne on the bar for you to your left. The music and television controls are right above you. Captain Dunham has asked that I deliver you safely to him in New York this evening," Cameron said, extending his hand to help me inside.

Before the limousine door closed, I smiled, watching Samantha out the corner of my eye blowing air kisses. She and Madison were slapping each other high five.

"Happy New Year Riley!" they screamed at the same time, both grinning, giggling and jumping up and down.

I waved goodbye. Chauffeur Cameron tucked my fur neatly inside neatly and closed the door. I tried to catch my breath. I poured myself a glass of champagne so I could calm down. I selected Sade to listen to during the ride. My iPhone buzzed with a text from Madison.

Scared of you, Riley. New Year's Eve with Chocolate Thunder, baby . . . lol . . .

I texted back: Yep. My own BMW . . . Lol . . . Beautiful Mister Wonderful.

CHAPTER 12

NOAH

"Welcome back to JFK International, Captain Dunham," the beautiful sapphire-eyed concierge said softly as I made my way into the American Airlines One World Lounge.

"My name is Kelly. How can I help you this evening sir?"

"I'd like car service to the Rihga Royal Hotel please, on 54th Street."

"No problem, Captain Dunham. May I get you anything while you wait, sir? Perhaps something from the bar this evening?"

"I'll have a vodka martini with a twist, thank you."

"Make yourself comfortable sir, and I'll have Jeffrey take care of you right away."

"I'll be over there," I said, pointing to a more private area across the room.

I eyeballed a large comfortable brown leather chair, and strolled across the room. I sat down next to a mahogany end table, grateful to have a moment to change gears from the long flight. This week's copy of the New York Post was setting on the table. I flipped through the pages, taking note of the gossip section *Page Six* peeking out the side of the paper. I couldn't help but recognize a photo of Nicholas Becker in the top right corner of the magazine with a headline that read *"New York's Most Eligible Bachelor Nicholas Becker is Rumored to be the Next Guardian Angel over James E. Beard's Hottest Food and Wine Nominee Riley Cook. Is Becker Hungry For More? We Wonder What's Really Cookin' With Ms. Cook? Sounds All So Delectable!"*

"Jesus, what the hell?" I mumbled out loud. I couldn't believe the news of Riley's collaboration with *Milk Money* had trickled out to the gossip mongers already. Between the gossip columns, Facebook and the internet, was there anything sacred anymore? And the mere idea of linking my Riley with Nicholas caused my blood to boil.

Pushing down my own frustration of the thought of Riley being romantically linked with anyone but me, I set the paper down and picked up the Wall Street Journal. Thankfully, my drink arrived.

"Thank you dear," I said to the server, taking a healthy swig. "My compliments to Jeff."

"Thank you," she said happily, grateful for the big tip.

Seconds later, I heard a familiar voice.

"You never know what the wind is going to blow in now do you? Gee Mico, we have to stop meeting like this my darling. Who knows, you and I might end up one day in the columns of *Page Six*."

I spotted those lean, smooth athletic legs of pure female temptation, my eyes lingering over those curvaceous hips, towards the tiny waist, past the full cleavage adorned in the American Airlines uniform and gazed into the face of Leah Chen. I stood, rising from my chair, towering over her in the most intimidating stance I could muster, noticing her long black hair rippling across her breast in waves.

"I doubt anyone in their right mind would consider you and I in the frequent flyer lounge of JFK Airport to be news of any consequence Ms. Chen."

"We could make some news of our own Mico," she said, cocking her head a bit to the side, in what clearly sounded like an invitation.

"What's wrong Leah? You and Warren run out of new tricks to play?"

Leah batted her eyes, flipping those luscious black waves of curls nonchalantly as if I had mentioned someone who name was of no consequence to her. I found that interesting. I didn't trust it either. Maybe she and Warren were mere fuck buddies. I had her pegged right the first time. The hottie with the wandering eye.

"And again, the name is Noah to you."

"I guess you haven't heard baby, tricks are for kids," she

said, stepping closer to me, rising on her tiptoes and leaning into my lips with both her hands placed on my chest.

I grabbed her hands tightly by the wrists, taking them off my chest, pulling them to her side.

"You should know Leah, I of all people know a trick when I see one."

Leah moved to slap me across the face. I caught her left wrist seconds before she made contact.

"Let it go Leah," I said sternly. "I'm not easily entertained by the games you play."

I was forcing myself not to get lost in her cleavage. She was teasing me mercilessly, positioning her body dangerously close to mine. I prayed that the torpedo would not come to attention.

"Warren is right after all," she huffed, drawing back in surprise. "You and that Riley woman think you're all high and mighty. And, in the words of Warren, "Oh how the mighty shall fall,"" she said, studying me for a beat.

"I'm disappointed in you Leah. Warren's opinion counts for nothing. He wouldn't know mighty if it came up and smacked him in the face. But he might get his chance."

"Yeah well when you get tired of playing around with boring little Riley Cook and want to spend some time with a real woman, call me, baby," Leah said shrugging her shoulders in annoyance. She turned her body away from me, rubbing her breast against my chest in the process.

I grabbed her arm hard, bending my head down and leaning my mouth into her ear whispering, "You can tell your boyfriend that if he gets anywhere near Riley or her family again, I will personally see to it that he will regret the day he ever met her. You would be wise to heed this advice as well," I hissed.

Leah never turned back around. I pushed her body away from mine, brushing myself off, straightening my tie as the Concierge Kelly approached us.

"Hey Leah, you coming or going today?"

"Why coming, of course," Leah said, turning her head around, staring at me while placing that well-manicured cherry red fingertip in her mouth. "Coming all over myself in fact," she said slyly, winking back at me.

"Captain Dunham, your car has arrived sir," Kelly said blushing, turning ten shades of red. She then lapsed into silence, but not moving on. Maybe it was shock from Leah's comment.

"Thank you, Kelly," I said dismissively.

I left money on the table for my bill and walked out the double doors of JFK. This madness with Leah and Warren was starting to feel like two bad pennies that kept showing up. I wasn't convinced it was a coincidence seeing her here today, but I couldn't say for sure since she worked for the airlines.

But one thing that I knew from Leah's words was that Warren wasn't finished with causing Riley anguish. With everything I knew about him, I wasn't surprised. I was going to have to pull closer to Riley. I would have to work harder to keep her and the kids safe. I had promised Lucas. I had promised myself.

My anxiety was building within me from merely thinking about the things I needed to share with Riley. But I didn't want to burden her right now. She was under so much pressure with all the long hours she had been putting in with Reese preparing for her pitch. It was more important that tonight go well. What I needed to share could wait.

I needed to shake my concerns off, pick up Riley at the hotel, give her a minute to re-group from her trip, and then we both head over to Nicholas's for the pitch. I was glad Reese lived in New York. Reese was joining us at Nicholas's for dinner. He would be able to answer any questions regarding Riley's business financials.

I couldn't wait to see Riley. The last couple of weeks had gone by too slowly for my taste. I threw myself into my work so I wouldn't have to think too much about how much I missed her. If the evening went as well as I planned, I'd be beginning this New Year in a way I never had. I'd make Riley mine.

CHAPTER 13

RILEY

The limousine cruised out of Lincoln Tunnel into Manhattan, as Sade's *"Lovers Rock"* was playing softly over the limousine speakers. Peeking out the window taking in the glow of the street lights, I rehearsed my pitch in my head one last time. I so need this presentation to go well.

The ringer on my phone pulled me out of my thoughts. It was Reese.

"Hey Reese, what's up."

"I'm checking on your 411 so I can time my arrival. Noah told me he sent a car for you," Reese said.

"Well I can't say it's any old car, baby brother. More like a Rolls Royce Phantom Limousine," I whooped cheerfully.

"Well, that's one way for a man to express his interest in a woman. I'll have to remember to add that move to my playbook."

"Yeah well take it on firsthand experience. It's a move that works. I've been floating on cloud nine ever since I got inside this baby."

"At first I wasn't happy about Noah's involvement in your business affairs Riley, but I can tell he's being supportive, so I guess I'll give him a pass. But if he hurts you or your business dealings in any way, his ass is mine, do you hear me?"

"I hear you, but remember Reese, Noah was Lucas's wingman. Lucas trusted him so why shouldn't we? Besides my world's gotten complicated pretty fast. The James Beard Nomination, an angel investor in the wings, all the funky publicity, and a new man in the mix. I've got to start trusting in others at some point."

"You're still a strong contender for the Beard Foundation nomination. The craziness at the gala hasn't diminished your chances any, so stop saying the publicity is funky," Reese said.

"Yeah well thanks to you. If it weren't for your blogger connections in the food industry orchestrating a substantial amount of good press about me, pushing the Warren Shaw funky publicity to the back pages, who knows how this picture would have turned out?"

I breathed a sigh of relief. Thank God I had my brother on my side.

"That was good for both our businesses, seeing how I was plastered across the pages in that ugly scene as well," Reese added. "Unfortunately father didn't see it that way. He caught wind of the bad press, called me up last week and read me the riot act," Reese chuckled.

"Oh he called me too Reese," I laughed. "He went on and on about the family name, how we both had completely lost our minds showing out in public. Dad is going to be looking over our shoulders no matter what. The Lt. Colonel is not to be stopped."

"I'm still puzzled how that news reached him even to this day. That man has spies everywhere. It's the same as if when we were kids," Reese laughed.

"Yeah Lucas used to say Dad had his own intelligence operation when it came to his family."

"Well sis, I need to tell you since you're coming into the Apple tonight, *Page Six* has gotten wind that you are now tied to Mr. kingpin playboy Nicholas Becker. Apparently they are linking you two together and I don't mean business related."

I laughed in Reese's ear at the absurdity of anybody putting me and Nicholas Becker together. Hell, I hadn't even met the man yet for goodness sake.

"Jesus Riley, Do I have to put you under guard or something, sister?"

"Oh stop it Reese. Those are rumors. These media talking heads don't have anything else to do with themselves, but seemingly mind my business, which is frankly no business of theirs. It's enough for me to keep up with me," I chuckled keeping the mood light.

The last thing I needed was for Reese to switch into overprotective mode tonight.

"Reese I'm coming into Manhattan now, honey."

"Okay Riles. I'll see you soon. Everything looks good. Don't worry about anything. You've got this in the bag baby big sis. Oh, and Riley?"

"Yeah?"

"I'm bringing Harper Carmichael Montgomery with me tonight as my plus one. I managed to talk her into doing a final review of your numbers for me on the company so as to confirm my projections."

"Oh cool. It's been ages since I've seen Harper. It'll be fun to catch up."

"I'm sure she'll be happy to see you too. Listen I'd better run, or I'll be late picking her up."

"No problem. Thanks Reese for everything. I love you."

"Love you too Riley."

I hung up, peering out the window, noticing the light snow that was falling as the limousine headed through Manhattan. The night was quiet. The music soothing. How I so loved snowy nights. My own excitement level was building again in anticipation. Tonight's pitch was going to be coupled with an intimate dinner for six. I was thrilled to hear that of all the women Reese had decided to accompany him, he chosen Harper Montgomery. Harper was by far no slouch.

She'd attended Columbia University's business school when Reese was a graduate Adjunct Professor mentoring some of the of the university's new business interns. The daughter of a U.S. Senator from the State of New York, Harper was a rising star, and now CEO of her own company, The Montgomery Consulting Group. She specialized in consulting, risk management, and turnaround services catering to the nation's top Fortune 500 companies. Harper had recently moved up to number twelve on Forbes' top thirty over thirty list this year. She was the first African American woman ever to make the list. The more I thought about it, the more I thought she'd be a great addition to tonight's activities. I was pretty sure I could count on her to be supportive. I wasn't surprised that Reese had run my financials by her. Those two number crunchers were cut from the same cloth, often sharing professional opinions with each other. I never could quite get a handle of if there was something more to their friendship than business.

"We'll be at the hotel shortly Ms. Cook," my driver Cameron said, slightly lowering the privacy window, pulling me out of my thoughts.

"Great Cameron," I said, smiling at his huge grin reflecting off the rear view mirror.

He nodded, raising the privacy window back up slowly. I was on pins and needles at the prospect of seeing Noah again. Even though we'd been speaking by phone daily, I was still anxious about him seeing me in business mode. It had taken me a bit, but I had come to terms with myself that I was obviously too attracted to the man to even entertain this crazy idea of mixing business with pleasure. Whatever doubts I had, it was too late to turn back now. I had gone out on this limb. I had no choice but to go forward. There was too much at stake.

Noah's stock had gone up considerably with me these last couple of weeks. He was kind. Thoughtful. Handsome as sin. I took a deep breath, reminding myself to step up to the plate. I needed to deal with this new combination of mixing business with the heat and roar of Chocolate Thunder.

My limousine pulled in front of the Rihga Royal Hotel on 54th street. Chauffeur Cameron opened the door of the limousine. Noah was standing in the cold outside the hotel's double doors waiting for me. He looked FINE AS HELL.

"Hey gorgeous," he said, grabbing my hand, pulling me close to him. "I've been dying to see you."

"And I you," I blushed, aware of the heat rushing to my cheeks.

Noah kissed me on the lips softly.

"Let me get you out of the cold baby."

He ushered me into the hotel's piano bar. A female lounge singer dressed in a beautiful gold lame dress was singing soft music. Noah ordered for the both of us, asking the bartender for a brandy for me and a vodka martini for himself.

The lounge was neatly arranged with two-seater chocolate leather love seats placed around the room at different angles. Cherry wood cocktail tables, some high, some low, were set up around the room facing the microphone and baby grand piano. The room was filled with the hum of the New Year's Eve revelers, all seemingly engaged in social chatter while the bustle of wait staff eager to serve them moved quickly around the room. I loved lounge music. It was my favorite.

The female singer was singing Michael Frank's familiar song *"Leading Me Back To You."* I recognized her voice.

It was the sounds of saxophonist Candy Duffer and neo-soul vocalist, the renowned "jazz goddess of love," Sable Winters. Both were two of my favorite artists. Xavier would be so jealous of me right now. He loved Candy Duffer and I loved Sable Winters. Noah and I sat close to each other, holding hands while taking in the intimate atmosphere. I speculated internally about his perfect start to a romantic evening. *Whoa. There you go again Riley. This is business. But it's also New Year's Eve.* My mind was in a chaotic state of conflict with this whole business of balancing business and pleasure. I felt like a neophyte negotiating with my own emotions.

"Riley, you look stunning tonight. No doubt I'm going to have to bat every man off of you."

"Thank you. You're pretty handsome yourself tonight," I said, sipping my brandy slowly, feeling my blood heating again.

Noah was wearing a dark blue suit, a light blue shirt with his initials monogrammed on the cuffs, and a dark blue tie. I glanced discreetly at his feet, his legs crossed one comfortably across the other. I took note of his black leather shoes with the Italian designer Bruno Magli insignia on the soles. Mother always says you can judge a man by his shoes. It occurred to me that he had a certain James Bond allure about him, looking as if he had stepped off the cast of Casino Royale.

The waiter returned with another snifter filled with B&B for me, and a vodka martini for him. A bowl of salted pretzels were placed between us. I sipped my drink, feeling the heat of the amber liquid warming my inners. I took in the ambiance of the room as the vocalist sang some of my old favorites with Candy playing the saxophone like it was a work of art.

"How are you doing Riley? You're quiet. Are you ready for tonight's pitch?"

"I'm ready. But I shouldn't have any more brandy after this. I want to keep a clear head. But it's helping to take the edge off my nerves."

"You're gonna be fine. Nicholas is a down to earth guy. He has a way of making everyone around him feel comfortable."

"That's comforting."

"He comes across as playful kind of guy, but from a business perspective he's as sharp as a tack. There's no one smarter, so be mindful of keeping your focus. Reese and I will be right by your side supporting you."

"Did I ever tell you how much I love piano bars?" I said, changing the subject quickly so as to stay as relaxed as possible. "They are my favorite. I use to beg Lucas whenever we had date night to choose a piano bar for after dinner drinks," I babbled, curious whether Lucas had shared that tidbit with Noah.

Who would know that about me, or was I predictable? An educated guess perhaps?

"I miss Lucas every day," Noah sighed, taking a huge gulp of his martini, tossing the lemon twist aside. "Do you still miss him?" Noah asked.

"Oh I suppose I have my days. But he left pieces of himself behind. I see the reflection of him every day in his children. I thank him for that, but I've gone on with my life."

Noah was still holding my hand now, moving closer to me. I mentally noted his affectionate side. I found it endearing. He turned slowly towards me reaching in his pocket.

"I have a little something for you Riley."

Noah handed me a tiny blue box tied with a stark white ribbon. I blushed, recognizing the Tiffany brand. I tugged on the white ribbon slowly, lifting the lid carefully.

"It's something that I hope will always remind you of our first two evenings together."

I was breathing unevenly. I opened the dainty gift box, lifting out a lovely gold charm bracelet with a single 18k gold diamond champagne bucket dangling off one link and an 18k gold apple dangling off another.

"I plan to fill this for you with reminders of everything wonderful that we share beginning with the first night we met at the gala. Wear it in good health, sweetheart."

Noah kissed my lips softly. "I hope it will bring you good luck this evening."

He kissed the top of my knuckles.

"Thank you Noah," I said, feeling that magnetic pull again between us.

My body lit up as if an electrical current had passed through it. Oh my. I felt the bolt of lightning that went along with that Chocolate Thunder!

"I love it. I will cherish it along with tonight's memories."

I kissed him back sweetly on the lips while he moved to put the bracelet on my wrist.

"We're scheduled to meet Reese, Nicholas and his people for your presentation and dinner soon. I expect it to be a long night. I promise I'll personally get you home safely in time for breakfast with your family."

"Sounds fabulous. You've done a lot already. I'm happy to be able to share the evening with you and to bring in the New Year together. New Year's always represents new beginnings to me."

Noah grabbed my charm laden wrist, turned my cheek towards him and kissed my lips again.

"I will see to it."

CHAPTER 14

RILEY

"Bellissima," Nicholas said, speaking in Italian, "It's a good thing Mico failed to tell me of the beauty of Lucas's widow. But for the fact I was studying back then, I would have gone to that Navy game myself, forgotten all about my friendship with them both, and made you mine. But all's fair in love and war," Nicholas laughed mischievously, kissing me on both cheeks.

Nicholas was still holding my hand tight, when I responded back in Italian.

"Lucas was the love of my life. His memory I shall hold dear to my heart as mother of his children. And, as far as Captain Dunham is concerned, he appears to have my best interest at heart setting up this opportunity for me to meet you and to discuss my company. For that I am extremely grateful to both you and him."

"Ahhhh Mico," Nicholas said, switching back in English, "you failed to mention that our lovely Riley here is not only beautiful, but smart, charming, and gracious too."

Noah straightened his back, sending Nicholas a shrewd smile, a bit of feigned annoyance flashing across his face.

"Come in my friends. Happy New Year. Welcome to my home," Nicholas said with the utmost joy, flashing his warm million dollar smile.

Nicholas helped me out of my fur, handing it to one of the servants who moved quietly about without notice.

"Thank you," I said politely, nudging Noah to hand Nicholas a gift-wrapped box.

"I'm warning you man, I don't want to have to use this gift on your head," Noah grunted, unsure of what our Italian exchange was about, but obviously trusting his gut that some flirtation was had by his friend.

Nicholas slapped Noah on the back laughing the whole time as if he knew he had pushed Noah's jealousy button. Noah handed him a bottle of fifty year old scotch wrapped in a red bow, a holiday gift from the both of us.

"It's good to see you again Nicky. It's been way too long man."

"I've missed you too Mico. This is such a treat," he said, slapping Noah again on the back.

Noah embraced Nicholas, giving him a big man hug.

"It feels like old times Mico. You're making my New Year's, brother."

A gentleman dressed in all black with a server tray walked over and handed Noah a vodka martini.

"I have to apologize to you Riley," Nicholas said, turning his attention to me. "My schedule has been so damn tight. I'm headed out of the country tomorrow night."

Nicholas's eyes did a body scan of me that ended at my breasts. His lush eyelashes and deep emerald eyes were magnetizing. Any woman would with a brain would willingly drown herself in them and not ask for a life preserver.

"Tonight was the only window of opportunity I had to meet you in person. I promise I'll make it up to you by ensuring that your evening will be a most enjoyable experience," he said, handing me a flute of champagne.

His emerald eyes were beaming at me again from someplace in between seduction and delight.

"The pleasure is all mine," I said, blushing, taking the champagne but reminding myself to drink slowly.

I still had to get through this presentation. I needed all my senses operating on high alert.

"Mico has spoken very highly of your company," Nicholas continued.

"I'm beyond grateful that you've gone out of your way to see me."

I was hoping that I was still breathing evenly from the intensity of his gaze.

Lord have mercy. My man karma must have gone into overdrive this month. Perhaps that Cupid Lily really had cast a huge heart-stopping spell on me or something. Yet another beautiful man was in my orbit. It was more than my fragile heart could handle. I wasn't sure my heart could take the pressure.

Madison was right. I have been too cooped up with work far too long. I'd apparently missed out on all the eye candy running loose.

Who could doubt that Nicholas Becker was walking heat. He was slightly taller than Noah, but had more of a muscular build. His dark brown hair was cut short and layered, but still long enough to run your fingers through. The fresh scent of the mousse in his hair coupled with his familiar Hugo Boss cologne invited you to take in his full essence. His five o'clock shadow accentuated his strong chin; his jawline revealing a hint of a dimple on the left side that made you melt when he smiled.

Nicholas was wearing a dark charcoal grey jacket with perfectly creased pinstripe pants that rode low on his hips. His crisp white shirt was opened just enough to reveal a thin gold rope chain encircling his neck as his chest hair made a peekaboo appearance through the open neckline of his shirt. Nicholas Becker radiated power, wealth, and raw passion. Beneath the surface you knew there was mischievous bad boy ticking like a time bomb waiting to escape that refined exterior. It wasn't lost on me that he possessed a certain sexual power that radiated like a beacon almost invisibly from his body igniting every woman's wantonness. Had the man been born centuries earlier, he would have led every woman within his grasp right along the path with him, straight into Dante's Inferno. He was a burning flame of insatiable heat and seduction.

"I'm glad Mico called me to tell me about your company, Riley. Far be it from me to miss out on a wonderful investment opportunity for *Milk Money*."

"I'm glad too," I smiled, turning my eyes toward Noah.

Noah pulled his body closer to mine, wrapping his arm around my hips playing the "this is mine" card that men play when marking their territory, making sure Nicholas knew I was off limits.

My heart galloped at Noah's touch. I felt that familiar jolt pulse through me as he tucked my body closer to his. One thing for sure, even in the presence of the infamous playboy Nicholas Becker, I couldn't deny my attraction to Beautiful Mister Wonderful. I fingered the new charm bracelet on my wrist nervously in front of me. The rush of excitement that coursed through my body from his nearness left me desirous of exploring the possibilities between us for more.

"Good, it's settled then," Nicholas said clapping his hands together. "We shall have a wonderful evening."

Nicholas shuffled us into the Great Room, walking down the long hallway with the grace of a pure bred stallion.

"Riley, I understand from my concierge that your brother Reese is on his way up," Nicholas said, leading us through the penthouse foyer. "We'll get started once he arrives. Meanwhile, I'd like to introduce you to my business partner Lucia Falco. She's waiting to join us."

I had done my research before coming to New York. Nicholas Becker lived in the infamous Becker Towers located in the ultra-luxurious condominium building of Central Park West at 61st Street in an 8,000 square foot penthouse Presidential Suite. His family owned tons of real estate in New York. I knew from earlier conversations with my brother Reese that celebrity residents Sting and Alex Rodriguez lived in his building. The building was well known for its breathtaking panoramic views of Central Park and the glittering New York skyline. Many of the resident's homes were often featured in Architectural Digest. Nicholas resided on the 86th floor, so it would take several minutes for Reese to arrive on the Penthouse floor once security was given the authority to let him pass.

Nicholas, Noah, and I entered the great room. The penthouse decor was obviously a reflection of his outgoing personality. His home reflected an impeccable design with fourteen foot ceilings, track lights and sixteen inch windows offering a 360 degree breathtaking views of Manhattan magnified with the help of several well positioned telescopes. Some of the most famous artists in the world's artwork hung on his walls.

Filled with every amenity one could only wish for in a home, the spacious penthouse suite had a large living area filled with unique artwork, handcrafted rugs, marble floors, and beautiful contemporary furnishings all tied together by a grey and white color scheme accented with luminous brushed silver accessories. Bang and Olufsen high quality audio and television systems were situated in every room with an interactive entertainment center that controlled each room. The floating staircase leading to the second floor was flanked on both sides by tall vases of white orchids.

A beautiful melodic version of "I wish you love" was playing softly in the background on the black baby grand piano positioned in the suite's corner. There were elegant New Year's black, white, and silver decorations everywhere. A twelve foot white Christmas tree was beautifully decorated with silver balls, black and silver silk ribbons, and silver turtle doves. I had to catch my breath the tree was so spectacular. A lit see-through glass fireplace separated the Great Room from the dining area, the crackling flame visible on both sides of each room. The dining table stretched the length of the room, easily able to seat fourteen. Tonight the majestic dining table was beautifully set for dinner service for six.

A spectacular diamond-studded chess set glimmered in the corner on a glass table, catching my attention. Nicholas must have noticed the look of awe on my face. He moved towards the chess table, picking up the black king, twirling it in his hand, the light dancing off the piece.

"Do you play Riley?" he asked, his head tilted to the side.

"I do," I answered, my skin flushing from my embarrassment of having him caught me drooling over his chess set.

"Hmm. Brains and beauty. A wonderful combination," Nicholas said, his voice expressing a hint of intrigue.

Noah kissed side of my head, his arm still possessively wrapped around me, his eyes narrowing at Nicholas.

A tall, poised, elegantly dressed woman approached us, extending her hand in greeting.

"Riley, May I introduce my business partner Lucia Falco. Lucia is my alter ego at *Milk Money*," Nicholas bantered, setting the chess piece back down, grabbing Lucia, pulling her close to him and kissing her on the cheek.

"Hello Riley, it's nice to meet you," Lucia said in a very heavy Italian accent, dismissing Nicholas with a nod.

"It's nice to meet you too," I said politely.

"I'm pleased to see you again Noah," she said, extending her hand, kissing him on both cheeks. I've heard much about your recent travels from Nicky. He speaks of you often, your days together at the Naval Academy," Lucia said.

"Well it's great we can all catch up again," Noah grinned. "It's been too long."

Lucia looked elegant wearing a gold silk sleeveless sequin dress with a high neckline and graduated white sparkled layers. She wore gold metallic gladiator leather stilettos that zipped up the back, complimenting her lean legs. I readily recognized she was wearing Oscar De La Renta. She was absolutely dazzlingly, the epitome of Italian beauty.

Her straight dark brown shoulder length hair framed her face in a way that gave her a professional look, as dark inky eyes peered through black Prada eyewear with just the right amount of confidence. It was obvious from her serious demeanor that she was business-like, yet at the same time welcoming, respecting the evening. Apparently, Nicholas surrounded himself with both brains and beauty.

"Riley, thank you so much for sending your pitch by courier," Lucia said, turning her attention back to me. "It was helpful having the advance copy of *Black Sequinned Bows and Champagne Night's* financial and business portfolio prior to tonight's meeting. It gave me a chance to review your portfolio more closely ahead of time. That was thoughtful of you."

"Well I wanted you to be able to digest my business plans absent the pressure of time constraints. That way I can answer any and all questions you might have tonight."

Noah beamed at Nicholas.

"I told you that this was an opportunity you shouldn't miss Nicky," Noah added.

"I wouldn't miss this for the world," Nicholas said flirtatiously.

Noah shook his head as Nicholas pulled Noah out of earshot.

I made small talk with Lucia, asking questions about *Milk Money*. A servant quietly moved about with a tray filled with champagne flutes, pausing briefly to freshen our drinks; taking Lucia's empty flute and handing her a new one. Noah and Nicholas were settled across the room at the fireplace catching up on old times, laughing in hushed tones between themselves.

Moments later I heard the arrival of my brother Reese and Harper being announced.

"Reese Nelson, Happy New Year," Nicholas said. "Welcome to my home."

"Thank you for having us," Reese said, entering the great room, hand in hand with Harper.

"May I introduce—"

"Well, well, well," Nicholas said, interrupting Reese. "What a delightful surprise. The ever beautiful, never to be underestimated Harper Carmichael Montgomery," Nicholas said with a smirk.

"Oh I didn't realize you two knew each other," Reese said with a look of curiosity, offering Nicholas a decorated bottle of Bollinger Champagne as a hospitality gift.

Nicholas shook Reese's hand. He kissed Harper on both cheeks, holding her in his arms longer than I would have expected between casual acquaintances.

"Yes we indeed know each other," Harper said, never unlocking her gaze from Nicholas. "I keep my friends close and my enemies closer," she winced, looking Nicholas up and down with the fierceness of a tiger stalking its prey. "Hey Riley. So good to see you again," she said. "And aren't you the surprise tonight captain," she said, acknowledging Noah, kissing both sides of his cheeks. She re-directed her attention back to Nicholas, whose intense glare at Harper was mind-boggling.

Nicholas stepped closer into Harper's personal space.

"You knew how much I wanted that Ernie Barnes piece my dearest," he said gritting his teeth. "I had plans to donate that artwork to the kids community center in Harlem on behalf of my foundation."

"And you knew how much I wanted those shares of Gilliam Global last month my dearest," Harper squinted with a bit of sarcasm shoving her short chinchilla jacket in his chest. I watched them stare each other down as one of the servants quickly took Harper's fur off Nicholas' hands.

Nicholas closed his eyes. He paused a beat. Silence.

"It was for the KIDS, Harper. Cut me a break," he gritted in a furious whisper.

"Who knew?" Harper shrugged. "You're not going to be a sore loser now are you Nicky?" Harper said dismissively. "I never knew you to be so touchy over a little piece of art. Buy another one Nicky. What's a million and a half to you? It's just a piece of art," Harper hissed, waving her hand in the air.

"You know that's not my point," Nicholas gritted, pinning Harper down with a look of disdain.

"For you, that's—what is it you say?—Milk Money, baby," she said, winking. "Get over it."

"That wasn't any old piece of art, Harper," Nicholas fumed, his voice elevating as he ran his fingers through his hair.

Harper cocked her head to the side. She planted one hand on her hip, looking him up and down. I thought for sure she was going to start snapping her fingers at him in the air next with the stance she took. Us black gals knew that stance. Well, at least the half black side of me did. I was a bit uncomfortable watching their interaction. It felt intimate on some level. What was it with these two?

"I wanted that particular piece of art. I promised that piece on behalf of my foundation for those kids," Nicholas said raising his voice, unleashing several swear words in Italian.

Oh my. This exchange was not pretty. Harper knew Italian too because those big brown eyes of her narrowed before he could finish his sentence. Part of me wanted to excuse myself and run.

"Pick up your marbles, Nicky," Harper gritted. "Game over, love," she said sternly, patting Nicholas on his cheek.

With all heads turned on Nicholas and Harper, not sure where this flurry of words was headed next, the room had turned almost arctic except for the heat passing between Nicholas and Harper. Lucia interrupted them both speaking as the voice of reason.

"Now Nicky, Harper's right. You lost the bid. Another day. Another time Nicky," she said smiling at Harper with a look that spoke, "This isn't over yet."

Nicholas didn't budge. He stood eye to eye with Harper with a ferocious look of intimidation. Harper didn't move either. She gave back everything he brought to their unspoken communication and then some. Silence passed between them, neither of them budging.

"Your objectives are different this evening remember," Lucia said, urging Nicholas again. Lucia grabbed Nicholas's arm gently nudging him to step out of Harper's space.

"Yes Kitten," Nicholas said to Harper with a sly grin, running his fingers down her cheekbone. "You're right. He who learns to walk away lives to fight another day, my lovely."

"No harm no foul," Harper said in Italian, slightly leaning into his touch.

"You do keep my senses sharp, Kitten," Nicholas sighed with exasperation.

"I'm not your Kitten," Harper hissed.

Nicholas grunted. Harper rolled her eyes.

Wow. That was interesting. Reese and I looked at each other, wondering which one of these two were going to strike back first. The Shark or the Barracuda. Talk about persona non grata. Noah and Lucia however treated this little tête-à-tête between Nicholas and Harper as if it were business as usual between them. I sensed they knew something I didn't.

"May I offer you a martini, Harper? You, Reese?" Nicholas said shaking it off.

"Sure thing. You two are making me cranky," Reese growled, his tone chilly. "This is supposed to be a professional yet festive evening, right Riley?" Reese said looking frustrated.

Reese had eased himself away from Harper's side. He was standing next to me now. He pulled me close to him, giving me a kiss on the top of my head. I knew he was uncomfortable watching that scene. Somehow, he'd at least managed to pause long enough to greet Noah and shake his hand. I however, was still stuck in my wow moment. The dynamics in the room had really taken a strange turn fast tonight.

"Well in the words of Dorothy Parker," Harper said, her hips swaying gently across the room in front of Nicholas, her four inch hills clicking on the marble floor, the scent of Chanel drifting in the air as she moved, "I'd like to have a martini, two at the very most. After three I'm under the table, and after four I'm under the host."

Harper began laughing gleefully, waving her hand dismissively at Nicholas knowing she had won the battle but perhaps not the war. He flashed a smile at her that didn't reach his eyes.

Harper had on the perfect black lace strapless dress that had a flared pleated skirt fitted at the hip with a black ostrich feathered hem. She sat crossing her legs looking every bit the well-bred debutante that she was. She sipped her martini, rolling the green olive in her mouth so seductively it was hard to tell if she was being demure or had just jumped off the centerfold pages of Penthouse.

Heir to the Carmichael Ketchup Empire and daughter of the only African American U.S. Senator's from Georgia, Harper Montgomery was filthy rich in her own right. Her family was old Georgia money. It was widely known that she was not to be monkeyed with in matters of business. Harper was bright, wealthy, and breathtakingly beautiful.

Her long black hair fell like a waterfall of curls, framing her delicate face, accentuating her caramel-colored skin and big brown eyes. She strutted her long lean legs like a thoroughbred stallion. The gossip mongers typically characterized her as every man's desire and every woman's envy.

Few would ever deny that she had a unsurpassed network of Who's Who in her back pocket, coupled with a little black book of contacts, the reach of which was the envy of every New York businessmen. When Harper Montgomery was in play, you'd either better win the game or get off the playground. She typically took no prisoners. And from what I had read, Nicholas Becker was the only businessman considered to be a worthy opponent, not much of a surprise since they each acted as if they were seemingly out to annihilate the other.

I sipped my drink, pondering the interpersonal dynamics between Harper and Nicholas. While I knew that Reese and Harper were longtime friends, I was never quite sure whether my brother was romantically involved, a friend with benefits, or neither. Reese played his so cards close to his vest when it came to his women. But this thing with Harper and Nicholas, that somehow felt like something else. Something personal. Something dangerous. Maybe those two were 'frenemies.'

I decided to forget about it, knowing I had my own issues to worry about this evening. Noah must have anticipated that my anxiety level had gone up, because he pulled me closer in his arms, anticipating my needs as if protecting me from the blazing bantering line of fire between Nicholas and Harper. Somehow I sensed Noah knew their story. He hardly seemed phased by their interpersonal dynamics.

"Well, let's all move to the dining area shall we?" Nicholas said very playfully, his mood having shifted again. "Our dinner buffet is ready. Take a seat and let's talk about *Black Sequinned Bows and Champagne Nights* shall we? After all, it's not my business that's important here tonight."

We entered the dining area, where a buffet was set full of beer battered coconut shrimp with rémoulade sauce, mounds of three pound lobsters flown in from Maine, black pepper crusted beef tenderloin with chimichurri sauce, hot roasted potatoes, Brussel sprouts with pancetta and pearl onions, apple and escarole salad with blue cheese and hazelnuts, and hot loaves of bread.

We each filled our plates and took our seats. I knew the spotlight would turn to me next.

Nicholas sat at the head of the table, Lucia sat at the other end. Harper and Reese sat opposite of Noah and I. Nicholas sat Harper closest to him at the long dining table which was elegantly decorated in a festive black and silver theme, white candles, with a silver runner draped down the long table from end to end.

"I must say Riley, you've done a wonderful job with your company over the last decade. I liked your strategic business plan and your identifiable goals for the future of the business," Nicholas said. "When you win the James E. Beard Award, what are your plans for leveraging that honor, my darling?"

Oh gee, I was stuck under the glare of this God-like Adonis, Nicholas, and the Beautiful Mister Wonderful. I reminded myself again that I needed to focus my thoughts.

"Well actually, whether I win the award or not, I plan to take my business international, expanding first into the UK and then later into Asia. I have a ten year goal to complete the international transition. Winning the Beard award will boost my credibility, helping make my entree into the global markets a lot smoother."

Noah had a comforting supportive smile on his face. Reese appeared pleased with my answers wearing a look of pride on his face. Harper gave me a wink. Lucia's face remained stoic.

"And how do you plan to handle the management duties? Such an expansion will take up a great deal of your time will it not?" Nicholas asked, nodding at the server to add more lobster to his plate.

"Hence my desire for an investor. The business will need a significant cash injection to cover the cost of an additional management team that can hit the ground running overseas. Thus, I won't have to have an everyday presence, though I do plan on moving about between the U.S. and any international locations."

I was hoping I was winning Nicholas over to my side of thinking.

"And, may I add," Reese said, holding his fork with a chunk of lobster still on it, "Riley's company has plenty of cash reserves on the side to withstand any fluctuations in the currency market should the value of the dollar fall. Thus your investment would be at a much lower risk, than say a traditional funding source," Reese continued, wearing his financial hat now.

"Well I'm not sure I agree with that." Lucia, interjected.

"What do you mean?" Reese said, shockingly surprised that his financial acumen was being question.

"We plan to invest in ten new businesses next year, and we have one slot left to fill with the right business that has a future for profitability. From what I can tell, her company's debt to equity ratios are a whole lot higher than I expected, actually making me question whether *Milk Money* should invest in this business at all," Lucia said.

"And what business school did you attend? Nick At Night School?" Reese snapped back at her. "Have you even read her financial statements? I did them myself."

"Forgiving your momentary bout of delusion," Lucia snapped back at Reese, the insult not sitting well with her. "I fail to see another Rhodes Scholar seated at this table here tonight," Lucia said coolly, looking side to side, then shooting daggers at Reese.

"Such a strong assertion, Lucia. Would you care to elaborate further on your thinking?" Nicholas said, unmoved by the difference of opinions.

Lucia cocked her head to the side at Nicholas, looking at him like he had two heads. The room went silent as forks failed to reach mouths waiting for the next shoe to drop. Nicholas rolled his eyes to the top of his head, stretching his neck from side to side in acquiescence.

"Okay, so your IQ is no doubt fifty points higher than everyone in this room. I get it. Please enlighten us my darling," Nicholas said to Lucia, urging her to explain.

I glanced at Reese. He was fuming. No one had ever outwardly questioned his abilities, ever. I however, was confused. Noah was no help. His face was as blank as a man pondering his hand at a poker table. Harper however looked to be enjoying this showdown immensely, sucking a piece of lobster in her mouth like it was a popsicle, directing her lobster foreplay at Nicholas.

"Yes, please do," Harper insisted. "And by all means, remember Riley, *Milk Money* isn't the only game in town," Harper added with glee, rolling her eyes at Lucia. "My company, *Montgomery Consulting*, would be happy to arrange a proper cash injection into your business, should *Milk Money's* management team here fail to see the light," Harper added coolly.

"Stay out of this Harper," Nicholas said with fierceness.

"I've seen the financials. I recognize a good investment when I see one," she said, tossing back her martini. "Unlike some people we know whose heads get stuck up their asses," Harper said, stuffing a potato in her mouth, glaring at Nicholas, daring him to challenge her.

"My company is financially sound and has been for years. Surely you're mistaken Lucia," I said, maintaining my composure, forgetting all about the fact that Reese was not going to maintain his.

"I'm sure there's a logical explanation for this misunderstanding," Noah said, giving Nicholas a chilling glare.

Nicholas stopped eating, rested his silverware, and pulled his high back chair away from the table.

"Lucia. Share your analysis with us please?" Nicholas said calmly, but more demanding.

Watching Nicholas keep his composure, I better understood how he'd managed to be so successful in business. He'd maintained his poker face throughout what was turning into a contentious heated dialogue between Lucia and Reese. It was interesting to watch his level of calm, despite the fact he had become unglued earlier with Harper.

Lucia politely excused herself, returning with two copies of the what were supposed to be my financial spreadsheets. She handed copies to both Reese and me.

"These aren't the company's financials," Reese and I both said in unison.

"What's the meaning of this Lucia?" Reese snapped.

"I beg your pardon Reese, but this is what I received at the *Milk Money* offices by overnight courier from your firm."

"I've never seen these before in my life," Reese said, looking puzzled, passing his copies to Harper. I passed my copy to Nicholas.

"Is this some kind of corporate espionage or is this a joke?" Reese said.

"Where did you get these Lucia?" Nicholas said looking puzzled.

"I got them from that new guy Ross on Stephen's security staff," Lucia said calmly.

"Who's Stephen?" Reese injected.

"He's Nicholas's body man, aka security detail," Harper quipped, dipping more of her lobster in the herb-infused butter sauce.

"Ross was babbling about how it wasn't his job to play delivery boy, but that he didn't mind stepping into that role when the messenger was as beautiful and sexy as the Asian flight attendant that delivered it," Lucia said.

"Flight Attendant?" Noah and Reese said at the same time.

"Asian?" Noah said out loud, not really expecting an answer.

"According to Ross, some American Airlines flight attendant claimed it was a package that was left on her plane. She claimed she was coming this direction across town and thought she'd do whoever left it a favor by dropping it off," Lucia said, looking at Nicholas in puzzlement.

Noah and Reese looked at each other and said "Leah Chen."

"Who?" Nicholas and Lucia both asked mere seconds apart.

They both looked as confused as I was feeling.

"Here's the mailing envelope," Lucia said ignoring Nicholas, handing it to me. "There was a card inside addressed to Riley. I wasn't sure what to make of it so I ignored it thinking I would give it you later," Lucia said.

I opened the card addressed to me. Inside was an un-signed card I read out loud that said "A whip for the horse, a bridle for the ass, and a rod for the fools back," Proverbs 26:3.

"Warren Shaw," I said in a low whisper, recognizing his handwriting. I handed the card to Noah. Reese slammed his hand on the table making the crystal jiggle.

"Calm down, Reese," Noah said. "This is fixable."

"Who's Warren Shaw?" Nicholas said.

"And Leah Chen?" Lucia added.

"A bunch of yahoo nobodies," Reese said.

"I saw her today in the JFK frequent flyer lounge on my way

here. I thought it was a coincidence, her being a flight attendant an all," Noah said with a look of disbelief.

Leah Chen? Noah saw Leah Chen? Here? In New York? When was he going to tell me that?

"In this business there are no coincidences," Lucia said. "You eat what you kill."

"Well what am I expected to be getting into here Mico?" Nicholas said, directing his attention to Noah, then to me, and back to Noah, not responding to Lucia's comment.

"Yes. What are we expected to be getting into here Noah?" I said, my eyes throwing daggers at him as if this were his fault. I slid his hand off my knee that had been resting on it under the table.

Okay. So, I would own the fact that Warren Shaw was part of my ugly past, but I'd be damned if I was gonna take credit for that bitch Leah Chen. Especially given the way she had her skinny arms wrapped around Noah's neck at the gala as if they had romantic history. No way in hell was I going to take that bitch on as my problem. No. She was Mister Mico's problem.

"Let's everyone take a moment here and slow down for a bit," Noah said, inserting himself back into the conversation.

"Oh this is the best New Year's Eve I've had in a long time, Harper chuckled. "Nicholas Becker's security must be off its game," she said, rubbing salt in the wound. "No way my security detail would ever take delivery of an unopened package and not know where it came from," Harper said, narrowing her glare again at Nicholas.

I had to hand it to Harper. Whatever Nicholas had done to her, he needed to fix it quick. Harper had turned my problem into his as if she were working some long standing vendetta against him.

"If anyone is vulnerable here, it appears things broke down at Reese's end," Nicholas said with all politeness. "And, Harper, I suggest you not worry your pretty little head about matters that don't concern you."

"Excuse me?" Harper said, with indignation.

"Enjoy your evening and make like the eye candy that you are, love," Nicholas said cocking his head to the side, grabbing her hand on top of the table, refusing to release it against her obvious efforts to pull it away.

I could see the fury burning in Harper's eyes, wondering

how this moment was going to end. Harper stood, pushing herself back from the table as Nicholas stood with her, his hand still clenching hers. She stepped closer to him, grabbing him between his legs, scrunching her hands hard against his balls making his face wince for the first time tonight. I felt my own face wince at the sight.

"You talk like a bad boy Nicky. You need a time out? You sound a tad misogynistic tonight," Harper said, obviously squeezing his balls harder as Nicky's face began to bear a frown. Nicholas tightened his grip around Harper's wrist, causing her face to squint.

"Nicholas. Harper. There are guests here," Lucia commanded.

There was silence. They both quietly released each other. Nicholas grabbed a decanter off the wet bar, and poured a huge amount in a cocktail glass and swigged it down. He sat. Harper fluffed her hair up with her hand, grabbed her champagne glass, and sat back down all lady-like as if nothing ever happened. She smiled politely at Lucia and nodded as if thanking her for the reminder. I thought it best I be the one to break the uncomfortable silence.

"Well for the record, I happen to have my flash drive on me with my entire pitch including the financials," I said, hoping not to let Harper start fanning the flames with Nicholas again.

I was getting nervous all over again. I needed Nicholas to stay focused. I didn't want my opportunity to gain an angel investor to get sidetracked by whatever this thing was between Nicholas and Harper. It was bad enough Reese looked like he had been a victim of shock and awe. And Noah . . . I could hardly look at him without fury in my eyes over this whole Leah Chen business. I was angry with myself because I'd been lusting after him in my mind all night. I was unable to deny my feelings for him but I needed to decide quickly how to balance my lust for him against my thoughts that he could possibly be trying to play me like a fiddle. I was never going to let another man do that to me again ever.

"Lucia if you could be so kind to let me print a copy of the digital file I have here on my flash drive, I'm sure we can put this whole matter to rest," I said, hoping my voice was still steady. I was so nervous I wasn't sure I could get through this craziness. I handed her my flash drive.

"No problem, Riley," Nicholas said. He was back to his original composed self.

Lucia proceeded to print copies of the right financials for herself and Nicholas. For the next thirty minutes I continued with the rest of my pitch as planned with everyone listening intently. Nicholas and Lucia bounced questions at me. They seemed to be happy with my responses. Harper even interjected complimentary remarks here and there throughout my presentation. I was confident in my finish, despite the fact my heart was beating wildly with anxiety and my palms were sweaty. But this is what I do well and I did it. I sealed the deal, despite all the obstacles.

But Warren was turning into being a huge freaking obstacle. Not only did I know that, but Reese did too. Reese hadn't shed his look of pissdom all night.

"Leave the original spreadsheets with us and we'll take another look at them," Nicholas said.

"If we have questions, Lucia or I will get in touch," he said. "For now, let's put this pitch to bed and everyone enjoy the rest of the evening. Your presentation was excellent Riley," Nicholas smiled. "I'm glad we got this sorted out. I like a businesswoman that knows how to pivot to Plan B, when Plan A goes awry. I'm impressed."

"Thank you again Nicholas. I can't tell you how grateful I am that you cleared your calendar on such short notice to see me, and for the wonderful dinner." I said, hoping I had adequately concealed the thoughts rolling around in my head that were making me crazy. I had done my best. Now I'd have to await his decision to see if my company would make the list for next year's angel investment. The thought of being railroaded by the likes of Warren Shaw and Leah Chen tonight were mind blowing. I was filled with a mix of emotion ranging from embarrassment to rage over their attempted sabotage.

Nicholas guided us back into the Great Room where a mini bar had been set up with flavored coffees, liqueurs, brandy, truffles, more champagne, and desserts. I downed several glasses of champagne to numb my pain. The last thing I wanted was for Warren to compromise the success of my business and to ruin my holiday. That was too much power to give him. I was determined to fight off the tears that had filled in the back of my eyes from my thoughts that were running wild in my head like a runaway train. I had given the moment my all. I needed to relax and have a good time.

Nicholas, Lucia, Reese, and Harper had gathered around a cart of humidors filled with a wide selection of cigars. A huge bowl filled with New Year's hats, whistles, glasses, and tiaras were passed to each of us by a female servant.

"It's almost midnight, and I prefer we all take our mind off business and have some fun," Nicholas said. "Let's have dessert, after dinner drinks, and watch the ball drop. There's nothing better than bringing in the New Year together with good food, good drinks, and good company."

Noah pulled me away from the group and closer to the windows overlooking the skyline. He put his arms around me and held me close.

"Riley baby, I can almost hear the wheels turning in your head right now. You did well tonight under difficult circumstances."

He kissed me on the top of my forehead. I said nothing in response.

"I will say this and keep saying it as long as I need to in order for you to be completely sure of me. There is nothing between me and Leah Chen. There is nothing between me and any other woman. There is only you. You are all I need and want. There is so much else to be said, but tonight is not the night. This is your night."

I looked in Noah's eyes to gauge the sincerity of his words. In my heart of hearts I knew he was being truthful. But putting my trust in a man was something I had no experience in since Lucas's death. Turning the corner was not going to be easy for me.

"Riley, you said earlier tonight that New Years was like a new beginning for you. I want that too. I want a lifetime of days and nights for years to come to begin and end with you."

And with that, Noah kissed me on the lips. I parted my mouth and let him in, kissing him back.

As the clock struck midnight, and the fireworks lit the sky, Noah held me in his arms. He clinked his glass against mine, and passionately kissed my worries away.

"Happy New Year, Riley."

I toasted with him, feeling a few fireworks of my own.

"To new beginnings, Noah."

CHAPTER 15

NOAH

"What time is it anyway? Shall we go somewhere and have another nightcap? We need to decide quick and get out of this snow."

The four of us were standing outside under the awning of Becker Towers hashing out our options as the wheels of the white Phantom pulled up in front to pick us up. The cold wind was biting, whipping against our faces.

"It's 4 am," I answered Reese.

"Whatever Riley wants to do is fine with me. It's her night, or shall I say morning. Either way, I'm going to escort your sister back to Pennsylvania."

"You all are welcome to crash at my place if you want. I've got plenty of room," Harper said.

"No way the senator and your Mom will catch me in my tighty-whiteys in the morning running around your Penthouse, Harper. I know how your people roll. Too much security for my taste babe. You guys are all welcome to stay at my place if you want," Reese joked.

I think Reese and Harper were buzzed from all the martinis and champagne at Nicholas's. Nicholas was the epitome of the party man. You go big with him or go home, and it was time to do exactly that, go home. Hell, I knew Riley and I were sufficiently buzzed, despite the fact I was trying to keep my wits about me, to keep this crew in line.

"So what, Reese? It's not like you're not practically family," Harper said. "I promise to make your favorite omelet," she grinned, cajoling Reese, twirling a lock of her hair like a schoolgirl.

"Man, drop us at Harper's place," Reese said, slightly slurring his words. "No way I'm turning down her omelets this morning."

"What do you want to do sweetheart?" I said, suspecting that Riley was ready to call it an evening.

I tucked the collar of her white mink coat up around her neck, brushing the snowflakes out of her bangs. I kissed the tip of her nose that had turned red in the cold. I wasn't sure what state Riley was in, and if you counted Nicholas and Lucia, I think it was safe to say we were all pretty much tore up. By the time Nicholas started playing Jay Z's *Empire State of Mind* on his baby grand, trying to rap, accompanied by Lucia having kicked off her golden stilettos, singing Alicia Key's part in Italian, I knew it was time to split.

Riley looked like she had it together, but at the same she had this look in her eyes that reminded me of a kid in a candy store and I was the candy. If she kept looking at me like that, I was going to lose all sense of control, quick.

"I'll pass. I don't know how much more of New York I can take tonight," Riley said. "I'm going to need help overcoming the embarrassment of tonight's financial statement fiasco."

She said that with such a great deal of seduction, I was confused. Was she embarrassed or freaking hot. Her eyes looked heated. Maybe I was the one screwed up.

Cameron walked briskly from around the driver's side, opening the limousine door. I guided Riley's hand, helping her inside while Reese helped Harper inside. Harper was starting to stumble. Yup, we were all fucked up. Nobody would deny we didn't bring the New Year in on a roll.

I was glad Riley didn't want to stay overnight in the Apple. I wanted her to get some rest. Riley was mentally and physically drained coming down off the adrenaline rush from the presentation. Not to mention, I was dealing with my own set of emotions wondering why Warren and Leah were coming after her with a vengeance.

Tonight almost ended up a total cluster fuck. Thank God, Riley was smart enough to have her presentation and clean financials on her flash-drive. Nicholas wasn't the type of man to waste time with folks playing games. He had stepped out on a limb sight unseen for me as a favor. The fact that this fucktard Warren tried to sabotage Riley, meant Warren had me to count as his enemy. He and that trouble-making fireball Leah Chen.

"I'm so sorry Riley, about the financials. I have no idea how Warren could have gotten the drop on me like this. I checked and double checked the financial package several times before it got picked up by the courier," Reese said remorsefully.

"It's not your fault, Reese," Riley said.

"If Warren and Leah are behind this, I'll be the first person to get to the bottom of it," Reese said, with a look of discontent on his face.

"I'm so embarrassed and angry at the same time," Riley repeated. "I'm going to need help getting over it," she said looking at me with those doe eyes.

Jesus. She said that again. Help getting over it? What kind of help? I'm here to help. Damn I'm fucked up. Hell this whole crowd is fucked up. Leave it Nicholas Becker to indulge us all with such excess of good food and spirits, none of us could think straight.

"It was a small glitch sweetheart in the scheme of things. You pulled it out fine in the end," I said.

"I did?" Riley said softly.

Whoa. She seriously needed to stop looking at me like that. All hot and bothered full of need. Desire mixed with wantonness.

"You couldn't have known either Reese," I said, trying to take my focus off Riley in front of her brother, concealing my thoughts, trying hard not to undress her with my eyes.

If these sparks kept up between us, Reese was going to forget about Harper's omelet and focus on me and his sister. I did not want to deal with his drunk ass getting a pension for protecting his sister tonight. She didn't need protecting. From now on, that was my job. Time for him to give up the reins. I got this. I promised Lucas.

"These things happens sometime. Keep your eye on the prize," I said, patting Riley's knee, feeling her flinch.

She crossed her legs my direction. I was a student of body language. I knew that was a good sign. Hell, Riley was the prize. It was hard for me to say those encouraging words and not think that I was the one that had won the lottery.

"Don't worry 'bout any of that mmm . . . madness Riley," Harper slurred, tripping over her words. "Nicholas is a lot of things, but a fool he's not," she said waving her hand dismissively, giggling to herself as if she told a private joke. "Nicholas knows a good investment when he sees one. He'll come through I'm sure of it. Besides, he definitely doesn't want to lose your business to me."

"Yeah Harpie, I was wondering that myself. What is it with you and Nicholas? This dance that the two of you do with each other . . . what's that about, exactly?" Reese said, tilting his body closer to hers.

Harpie? Damn we were all plastered. Every-time I stay in Nicholas's space too long, this happens. I hoped this conversation didn't go off the rails, Reese inquiring about Nicholas and Harper. I knew the deal, but I was sure no one else did.

"Such an explanation would require a lesson in hissstoooory," Harper said smugly. "Get it . . . his story . . . ," she laughed uncontrollably.

Jesus. Harper looked at me knowing I already knew the answer to that question. Nicholas and I go way back. Very few people knew that despite a decade gone by, Harper and Nicholas had never gotten to done.

"Why don't you educate me," Reese said, determined not to be denied, grabbing Harper's hand, fingering the diamond studded cuff on her wrist, pressing his head against her shoulder, letting it rest on her breast like a little kid.

"I see no reason for us to go to school tonight Reeces Pieces," she laughed.

Reeces Pieces? Yup. Harper was toasted all right, and Reese was shit-faced enough to get sucked into that web of complexity called Harper Carmichael Montgomery.

"Oh you gonna play that card tonight," Reese said grabbing Harper, tickling her as she laughed wildly, blowing a New Year's paper horn in his face.

Riley looked at Harper, and then at Reese. She was studying them as if she were trying to figure out if they were kiss-in cousins or friends with benefits. I knew better. Anybody trying to take Harper to school was going to have to deal with "The Teacher," and his name was Nicholas Becker.

"We're here sir, Soho," Cameron said.

"Well I guess that's meeeee," Harper said. "You coming, egg man?" Harper said playfully to Reese. "Or do I have to scramble you?" she giggled, grabbing her red-bottom shoes off the floor.

"I'm right behind you Harpie. Over easy baby," Reese said, laughing playfully.

"Have a safe trip back sis," Reese said, kissing his sister on the cheek before stepping out the limo. "Take care of her Noah," Reese said, his eyes squinting, shaking my hand on the way out the limo.

Somehow I knew if I didn't do right by Riley, Reese would be the first in line to deal with me. He was beyond overprotective of his sister. Straight off the radar with his shit, that one was.

"I'll be back in Washington's Crossing before you get a chance to miss me Riley," Reese said, turning to his sister.

"I know you will Reese," Riley smiled back at him lovingly.

"Happy New Year people," I said waving good-bye to Harper and Reese, hoping they'd hurry and get out so I could close the door to protect Riley from the blowing wind gusts.

"Bye Harper. Love you Reese," Riley said to them both.

I said my good-byes to Reese and Harper. I moved closer to Riley, pushing a button, raising the privacy glass. I dimmed the lights, pushing the on button for Al Jarreau's track *Teach Me Tonight* to begin to play. I poured her a brandy to warm her up.

"We should share this," I said, not wanting to get her any more plastered.

I handed the brandy to her, stroking my finger down the side of her cheek, leaning forward touching her lips next to mine. I watched as she took a sip of the brandy. I took a sip, then sat the brandy snifter in the glass holder. I kissed her deeply, tasting the combined sweetness of her and the brandy. Riley ran her hand across my shoulders and down the sides of my arms. I kissed the side of her neck. I dropped my hands and slid them between her hip and thigh, touching her lacy black garter, my fingers exploring the wet places.

"You're beautiful, Riley. More than any man could want," I whispered.

She looked up at me flashing those big come and get me eyes, swallowing hard.

"I've not been with a man in years."

My eyes scanned hers. She looked back at me penetrating the little of what was left of my suit of armor, looking deep into my soul.

"We can take things slow baby. "We've got all the time in the world. There's no need to rush. Nothing will happen before you're ready."

The last thing I wanted was for Riley to panic, feeling like she had to live up to my expectations. I wanted her in my life for the long haul. I was willing to give her all the time she needed.

"Does that mean we can cuddle and play on the ride back?"

she asked.

Cuddle and play? My kind of night.

"We can do whatever you want to do baby. I'm not planning on going anywhere," I said whispering in her ear.

She slid unto my lap, knowing just where to touch me, rendering my mind to nothing but mush. I kissed her for what felt like several minutes. Her taste exploded on my tongue. She teased my cock, rubbing me, caressing my cock with nothing but the fabric of my pants separating me from her touch. She fingered the zipper on my pants, and I grabbed both her wrists.

"If you do that I'll lose control," I said, slipping my finger deep inside her, watching her squirm on my lap. "I want you to be the one to feel good. I don't want to ever think about another man touching you."

I had fantasized about her more times than I could count. The thought of another man touching her made me nuts. My emotions were involved long before I'd ever touched her.

"No man has in a while," she moaned, biting the lobe of my ear, leaning forward, angling her body, giving me access to her pleasure center.

She laced her fingers inside mine, still nibbling on my ear, her breathing accelerating, moaning her orgasm in my ear. Our kissing became more passionate as we explored each other's mouth and body in unison. We lost awareness of our surroundings, immersed in each other. Somehow we managed to quell the heat and desire between us, repositioning ourselves. We both slowly drifted off to sleep.

As the cold January morning sun threatened to rise, the wheels of the white Phantom turned on to River Road and into Riley's circular drive. I awakened, noticing her head was still nestled against my chest, her body tucked tight to my side. I couldn't imagine a more perfect New Year's Eve. I chuckled to myself noticing she had a paper party blower still clutched in her left hand. The glittered oversized New Year's eyeglasses with pink and white paper blowers were tucked in the side pockets of her fur, her stiletto heels kicked off in front of me on the limousine floor.

Our whirlwind evening of business and pleasure came to an end with Riley and I teasing each other in a heavy make-out session. The Phantom came to a stop at Riley's front door.

"Babe we're here." I kissed the top of her head. "Thank you for a wonderful evening."

"No, thank you," Riley said, rubbing her eyes. "I had a wonderful time."

I leaned over, putting my arms around her, lifting her chin to mine and kissing her lips more intensely. She kissed me again, languishing this time.

Cameron opened the door. Riley slipped on her heels. Damn, I wanted those heels wrapped around my ears. She looked up at me with begging eyes as if she could read my thoughts. I grabbed her hand to help her out. It took her a moment to get her keys. We stepped on the doorstep together. I kissed her a third time. I knew her feelings of attraction were emerging into something more and that we was headed down relationship road.

"Sweet dreams baby. Get some rest."

I put my arms around her, hugging her, pulling her white mink close by the collar, not wanting to let go. I kissed her again.

I waited until Riley stepped inside. She turned back to wave at me. I stepped back inside the limousine, waving good-bye. I could feel myself moving down that sliding board of life, leaving that space of feeling completely comfortable being single to feeling completely powerless.

I've fallen in love.

CHAPTER 16

RILEY

"Hello Riley? This is Lucia Falco. Did I catch you at bad time? Are you free to talk?"

"Oh hi Lucia. I was just sitting here reviewing some of the changes on the layout for one of my new books," I said moving my phone to speaker so I'd have my hands free to write or take notes. "But yes, this is a good time."

I was nervous about getting this call. It had been a three weeks since I'd been in New York to pitch my presentation to *Milk Money.* I'd been on pins and needles awaiting the news as to whether my company had made *Milk Money's* list of ten companies for this year's angel investment.

"Good news Riley. Nicholas was totally impressed with your presentation once we got past the mix up in the financials. We both agree that *Black Sequinned Bows and Champagne Nights* is the best company to take the last slot on the *Milk Money* roster this year. Congratulations."

"Oh my God, I'm so thrilled. Thank you so much! Please thank Nicholas for me."

"He's still tooling around on *The Julianna* somewhere near Greece right now. Hold on and I'll patch his call into ours on three way and you can thank him yourself," Lucia said.

Oh Lord this was so exciting. I could hardly think straight. I cleared my throat in anticipation of Nicholas joining in on the call. Tears of joy were starting to well up in the back of my eyes. I needed to hold it together so I could get through this call.

"God Speaking," a sexy male voice said through my speaker.

"Knock it off Nicky. I've got Riley on the line," Lucia said, not at all bothered by Nicholas's greeting.

"Riley Mon Cher. Nicholas Becker here."

"Hi Nicholas. Good to talk to you again."

"Congratulations Riley. We're excited to have you join the *Milk Money* family," Nicholas shouted through the static on the phone that must have been coming from his yacht.

"Thank you so much. I'm pleased to be chosen. I promise I won't let you down. I plan to make a lot of money for the both of us," I said raising my voice a bit louder so he'd be sure to hear me.

"We plan to issue a *Milk Money* News Release with our roster of this year's ten companies. We wanted to give you advance notice."

"Yes, all the financial blogs will pick up our News Release, as well as the various social media outlets, so I expect things will start to move pretty quickly," Lucia interjected.

"We're injecting a two and a half a million dollar cash infusion into your company Riley. Lucia will send you all the appropriate paperwork that will detail the terms and conditions of our investment. Have your people take a look and call my people. The sooner we get things executed, the sooner we can move on your expansion plans," Nicholas said.

I could hear water splashing and girls giggling, and voices speaking in French in the background. I heard Nicholas say "Pas maintenant, mon amour," and what sounded like a slap on somebody's butt and then the sound of a kiss, which I knew meant he was keeping some woman at bay.

"I'll be back in a couple of weeks. we can talk more then, oui?" he said.

"Sounds great. I look forward to talking to you both again soon."

"Arrivederci amore mio," Nicholas said, and hung up.

An Italian, good-bye? I suppose that was for Lucia's benefit.

"We'll be in touch, Riley."

"Bye Lucia."

"Yes, Yes, Yes!" I screamed so loud, jumping up and down in a way that even Stogie and Cleo both woke out of their slumber and began barking loudly.

"Party over here," I said out loud to both the dogs who were looking at me, both jumping up and down themselves totally joining in on my excitement.

I sent a text to Madison, who sent a text to Lily, who sent a text to Zoe. Before I knew it a flurry of text messages started between us. Congratulatory remarks were flying back and forth. We were all thrilled. My gals were as excited as I was. As soon as our texting frenzy started to calm down, my landline phone rang. It was Reese.

"Hey sis. I heard from Harper that you landed on *Milk Money's* angel investor roster. Congrats Riley. I knew you could pull this off."

"Geez Reese, I found out myself less than an hour ago. How did Harper hear the news already?"

"Apparently *Milk Money* issued a news release. In this business news travels fast, honey. Harper sends her congrats."

"Do tell her I said thanks. I hope to see her again soon, yes? It was fun hanging out with her on New Year's Eve."

"Hard to say. She's a busy woman. Speaking of New Year's Eve Riley," Reese said quickly changing the subject, "I hired a private investigator to look into the attempt at sabotaging your financials."

"I really don't think you needed to do that Reese. Besides, everything worked out in the end since I had the correct data on my flash drive anyway."

"No, honey. The fact that could even happen at all was a reflection on both our businesses and my security systems. If it had to happen at all, at least it went down with friends and not with one of my paying clients, if you know what I mean."

"I suppose you do have a point there. Did you find out anything yet?"

"Yeah. I discovered that one of the gals in my clerical pool called out sick the day I sent the financials to *Milk Money*. A temp had been sent to replace her. Apparently the temp was a cousin of Leah Chen's. Some gal who was here on an educational visa from Beijing. She left the country at the end of the semester."

"So Warren Shaw really was behind this?" I interrupted.

"Well the trail goes dry from there, but it doesn't take a degree in rocket science to put two and two together Riley. That douchebag was definitely behind this. Either way I fired the woman in my clerical pool, discontinued my business with the staffing agency, and the woman in charge of my company's clerical pool is on notice that she's next if anything like this ever happens again."

"Well what do we do about this Reese? Should we report this information to the police?"

"We were in New York Riley. Kind of outside of Pennsylvania's law enforcement jurisdiction. I think the best we can hope for now is to be vigilant and make sure Warren and his little minion, don't get anywhere near you again. If he does I swear I'll ... "

"Hold on Reese," I said, my eyes glued to another text that flashed across my cell. It was a smiley face from Noah. My phone beeped in my ear. I pulled the phone away from my ear, looking at the caller ID that read Noah Dunham.

"Can we finish this later Reese? Noah's calling and I'd need to take this call."

"No problem Riles. I've got somewhere to be anyway. We can pick up on this conversation later. Riles?"

"Yeah?"

"Be careful baby."

"I will Reese."

"I mean with your heart."

"Don't worry Reese. I know how to take care of myself."

"I know Riles. It's just that when you fall, you tend to fall hard."

"Yes, Reese but I've since learned that if I must fall to land looking up," I said, chuckling. "Talk to you soon baby brother."

I hung up with Reese, hitting the flash button on my phone.

"Hey gorgeous. Congratulations." Noah's sexy voice echoed through my phone.

"News does travel fast, doesn't it?" I teased.

"Yeah, Nicholas called me from *The Julianna* to tell me the good news. He's pretty excited too. He believes in you and so do I."

"I have you to thank for putting me in touch with his company," I said softly.

"Anything for you Riley," Noah answered sweetly. "I'd hang the stars and the moon for you baby."

I wondered if Noah could see my grin through the phone. God that man always knew what to say to heat up my body and scramble my brain.

"Any word on the Beard Foundation nomination yet?"

"Not yet, but I hope to hear some news any day now. Luckily the funky press I got at the gala from Warren and Leah's appearance died down pretty quickly. The New York media didn't pick up on it. They seem to be more interested in the nature of my business with Nicholas Becker."

I could hear Noah pull in his breath. I wondered whether his angst was directed at Warren or Nicholas?

"Not to worry sweetheart. No news is good news."

"I spoke to my brother Reese a few minutes ago. He did some checking of his own, and it looks like Warren and Leah were behind that little stunt of swapping my financials. I'm just scared that . . . "

"Don't be scared Riley. I won't let him or anyone else hurt you, your business, or your family. You have my word. Enjoy this happy moment and don't think about those two vipers."

"You're right. I need to put those scary thoughts behind me."

"I want to see you Riley. Can I twist your arm and get you to clear your calendar so we can have some one on one time together without a crowd? I promise I'll make it worth your while."

"Well since I'm in such a great mood today, and given that I owe you a huge thank you, I think that can be arranged," I giggled.

"Good. Shoot me some dates when you're available and will make it happen darlin'."

"Open this damn door Riley, it's cold out here ."

"Who the hell is that, Riley?"

"It's Madison. She's banging on my back door to get in to celebrate. She's outside on my back patio yelling like a crazy woman," I giggled.

"No problem baby. I'll call you later tonight and tuck you in. Go have some fun with your posse."

I was already moving to the back door to let Madison inside. I looked at my watch, realizing it was after four-thirty and school was out. Madison must have run straight home shortly after my flurry of texts with her, Lily, and Zoe.

"Aye Aye Captain. I look forward to talking to you later tonight, especially when we get to the part where you tuck me in," I said, letting out a soft giggle.

"Bye baby."

"Ohmigod Riley, you're on your way to the top, roadie," Madison squealed.

"I sure hope so Madison. I feel like all the numbers are rolling by way, kiddo. I'm beyond thrilled. Time to clink the Ridel's."

"You took the words right out of my mouth. Pop the corks."

I led Madison through my home office area and into the kitchen.

"I haven't had a chance yet to tell the kids yet. Samantha's working late, Xavier's at the gym, and Claire's doing an overnight with one of her friends. I was starting to feel like I'd have to celebrate alone."

"The best part of our living on the same cul-de-sac is that we're never alone.," Madison said, pulling a bottle of Verve Cliquot out of the refrigerator, knowing I kept at least two bottles on constant chill.

I grabbed two champagne glasses out of the cabinet, and instructed Madison to pull a round of cheese and some Greek olives out of the refrigerator too, while I moved to grab a loaf of country french bread out of the bread bin.

"I tell you Riley, there's nothing better than having a BFF that's in the food and wine business. I stay in heaven at your house."

"That's just because you're a foodie at heart, Madison. Stick around here long enough, you'll catch Xavier insisting that we need more boiled eggs, and protein drink instead of all these gourmet dishes. And Claire . . . all she wants are chocolate brownies twenty-four and seven. Samantha, that one is a salsa and nacho freak. If I didn't have you around, there'd be no one to appreciate my gourmet sensibilities," I muttered.

"Color me your devoted foodie guinea pig, Riley."

"I love you Madison, for eating all my bad concoctions in college. Do you remember when folks use to make excuses to leave our apartment whenever I went into the kitchen?"

"Yeah, but you kept at it, perfected your skills, and here we are years later, and you're a Beard Foundation Nominee. The joke's on them, Riley."

Madison popped the cork on the champagne and took a swig out of the top of the bottle. I shook my head at her and shrugged my shoulders wondering what I was going to do with her. I snatched the bottle from her and poured both of us glasses.

"Here's to you Riley Cook. May you have many years of health, wealth, love and success."

We clinked our glasses. I took a gulp of my champagne, nodded, and tossed a Greek marinated black olive in my mouth, falling deep into my oversized stuffed chair in front to the fireplace, kicking my feet up on the ottoman. Madison plopped down on the nearby loveseat next to me.

"I guess I did stay devoted to the craft of perfecting my food and wine knowledge."

"Yes you did Riley, and in all that effort and devotion, you've managed to land a two and a half million dollar investment from Mr. Hot Guy himself, Nicholas Becker, all while having the Beautiful Mister Wonderful Chocolate Thunder himself worshiping at the altar of all things Riley," Madison giggled. "Noah's nose is so far open you can run a Mack truck through it."

"Oh no it's not," I said, trying to play Madison off.

"Girlfriend, did you think I didn't notice that little charm bracelet with the gold apple dangling off your wrist that you've been wearing since you've been back from New York? Uh huh. Shovel that shit to someone else. This is me you're talking to. Spill it Riley, did you knock boots with the captain or not?"

"Madison, you of all people know I don't mix business with pleasure," I grinned. "But I can't deny things didn't get a little hot and heavy on the way back. It was a long ride, Maddy," I was chuckling more loudly now.

"Obviously not long enough," Madison giggled. "What the hell is wrong with you, girl? I told you to get you some. You've been on a permanent dry spell since you and Warren busted up."

"Oh God, please don't mention that sicko Warren's name. I talked to Reese right before you came in, and he found out through a private investigator that Leah Chen and Warren were connected to the issue of my financials being swapped ahead of my presentation with Milk Money. God Madison, Warren's actually trying to hurt my business."

"Well it was all over the media and the internet Riley, so

Warren couldn't have missed knowing that there was something big going down with your business and Milk Money. But to pull that corporate sabotage rabbit out of his black hat, was downright treacherous. Isn't there a law against that?"

"I'm sure it is if one could prove it. Between that little stunt with the gift basket, and the financial document swaps, this is getting downright spooky scary annoying. Oh, and both times he's pulled this crap, there's this religious scripture handiwork cards of his enclosed that sound pretty threatening."

"Maybe that asshole is getting mental. You think?"

"Mental? Yeah I got his mental," I said, taking more gulps of champagne, shoring myself up with liquid courage. "He doesn't know me now Madison. My relationship with him was a long time ago. I'm not that same weak woman anymore that he treated like dirt under his feet. I'm all grown up now with no intention of taking on his shit now or ever."

"I believe you girlfriend. He's the one that should be scared. Hell you've gotten downright intimidating with your grown up self," Madison laughed. "Hell I'm scared for him."

Madison and I slapped each other five and fell out laughing again, just as the doorbell rang.

"It's Zoe," I said, looking through the peephole and seeing my sister-in-law standing on the porch looking her usual beautiful self.

I quickly opened the door to get her out the January chill.

"Oh Riley, I'm so excited you made the roster for the angel investor funds, but don't you think building a floral shop in your home is a bit extreme?"

"What do you mean Zoe?"

She stepped aside and an entire procession of yellow roses in beautiful vases were headed up my walkway.

"Flowers for Ms. Riley Cook," the teenage driver said, forcing a clipboard in my hand with a pen for me to sign.

"Oh my God," Madison squealed. "I bet I can guess who these are from Riley."

No sooner had I finished signing the floral driver's clipboard, about six more vases were carried inside my home, each in different colors creating the look of a rainbow. Red roses, yellow rose, white roses, pink roses. All the flowers were in beautiful crystal vases, each different with gold and silver ribbons tied beautifully around each of them.

"It's starting to look like a floral shop in here Riley, where's the card, honey?" Madison said.

I searched for the vase with the card. Madison looked so thrilled I thought she was going to burst open in two from her own level of excitement. Zoe had a blank look on her face, waiting patiently to hear who was responsible for this god awful beautiful display. The fragrance from the roses were filling the room. My heart was beating rapidly.

"They're from Noah," I grinned.

"What does the card say Riley?" Madison prodded.

"It says '*Rest your eyes on beauty and know that I feel the same emotion whenever I look at you.*'"

"Ahhhh, that is so sweeeeeet," Madison said. "That man is going for the heart-lights Riley. He's gonna turn those babies on high beam and drive you at warp speed down love's highway," Madison chuckled, pouring herself more champagne, sitting down and kicking her feet back up on the ottoman.

"Nice," Zoe said curtly, moving her eyebrows up a fraction of an inch. She glided across the room, grabbing a champagne glass and pouring. She topped my glass and Madison's.

For a moment none of us said anything. I could hear the crackle of the fireplace. The silence in the room was deafening.

"So Zoe," Madison said. "You know the captain. You think this guy is serious or does he manage all of his relationships this way?"

"He was my brother's best friend. You'd have to ask him. And of course we can't do that now, can we?" Zoe said, her voice creating an arctic chill in the air.

"Is there something wrong that I should know about, Zoe?" I asked softly. "I'm not trying to check into heartbreak hotel again anytime soon," I grinned, trying to tease her, but still expecting a serious answer.

"Not at all, Riley. Noah was my brother's wingman. Lucas trusted him with his life and everything he held dear. Don't pay any attention to me. It's just that I miss Lucas and I love you. This is your time and you should enjoy the moment."

I looked at Zoe hard, not sure whether she had convinced me or not. Intuitively, I felt like there was something more that was going unsaid.

"Really, it's all good honey. Don't mind me. I'm wound up from a tough day at work. Julian's writing some new music for the group and he's overworking us all," Zoe said casually.

She sounded a bit more relaxed, so I guess she was probably right. Maybe this really was about her being tired and not about me getting involved with her twin brother's best friend.

I grabbed my iPhone and sent Noah a text message.

Thank you for the flowers. I love them.

I paused and waited for him to reply, sipping my champagne, listening to Zoe and Madison chat in the background. They were texting Lily, letting her know that Noah had set up a flower shop in my home.

You deserve every rose. Congratulations, baby.

Thank you. Are you still tucking me in tonight?

Wouldn't miss it for the world sweetheart. Call me when your gals leave. Talk to you soon. XOXO.

XO

"So what did *Chocolate Thunder* have to say Riiiilllley?" Madison said teasing me.

"I thanked him for the flowers. We're gonna talk later tonight, thank you. Mind your business Madison."

"Your business is my business Riley, and my business is your business. Did you forget the pact we made when we were kids? Need I remind you?" Madison giggled.

"One for the money and two for the road," Madison and I both said together laughing out loud, slapping each other five.

"What is with you two?" Zoe said. "You guys are back to your inside jokes again?"

"Something like that Zoe," Madison chuckled.

"Time for me to split then Riley. You and Maddy's inside jokes are getting old girlfriend. I gotta run, Riley."

"Oh Zoe don't leave. Don't mind us," I said, pleading. "Stay and hang out with us some more."

"Nope, not. Julian's called a session tonight so I've got to catch up with the band. Thanks for the champagne though. Congratulations honey," Zoe said giving me a hug, kissing me on the cheek.

"I'll walk you out Zoe," Madison said. "Time for me to get home too so Riley can get back to thinking about taking that BMW out for a riiiiiddddddeeee, if you know what I mean."

"What BMW? You get a new ride Riley?" Zoe said.

"Beautiful Mister Wonderful," Madison and I said at the same time. We both laughed gleefully again. The three of us hugged and kissed each other good-bye.

"Hey baby. Your posse gone?"

"Yeah," I said pulling the thick white down-filled comforter over my waist and sliding in between the sheets to get warm.

I waited until Madison and Zoe left to get comfortable and call Noah back for my "tuck me in call." I was buzzed from the all the champagne the gals and I drank. I was feeling giddy like a school girl. I couldn't wait to talk to Noah and hear his voice again. I was still floating on cloud nine from all the roses he'd had sent today. Samantha and Xavier had come home late and were both surprised when they walked through the door, noticing the house looking like a floral shop. Samantha was tickled pink. But Xavier was hardly impressed. He kept babbling about how wide Noah's nose must be open to build a flower shop in my home. I teased him, suggesting he take note on how it done when a man properly woos a woman and that he could stand to rip a page out of gentleman's handbook. Xavier was as overprotective of me as Reese. I wondered if he and Reese had made a pact to scare all men out of my life.

No doubt when Claire gets home tomorrow from her overnight, she'd have nice things to say. She was always wanting me to "get a life," unlike my son.

"Tell me what do you have on, love? Something sexy I hope."

"I have on something black and lacy just for you," I giggled.

"Ummm, short or long?"

"Baby doll."

"Oh Lord, the thought of you in a black lace baby doll nightie makes me crazy thinking about it," Noah said. "Sugar and spice and everything nice. I want you here with me Riley."

"Well it's not like I'm around the corner. There are a lot of miles between us Noah, but I suppose a visit could be arranged," I teased, twirling a lock of my hair around my finger.

"There aren't enough miles to keep me away from you babe. When can you come visit? I'll send you a ticket. A weekend together would be nice don't you think? I haven't seen you since New Year's Eve," Noah said, rattling a ton of questions at me nonstop.

This must be his excited voice, husky and incredibly enticing.

"That was only three weeks ago, Noah."

"Really? It feels like a lifetime to me."

"I can come two weekends from now if that works for you. I need to make arrangements with Zoe to see if she can watch Claire for me."

"I'd love to meet the kids at some point too, Riley. I doubt Xavier will take too kindly to some strange man he's never met whisking his mother off. Or Samantha either for that matter. And Claire . . . she was all Lucas ever talked about in our last months together," Noah said, his voice dropping to a whisper, sounding a bit introspective.

"For the record, I'm not one to expose men to my kids until I'm at a place that I'm comfortable that we're going to be something. . ."

"Something what?" Noah asked.

"You know . . . something . . . more," I whispered softly, hoping I'd said that in a sultry way.

"More . . . yes . . . I'm all for . . . more, Riley. I can be good at more," Noah said.

"Are you teasing me?"

"No baby. I'm serious as a heart attack," Noah laughed playfully.

"That's good to know," I said, my lids starting to get a bit heavy. My voice was starting to sound sleepy even to my own ears.

"It's time to tuck you in baby. You sound tired."

"I'm sorry, it's been a long day. I guess I'm more fatigued than I thought. It's not every day I gain an angel investor, get flooded by a rainbow of roses, and have a champagne-filled evening with my gals. I guess I'm a little worn out."

"No problem baby. I'm tucking you in now. I'll call you

tomorrow about your ticket, okay?"

"Okay Noah," I said sleepily. "Hugs."

"Kisses," Noah said, making a puckering sound with his lips.

"More," I said.

I hung up my phone and slowly drifted off to sleep, imagining those luscious lips on mine and those strong chocolate arms around me.

Noah was right. Sugar and spice and everything nice.

CHAPTER 17

WARREN

"It's all over the blogosphere. That bitch got her ass an angel investor. Your girl was supposed to swap the financials. What the hell happened?" I yelled.

"She did swap them. I saw to it myself. My cousin switched the spreadsheets. It's not our fault Warren. Maybe that uppity bitch had an extra copy or something," Leah said casually, ignoring my anger, flipping through some magazine called Cosmos, popping gum in her mouth like a kid.

"Look Leah, this is not some game of Tiddlywinks. I want to bring Riley's company down to its knees. Those fake financials were supposed to put a nail in her coffin. Instead she ends up with a motherfucking investment for two point five million dollars. What the fuck?"

"Jesus, Warren. Why are you so obsessed with this woman and her business anyway?"

"None of your business. What do you care?"

"I don't care, I'm just askin.'"

"You don't get to fuck over Warren Shaw and get away with it. Riley fucked me over and this is called payback time. You'd be smart to remember that too, woman. File that away somewhere in that little pea brain of yours," I said, grabbing her by her ponytail, pulling her head back hard, pushing her lips close to mine.

Leah was on a layover hanging out with me between flights. She'd knocked on my door, crawled in my bed and we'd fucked like jackrabbits all weekend. Except now I was getting frustrated. This thing with Riley was getting to me.

Riley's success with an angel investor was all over the internet. Good things were happening for her left and right. She thinks she's hot shit tooling around with that new captain fella she brought to the gala. Yeah, I checked out the graduation ring on his finger from the Naval Academy. I even saw the year that asshole became an officer and gentleman. He's practically the same age as me. I don't know what she sees in him that she didn't see in me.

One thing for sure, I'm not going to go crawl into some hole and go silent. No, I'm not done with her yet. And I damn sure are not done with Captain Asshole. This shit is not over until I say it's over.

"So what's your plan now Warren? You've been up to bat now twice. Three strikes and you're out loverboy," Leah said, biting slowly on my ear lobe.

She rubbed her hand against my cock, her way of getting me to calm down. I felt her hand against my cock realizing she knew I had turned solid as a rock. I couldn't hide the fact that she turned me on whenever I was in her presence. I struggled to maintain mind over my flesh with her, but I could never get my cock to behave whenever she was around. Personally I didn't give a damn about her. But there were fringe benefits to keeping her around longer. I got that Leah was using me as much as I was using her.

"I'll tell you what the plan is Leah. Next time, I hit this out the ballpark. Sometimes if you want something done right you have to do it yourself."

"Meaning you're going to start carrying your own water this time?" Leah said, shrugging her shoulders nonchalantly as if she didn't believe me.

"I plan to hit her where it hurts this time. That shit-head brother of hers won't be able to help his sister either. This time I'm taking her down for good."

I pushed Leah down to her knees, unzipped my pants, and whipped my hard ass cock out.

"You know what to do," I said.

Leah was starting to piss me off. She had no real respect for me or what I was trying to do. I'm not sure what made me think she was going to be in this with me for the long haul. This bitch was totally self-serving. Loyalty didn't run through her veins.

I grabbed the back of her hair and pushed my hard cock further down Leah's mouth. She was good for something.

"Say my name Leah."

"Yeah, Daddy."

"Right. Now act like you know. You gotta remember to dance with who brung you, woman."

Leah let out a wicked laugh. I was right. She wasn't in this with me for the long haul. But what did I care. The only thing I cared about right now was bringing Riley Cook to her knees.

Maybe I'd make Riley say my name.

CHAPTER 18

NOAH

The last few weeks had been hectic for both Riley and me, but we were both committed to making time for each other. Our relationship was blossoming. I officially turned in my Noah Dunham bachelor card. I was keeping my promise to Lucas to look after his most prized possessions.

I knew my playa days had come to an end by virtue of the fact that a few of my old flames had called me to be their "plus one" at this or that or event and I declined. It wasn't a secret that I had a penchant for beautiful women, but I was taking the exit ramp off the fast lane. The last thing I needed was a female blast from my past resurfacing, interfering in my relationship with Riley. I respected what we had far too much for conjured up nonsense. I had cut all ties with the fast and now furious women from my past, many of whom were having trouble accepting that I was off the market. Riley was a keeper. I wasn't letting anything or anybody get in our way. My love for her had taken root long before we met. I intended to nurture and cherish it.

I jumped into my new Carrera, my heart practically thumping out of my chest, and headed to Reagan International Airport. Riley and I were officially a couple. Having landed *Milk Money* as her angel investor, she'd been busy getting new staff in place for her company. She'd finished her book and was on a short book tour for the launch. I had made it a point the last few weeks to fly to whatever city she was in and to meet her for lunch, dinner, vintage shopping and to share whatever breaks her schedule permitted. In each city that I managed to juggle, I would get in line, wait my turn with most of her followers, purchase her book and have her autograph each one. So far, I had nine copies, each with a handwritten note inside. Some of those notes were funny, others were steamy, most were passionate, but they all made a footprint on my heart.

In between my visits, we'd have marathon late night phone chats with some phone sex on the side, picking up where we left off New Year's Eve night in the limousine. Whenever we spoke, she told me where the tour was heading next. Sometimes I would tell her I was coming and other times I'd show up and surprise her. Her book tour drew large crowds. I often had to squeeze myself in the room. By now I knew her book inside out. I think I loved *"Wining and Dining with Riley"* more than she did. I had her book down pat. I now knew what to drink with what to eat. Now that the tour was over, Riley was coming to D.C. to see me.

I had started to seriously consider transitioning out of the Navy and into civilian life. I hadn't told Riley yet, but I had sold off all of the investment property I owned in the Carolinas. Now that the housing bubble had burst, I decided my future wasn't going to be located in an area with me swinging golf balls every day at Hilton Head. I planned to take the proceeds of my property sales and purchase land in Upper Makefield Township, PA, near to where Riley resided.

While I knew she loved the home she and Lucas built, I was thinking about building a future with her and the kids. But I didn't want our future to begin in Lucas's home. Lucas was my boy and all, but even he'd agree Riley and I should have our own home. A fresh start. After all, Lucas made me promise to do whatever I could to ensure her happiness. Now that she was coming to D.C. for the weekend, I pondered whether this would be the right time to share this information with her. I was looking forward to the fact that we were going to have the whole weekend together. I didn't want to get too heavy and scare her off.

Because her schedule had been arduous and mine had been no cakewalk, we agreed our time together should be low keyed, relaxed and spontaneous. February was known to be bitter cold this time of year, so staying in and relaxing sounded good to the both of us.

I'd arrived back in town myself only a couple of nights before last, having taken the red-eye in from Los Angeles. My plane was half empty except for the presence of California's governor and some of his staff, who'd spent most of their time talking and walking up and down the aisle discussing politics loudly. A few of them sounded quite tilted, bitching about having to come back to D.C. for some kind of boondoggle with all the other governors in the country. I managed to close my eyes on the plane and put their bitching aside. All I could think about was the fact that Riley and I were overdue for some much needed down time. The fact that we could take a breather together was what the doctor ordered.

I arrived at the airport in time to catch Riley walking out to the curb. We'd planned in advance to meet so as to avoid the parking maze. Surprisingly, American Airlines was right on time and so was I. I waited impatiently, standing next to the door of my new Carrera that I'd christened "The Commander."

There she was. Beautiful as ever wrapped in a camel colored cashmere coat with a fur trimmed collar. I scurried briskly her direction, cutting the distance between us in half. I reached out, leaning over to hug and kiss her softly on the lips, unable to control my excitement at seeing her again.

"You ready, gorgeous?" I said, grabbing her weekender bag, guiding her toward my new car. I opened the door, helping her in, admiring those beautiful lean legs peeking out from under her wrap coat.

"Here baby, let me help you with the seatbelt," I said, clicking her belt, letting my right hand rest briefly on her knee. I so wanted to rip that crisp white shirt straight off her, hike that beige skirt of hers over those curvy hips and sit her right on top of the "Torpedo."

God she was beautiful. I loved her body. I loved her mind. I loved everything about her. I was talking to myself overtime in my mind, forcing myself to mentally slow myself down. But it was tough, because I had missed her. She was hard to resist. Both smart and beautiful, Riley was any wise man's wet dream.

Rapper 50 Cent was playing loudly through my speaker system, singing *"Let me take you to candy shop"* because that was my happy song, and I was happy. I pulled out of the airport area and hit the highway at high speed.

"Noah dear, do you typically drive this fast?"

I glanced at the speedometer, noticing I was flying a little over a hundred. I kicked myself mentally for not being more mindful that I had Riley in the car. I slowed the Commander down to around eighty miles per hour so as not to set off any more alarms with Riley. Not to mention, we had a thirty minute drive, a storm was brewing, and it was starting to rain cats and dogs. Slowing down was not a bad idea even though it was generally against my nature. I was certain I was scaring her.

"Tell me what you've been up to since I've seen you last baby," I said, hoping to relax her a bit.

Riley starting chatting about the book tour. I listened attentively, unable to help myself from rubbing my hand on the inside of her upper thigh. She was going on and on about having sold several hundred books. Her publisher felt the tour had been a success.

Riley removed my hand from her thigh, picked it up and kissed it softly against her lips, still chatting about the tour and changes she was making with her company. I was blowing down the highway at full throttle again up until we both noticed another vehicle had hydroplaned on the highway. I couldn't tell if the stroke of my hand was making her uncomfortable or my driving so I broke my speed down yet a second time, reminding myself not to be a show-off and to reel myself back in and focus.

Riley was aroused. Her nipples were starting to peek through that crisp white shirt she was wearing every time I attempted to stroke her leg. My overall excitement to get her home was tempting me to race down the highway, put the pedal to the metal, and get her home as soon as possible.

This was the first time Riley was coming to my home. It was also the first time in years that I literally unpacked my home. I'd unpacked each box carefully, putting every piece of furniture and all the knick-knacks in their proper place. I had even put fresh flowers in the Steuben vase that I had once given to my ex-wife that she had managed to leave behind, not wanting any reminders of me in her possession. I knew women had a tendency to scrutinize a man's place so I wanted everything to be right. I did not want to disappoint.

"Are you hungry? We're coming into Alexandria. We can stop and get something to eat if you want."

"I'm hungry but I'm not really up for having a huge sit down meal if that's okay with you," she said. "I'm kind of burnt out on all the heavy meals from the book tour," she sighed. "Can't you tell I've picked up a couple pounds?"

"All in the right places, sweetheart. You're looking beautiful as ever to me," I said, tapping her knee gently. "Perhaps we can get something simple that we can take with us?"

"There's a Subway around the corner from my townhouse. I'll grab a couple of foot-longs. I have some champagne on ice. We can go home, watch some movies and chill."

"That sounds perfect."

"You're shivering. Are you cold?"

"I have a slight chill, yes. It's been a long flight and fatigue has set in," she said, turning those big brown saucy eyes my direction.

"I'll turn the heat up a notch. We're almost home. If you're still cold when we get there, I'll warm you up."

I shot my best my bad boy smile at her.

"Umm. Does that include cuddling? Cuddling sounds good, right?"

"Yeah, baby we can cuddle. Cuddling is good," I said with a laugh.

I knew where the torpedo was going to cuddle all right.

I stopped at the Subway and grabbed a couple of turkey and cheese subs, chips, and two large chocolate chip cookies. I picked up a couple pints of H⬜⬜gen Dazs Rum Raisin. For some reason the Subway was particularly crowded and the cashiers were moving slower than usual. I could feel the excitement in me building. I wanted to get back to my woman.

Riley glanced at me with that loving smile of hers as I was coming out the store's double doors. *Man, stand the torpedo down, dude.* I smiled back at her, jumped back into the Commander, speeding around the corner into the gated community of Piedmont Estates.

My automatic garage double door opened as I pulled into my development. I parked the Commander next to my everyday car, a Lexus GS Hybrid, and helped Riley out of the Carrera. I caught a hint of her cologne. She smelled like the clean fresh notes of the ocean with hints of lavender. So enticing.

I guided her thorough the back door entering my home through the basement. I led her up the stairs to my four level townhouse.

"Welcome to my home baby. What's mine is yours, so make yourself comfortable."

"You have a nice place, Noah."

"The main living area is my idea of picturesque. With the floor to ceiling vertical window blinds, I have a breathtaking view on all three sides. Maybe we can have morning coffee and look out on the grounds together," I said, arching my eyebrows upward. "I'll give you the tour, sweetie."

I started with the living area, the largest space, with beautiful lamb-skinned rugs adorning the rich dark hardwood floors. Next was the kitchen area, equipped with state of the art appliances and granite counter tops revealing my lack of use as the kitchen and greenhouse breakfast area still looked fresh and unused. A low breeze swept a strand of her hair from the white ceiling fans that hung from the thirteen foot cathedral ceiling that were turning quietly in slow motion as the rain pattered against the skylights. It had taken me a while before Riley's arrival to unpack four bedrooms and to remove all the tarps on the furniture in the living area,but I had somehow managed to put everything pretty much in place. If I must say so myself, I was pretty proud at how things had turned out. Home decorum was not my interest nor my strong suit. I must have drank a whole bottle of Stoli's by myself the night I unpacked the house, cursing each full box out, asking it where the hell did it come from and why was it here. It took me a while but I finally resigned myself to the fact that unpacking was a necessary evil. I had grown far too accustomed to living out of hotels on the road while my stacks of boxes at home remained untouched. Worse, my cupboards were filled with cheerios, cereal, popcorn, and Stoli's. My only home staples. I reminded myself to purchase some food or I'd need to order in later. I couldn't ravish her body for days while expecting her not to sustain on food.

"Make yourself at home darlin.' "

"Your home is lovely. I'm impressed," Riley said, moving towards me kicking off her heels, standing on her tiptoes giving me a soft peck on my lips.

I responded, kissing her back on her nose. I grabbed Riley's weekender bag to take upstairs to the master bedroom, but not before noticing that she was moving around the room, slowly checking things out. Riley was looking at several of the pictures of Lucas and I that we'd taken together through the years. I glanced her way, noticing as she moved towards the family photo of she, Lucas, and the kids.

I moved across the room to cut the fifty-five inch television off that I'd left playing before going to the airport. I turned on the Bose player with my iPad docked and selected my "Music for Riley" Playlist. I had made the playlist especially for Riley that started with Weeknd's new hit single called *"Earned It,"* followed by old school Vanessa Williams's *"Everlasting Love."* My entire playlist was filled with melodic harmony with only her in mind. I'd even added Nicole Henry's *"All The Way."* I had hoped she was okay with my taste in music.

I wondered if she thought my townhouse looked too much like a man cave versus a space that a strong independent woman could see herself spending time in with me.

Just as that thought flashed through my head, Riley said, "I feel so relaxed here."

"Thank you, babe. I'm glad."

I was grinning now.

"I love Nicole Henry's song," she said.

"Good, it's our song then."

The dark hardwood floors helped to accentuate the light beige overstuffed sofa that wrapped across the entire back wall facing the fireplace. Matching oversized ottomans sat at the foot of each end of the sofa pieces. A dark brown and cream colored lambskin rug sat under the large smoky glass cocktail table. I knew she was cold, so I lit the fireplace ablaze, then poured her a glass of champagne and dimmed the lights. I made myself a vodka martini and grabbed a couple of plates out of the kitchen for our foot-longs.

"You need some help Noah?"

"No, I think I can manage a couple of sandwiches, but I won't make any promises," I chuckled.

Riley walked into the living room, sipping her champagne. She began picking up pictures this time.

"I see you have quite a few pictures of you and Lucas."

She moved toward the family photo of Lucas, her, and the

kids.

"You know this family photo of all of us was taken shortly before he passed. Oh, and this one is of he and I taken on our honeymoon," she said with a bit of surprise.

"You know Riley, I can move these pictures if you like."

"Not at all. I can see that you and Lucas had a special bond. You know that makes you all the more special to me as well."

I knew damn well I was in love with Riley. I wanted every moment of this weekend to go right.

"My home is your home. I want you to be completely comfortable this weekend. Come honey, let's eat."

I sat our food down on the table in front of us. I placed another log in the fireplace using the iron rod to stoke it a bit. The fire made a crackling sound.

It was still chilly. Riley had wrapped her hands around her arms, warming herself.

"Can you point me to the powder room, I'd like to wash my hands."

"Sure thing sweetheart."

I led her to the bathroom near the foyer. I busied myself nervously grabbing some toss pillows out of the bay window and putting them on the sofa so as to make sure she was completely comfortable. As she exited the bathroom, I came up behind her and ran my hands gently up and down her arms to warm her. Barbra Streisand's *"Love Dance"* was playing softly in the background.

"Are you warming up now baby? Let me warm you up some more," I said, still rubbing my hands up and down on her arms.

"I'm much better now."

We sat on the sofa and began to gnaw away at our foot-longs. I asked her about the kids. She brought me up to speed on how things were going with Xavier, Samantha, and Claire.

"Xavier is spending a lot of time occupied with Nena. Samantha is starting to write poetry, busy participating in a few poetry slams, and Claire is taking Martial Arts classes."

Riley and I had agreed in one of our many marathon video chats when she was on tour, that the timing was good for me to personally meet the kids in our next window of opportunity. Her children knew that we were dating and were starting to inquire as to when they were going to meet me.

"What do they know about me so far?"

"I brought them up to speed on the fact that you were a close friend of their Dad's and that you knew their Aunt Zoe well."

"I'm looking forward to meeting them. I want to become a part of their lives."

I thought about the fact that I knew most everything about them growing up anyway from Lucas. And now we were actually going to meet. I was pretty good with kids. And these kids were particularly special to me.

"They want to meet you too," Riley said, pinching the corner of bread off the tip of her hoagie.

I wiped a couple crumbs off the side of her mouth with the back of my thumb, planting soft kisses across her jaw. We finished our food. I grabbed her hand, pulling her close to me, sweeping her up off her feet signaling that I wanted to her to dance with me. Sade's *This Is No Ordinary Love* was playing.

In my heart I had danced this dance with Riley a thousand times, time and time again in my imagination. And, now this moment was no longer a figment of my imagination. It was real. I could feel my heart beating and the torpedo pulsating. Riley was in my arms for good. She exhaled. I could feel her heart thumping. This was our time. Our moment. I wanted to make love to her. Right now. Right this minute.

I had an unstoppable longing for our bodies and soul to join. I needed the contrast of my chocolate brown complexion against the hue of her fair caramel-colored skin. I'd lit candles in the room earlier. They were fluttering softly in the room, creating an intimate ambiance that I had hoped she might like.

Riley was responding to me as we danced. I knew she could feel the torpedo growing hard next to her. I kissed her lips tenderly, working my way to nibbling on her ear ever so softly. I planted kisses on her lips heading down along the nape of her neck. I could hear her breathing starting to pick up. We were both silent. We were both in a desirous place. We were communicating in a language that only lovers understood.

"You feelin' the music?"

"Um hum," she murmured. "You feelin' it to?"

"I'm feelin' you. I feel you in every crevice of my heart, filling all the empty spaces with your love."

I took Riley's hand and led her to the couch, tossing the oversized pillows on the floor. I sat her down. She wasn't cold anymore because I could feel her warmth radiating. I rose to pour her another glass of champagne. I focused on those sweet succulent lips, watching as she took a sip of her champagne. I headed to my wet bar and cracked open a chilled bottle of Grey Goose. I pulled out a martini glass from the over-hanging rack. I grabbed a couple of Greek olives from the mini-fridge, poked a toothpick through them and slid them in my glass. I took a sip. I couldn't take my eyes off her.

Sade's *"This Is No Ordinary Love"* was still playing, perfect for the mood. She was casually thumbing through some GQ magazines I had lying about. I paid close attention to all her idiosyncrasies. The way she flipped the pages. The way she tilted her head. They was she wet her lips. I sipped and I studied her. I didn't want to miss a thing. I wanted to take in every bit of her essence. The feelings I had for her were beyond intense. Soon I wouldn't be able to hold back on my expression of love for her that I know needs to be said. That I know she needs. She needed to know she was worthy. Deserving. Lovable.

Noticing my silence, Riley looked up at me, flashing that 'come and get me' smile. That look did me in every time. I grinned back at Riley trying to contain my exuberance and to savor that look. I winked at her to lighten the mood. Then, I started dancing to the music in front of her, swaying back and forth.

She giggled.

"You bad boy, you. You must be feeling that martini," Riley said, totally in command.

"Oh, yeah, I've got my bad boy hat on for sure."

I pretended like it was karaoke night, holding an imaginary microphone in my hand, singing to the top of my lungs. She was laughing at my shenanigans. I loved to hear her laugh. We were having fun. I was seducing her, pulling her in slowly.

I continued swaying to the music while slowly unbuttoning my shirt, pretending I was a male stripper. Taunting her. Teasing her. She tossed her hair back and took another sip of champagne, her eyes studying my body.

"Work it baby!" she whooped.

I was fully buzzed and motivated now to begin to cut up. I unbuckled my belt and hung it out to the side turning it around and around. I dropped my pants and was standing there with my shirt opened revealing my trained biceps, six pack, and my Hugo Boss boxer shorts with the torpedo peeking through. The torpedo had come to attention and I no longer had control over him. Riley was looking at me with that school girl look that was someplace between shock, awe, desire, admiration, and affection.

Damn, she was looking at me with a look of intensity I had never seen on her face before. I think she might be getting ready to turn me out. I'd become the prey. These tables had turned on me quickly. I was starting to have a moment.

My insecurities swept over me. I wasn't quite sure if I could rise to the occasion. I gave my face an imaginative slap. *Get it together man,* I told myself. *This is not the fucking the moment to wussy out.* I came back into my present moment and regained command over myself.

Riley curled her well pedicured toes. Her legs were smooth and lean. I was out of control. I wanted to part her legs and comfortably land myself right in between.

Carlos Santana's "Smooth" was playing now. We were both feeling our passion and desire for each other. Riley got up, shaking her head from side to side, keeping time with the music. She danced this little salsa move, making her way towards me, swaying her hips slowly with her arms held high over her head. Damn. She was burning a path with every step she made towards me, pursuing me, setting me on fire. Riley was in complete control. And I was losing my control.

She took my hands, placing them on her hips; acting as my guide, helping me to help her slip down her beige pencil skirt. Her white shirt was fully unbuttoned now. Her black lacy bra was mine for the taking. I unsnapped her bra, my eyes pinned to her soft breasts, her caramel nipples peaking, begging for my attention.

I stared eyeball to eyeball with her, kissing my way down her body, starting a long melodious trail down to her stomach. I knew she wanted me as much as I wanted her. An electric charge passed between us. We were both burning with desire. My eyes drifted over her breasts. She put her hands on the side of my face pulling my attention back to her. Our eyes met again in our brief moment of silence.

"Do you want me?" she asked softly.

"I want you more than I want air right now."

"I want you too Noah."

I was crossing terrain with her I had never crossed before. I was in heaven. Lord have mercy on me. I kissed and fondled her breasts, giving both of them my full attention, swirling my tongue around each nipple, sucking her hard. I was starting to knock things awkwardly off the cocktail table, pulling the waistband of her saturated Victoria's Secret black-laced panties, ripping them off. I dipped my finger inside her. She leaned in closer to me. I laid her down spread eagle before me, opening her legs, crawling between them. She pushed my shirt open impatiently.

"Oh God no," she muttered.

"Oh yes baby," I answered.

With the tip of my tongue I assaulted every inch of her, torturing her with every lick. She panted and moaned more loudly now. Groaning in pleasure, her sweet juices tasted like honey, making me hyper aroused.

The more she moaned the more I let my tongue devour her sweet sex, her juices flowing like a honey faucet. She quivered, tightening her thigh muscles around my head. Her back arched as she held my head, urgently commanding my tongue further inside her.

"Oh God, that feels so good baby," she whispered, as if she were in her own little trance. The sounds of her moans were making me more excited. She sounded so good, I could go on all night with foreplay just to hear her moan for me. She let out a scream as I continued to feed on her clit. She tasted oh so ever sweet. I moved my mouth to fondle her breasts, my hand between her legs.

"Look at me," I ordered.

Riley looked at me as if I were something good to eat.

She grabbed the torpedo and plunged the shaft deep inside her and began gyrating rhythmically.

Whoa.

"Condom," I said.

"Pill," she said.

Bareback? Oh hell yeah. I slammed the torpedo against her pelvis, grinding deeper inside her. The sensation was euphoric. I couldn't remember how long it had been since I had made love to someone I thought was "special." God, I was so high on her love. She gazed into my eyes and neither of us could stop the unbridled passion.

I flipped her over and smacked her round bottom without ever losing rhythm.

"Oh," she moaned.

"You like that baby? You like the torpedo?" I said smacking that round beautiful full bottom another time.

I could feel the torpedo hot and heavy against her belly now approaching her from the rear doggie style.

"Yes Noah," Riley moaned. "You're doing me so good baby," she grunted as I quickly thrusted the torpedo in her, moving now with long slow strokes.

"Awh man," I said, slamming my pelvis into her as my balls smashed against her ass. The sounds she moaned let me know to continue to take long deliberate strokes now. I knew I was gonna explode as my balls were starting to fill up. I was sprung. Riley was screaming for mercy now. That was my cue. I scooped her up and took her up the stairs with me still inside her. I got to the top of the stairs and held her over the stair railing. Her fingernails were digging into my back. I was moving in and out of her now like a wild man. She was struggling to accommodate me and take me all inside of her. She grabbed hold tight to me as if her life depended on it while I pumped the torpedo at a very fast pace. I heard Riley moan and scream with a sound I didn't know it was possible to come out of her. I felt her legs trembling as her backbone was hanging over the railing.

She might have been unsure if I could hold her but that was exactly the emotion I wanted to evoke in her, that I had her and I was never gonna let her go, all while the torpedo romanced her sensitive tissues until we could get horizontal. I was rock hard inside of her. That petite frame was not leaving my grasp. She screamed my name, out loud, "Noah," grasping my neck for dear life. I pulled her back over the rail and carried her into my bedroom so she'd feel safe.

My own sounds were now deep and resonating thorough the entire bedroom. I had reached all the right spots. I had hoped the torpedo had done his job. I gave her a moment to adjust to the torpedo lengthening as I felt myself as I hit bottom and could feel both our organisms approaching. Riley had unbridled access to my heart and now she was taking my body. Riley swung around me, and got on top. Got damn, I was mush now. Riley turned into a wild woman. She was scratching my chest with her fingernails, with her head thrown back as her soft dark brown mound glided up and down on my shaft, sucking every last bit of juice out of me. We were in an intense moment that was escalating and I could no longer muffle my own moans. I could feel the torpedo lengthening. Now I was the one moaning for mercy. I turned rapidly around, putting her underneath me. I wrapped my large muscular hands around her, plunging deeper and deeper. Both of our breathing quickened and I exploded. I heard her scream out in ecstasy. Her body was wet from my sweat dripping off me and onto her. Riley and I were in unison. I grabbed her, slapping her ass.

"Yeah baby," I uttered out loud.

She wound my excitement down slowly and laid soft kisses on my forehead, nibbled on my ears, kissing my lips passionately. The torpedo fell limp. Riley was still on top of me, neither of us able to move. She started to move. "Whoa baby. Slow down, I'm not ready."

I pulled out of her slowly. Her groin was sopping wet, her thighs filled with sweat. I could feel the sweat beads bouncing on her back. She plopped down beside me and our heartbeats slowed. The sweat was breaking on my six-pack and forehead.

"I'm going downstairs for that Rum Raisin," she whispered.

I watched as Riley wrapped a sheet around her, and headed downstairs.

What the fuck? She has energy to walk downstairs for ice cream? Oh hell no. The torpedo is off his game. Shit. She's got energy to walk! What the fuck? I can't move.

"Oh hell no dude," I mumbled to the torpedo. "We have not knocked it out the park yet. She is not supposed to be moving."

I opened one eye slowly eyeballing the torpedo. Hmmm, not done yet. Get you hard ass in gear, brother. We are not going out like this. My manhood is on the line here, torpedo. Straighten out. She's walking around to get ice cream. Dude we ain't' done yet.

Come to attention, bitch! I command you, muthafucker. The torpedo was limp. He had a mind of his own.

"Fuck you Noah."

CHAPTER 19

RILEY

Oh my god. Noah was all that and then some. I've never been made love to like that since . . . I don't know . . . my thoughts were distracted by my need for something sweet. I opened his refrigerator to scout for the H⬚⬚gen Dazs. Damn, he was good. And to think, I remember the days when I actually thought Warren was decent in bed.

Frankly, I can't remember when I've been made love to like that. I think I shall have some more of that, Mister. I searched for a spoon, finding one and dipping deeply into cold Rum Raisin. I chuckled to myself. Noah was um um good. It's been a long time since I felt comfortable enough to share my body with a man again. I struggled to remember any man making love to me like that. My mind drifted back to my lovemaking with Lucas.

I was a virgin when I married Lucas. Lucas and I were young. I was a sexual novice, only knowing what he had taught me, which wasn't a whole lot. After his death I found my sex life with Warren to be a bit more exciting up into the point our relationship crashed and burned.

One night shortly after making love, Warren made a painful disclosure. He hinted that he didn't know whether he wanted to be in a relationship with a man or a woman. I was in shock and devastated. That was the night I painfully ended my engagement with him.

Warren would later admit his confession was all a ruse. A story he made up to cover up an out of town visit from another woman with whom he was having an affair. Allegedly his story was designed to get rid of me temporarily. He had plans to pick me back up once his out-of-town boo was gone. I was beyond crushed. I broke off the engagement, picked up was left of my shattered heart and colored the two of us done.

Ugh, such bad memories. I literally shook myself off while peeking my head back in the freezer.

"Thank you again Jesus you didn't let me marry that man," I whispered to the heavens.

But I was back in the saddle again doing what I promised myself I wasn't going to do. Stirring the pot of the contented life I'd built for myself and the kids. I'm adding a M.A.N. to the mix. Maybe this is a mistake. But then again, maybe I've been wrong all these years. Maybe I could find true honest, loving companionship. Maybe happiness with a man was in my future.

I spooned more ice cream in my mouth. I couldn't wait to talk to Madison. She was going to prod every last detail of this weekend out of me, I knew. I could hear her voice now in my head saying, "Bitch, grab that ice cream and go get yourself some more of that dick. Whip it on him and go turn that party out, girlfriend. Take hold of what's yours Riley."

Okay. Okay Madison. You're all in my head. Shut the hell up. I licked the back of my spoon noticing my high heels on the floor. I dropped the sheet around me and slipped them on my feet. I grabbed Noah's blue shirt laying on the floor, slipping my arms through the huge sleeves, tugging it over my shoulders to knock the chill off me. I grabbed the Rum Raisin and more champagne.

I headed up the stairs with the ice cream and spoon in my hand. Noah had fallen asleep, sprawled out on the bed still naked. I drooled over his chocolate-skinned six pack. His military trained biceps were bulging, still glistening with sweat under the dimly lit hue of lights glowing in his bed headboard. I noticed his left arm was imprinted with the same Wingman tattoo that both Lucas and Xavier wore.

Oh my god. My husband, my son, and my lover all have the same tattoo. How did that get by me? Riley, this is information you're supposed to know what to do with, girlfriend. Between the champagne, the lovemaking, the music, the moment, I was emotionally foggy. This had gotten by me. I ran the tip of my fingernail slowly over the crossed naval swords on his tattoo.

Lucas and Noah really did have some kind of bond that I intuitively felt I didn't fully understand. They were closer than I had imagined. I knew what that tattoo meant to Lucas. I knew what it meant to Xavier. What I didn't know, was what it meant to Noah.

Noah turned over slowly opening his eyes. His eyes followed mine as I fingered the outline of his tattoo sensually. Pull it together girl I said to myself, feeling as if I were having an emotional moment as a flood of memories coursed through me.

I spooned rum raisin to my lips to keep from having to form words, and then spooned a scoop to his. Noah took the cold ice cream from my hands, setting it down on the nightstand. He pulled me further into the bed, positioning himself in front of me, spreading my legs. He pulled his sky blue monogrammed shirt off me slowly running his hands down my legs, slowly admiring the heels on my feet. He grabbed my left leg, slowing kissing my ankle, making his way up my calf, the backside of my knee, and then to my upper thigh, He pulled the sheet over his head and went down on me. Oh, sweet Jesus. *Can you it make easier on me?* I thought. Noah's tongue was talking to me. He was claiming me. His tongue was circling my clitoris demanding, instructing, commanding that I was his. Begging me to belong to him. I pulled the sheet back and had wrapped my high heeled legs around his neck. He lifted my butt up towards him. Over and over again he was marking his turf and making himself clear. As my body exploded under the weight of multiple orgasms, I surrendered over to his silent command.

As my heartbeat slowed, I faced the fact that I was officially exhausted. I was done. Sated.

"Were we what you expected?" Noah panted, plopping on his side, and spooning me from the back.

"Better than I'd imagined," I replied.

I belong to you and with you, Noah.

For the remainder of our weekend Noah and I pretty much never crawled out of bed except to eat and shower. We watched movies, played chess, and read our favorite magazines and newspapers. But mostly we made love. I watched him doing his daily morning pushups, teasing him about the fact that he had the same macho habit as Lucas's of gargling with vodka after brushing his teeth. I figured it was some Navy ritual the two of them must have shared. It gave me the willies when Lucas did that shit and now Noah was doing it too. *Some kind of macho man thing.*

It was wonderful to be able to chill, make love and pretty much do nothing, but our time together was up. It was time for us to get back to our daily lives.

"I don't want to let you go," Noah said.

He had complained the entire drive to the airport, talking mostly about not wanted us to be separated again.

"It's going to be hard for me to leave," I said standing next to the Commander as he pulled my wheelie out of the back.

I could feel the tears filling in the back of my eyes.

"I'll be back in Pensie before you know it," Noah pulled me close to him in a hug, whispering in my ear. "We're going to do this family thing next time."

"I know, I know."

I dropped my head down so as to not let him see me tearing up. I felt silly and emotional. He pulled my chin up to his face and looked me in the eye.

"You've built a bridge to my heart. It beats for you and only you."

He wiped the tear that had fallen on my face.

"Go now, Riley before we change our minds."

"I know. I know."

I kissed him, turning to pull my Jackie O-looking sunglasses on my face to hide my emotions. I hated good-byes.

As I boarded the plane for the ride back home, I knew I was in love. I knew he was too. We'd solidified our plans for him to meet the kids. We agreed to talk later about how we thought they each might handle the news of our being a couple. It would be a few weeks before we could make the family introduction visit happen. Noah was headed to Missouri for a few weeks to spend time with his elderly father who was ailing.

I put my weekender bag in the overhead compartment. My having to leave Noah felt bittersweet. I loved our time together but I was sad at the same time to be apart. I was going to have to get stronger if I was going to throw myself head first into a commuter relationship.

I reached in the left pocket of my trench coat to grab my boarding pass. To my surprise a little blue box wrapped in a white satin bow was tucked in my right pocket. I opened it slowly as I heard the sound of the wheels of the plane lifting up in their lock position. I gasped and my heart fluttered wildly.

I opened it. It was another beautiful eighteen caret gold Tiffany charm. But this one was even more special than the last, a heart-shaped tag engraved with the words "I love you."

I peered out the window of the plane watching the white clouds float silently by. It was me that was floating on clouds.

I love you too.

Chapter 20

Warren

"I'm really getting bored with hovering outside this woman's house all the time."

"Deal with it Leah. It's not like you have anything better to do today."

"Warren, I don't appreciate spending my weekend off stalking Riley Cook's home on a Saturday night," she said, opening the glove compartment of my Escalade nosing so as to peer at whatever I had inside.

"What are you doing?" I snapped, knowing the only thing Leah would find would be a few autographed copies of my paperback and a couple of half smoked joints.

"I'm hungry. You've been stalking this woman off and on now for a couple months. I'm surprised she's not on to you by now. She's supposed to be an ex-girlfriend. What's your problem? This woman has turned into some ugly obsession with you," she grumbled, tossing the contents of my glove compartment around.

"Stop being a bitch Leah."

"Well bitch trumps stupid motherfucker every time. Besides I haven't eaten anything all day."

"You can eat later," I said, ignoring her comment.

Leah thought I was obsessed with Riley. But her opinion didn't matter. This was payback time. I was gonna make Riley pay for thinking she and her family could thumb their noses up at me as if I were a nobody. She and that joke of a brother of hers both thought they were better than me. And now that she was cavorting around with that new Navy Captain dude. I was going to wait patiently in the wings until I caught both of them on my radar and made them pay. The last thing Riley was going to get was her happily ever after with some high ranking Navy flyboy.

Again.

"I'm hungry Warren," Leah whined, spotting the joints, reaching for the Bic lighter and firing up the old roaches.

Leah reared back in the seat of my Escalade and blew smoke rings in my face. My patience was wearing thin with her. I was getting as bored with her as she was with me. Leah moved to turn the music up louder, blowing smoke and fogging the windows. I might as well have been babysitting a petulant child.

"I'll be on flight duty, headed to London for the Easter holiday," she coughed. "Don't look for me to be around to play these games with you and your ex-girlfriend when I get back Warren."

Leah looked my way, offering me what was left of the joint, but I shook my head in denial. I pulled the little black binoculars I had wedged between us and aimed them at Riley's house. There were no visible signs of activity anywhere. I began to wonder if Riley and her family were even in town. Perhaps they got an early start on the Easter holiday and left town. It was the middle of April. It wouldn't be uncommon for her to take off early to beat the holiday crowds. Maybe Leah was right. Maybe it was time to end my surveillance for the day.

"As a matter of fact Warren, don't look for me at all after this. I think it's time you and I part ways in this relationship honey," Leah said, dragging on the joint hard again. The joint was so small now she was going to need a clip to finish it, lest she burn those pretty nails of her.

"Oh you're gonna bail out of this relationship now, right when things are getting good? It must be true what they say. When the going gets tough, the tough get going."

"Well the going can get tough without me Warren. I need a new scene," Leah shrugged.

"Whatever," I answered, rolling my eyes up in my head, not really taking her seriously.

It didn't matter. If Leah was going to leave me, then fine. I was going to stay focused on my mission with or without her. No way in hell, Riley Cook and that new asswipe she was seeing were going to ease on down their little yellow brick road trippin' on happy if I could help it.

No damn way.

CHAPTER 21

NOAH

The wheels of the Commander couldn't get me to Pennsylvania fast enough. I was blowing the doors off most of the eighteen wheelers on the highway in my excitement to get to Riley's. I left Alexandria three hours ago. If it weren't for all the traffic in Baltimore with folks headed to the Camden Yards to watch the Orioles and the Phillies play, I would have been here seeing my woman a whole hell of lot sooner.

It was a beautiful June day. Riley was throwing a casual barbecue this weekend for me to meet the kids. They were given advanced notice that I was coming. A couple of times when Riley and I were having one of our marathon calls, she would put me on speaker phone with whichever one was around, letting them and me say hello. Lucas would be pleased the kids turned out so well. They appeared to be a well behaved well-mannered troop. I think Lucas knew deep down when he made me promise to look after Riley that I would fall in love with her and she with me. He was very adept at orchestrating outcomes. This wouldn't be the first time that Lucas had orchestrated an outcome and it wouldn't be the first time that I had honored his wishes. Lucas frequently told me Riley and I had more in common than we knew and that if he died in action, he wanted me to be the one to step in, grab the reins and pick up where he left off. I use to think that was his way of getting me to commit to keeping my promises to him, but I didn't need a whole lot of convincing. I would have done anything for Lucas. And hell I thought Riley was beautiful from day one. Lucas valued Riley's happiness. So did I. I hoped the Cook troops agreed.

As I turned down River Road, and into Riley's cul-de-sac, I could see Xavier in the driveway polishing his black and red Ducati. A little white poodle was stretched out with hind legs behind it, watching over Xavier. I parked the Commander up behind him, being careful not to crowd him. As I tilted my head down peaking over my aviators, I could see the resemblance of Lucas in Xavier. I tried to dress casual and not look too stuffy simply wearing a pair of dark blue jeans, a black muscle shirt, and gym shoes.

"Hey man," Xavier said. "The whole house has been waiting on you."

He moved in close to the car door to greet me. The little white poodle was barking up a storm and circling at my feet.

"Cleo, sit," Xavier ordered. "We have two dogs. This one takes a bit of time to warm up to strangers, but she's lovable at heart. For the record, she's easily won over with doggie treats."

"Good to know," I smiled, shaking Xavier's hand.

He had a strong grip like Lucas.

"You must be Xavier."

"And you're Noah. I recognize you by your "Rockin Wingman" he said, shaking my hand and leaning into my shoulder.

"So you're the man that gots my mother all starry eyed."

Xavier was as tall as me and pretty much able to look at me eyeball to eyeball.

"Your mother is a wonderful woman."

"I understand you and my dad were close friends," he retorted. "Did you guys fly together?"

"Yes we did. He was an excellent pilot."

"So I've heard," he said.

Xavier grabbed my bag out of the back seat.

"Everyone's out back. Get comfortable, grab a beer. Maybe we can shoot some hoops later. You're not too old to play a bit of b-ball, right man?"

"I can hold my own," I said.

Riley ran up to me, hugging me as soon as I entered the back yard.

"Hey baby," I said, as she pecked me on the lips quickly.

"I'm so excited to see you honey. How was the trip down?"

"I couldn't get here fast enough, frankly."

Riley blushed, turning as red as the sheer sleeveless polka dot dress she was wearing with a big red bow at the waist with a ruffle on bottom. Her swimsuit was peeking through underneath. She wrapped me in a huge hug while still holding a spatula in her hands, smelling like hickory chips from cooking the burgers that were sizzling on the grill.

"That's my daughter Samantha," she said pointing to one of the two young women in the swimming pool. "And that's Nena, Xavier's friend," she said pointing at the other.

Samantha and Nena were on floaters in the swimming pool. Samantha was clad in a black bikini, floating on a green lounger reading a copy of Vibe magazine. A golden Labrador was doing laps around her. Nena was on a blue floater in a very skimpy yellow thong swimsuit. She didn't look like a Cook, so I quickly deduced when Xavier threw her a towel that she was the girlfriend.

"X, can you please call Stogie out the pool," Samantha barked.

Unlike Cleo, Stogie the Labrador paid very little attention to me, enjoying the water, swimming as if he hadn't a care in the world.

I wondered somehow if Lucas was behind that dog's name. Lucas and I often had Stogies and vodka night during our down time at the Academy. Samantha gave me a wave from the pool.

"Hey Noah," she said, flipping her sunglasses up, giving me the once over.

"It's nice to meet mom's new boo," she yelled out. "I thought I was going to get to meet you New Year's Eve night but instead I only got to see that hunky chauffeur."

Riley's youngest child came out the back door kitchen.

"Noah, this is my daughter Claire."

Claire was a mini Riley. She had that same exotic look favoring her mother. She wore cut off jean shorts, flip flops, and a t-shirt that said "Take good care of me, I'm hard to replace." A Nikon camera with a long lens hung around her neck. She had a huge tossed salad in her hand, setting it on down with the other side dishes on the picnic table on the deck.

"Hello. You must be Noah, my mother and father's friend. I'm Claire."

"Hello Claire. Nice shirt," I said feeling the sweat beads that had accumulated on my brow, taking note of the lump in my throat.

"Thanks. My father bought it for me when I was first born. Every year on my birthday he would give me a new one. My sister Samantha has carried on daddy's tradition ever since."

"I like shirts that have important messages," I said anxiously, hoping Riley's kids would like me.

"This one's my favorite because it's purple. I love purple. It's a very royal color."

"Very much so. Fit for a queen," I said, thinking the apple doesn't fall to far from the tree. I chuckled out loud turning my attention back to Riley.

"Riley, she has both your beauty and your good taste."

Claire set the salad down and starting snapping pictures.

"You know I'm going to one day be a famous photojournalist," she said while snapping my picture. "I'm practicing food photography so I can one day help with Mommy's books. I'm the creative one in the family," she said loudly in earshot of Xavier and Samantha.

Samantha looked up from her magazine, lifted her glasses off her face, then rolled her eyes, and went back to reading.

"The rest of these clowns look to me for inspiration," Claire said.

"Knock it off Claire," Samantha yelled as she got out the pool and reached for a pack of Newports laying on the patio glider.

"You know I'm right Sammi," Claire laughed.

As Samantha turned, Claire snapped a picture as she bent over.

"Miss hip hop wedgie booty," Claire laughed.

Samantha fell out laughing.

"Tell her to stop, Mother," Samantha said, pleading with Riley.

Xavier reached in the cooler, handed me a beer while grabbing himself one.

"Mother do something with those two."

"Mind your business X," Samantha howled.

"Yeah X, mind your business nappy head," Claire added, setting her camera down on the picnic table and arranging the napkins on the table.

Xavier walked over to Claire, picked her up, and then did the same to Samantha, propping them both under his muscled arms. They both were screaming and moving their legs wildly in his arms.

"Xavier, please, don't egg them on. You know how they can get," Riley pleaded.

Xavier threw them both wildly into the pool. He then dove

in, dunking both their heads under water. Stogie flew in next. Water splashed up high, landing all over the grill. Cleo was running up and down the side of the pool barking as if she were a big dog. I sat down at the table, enjoying this moment of watching the kids at play.

Riley threw up her hands. She came in my direction, wet from the splash, and sat on my lap. I rubbed my hands on the sides of her thighs and patted her twice. I was mentally pleading with the torpedo to stand down.

"Now you've met the family Noah. They appear to be in full form today as usual." She gave me a quick peck.

The kids eventually made their way out of the pool and begun to devour the picnic table full of burgers, corn on the cob, baked beans, and salad. Xavier had managed to talk me in to a quick one on one basketball. He was pretty much whipping my ass on the court despite the fact I thought I played a pretty good game for my age. After we finished basketball, the kids started to make their way inside which left Riley and I to have a few quiet moments alone. The sun was beginning to set.

"Dear you haven't eaten much today," I said.

"I've smelled the food so long cooking it, I don't feel hungry now."

I relished the fact that Riley was a great cook. I could see why her food and wine business was a success. Noticing the ice tub filled with a several different wines, I pulled out the Pinot Grigio to pour her a glass.

"You should at least munch on a burger a bit."

"Good wine choice," she nodded, taking a sip of the cool Pinot Grigio.

I poured myself a glass. I was proud I now knew which wine to pick having previously read all those copies of her book. A nice breeze had picked up in the air, and Riley's brown locks were blowing in the soft breeze.

"Riley, you know I've been thinking for some time now that it is getting time for me to move on from the Navy. I wanted to tell you this in February when we were together, but I thought it best to wait and to give us more time. But I think now is as good as time as any."

"You want to retire?" she said, her expression registering curiosity.

"I've sold all of my investment properties. I have purchased some land nearby here in Bucks County. I'd like not to have do this commuter relationship thing next year. I'd like to be here for you and the kids now."

Riley took another huge gulp of her wine. She was listening intently but still hadn't spoken.

"I'd want to know how you feel about that," I said while grabbing her hand and placing it in mine.

"Noah, I'm very lucky to have you in my world. I want you to be here right by my side. Your coming into my life has helped me to believe in love again. You were special to Lucas then and are special to me now," she said, smiling softly.

I held her a bit more closely.

"Riley, I want to be a part of yours and the kids future. I don't want to take you any faster than you want to go, but I need to be close by . . . here with you now. I love you Riley."

"I love you too Noah."

Riley gave me a long passionate kiss, our tongues exploring each other's mouths in the night air in the dark, a hint of light reflecting off the pool and the solar lights around the deck.

"This is going to be hard having to behave all weekend in front of the kids baby. "

"You don't have to tell me," I said, as I held my arms tightly around her as she sat in front of me now.

"I've been arguing with the torpedo all day," I whispered in her ear. "He's been giving me grief about missing his little friend."

"I suppose we just have to catch as catch can," she said with a smug smile, biting her lip.

"C'mon, I'll help you put the food away. You can show me where you want me to lay my head."

"You know where I want you to lay your head," she groaned.

"Stop it woman," I smirked. "This is hard enough. You need to take it easy on me."

I followed Riley into the house helping her to wrap the food, clean the dishes and put them away.

Changing the subject, she said, "Zoe and Julian, Madison, and Quentin are all coming over tomorrow. We thought we'd meet up with Lily and all of us do after dinner drinks or something. Zoe and Julian are back from their tour."

"Oh yeah?"

"I told them you were here for family time with the kids, but I thought we could squeeze in something much later in the evening. "Is that okay with you?"

"Whatever makes you happy baby," I said drying my hands.

I walked into the living area noticing the wedding photos of Lucas and Riley on the wall. There were numerous pictures of the kids in various stages of their lives at all different ages. I picked up the wedding photo of Lucas and Riley. I remembered when they got married like clockwork. I was supposed to be his best man, but had gotten called out of the country unexpectedly. So Lucas and I got drunk before I left and tattooed ourselves with the Rockin' Wingman Deuces tattoo as our way of sharing his wedding moment together at least in spirit. I would be there with him right on his arm. We never initially intended that I stay in the background from this part of his life. Over time, things had started to get convoluted in his life, but I remained committed to holding up my end of our bargain. There were things between Lucas and I that no one besides us shared or knew. I had remained ever loyal to him up to the bitter end. I know it must have been strange on some level to Riley that I could be Lucas's very best friend in life and she not know of me or about me, but we had our reasons. Sometimes life throws you curve balls. You play the hand you're dealt.

Initially it was a matter of inconvenience that Riley and I hadn't met, but later it became more a matter of purpose. Lucas insisted that we choose to let sleeping dogs lie. He both knew in the deep recesses of our heart that the day would come where I would finally get to openly introduce myself to Riley.

Lucas was good about sharing everything about Riley with me by story, letter, and in person, in anticipation of our one day meeting and loving each other. Lucas was a big letter writer.

Riley and I were meant to be at this place at this point in time in our lives. Lucas had seen to it. I picked up the photo and looked at he and Riley. I mumbled to myself, "Man thank you. She's every bit of the gift you said she would be. I miss you and I love you. Deuces Rockin' Wingman."

Claire walked in the room dressed in her martial arts gear.

"What's up Claire?" I said, her presence pulling me out of my private thoughts of Lucas.

"Oh, I've been down in the basement practicing my moves. I hear you're a black belt like my dad."

"Yeah, he and I use to keep our skills up working out with each other."

I hadn't told her Lucas and I had invested a lifetime of training into martial arts. We both had the ability to pull a man's heart out of his chest without breaking a sweat.

"I'm taking martial arts classes now, following in my father's footsteps. Would you like to come downstairs and help me practice?"

"Sure thing."

After all, I was supposed to be making full use of my quality time with the kids. Claire led me down the stairs to the basement that was set up like a huge recreational area. There were mats, sparing bags, pin ball game machines, a pool table, and a home theatre system. Claire went to the edge of one end of the mat. I took my shoes off before stepping on the mat reminding myself to be gentle with her since I had drank a couple of glasses of wine earlier. I wanted to be mindful of my strength. I stepped to the edge of the mat. I wanted give her a lot of leeway for attack being mindful of the differences in our experience levels.

Claire and I bowed, never taking our eyes off each other. Three quick hand defensive motions and a roundhouse kick from Claire and the next thing I knew I was on my back.

"Oh shit," I said out loud.

"You okay Mr. Noah?" Claire asked.

"No problem," I said shaking myself off.

I tilted my head side to side so as to stretch my neck muscles and loosen up a bit. We bowed a second time politely.

"Hah! Hah! Eweh! Hah," Claire said as she accidentally kicked me in the groin from a side kick that was way too low.

I fucking hit the mat dead on my back again with this kid. I knew I couldn't go full out mano e mano and be on full attack mode with this kid, but damn she was beating me, tearing my ass up with her foot on my throat and me now flat on my back.

"How are you doing Noah?" I heard Riley say sternly. She was coming down the stairs having finished in the kitchen.

I knew for a fact I was looking at Riley with a looked that revealed I had everything under control. Slap. Pow. Slap. I was immediately pulling the punch and now Claire was on the mat. Fuck it. This was starting to get a bit embarrassing to let a fifteen year old kick my ass. Riley was squinting, her eyes narrowing, looking at me with a look of a concerned cat watching over her cubs.

"We're good babe," I said, trying to reassure her.

"Yeah Mom," Claire said. "Don't worry, I got this."

Did she just say I got this? What am I, chopped liver?

I could tell Riley was not happy with any of this. After all, this was her baby. Claire and I bowed a third time. I was mentally cussing myself out knowing that I had to exercise restraint giving Claire leeway to kick me in the chest while at the same time providing instruction.

"Noah , don't you hurt my baby."

Was she kidding? Riley's mini-me was a petite kick ass green eyed ninja that was pounding my old ass into the mat and in no way about to get hurt. Besides I too had a vested interest in ensuring Claire's safety. If she aspired to be an expert in martial arts like Lucas and me, I was going to personally help her reach that goal. Claire and I bowed for a fourth time. Pow Pow, slap slap, kick jab, kick slap, pow, kick slap, jab. I felt like I was the gnat and Claire was swatting my ass. We were moving a whole lot quicker and faster now. God Damn. I had underestimated Claire's training and passion. I dropped my guard casually so as not to hurt her, but that was a mistake. She swirled around quickly kicking me upside my head.

My head starting ringing. I hit the ground hard and fast. I heard Riley say, "Noah are you okay babe?"

I shook my head, got off the mat, and bowed to Claire who bowed back.

"Good job, Grasshopper," I nodded to Claire.

Xavier headed into the basement with Nena tagging behind him.

"Ah man, I hope you weren't' foolish enough to get on that

mat with Claire, dude," he said as he turned up a Corona. "Tell me Noah, you didn't make that mistake?"

"Yeah man," I said as I huffed and puffed and dragged myself up off my knees. I bowed kindly.

"Ms. Claire dear, I thank you for the workout. You're a force to be reckoned with much like your dad. You're progressing along nicely, Grasshopper," I said. "If you're interested, tomorrow I'd can show you some of my special killer moves," I said, breathing excessively and coughing.

My buzz was gone and I was fully sober.

"Noah," Riley said firmly. "That doesn't sound like a good idea to me," she said worriedly.

"Trust me. She's ready."

Claire bowed. I bowed politely and drug my ass off that mat. I don't think Riley was none too happy about anything going on in this picture.

I think Riley had mercy on me after my beat down from Claire. She didn't try to put her own on moves on me. She showed me to the guest bedroom that was tastefully decorated. The room had dark navy blue curtains that elegantly draped a bay window that overlooked the view of the backyard pool area. The was a corner fireplace that I thought was a nice touch. Beautiful artwork adorned on the walls. I recognized the artists. Sylvia Walker and Tom McKinney. I pulled off my tennis shoes and unzipped my blue jeans feeling good to be in my boxers, plopping myself down on the bed that had a navy blue and white pinstriped downs filled duvet. There were large overstuffed pillows filled with goose feathers that occasionally slipped out their casing when I punched the pillow to make myself comfortable. Riley and I had both agreed to try to get some rest respecting, the fact that it had been a very long day.

It was the early crack of dawn when I woke. The torpedo was still a little tender where Claire had kicked the crap out me. I could feel the heat of the sun peeking through the bay window. I sat up on the side of the bed and bitched with myself because I knew I had to get through my early morning pushup regimen. I was starting to question what had Lucas gotten me into as I hit the floor and began my pushups.

Lucas must have been rolling over in his grave in laughter right about now. Riley was fucking my brains out, Xavier was whipping my ass on the basketball court, and Claire was kicking the crap out of me and the torpedo with her martial arts training. The only person left to get a piece of my ass was Samantha. I was starting to speculate the range of possibilities of what Samantha could have had in store for me. This felt like an initiation of some sorts. I was starting to get a bit paranoid looking sideways at this entire family life thing. I completed my daily pushup regimen and limped to the shower. After all, family life was new to me and I had been knocked around this weekend like a dingy on the side of a huge vessel.

I had been a single man for many years since my divorce. I was having a weak moment, wondering what I was really getting myself into as I tucked myself into the hot shower. But my muddled thinking lasted about a single minute. Just as I was starting to enjoy the relaxing steam and hot water pouring on me from the from shower jets above, Riley joined me in the bathroom. She closed the door behind her. She took off her little white fluffy fleece robe revealing her nakedness, joining me in the shower.

"Good morning babe. I knew you were an early bird and would be up at the break of dawn before anyone else in the house, so I decided to come wish you a good morning."

The torpedo was standing at attention now.

"Good morning my love. My ass is sore. The Cook troops got the best of me yesterday," I said grabbing the torpedo and soaping him up.

Riley had her arms around me with her breasts pushed against my chest, her hands on the cheeks of my butt.

"Let me help you with that."

Riley bent down and starting working the torpedo with her lips. I felt like I had died and gone to heaven. The warm water was beating down on both our bodies. I knew I was going to a be turned up, a victim of an early morning turnout.

"Babe this feels like risky business. Do not let these kids know you are in here."

"Those sleepy heads? Are you kidding me? This is way too

early in the morning for them."

"I don't know Riley, kids have Mommy radar. Especially when they think their well settled happy home might be getting ready to take in a new addition. Don't underestimate those kids Riley. They are going to make my ass toe the line," I pleaded between my own moans.

Riley was gonna make me toe the line too, showing the torpedo who was the boss.

"I know a little bit about kids Riley," I panted. "Baby we need to be careful so as to not rock the boat."

Riley kept her lips wrapped around my shaft moaning "Um hum," like I wasn't saying anything of importance.

Fuck it. That's it. I'm already losing this debate. I whipped Riley around quickly and penetrated her soft sex mound from the rear. I put my finger in her mouth across her teeth to prevent the screams I knew I was going to pull out of her next. The warm water was beating down on the both us. I was riding her hard, waking up every inch of her body. I was stroking her long and hard. And she was hula-hooping on the torpedo.

"You want some of this?" I said as I pumped deeper, faster and harder. "You've come out to play this morning gorgeous, so let's play," I whispered in her ear. "The torpedo has missed his little playmate," I said, stroking her from behind with my fingers still in her mouth. She was biting on my fingers hard now but I was determined to keep my hand in place to make sure she didn't take the roof off the house with her screams because I was gonna tear it up this morning. After all, my manhood was in play now, and the torpedo takes it kind of hard when a woman gets the best of him.

Damn, she feels so good, I thought, as the torpedo said 'shut the fuck up man and focus.'

CHAPTER 22

NOAH

Riley and I were on day five of our family time. While Riley had gone grocery shopping, Samantha and I had a chance to have some one on one time talking about the hip hop blogging work she was doing. She'd been a featured blogger for Vibe Magazine's online community, reading me in on the rapper Jay-Z's historical journey from poverty to wealth.

I knew a bit about hip hop and was able to hold my own on the topic, bringing up my own likes about the hot new artist Drake. Xavier injected his feedback into our conversation, eavesdropping while eating in the kitchen, sharing his own theories about how the jazz genre had its influences on hip-hop and neo-soul. I'd promised Xavier he could take me for a spin on his Ducati later. Nena wasn't around, so it would be good to have some male bonding time alone with him. Claire had an oversized life size chess set that was practically half her size set up in the backyard. She and I were playing chess when Riley came home from the store.

"You guys need to end that game Noah," Riley said, sliding the back window open, yelling through it. "It's time to get dressed for the evening."

I was more than happy to get this chess game with Claire over. We'd been playing off and on for the last two days. Claire was a skilled chess player. On a couple of occasions, I had to sit down for a few hours and think deeply before I could move. She had a highly competitive nature. She hated to lose. It wasn't in my nature to lose either. I needed to find one thing that Claire wasn't good at, so I could at least mentor her on something.

I moved my Bishop, capturing Claire's Rook when Riley made her way into the backyard towards us. The reflection of the light dancing off the water from the swimming pool captured

Riley's beauty in a way I wanted to forever remember.

Riley reached over me, planting a kiss on my lips. Still standing behind me, she wrapped her arms around my neck, her face side by side with mine. I was studying the chessboard intensely. Riley's soft body draped around mine was affecting my concentration. Claire's expression revealed she planned to go in for the kill. We both had to stand up out of our chairs in order to move the huge oversized pieces.

"Don't distract me now baby," I said to Riley. "I'm getting ready to send Claire packing."

Riley sized up the positions of the pieces on the board.

"I wouldn't be so sure about that love."

"Oh yeah, I'm winning," I said proudly, my chest pumped up. "This game is soon to be over darlin'."

I grabbed Riley's hand swinging her body around to sit on top of my lap so I wouldn't be distracted further. Claire sauntered over to her Queen, setting it down next to my King.

"Game up, Captain. Checkmate."

"Damn, Riley. I told you not to distract me baby."

Riley laughed, hugging me gently.

"Don't feel bad sweetie. Claire beats everybody."

Good Lord. This petite ninja Claire is a mess.

"What doesn't she excel at Riley?"

"She excels at most everything," Riley shrugged proudly.

"You're a formidable opponent Ms. Claire."

I bowed to honor her win.

Claire pulled her Nikon camera up to her eye and snapped a picture of me and Riley. I grinned from ear to ear feeling much like a silly cartoon character.

"Come baby. We have plans," Riley spoke.

Riley had made plans for us to go out tonight to celebrate Zoe's birthday with Julian, Madison, and Quentin. Lily and Dr. Nathan had also driven down from D.C. for the occasion. I was hoping tonight would be a happy moment for Zoe, because as a twin, that meant today would also be Lucas's birthday as well. I didn't want Zoe or Riley to be sad. Nor did I.

"Lily's had made reservations for the eight of us at the Lambertville Station. Lambertville Station is a premier restaurant located on the riverfront in Lambertville, New Jersey, not too far from Washington's Crossing," Riley said.

"Looking forward to a good birthday party," I winked.

I headed up to the guest room to change for the birthday celebration. I was pleased the dress code tonight was business casual. I didn't feel up to wearing a tie tonight. I showered, dressed and headed back downstairs to wait on Riley.

Riley strolled down her spiral staircase wearing a black lace dress with gold insets on the sides. It was enticing. I imagined her wearing those sexy black garters underneath like she had on the night we were in the limousine coming back from New York City. I had to restrain myself from not slipping my hands under her dress to see.

Xavier had smooth jazz playing on her Bang and Olufsen. "*All The Way*" was playing. I stood as Riley entered the room, watching her glide closer to me. I grabbed her hand, held her close to dance.

"They're playing our song," I whispered in her ear.

"Yes, I know."

"I love you Noah," she said, looking at me with those big brown doe eyes.

"I love you too Riley."

It felt like a poignant moment. I suppose I'm an old school romantic at heart, but one thing for sure, I was in love with this woman. I wanted to grow old with Riley. I want to share her life, the kids. I wanted the whole kit and caboodle. I wanted to put a rock on her finger so big that it would ward off any man that gave a second thought to approaching her.

Madison flew through the door suddenly, with Quentin on her heels, interrupting our romantic moment. Did that woman ever learn to knock? Madison walked in and out of each other's homes as if they owned the place. I needed to get used to it.

"Hey good people. Let's get this show on the road. Break this lovefest up you two. It's getting too damn hot and heavy in here. You guys are like high school sweethearts that can't take their hands off each other," Madison goaded us playfully.

Quentin gave Madison a quizzical look. He was studying me and Riley in his shy laid back kind of way. I found it interesting

Madison was so outwardly outgoing and Quentin so shy and reserved. I made a mental note to ask Riley later what was the deal with those two. I wondered if Riley thought their relationship was going anywhere.

"Who are we waiting for?" Madison asked.

"No one. Lily, Nate, Zoe, and Julian will meet us there."

"Well let's get this party underway."

"Let me grab our gift," Riley answered.

Riley grabbed a crisp white shiny looking bag, with a black sequinned bow tied neatly off the side of one of the white handles. The bag had her company logo on it. I better understood why she was so successful in her business. She did everything so perfect.

RILEY

Noah sat up front in Quentin's black Mercedes, letting Madison and I have our girl time in the back seat.

"So what'd ya get Zoe?"

"Got her a set of crystal stemmed champagne glasses monogrammed with a Z on the front. She's always loved mine. Every New Year's she comments on them so I thought I'd get her a set of her own."

"What'd you get her, Madison?"

"I got her a sleek satin teddy with a matching panty that she can wear to light a fire under Julian," Madison said as we pulled up to the restaurant's valet parking.

Noah opened the back door, helping Madison and I out of the car. Madison and I giggled about the sexy lingerie as the four of us headed inside the restaurant.

The Lambertville Station had such colorful history. It was a restored 19th century train station on the banks of the Delaware river across from New Hope, Pennsylvania. The focal point of the restaurant was an etched glass encased railroad car that sits on the track overlooking a view of the quaint town of Lambertville, New Jersey. The surrounding decor is filled with gleaming brass and antiques and the food is pretty much American cuisine.

The Maître D set up a special area for us in the Victorian room that included a circular table large enough to seat eight. The area was fully lit by candlelight, the ambiance beautiful.

Zoe and Julian had already arrived. Lily and Dr. Nathan arrived shortly behind us carrying black, white, and gold happy birthday balloons. Noah placed an order for three buckets of Verve Cliquot Champagne. My favorite. Julian ordered multiple plates of oyster Rockefeller appetizers for the entire table. I grabbed an oyster off the plate, sucking it down slowly in mouth, the juice gliding across my lips. The oysters had a strong taste of the sea and were succulent in texture. When it came time to place our main entrees, I ordered the Chesapeake Lump Crab Cake while Noah ordered Bistecca Alla Fiorentina. Zoe and Julian settled on the Dijon Rosemary Encrusted Rack of Lamb. Madison ordered the Halibut. Quentin ordered shrimp and linguine.

A couple of glasses of Chianti later, Noah was eyeballing my crab cake. I lovingly fed him forkfuls of my entree here and there. Noah switched off from drinking wine and moved to a vodka martinis. I knew he was buzzed when he slid his hand under the table, rubbing my thigh.

"Behave yourself," I whispered.

"I'm checking for things I like," he said, running his finger under the top of the sheer black nylon attached to my garter.

Zoe was feeling no pain, enjoying her birthday celebration. Madison and Lily were engaged in conversation about both of their teaching experiences. The guys had somehow got on the subject of nearby shooting ranges. Noah got excited, mentioning that he owned the same Walther P99 gun that James Bond carried in all of his movies. The guys were cracking up with each other about their shooting experiences. I reflected momentarily thinking that Lucas too owned that same Walther P99 sidearm as well. I found that discussion most interesting. Did Lucas share with Noah the story about the night he held that unloaded weapon in his lap, pointed it at me, telling me to undress for him. Lucas pretended he was a cat burglar that night. He was successful at getting me to undress for him that night, ratcheting up the sexual tension between us. He'd even handcuffed me while he had his way with me.

Now that I think about it, both Lucas and Noah had wild bad boy tendencies. What did the Naval Academy do to its guys? My brother Reese, an Army officer, was much more restrained. There was something about Navy men that was distinctly different.

My thoughts veered back to the present as Noah ran his hand up my thigh again under the table.

"You're my own favorite Bond girl," he whispered in my ear.

"You're going to be my undoing," I whispered back, sliding his hand back on his lap under the table.

Quentin and Madison seemed to be enjoying each other's company. This was turning out to be a good night except for the fact that Lily and Nathan's relationship was strained. Only I knew they were on the outs. Nathan looked bored to tears, acting as if he didn't want to be here. Lily was acting like she wanted to be here, but not with him.

Quentin and Noah were bonding over some basketball game with LeBron James.

"Yeah Quentin, I purchased some land in Washington's Crossing. Maybe I could retain your real estate company to build Riley and I a home."

That conversation caught Zoe's attention. Actually it caught everyone at the table's attention.

"Oh really?" Madison interjected, her conversation with me coming to a halt.

I knew this subject was going to come up again sooner or later. I hadn't made time to bring my girlfriends up to speed on how far my relationship with Noah had progressed. Luckily, the wait staff interrupted the exchange, moving towards our table with a lit birthday cake filled with sparklers in the middle for Zoe.

"Happy birthday my lovely Zoe," Julian grinned. He kissed her softly, handing her his birthday present. We all gasped as Zoe unwrapped the most beautiful yellow canary diamond necklace that happened to match the lovely yellow spaghetti strapped satin dress she was wearing this evening.

One by one, we each presented our gifts to Zoe. We each watched with love as she opened them.

"I have another present for you Zoe. Come everyone. Follow

me to the wine cellar," Julian said.

The eight of us followed Julian to the downstairs wine cellar area of the restaurant. This part of the restaurant had exposed stone walls with arches and original beam work dating back to the 1800's. The furnishings were contemporary. The room was decorated in rich chocolate brown and soft turquoise that lent itself to a modern sophisticated feel. Wines from all the surrounding wineries in Pennsylvania and New Jersey were slotted in the wine racks all around the room. A baby grand piano was set up in the corner of the room.

We settled ourselves at a long wooden table. Julian sat at the beautiful black baby grand piano. He began singing a new song he'd written especially for Zoe. It was a beautiful song about a man who's love for his woman kept him warm on his most difficult days. The song was entitled, *Happy To Be Near You*.

Julian had recorded it especially for Zoe. The song was to be included in their new album. This was the first time Zoe was hearing it. Teary-eyed, I along with the other guests, each lifted our glasses at the end of the song for a birthday toast. What a wonderful gift.

Noah and I clicked our glasses together saying "Cheers" to Zoe and then we softly kissed. Zoe, clicked her glass against mine as Noah smiled at the both of us.

"To Lucas," Zoe said boldly. Zoe clinked her glass with his.

Noah gazed deeply into Zoe's eyes.

"To Lucas."

It was well after midnight when we left the restaurant. Rain was beginning to sprinkle down out of the clouds. Madison and I were feeling no pain. Quentin and Noah were having fun teasing the two of us, putting the both of us in the back seat of Quentin's Mercedes again, while they both sat up front talking basketball.

Madison and I were chatting it up when I passively focused on Noah's conversation with Quentin.

"What is it Q? Is there something wrong?" Noah asked.

"Probably nothing man. This SUV behind me has been riding

my tail ever since we left the restaurant. I get annoyed when these inconsiderate drivers ride my ass like this on this road in rainy weather."

Noah looked in his side view mirror on the right passenger's side.

"Looks like an Escalade. You know these drivers in these fancy SUV's think they own the road."

"Yeah man, but it's been like this for the last five miles. Maybe I should slam on my brakes and he'll get the message," Quentin grumbled.

"Nah, that's not the right move, lest he end up in your rear end. It's probably some young whipper snapper that's out in daddy's ride tonight that hasn't learned the rules of the road yet. You know how these kids are Q."

"Yeah, well maybe he needs a lesson in road rage tonight."

Noah and Quentin both busted out laughing, slapping each other a high five, before engaging back into their prior conversation again about basketball.

I focused back on Madison and our own conversation right about the same time we arrived back to my home. Rain was starting to patter down harder on the pavement as we pulled up into my circular drive on River Road. Noah and I just finished saying our good-byes to Madison and Quentin, when Nena came flying out the house looking as if someone could have cracked eggs on her head and they would have fried. She was shouting loudly.

"Leave me alone X," she cried.

It was obvious from Nena's anger that she and Xavier were having a fight. A loud clap of thunder rang in my ears from above. It shook me. I practically jumped out of my skin at the flash of lightening that flashed in the distant clouds.

"You need to calm down," Xavier pleaded with Nena. Unmoved by Xavier's pleas, Nena scampered hurriedly into her red Fiat, locking the doors, shutting Xavier out. She put the pedal to the metal, her tires screeching loudly. She sped off, accelerating in an extreme hurry. Before I could speak, Xavier grabbed his Shoal helmet off the back of his Ducati, and was revving the engine.

"Xavier, what's going on here?" I pleaded.

"Nena wait," he shouted out loud, ignoring my pleas.

Xavier lifted the kick stand on his bike.

"Xavier," I repeated. "What's going on here?"

"Nothing, Mother," Xavier snapped.

"Xavier Nelson Cook!" I shouted, commanding his attention.

Xavier wasn't listening to a word I was saying. That damn Cook temperament. The rain was pouring down more heavily the brewing storm worsening and more impending.

"Xavier man, hold on now son. Talk to me brother," Noah pleaded with Xavier.

Xavier, revved the engine like a crazy man, preparing to take off in pursuit of Nena. To my shock and surprise, Noah jumped on the back of the Ducati with him. Before I could say another word, Xavier and Noah were gone on the Ducati, lost into the night. I saw a dark blue Escalade pull out after them. Was that the same car I heard Noah and Quentin discussing on the way home? Maybe my imagination was running away with me. That was strange.

Confused and clueless, my heart was racing. I could feel it about to pop out of my chest. This could not be good. I stormed into the house yelling to the top of my lungs.

"Samantha. Samantha!" I screamed out loud to anyone who would hear me.

I threw my handbag on the table making my way into the kitchen. Samantha strolled in halfway between calm and concerned not fully aware of what was taking place.

"What the hell is happening here with Xavier? Do not lie to me."

"Mom, you know how X is, messing around. He got caught with his pants down again. He can't seem to keep his little head in his pants like most men. Always thinking with the wrong head."

"What do you mean?" I shouted, my voice still raised and animated.

"Nena got wind that he was messing with some girl at the gym named Sophia and the shit was on. They had it out."

I shook my head in disgust hearing this story.

"Xavier told her Nena she was too needy. She called him a manwhore. They were arguing back and forth. One thing led to another and she took off," Samantha replied.

"Good Lord," I mumbled.

"I never much cared for her anyway. That is my brother she was insulting. X is probably the one in the wrong, but little miss jazzy prissy doesn't get to talk about my brother. She's lucky I didn't give her the beat down, talking to my brother like that."

"Samantha, see if you can't get him on his cell phone please," I said shaking my head. "He needs to calm down. He is definitely Lucas's son," I sighed. "Neither can see the forest for the trees when they're pissed."

"Where's Noah?" Samantha asked, looking around the room.

"Jesus Christ, he jumped on the back of the Ducati with Xavier. They're out there together in this dreadful storm on that damn ass bike."

I could hear the rain crashing harder now against the skylights.

"I can't get X to answer," Samantha said, hitting the redial on the on the phone again.

"Keep dialing."

CHAPTER 23

NOAH

"Xavier, you need to slow this bike down son," I shouted through the fierce wind and rain. "This girl isn't going anywhere."

I caught a glimpse of Nena's taillights as her Fiat turned around the bend on the winding road. The rain was beating so hard on my face I could barely see. I only hoped Xavier could see. We were flying down Taylorsville Road in the dark. Xavier wasn't talking. His only mission seems to be to catch up with Nena. Someone was blowing up his phone. Probably Riley. None of this was good.

Xavier was speeding like a freaking mad man. This moment reminded me of how Lucas used to act when he got pissed. All he could see was red when he was mad. I seemed to be the only person that could calm him down and bring him back to his senses. I was hoping I could do the same with his son. There was a lot to be said about DNA.

"Listen man, there's plenty of other fish in the sea" I pleaded. "You don't have to wrestle with this one. Let her go, man," I shouted louder.

The road was hilly. Curvy. The rain was falling heavy and hard. The thunderstorm was way too strong for us to be flying on a bike chasing a woman in the dark at this high rate of speed. I heard the crack of a tree branch fall behind us as a bolt of lightning struck the ground. Fucking crazy ass kids. What happened to ice cream at Baskin Robbins where the woman gets mad and throws a milk shake in your face? These millennial kids are so fucking high drama. Too many hours spent watching reality tv. Nothing but drama with tomorrow's future leaders.

Xavier eased the bike up to the side of Nena's car. We were straddling the yellow line, edging into the lane of any on-coming traffic that might be headed our way. Xavier lifts the front of his helmet, the wind beating hard against the both of us.

"Nena," he yelled, waving his hand wildly. "Pull over."

I turned my head behind me. That same familiar Cadillac Escalade was behind us. Was that a coincidence? Why was this same vehicle on our tail? Xavier's phone rang again. He ignored it.

An on-coming pickup appeared over the hill, its highway lights blasting, flickering against the dark night sky. I suspected neither Nena nor Xavier could see clearly now. After all, who in the fuck would expect anybody to be out on the road in this kind of storm at this hour on a bike driving like a crazy person? Nena slammed on her brakes first, struggling to maintain control of the Fiat. Xavier sped up attempting to get out in front of her. The SUV behind us sped up, leaving us no room to navigate. Nena was trying, yet struggling, to maintain sense of control. The oncoming pickup truck had us squeezed in between it and Nena. Xavier moved to get back in his lane, but the SUV behind us sped up leaving Xavier no room to maneuver. Xavier attempted to position us in between Nena and the ongoing pickup. The SUV behind us flashed its highway lights, blinding the on-coming driver in the pickup truck. The pickup truck swerved our direction, hitting the SUV behind us instead, head on. I heard the sound of the crash behind us as Xavier accelerated, swerving ahead of Nena. Nena clipped the back of the Ducati. Xavier tried unsuccessfully to avoid skidding but he lost control. We hit the guard rail and immediately went airborne.

Everything was moving in slow motion now as if time had slowed to a snail's pace. The ride in the air was so long it felt as if it were taking a lifetime. Was this nightmare ever gonna end? I didn't know any prayers but one, but it felt like a good time to say one, so I said it to myself.

"The Lord is my shepherd," I prayed as Xavier and I went flying through the air, the Ducati tumbling out from under us. I felt an unfamiliar sensation of being held in someone's arms. Lucas? Is that you? I heard my own bones break as I tumbled to the ground. My last thought was of Riley.

Chapter 24

Riley

The next call I received was from St. Mary Hospital's Trauma Center in Langhorne, PA. Too many minutes later I was busting through the double doors of the hospital's emergency room. Madison, Quentin, Zoe, and Julian arrived shortly thereafter. Lily ran through the double doors next. Dr. Nathan blew past of us all saying,

"I got this Riley. Don't worry. I'm here for you."

Dr. Nathan tore through the next set of double doors, directing one of the emergency room nurses to follow. It was well after 2 o'clock in the morning. The nurses insisted I wait for the doctors, pushing me back out of the trauma center. I busted through the doors anyway, fighting my way past the nurses.

I heard the EMT yell out.

"We've got two John Doe DOA's and two in limbo."

Oh good Lord, please don't let them be dead. Who's dead? I began moving along the emergency room patient area pulling curtains back to see who was dead. A young nurse dressed in blue scrubs grabbed me.

"Ma'am, ma'am. You can't be here. You need to wait outside."

"I need to know. I need to know," I screamed in anguish. My son ... my ... my ... "

"What's your family member's name?" she asked, cutting me off. "Calm down. Let me see if I can get you some help."

"I need to know they're okay," I muttered, not making much sense, my arms flailing and my head bobbing wildly.

"We've got two dead on arrival. A black male and a John Doe, un-identified white male."

"You family?" the stout nurse asked. "Privacy laws don't let me discuss these matters unless you're family."

She cocked her head to the side peering at me over her

bifocals.

"My son? Noah?" I pleaded.

I couldn't wait. I tore past her, fighting to see who was in the next bed. I scrambled past the next set of nurses making my way to the patient area. No one was keeping me away from my son.

Finally, I found my son. Bloodied. Convulsing. Another body with a sheet over it was being wheeled past me. Who was the John Doe? I struggled to see what I could see. At least ten people in scrubs were all moving at lightning speed. Samantha was on my heels. She took one look at Xavier, let out a heart-wrenching cry and collapsed on the floor behind me. Thankfully Madison, Zoe, and Lily had managed to hold on to Claire. I looked to my left. The doctors had a crash cart with paddles. It was Noah. They were doing CPR on Noah. They were yelling loudly, each person moving in sync like a fine tuned orchestra.

"We need to get him to surgery stat," Nathan ordered, as he injected Noah with multiple needles, screaming for everyone to get him to the OR. A sea of folks in blue rolled Noah out on a gurney with a nurse in blue on top of him holding an oxygen mask, pumping it incessantly. A police officer ran to assist Samantha.

"Leave her. She'll be fine. I need to see to my son."

The police officer scooped Samantha into his arms, taking her back out of the patient area. Zoe, Lily, and Julian rushed to her aid. The stout nurse caught up with me, shoving me back harder this time. We were directed to go to the family waiting area on the third floor. I was hysterical. Noah was already headed up to surgery, and Xavier was headed there next.

By the time I reached the third floor waiting room, I was crying out loud in anguish. I could hardly catch my breath. Madison and Quentin were close on my heels.

"Oh, God. Please don't let me lose Xavier and Noah," I moaned. "Please Madison. Help me. I can't lose my son. I can't lose him. Them."

I shook my head in tears, sobbing in Madison's lap.

"We need to pray now," Madison said, rubbing my head. Claire and Samantha were both crying, huddled up in the corner of the room supporting each other. Lily put her arms around me.

"It's gonna be okay Riley. Nathan is with them. Nathan is not going to let anything happen to them Riley."

I nodded my head in agreement, still unable to speak,

profuse tears flowing down my face.

"The hospital has granted Nathan emergency privileges. He'll be in the operating room the whole time. Nathan will take care of them Riley."

By now even Quentin was pacing the floor. Zoe had pulled her rosary out and was fingering each bead repetitively. Silently. Julian was holding onto Zoe who was in tears.

"Mommy, I called Uncle Reese. He'll be here soon. He's flying down in one of the Milk Money private jets," Samantha said.

I nodded, saying nothing.

"He said to tell you he'll be here as soon as the weather breaks."

Every hour passed far too slowly. I was overdosing on coffee. It was eight a.m. and the nursing staff was changing shifts. We all were sprawled out in the third floor waiting room awaiting word from one surgical team or the other. The waiting area was small with a sofa, love seat, a small table, and several chairs lined around the walls. My friends and family completely filled the room, which was a blessing in disguise. There was no more room for anyone else besides us. I didn't want to break down in front of strangers. I occasionally stood up to look out the window which faced the hospital parking lot. We each seemed to have taken turns pacing the floor, in between a few hours of sleep here and there.

Nena had come in around seven a.m., but left in tears, too distraught to stay. I hugged her and told her what I knew so far. She was the only one that managed not to get hurt in last night's accident. She kept babbling about the driver in the Escalade that kept flashing its high beams, blinding the other drivers. She felt responsible for starting the chain of events on everything that happened last night. I wanted to let her know this wasn't her fault. But I didn't have enough words. I supposed she figured it wasn't a good idea to stay, especially since Samantha was throwing her daggers with her eyes. She finally left. The truth was, this was our family crisis. She couldn't help us. Hopefully she had family and friends of her own to support her through this melee. Our night had been filled with hours of crying, hugging and silent moments of reflection.

Finally, Nathan entered the waiting room in his blue scrubs looking drained, sweaty, and fatigued. He hugged me.

"Riley, Xavier is out of surgery. He's going to pull through but he's pretty broken up. He has several broken ribs. One of his ribs punctured his lungs. We had to remove his spleen."

"Oh good Lord," I spoke, covering my mouth with my hands to quell my moans.

"Thank God he had a helmet on. He's going to live, but he'll have a long recovery. His youth is on his side. He'll need several months of physical therapy."

I nodded, so grateful that Dr. Nate had said my son would live.

"What about Noah?" Lily said, asking the question I wanted to but was afraid to ask.

"Riley," Nathan said softly, still holding my hand. "Noah's not out of the woods yet. He has a severe head injury. We're working hard to address the hematoma on his brain. He didn't have on a helmet. He got thrown pretty far off that bike. There's swelling in the brain."

"Nathan," Lily said, not finishing her sentence.

"The good news is he managed to land on a portion of the river bank that was layered with sand in anticipation of some construction to be performed. That helped to cushion his impact," Nathan said, ignoring Lily.

"Thank you for all you're doing Nathan," I managed to get out, tears still flowing down my cheeks. I inhaled a deep breath, hoping to calm myself.

"The fact that he's physically fit for a man his age helps. He's going to need a lot of blood. I expect him to be in surgery for several more hours before I can answer what his chances are Riley."

Lily, stepped closer to her husband.

"Well Nathan you just fucking get in there and see to it that he pulls through, you hear me. You see to it that Noah pulls through!" she cried. "You see to it Nathan!" she ordered, collapsing in the chair.

I put my hand on Lily's shoulder to calm her down and to keep her from whipping Nate's ass. Lily was already angry with Nathan generally at this point. He ignored Lily's demands and kept his eyes focused on me.

"I'll give blood," Quentin spoke up.

"Me too," Zoe added.

"We'll all give," Samantha added as the tears rolled down her face.

"Okay, I'll send someone up to take care of it and you can all give. That would be great," Nathan nodded solemnly.

"Can I see my son?"

"Sure, I'll come back and get you when's he out of recovery Riley."

I don't know how long I'd been nodding off when I heard Claire's voice jostle me out of my sleep.

"Uncle Reese."

I opened my eyes to see Reese hugging both Claire and Samantha in an embrace.

"I'm here for you girls. Your brother's going to be fine. I promise you."

I bolted out of my seat, rushing into my brother's arms. I was uplifted by his unwavering faith regarding Xavier's prognosis. I prayed my son would live, but I was uncertain as to what to expect for his long term recovery. Reese was the beacon of strength I needed to get through this adversity.

"I got here as fast as I could Riley. Nicholas loaned me the use of his jet. He's in Rio on *The Julianna*. I promised him I'd keep him informed on Noah and Xavier's status. This storm is battering the entire East Coast. It took hours for us to get clearance to take off, but I'm here now. How's my nephew?"

"Nathan said he's going to pull through. Noah's still in surgery," I muttered before breaking down again, hardly able to get the words out past the lump in my throat.

"Let's hope for the best. Nicholas was beside himself upon hearing about the accident from Harper. I was with her when I got the call. Nicholas is practically ready to send in an army of the best team of doctors and medi-vac them to New York," Reese sighed, rubbing his hand across his clean shaven head.

"I'm the one that is beside myself," I moaned, breaking down in tears again.

"Let's hope for the best for the both of them Riley," Reese said, pulling me close to him, hugging me. "Where's your posse?"

"They went for coffee downstairs in the cafeteria. Do you want me to have them bring you anything up?"

"No, I'm fine," Reese said, tossing his weekender bag in the corner. "Tell me what happened Riley."

I spent the next thirty minutes bringing Reese up to speed on the birthday party and the drama that was underway when Noah and I arrived back home. Reese listened intently, holding my hand throughout my recount of last night's events, right up the point of which we were all asked to give blood.

"Warren is dead," Reese said somberly.

"Warren? What's Warren got to do with this?"

"I checked with the police captain here while I was waiting on the tarmac for hours. Warren was the driver in the Escalade. He'd been following you guys all night. He followed you guys from the restaurant back to the house. He was killed, Riley."

All of a sudden it hit me. Warren was the black male John Doe. Dead on arrival. DOA. My senses were back on overload again.

"What does this have to do with Warren, Reese?"

"A while back I told you I hired a private investigator to look into his sabotaging your presentation. My investigator's been compiling a case against him that would hold up in Pennsylvania. Warren's been stalking your moves, off and on for the last year. The fact he showed up at the gala was no accident."

"Oh my God," I gasped, placing my hand over my mouth in disbelief. "Why didn't you warn me?"

"I didn't tell you because the investigator said he was no longer a real threat. His girlfriend Leah Chen left him. He stopped snooping around right about the time my investigator was ready to pull out all the stops and close in on him. We figured he knew we were on to him. We had enough on him to have him arrested for stalking. But he stopped cold. He hadn't been sniffing around so he was back off our radar. The investigator figured he lost interest and moved on. Unfortunately, that wasn't true."

"This is so hard to believe Reese."

"I only have the preliminary details, but Warren was the main cause of this accident."

"I can't believe he would stoop so low. Did he hate me so much he would try to kill my son? Kill Noah?"

"Warren was a bad person. He was selfish. Jealous. He never had your best interests at heart Riley. He only cared for himself. I can't say that I'm sorry he's dead. The world is a better place without him."

"Warren was a lot of things, but I would never wish him dead."

"I can't say I share that emotion, but okay Riles. I'm a man. I know what he was capable of here. He meant my family harm."

I was glad my brother was here. I needed him. Whatever happened next, I knew I could get through it with Reese at my side. I couldn't believe Warren was dead. My mind and body were numb to the news. My love for him was long gone. He felt like a stranger to me, a bad apple that meant me no good. The universe had protected me from marrying him. For that I was grateful. But part of me was sad that as a grown man, Warren never evolved into being a good person. I prayed that his soul would have peace in the next life. At least my brother wouldn't have to go to prison for killing him. I sat back down in my chair to collect my thoughts. Reese sat next to me holding my hand while I rested my head on his shoulder.

A young professional looking woman in a grey suit arrived hours later. She identified herself as the hospital's Patient Advocate assigned to our family. Her job was to shuttle each of us individually to the laboratory area where a phlebotomist would draw each of our blood. I signed permission slips and a waiver allowing an insistent underage Claire to give blood. Reese was first in line to give. Everyone else followed.

A few hours later, Nathan returned.

Chapter 25

Riley

"Riley, you can see Xavier now. We have him heavily sedated, so I doubt he'll know you're there," Nathan replied.

"He'll know," I stated, pools of tears forming in the back of my eyes again. "Any news on Noah, yet?"

"He's headed to recovery. I expect to get an update any moment now Riley. I'll keep you informed. You'll be the first to know," Nathan said.

"I'd like to go see Xavier first by myself, if you guys don't mind," I said turning to everyone in the waiting room.

Reese nodded in agreement.

"Zoe, you and Reese take Samantha and Claire in next when I come out."

Samantha had been chain smoking Newports all night. She was jittery from the excess coffee and cigarettes. I figured it was a good idea for her to see her brother with her Uncle Reese and Aunt Zoe rather than go it alone in case she felt faint again. Claire was a real trooper. Tough as nails. I knew she'd be a source of support for her big sister.

I walked down the long hallway to the patient room where Xavier was resting. My nerves were frayed. I thanked God silently again for sparing me my son. Now I wanted him to spare my man.

"Please Lord," I whispered, quietly opening the door to Xavier's room, "Don't let me lose Noah."

I can't say I was fully prepared to see my beautiful darling son like this. It felt cruel. Xavier was black and blue. His beautiful locks were gone. His head had been shaved to get pieces of metal and glass out of his head. Oh, God, he's gonna be so pissed when he finds out his locks are gone. I rubbed my hand across the cast on his arm which stopped just short of his rock-in wingman tattoo. His eyes were closed.

A nurse entered the room to adjust the intravenous tubing that was coming out of his left arm.

"We're giving him Propofol."

"Isn't that the drug they gave Michael Jackson?"

"Yes, but it's very safe. Not to worry, mom," the nurse replied gently.

I put my hand in my son's hand.

Lucas, watch over our boy. He is my first born. Watch over him Lucas. The tears rolled softly down my cheek. I feel like this is a nightmare Lucas.

"Xavier, I'll bring you some jazz up tomorrow to listen to baby. I know you'll like that."

I spoke expecting him to hear me. I needed him to hear me.

"You're going to make it through this baby. Mother's going to help you get through this baby."

Behind Xavier's black eye, I thought about how much he looked like Lucas. I pulled the sheet back slightly. His muscular chest was tightly bandaged. I hoped he was warm. He didn't have a whole lot of color in his skin.

A nurse stepped in startling me out of my thoughts.

"I need to change his catheter. You might want to step out for a bit."

I nodded okay, and quietly headed back to the waiting room to join the others. Nathan was arriving the same time as me. His face looked tense and strained. *Please lord, let this be good news. I know you don't put more on us then we can bear, but I feel like I've reached my limit as to what all I can bear now Lord.* The look on everyone's face was quite indescribable. I lacked a label or proper emotion to describe the air filling the room. I looked for my brother Reese, but he was nowhere to be found. Instead, I looked back and forth between at Zoe, Lily, and Madison.

"What is it?"

"Let's sit, Riley," Nathan said.

"No I'll stand," I said, intuitively knowing to shore myself up.

"Okay, then." Nathan exhaled.

"Riley, Noah is in recovery. He's pulled through the surgery. He is in intensive care. The next 48 hours will be critical. He's lost a lot of blood but his chances are good."

"Oh thank God." I let out the gush of air I'd been holding.

"There's one thing Riley."

Nathan paused, dropping his head a bit.

"Go ahead. Spit it out Nate," I snapped nervously.

"Okay then."

He paused again. I waited.

"Regarding his blood, Riley . . . ," he said, pausing slowly. "Noah has a rare blood type, and only one of you here in this room was a match."

"What? What do you mean, rare blood type?"

I felt confused.

"Riley, his blood type is rare. Not many people have it, which makes donors more difficult to find."

"What exactly are you saying, Nathan? What do you mean? There's no blood?"

Nathan cleared his throat. Lily was staring at Nathan like a cat readying itself to leap on its kill. Still Nathan had not spoken.

"No, we have a donor."

"Who?"

My mind was working overtime. Who in this group of friends and family could have a rare blood type the same as Noah's? Lucas and I were O Positive. Was someone in here related? A sister, a brother perhaps? I didn't get it.

"It's Claire, Riley. Only Claire is a match."

"Claire?"

A pregnant pause followed by complete silence fell over the waiting room.

"Claire?" I repeated. "What does that mean exactly, Nathan?"

Zoe backed up ten paces as if to be teetering on falling, her knees perhaps about to give out.

"Claire and Noah, Riley," Nathan said, grabbing my elbow in case I needed support. "Claire and Noah are father and daughter."

The silence was suddenly deafening. You could hear a pin drop in the room, even though a train was roaring through my head. My mind went into overdrive. I glared at Nathan as if he were speaking a foreign language. I simply could not process what he was saying. Claire turned her attention from the magazine she was reading and rolled her eyes side to side, gauging first my expression, then Zoe's.

"Noah and Claire are father and daughter Riley. They are 99.999% match. I've run the blood tests three times. I'm certain of it. I'm sorry you have to hear this information this way."

"Oh shit," Madison said, falling back to her seat.

"Nathan what in the hell are you saying exactly?!" Lily yelled. "What the hell, Nathan?!" she yelled at him again.

"Shut up Lily. I've run the test three times, so get the fuck off my ass will you?!" he shouted back, stepping closer to her.

Lily and Nathan were practically in each other's face now

"It's been an emotional time for me too Lily Maria DeLuca," he snapped back at her.

"Fuck you Nathan!" Lily screamed at him.

I couldn't tell if this was still about Noah and Claire. Whatever was going on between Nathan and Lily, it felt like something else.

Nathan was shouting at Lily in Italian now. Lily was arguing back at him in Italian. I hated that I understood what they were saying. It was too personal. None of it any good. Lily turned her back on Nathan, folded her arms and walked towards the window. We were all stressed and way too fatigued.

"You people really know how to keep shit real around here," Samantha grumbled. "Fuck this. I'm going outside to smoke. And then I'm going to see X," Samantha said, stomping towards the door appearing totally out of control.

"Samantha," I snapped.

"This is some goddamn Billie Jean shit," she shouted back at me.

Samantha plain lacked the ability to cope with what she just heard. I reminded myself to give her a pass for her outburst. This was hard on everyone. Samantha was never quite as strong as she liked to present herself.

"I need to get back to Noah," Nathan mumbled.

He left our waiting room totally overwhelmed.

"Maddy, I need to tend to some things," Quentin said. "Is it okay if I take a break?"

"Go ahead," Madison said, waving her hand at him to move on.

Quentin kissed Madison on the top of her head on the way out.

I paced slowly around the waiting room, my eyes landing on Zoe. Tears were running down her face and she was shaking her head.

"I know you don't understand, Riley," Zoe said, between her sobs, crying even harder now.

"Zoe," I said softly. "What don't I understand?"

"Huh," she said, her eyes still not looking at mine.

"Tell me Zoe."

"Yeah Zoe, tell us," Madison snapped.

Madison, Zoe, Lily, Claire, and I were the only ones left in the waiting room now.

"Claire, baby will you check on your brother for me please? I need to talk privately with Aunt Zoe."

"Okay Mom, but maybe you and I can talk privately later."

"Absolutely sweetie."

I reached over and hugged Claire, my eyes following her as she headed down the hall towards Xavier's room.

Zoe was still crying and babbling, making no sense at all.

"Tell me Zoe," I said as calmly as I could trying to slow Zoe's babble down. "Tell me what I don't know."

Zoe was shaking her head no back and forth as if she didn't want to speak.

"I know you know. Lucas *always* told you everything. You two *always* kept secrets," I said with an acute sense of purpose. I wanted to know exactly what Zoe knew.

The three of us were crowding closely around her. Madison had crossed her arms and was biting down hard on her bottom lip, a look of contempt flashing across her face. Lily just plain looked like the deer in the headlights.

"HE COULDN'T HAVE CHILDREN, RILEY!" Zoe screamed. "LUCAS WAS STERILE, OKAY?" she shouted as she collapsed backwards in a nearby chair.

The tears were streaming down her face and snot was running out her nose.

"What else Zoe?" Lily said with anticipation, her hands revealing a slight tremble as she leaned in resting her hand on Zoe's shoulder.

"Yeah, what the fuck else?" Madison said, totally agitated, a look of frustration mounting on her face, her foot tapping nervously.

I gazed deeply into Zoe's eyes, searching for truths.

"Give it to her Zoe," Julian said, moving from across the corner of the room, towards Zoe to console her.

Damn, in my hysteria, I hadn't noticed that Julian had re-entered the waiting room. How long had he been here?

"Give me what?"

"There's a letter," she sobbed. I've been carrying it in my purse for several days now. I figured since you and Noah were getting close, maybe this was a good time for me to give it you."

"A letter," I whispered out loud.

"It's a letter from Lucas," she wailed. "Lucas gave me a letter. He said *'The day may come when you might have to give this letter to Riley, Zoe,'*" Zoe said, attempting now to pull herself together.

She coughed to clear her throat and straightened her shoulders. She was now sitting more erect. She was more in control.

"He told me you didn't know he was sterile. He wanted to tell you, but you were so damn determined to have another baby. You wouldn't leave it alone. You kept pushing and pushing him to have another," she said curtly, as if she were annoyed with me.

"You kept this from me?" I said in disbelief, feeling a sense of betrayal sweeping over me. I was starting to feel light-headed from listening to her words.

"I kept my brother's confidences Riley. I'm not a snitch. If I were, then I would, but I'm not, so I didn't. Okay? We fought over it. I wanted him to tell you. But he's my brother. He's my twin brother, Riley," Zoe said with a lot more authority, daring me to challenge her loyalty to her brother.

Julian handed Zoe his handkerchief. She wiped her nose then cleared her throat.

"Lucas said "One day you'll know when it's the right time to give her this letter." That's all I know Riley," she hissed, blowing out a noisy breath and flipping her hair. "Riley. I know nothing more. This business with Noah and Claire, I know nothing else," she shouted.

Julian gently putting his arms around his wife in his efforts to calm her down.

"It's okay now, Zoe. What's done in the dark is coming to the light. This will all be okay baby. You don't have to hold this in anymore."

Zoe reached in her purse and handed me the letter from Lucas. I stuffed it in my jacket pocket. Then I tore out of the waiting room.

CHAPTER 26

RILEY

I walked out the double doors of St. Mary's Hospital emergency room doors certain I was caught in a some kind of horrible nightmare. My head was spinning. I felt certain I could feel my blood pressure rise. It was late afternoon. I was beyond tired and emotionally spent. I drove down Route 332 and headed straight to Home Depot in Langhorne. Lucas's letter was burning a hole in my pocket.

I pulled into Home Depot's parking lot and opened my trunk. I pulled out my white workout gym shoes and put them on my feet, throwing my heels in the trunk. I realized I still had on my cocktail clothes I'd worn to Zoe's birthday party. I made my way through Home Depot and went straight back to the hardware department. I found a scruffy kid salesperson walking down the aisle dressed in one of those little orange jackets.

"Can you show me where to find the hammers?"

"No problem, Ma'am, we have them right here."

I peered at the selection of choices, as he grabbed a hammer down off the top shelf.

"No I'm going to need something a bit bigger."

He look at me puzzled, not quite sure what my needs were. I walked further down the aisle until I found what I needed. I made my purchase and left the store.

I got back in my car, headed to Newtown. The short fifteen minute ride felt like a lifetime as my car passed through the black wrought ironed gates. Average White Band's old school song *Cloudy* was playing on my radio. The song seemed oh so fitting for this particular moment in time. As I listened to the melody, I never felt more alone in my life. I felt lost. Confused. Broken. Betrayed. Who could be trusted?

I made a left turn at the entrance of the black rod iron gate. I drove down three rows. I parked my car. I turned the radio up loudly, rolling my window down so I could hear the music play outside of the car.

I stepped out on the thick green grass that looked as if it had been freshly cut. Well-manicured. The smell of fresh flowers floated in the air. I was comforted by the fact that Newtown Cemetery was still as peaceful as I always remembered. It was one my favorite places to come and think. To talk to Lucas. But in my heart I knew I would not be returning for a while after today.

I leaned up against the side of my car, taking in the view before moving to the rear of my car, opening my trunk. I pulled out the newly purchased sledgehammer that still had the Home Depot sticker affixed to the side of the thick wood handle. It was time for me to talk to Lucas.

"Lucas, it's me, Riley."

And then I swung that fucking sledgehammer hard enough to chip a corner piece of the granite stone off.

"Why Lucas? Why would you do this to me?" I cried.

I swung hard again.

"You bitch ass mutherfucker you. Secrets, Lucas?"

I swung hard again.

"You've got secrets now Lucas? Fuck you Lucas," I wailed, crying harder now. My nose was starting to run, snot running from my nose. I was wailing to the top of my lungs while dropping to my knees. My tears were streaming heavily down my face.

"You sorry piece of shit!" I yelled up to the heavens, shaking my fists in the air. "You've got something to say to me now, motherfucker after all these years, do you? Well let's fucking hear it now you bitch ass mutherfucker."

I stood up. I took another hard swing chopping another large chunk of his tombstone off.

"And for the record muthafucker, if I don't like what you have to say, I'm gonna beat you with this sledgehammer some more motherfucker."

Half of Lucas's tombstone was cracked off but I didn't care.

"I want some fucking answers motherfucker. How could you betray me like this, Lucas. You and your fucking grand schemes. Always trying to control some shit. You're not in charge here Lucas, you hear me. You are not in charge!" I screamed as I swung yet another time.

"Fuck you, Lucas."

I dropped the sledgehammer down on the ground, and walked back towards my car.

"And you'd better see to it my Xavier doesn't die, you sorry piece of shit."

I turned, walking back two feet to the mess of chipped concrete on the ground, picking up the sledgehammer and cracking his tombstone two more times.

I returned to my car, putting the sledgehammer in the back seat and drove home.

CHAPTER 27

RILEY

I wondered if this day could get any hotter. It was August. Today was my birthday. I wasn't in a celebratory mood. I preferred the day come and go without much of a fanfare. I hadn't talked much with anyone the last couple of months. I'd spent most my days and nights the last few months at the hospital.

The best present I could ever have was outside at poolside catching the sun's rays. I glanced out my kitchen window for the third time. My son was home. His crutches lay at his side next to a wheelchair that Samantha wheeled him in around the house. He was going through his exercise regimen with the help of one of his friends, Dr. Elliot Fischer. Elliot was in his last year of residency in obstetrical medicine at a New York hospital. He'd come down several weekends to help Xavier with his therapy. I was pleased he had another male around to encourage him. I was pleased his therapy was coming along well. He was walking much better and picking up some much needed weight. His hair was still extremely short, but he was wearing it straight now. My brother Reese was calling him every day, prodding him about getting back to his game weight so he wouldn't feel so guilty about wiping him up on the basketball court. Xavier seemed to work extra hard with Dr. Fischer on the days he talked to Reese. I suppose that was some testosterone thing between them. It seemed silly to me, but whatever worked, I was all for it.

Samantha told Xavier how handsome he looked every chance she got, secretly hoping he wouldn't grow his dreads back. She tended to his every whim, short of tending for an invalid. Xavier couldn't get too far out of her sight. She screened all his phone calls, ordering the flood of girls that were calling to call back at another time. Surprisingly Xavier was letting

Samantha have the reins. He claimed he wanted time to heal and to digest the loss of his relationship with Nena. He said he was enjoying being a single man again.

I hit the play button on my answering machine. It was Madison. She was starting to sound like a broken record these days.

"Riley, girl, read the letter. It's time. Read the letter Riley. It's time to put this behind you."

I hit the delete key. I realized on some level Madison was probably right, but there was only so much information I could take in at one time. I reached inside my refrigerator, looking for the picture of lemonade I'd made earlier in the day. I poured myself a tall glass, glancing out the window at my son who was trying to lift the weights while Dr. Fischer was spotting.

The doorbell rang, which thanks to Claire was now playing "Happy Birthday To You" all month. I wasn't much in a birthday mood. Claire however wasn't going to let my birthday go by unnoticed. I suppose it was her way of keeping my spirits up. But the reality was I was just plain numb.

I opened the door finding a young professionally dressed twenty-something woman on my doorstep.

"I'm looking for Ms. Riley Cook."

"That would be me," I answered casually, still holding the cool glass of lemonade in my left hand as I propped myself up against the door jam.

"Ms. Cook, I'm a personal shopper. Some time ago, Mr. Noah Dunham made arrangements for you to receive this package. I've been unable to reach him. But I'm still following his strict orders to see to it that you get this."

She held up the signature teal blue bag with a white corded handles from Tiffany's.

"But I'm certain he would want you to have it. I recall him saying he was buying it for your birthday. It is your birthday today, right?" she said.

"It is," I answered.

"Oh great," she said, looking relieved. "I thought since I lived in the area, I'd make the delivery for him. Is he okay or perhaps out of the country?"

"No, he was in a terrible accident. He's been in a drug induced coma now the last couple of months."

"Oh my goodness. I'm so sorry to hear it. I sure hope he is going to be okay? He seems like a really nice guy and it's clear you're someone very special to him," she said, her voice filled with concern.

"Well we're all hoping for the best, yes."

"Well happy birthday Ms. Cook," she said, handing me the tiny blue gift bag.

"Thank you very much."

I watched as the young woman headed back down my driving way, a lump gathering in my throat. *Do not cry again Riley.*

I headed upstairs to my bedroom, plopping myself down on the chaise, sighing a bit before opening the gift. I slowly pulled the white satin ribbon off the tiny blue box. It is a beautiful charm inside a turquoise blue porcelain jewelry box. A lovely 24k gold birthday cake with a lit candle sticking out the top. I pulled the tiny white card out of the envelope.

"Happy Birthday Gorgeous. May I always be the one to fulfill the silent wishes you make. Forever Yours, Love, Noah."

I pulled down my large wooden hand-carved jewelry box resting on the top shelf of my armoire. I put the new charm next to Noah's bracelet that was adorned with the other charms he'd given me. I placed the larger wooden jewelry box back on top of the shelf of my armoire, closing the double doors shut tight. A small tear that had pooled in the back of my eye escaped and stained my cheek. I quietly wiped it with the back of my hand.

My phone rang. It was Lily.

"Happy Birthday Riley."

"Thank you Lily."

"Don't you think we should do something to celebrate Riley?"

"Not in the mood."

"You've been depressed for a while now Riley. It's time to snap out of it girlfriend."

"How are things with you and Nathan?" I asked, changing the subject, hoping to distract Lily from talking about me.

"They're going. I think Ms. CNBC has left him."

"Really?" I asked, quizzically.

This was a surprise. New news indeed.

"Yeah I think Nathan spent so much time there in Pennsylvania making sure Xavier and Noah were gonna make it out the woods that I think she decided he was trying to make up with me," Lily giggled.

"Get out," I chuckled back.

"Yeah, from where I sit, it doesn't seem like things are going so well in MS. CNBC's paradise."

"How's Gabriel?"

"He's surviving. He's got his head in some new research on pancreatic cancer. I think his own relationship has hit the skids. I overheard him a couple of days ago, talking on the phone with his med school classmate Elliot Fischer about looking moving to New York at the end of his Doctors Without Borders stint and hanging out with him and X. A move to New York would be good for him right now. He's not too happy about the marital discord between Nathan and me, but it is what it is."

"And what about you Lily? How are you doing?"

"I'm taking it one day at a time Riley."

There was an awkward moment of silence.

"Riley have you read the letter yet?"

"No I haven't."

More silence.

"I finally got around to buying Lucas a new tombstone

though. I thought since Xavier was coming home, if he paid him a visit, I didn't want to upset him. So I had a new one put in to replace my makeover."

"Well that was the right thing to do Riley. No need to go to war with the kids over your crazy moment of trying to kill the dead. But I feel your pain girlfriend. Nathan's lucky he still has both his heads," Lily laughed.

"Nathan's a lucky man indeed," I grumbled.

"I think he sleeps with one eye open now. After he heard what you did at the cemetery, he's afraid I might take a notion to starting my own chop shop on that little head of his."

"Well in my case I eventually made improvements. I added one of those nice granite seats so we could have a place to sit down."

"Hmmm. Improvements. Now that's a thought. A new and improved version. I can get with that," Lily laughed.

I was laughing myself now at Lily. It felt good to laugh.

"You're making my day Lily. Nate will come around. You'll see. Give him time to come back to his senses."

"Riley you know Madison and I are your closest friends. We've talked it over. We both agree you should read Lucas's letter."

"I'm not sure I care what Lucas has to say at this point," I said taking a huge swig of my lemonade, and stretching across my bed.

"And you know Riley, not for nothing, Zoe's taken this whole thing real hard. It's her twin brother. You know she needs information too Riley. She has her own level of pain behind this whole matter."

"Don't we all," I said dismissively.

"Maybe today would be a good day to gift yourself the gift of moving on."

Moving on. Now that was a concept that would scramble my brain into oblivion. How does one move on from finding out that their child is not their husband's child. A dead man can't talk any more than one in a coma.

"C'mon Riley. You gonna read the letter or what?"

"Perhaps. I've got to run now Lily," I said, eager to get off the call.

"Thanks for checking in with me."

I hung up. I knew Lily and Madison were right. I just didn't know where to start. It had become increasingly difficult for me to separate the present from the past. Sadness had nestled inside my heart and made a permanent home. My dead husband's best friend is my lover. And unbeknownst to me, the father of my child. Lucas is dead. Noah's in a coma. Everything has gotten so complicated with our lives. My present so tangled with my yesterday's that now have to be taken apart. And to think I always thought Warren Shaw's betrayals were a result of my own poor judgment clouded by my vulnerability and grief from the loss of Lucas. Who knew years later I would find myself betrayed yet again. Except now the betrayal is by the hand of Lucas and Noah. Right when I finally felt I could trust and love again, sadly, I find my heart shattered yet again.

My feelings of disgust and aloneness resurfaced again as I walked back outside to the pool area. They were familiar emotions that appeared everyday almost like wearing an overused worn sweater. Stogie was in the pool again. Cleo was in Xavier's lap licking his face. Dr. Fischer was gone. I walked over to Xavier and gave him a kiss on his forehead.

"Mother, you are the best mom in the world. Priceless. I can't imagine my life without you."

"I couldn't imagine my life without you either, son."

"Mother, I feel I need to say something to you."

"What is it honey. You feeling okay? Should I be worried about you?"

I pulled up one of the wooden lawn chairs and sat down in it next to my son.

"No, it's you I'm worried about. Mother, you know Noah loves you deeply. He got on the back of my Ducati that night for you. He was trying to protect one of your prized possessions," Xavier said.

"I don't know that I can talk about this yet baby. It'll only make me cry again."

"The man has something to teach all of us about love. Maybe you should try harder to see your way to forgiving him and Dad.

Dad is dead, but Noah is not. He's going to pull through, I know he is."

I nodded my head silently in agreement but no words came out of my mouth.

"And when he does, you will need to decide if he is going to have a place in your life. One thing this experience has taught me, is that life is too short. And it's especially short to be without someone who loves you like that."

I squeezed his hand tightly, fighting back the tears that were forming in the back of my eyes.

"I know you're in pain Mother, but please try. Do it for me. I want you to be happy. Noah made you happy. I'm a grown man. You can't sit around here and coddle me all your life. You need someone to be there for you sometime. You're a beautiful woman and you're not dead yet," Xavier huffed.

"How did you get to be so wise, son?"

I grabbed Xavier's hand, putting it to my lips, kissing it softly. I was moved by his profound sense of wisdom at such a young age. I was certain his near death experience had matured him some more.

"I'm gonna run out for a bit, okay. Are you going to be okay?"

"Yes mother. I'll be right here waiting for you when you get back. Besides, Samantha's not letting me get too far out of her sight. She's screening all my calls. I have a lot of motivation to get well. Samantha screening my calls is a huge motivator. Trust me," he said, heading towards the Jacuzzi.

I smiled lovingly back at him. I grabbed my handbag, sunvisor and sunglasses. It was time to take a ride.

CHAPTER 28

RILEY

I rode around for hours, not stopping until the wheels of my X5 turned through the black wrought iron gates. It was time to read what Lucas had to say to me. After all, this year's birthday couldn't have gotten any more somber.

I drove down the third row and parked. My eyes were tired. Hell, I was tired. I took my contacts out and put on my reading glasses. I opened the trunk, lifting the lid to the hidden compartment where I kept my gym shoes. I pulled out Lucas's letter. I walked over to the new granite seat, sitting, glad that I didn't have to sit on the ground for this moment. The hard stone felt cool against my thighs. I took a deep breath and exhaled and looked around. An old man and his dog were walking quietly through the cemetery in the distance. The dog barked once as if to alert his master to my existence. He glanced up at me but continued forward on his stroll, respecting my moment of solitude and reflection.

"I'm ready to hear what you have to say now Lucas."

I opened his letter, and I began.

My Dearest Riley,

You have been the love of my life from the day I first laid eyes on you at the Army-Navy Game. If you're reading this letter it means that I have passed on. I have asked my sister Zoe to retain this letter for me until she deemed it to be the right time to give it you, conditional only upon your having met Noah. Hopefully you've come to know Noah by now. I hope he has a special place in your heart just as he has had in mine. Noah has been my confidante. He's been the best wingman anyone in life could have. He's been the brother I never had.

Throughout my days at the United States Naval Academy and for the duration of my career, I've shared most every detail about my life with him. I've also shared my every feeling of love I have for you and the kids. I've shared my photographs, our stories, and our dreams. My love for you runs deep and unconditional. In his own special way, Noah has loved you too. I have seen it in his eyes every time he lights up at the mention of you and the kids. While you couldn't possibly know this or perhaps even understand, you've been his family too. Vicariously by my own design.

Riley, sometimes life throws us curve balls. And this is ours. I'm sure you are aware that Zoe has known Noah for years. There were legitimate reasons as to why you've never met Noah before now.I'm not perfect Riley. I've made my share of mistakes in life. One such mistake was not sharing with you that I am sterile and unable to father any more children subsequent to births of Xavier and Samantha. My sterility was at the hand of my own stupid mistake.

I was out one night with some of the other officers in my tactical unit during my second tour of duty. Several of us got drunk at some dive bar in Malaysia. We decided to haul ass over to a nearby beach and take a late night swim. To make a long story short, I was showing off attempting to dive off a lifeguard tower. I fell and injured myself. Perhaps the universe was protecting me from drowning in my drunken state. Nonetheless, the injury resulted in my sterility.

It was during the period of time shortly before my third tour of duty and right around the time you were pleading to have another baby. I knew how badly you wanted that third baby, Riley. I went along with your idea to freeze my sperm in the event I didn't return from the tour. It was a great idea except that I had no viable sperm to freeze. I was fortunate that the sperm bank we chose wasn't appointment intensive. It was a stroke of luck to be given the choice of producing the sperm at the lab site or collecting it privately at home complete with a set of instructions on handling the collection. It made it easier for me to hatch my plan of subterfuge.

I figured while I was gone on tour you would abandon the idea of having another baby and our life would go on as usual. So I convinced Noah to be the sperm donor in my place. I thought that it was the right thing to do. Not so much due to any doubts I had about not returning, but more so out of my fear of having to face your disappointment. I knew I could not impregnate you. I hoped when I returned we could discuss the issue further before going forward with any artificial insemination procedures. Maybe even put the idea to rest once and for all. Never in my wildest dreams did I expect you would go forward with impregnating yourself without me as a homecoming surprise. The thought of you going it alone never crossed my mind, and certainly not Noah's. When I returned home, you were seven months pregnant, glowing, and happy. I was in fear that if you knew the truth of what I had done, that I would lose you. There was no way I could ruin your joy, not to mention contemplating a life without you. Noah was as shocked as I was upon learning the news. But at the end of the day, he considered the baby his gift to us. One that bonded all of us in an incredibly special way.

Riley, I asked Noah to act as my sperm donor. He did this for me Riley. He wanted me to be happy. He knew it made me happy that you were happy. And we both wanted your happiness.

Because I am not Claire's biological father, Noah and I agreed that we would take this information to our graves with only two exceptions. Noah promised to only act on this information in the event that I was deceased. In the event of his death, I in turn promised to share this information with you, and we could both manage how to handle the information with Claire. We both knew the day would come where you would one day know the truth.

I've always known Noah to have a deep care for your well-being. He has given his word to make every effort to watch over you and our kids, as any loving brother would do. He would do everything in his power to keep you and the kids safe and cared for in the same way he knew I would have but for my death. He knows he is Claire's biological father.

Riley this has been a heavy burden to carry. I hope one day you can forgive me. Zoe does not know about Claire's parentage. As far as she knows, I am Claire's biological father. So please don't kill the messenger. I know it's not beyond you to try. I expect the contents of my letter will be difficult for both of you to absorb. But Riley, Zoe is my twin. We shared a womb together. Zoe's loyalties have been to me in this matter. I hope you can one day come to understand.

It is my desire and hope that you can find love with Noah. He's a good man. I want you to be happy. I don't want you to be alone. I cannot think of a better man for you to share a future. I trust in his ability to protect my family. Should the two of you be able to find real love, you and he have my blessings.

I hope with these words you can now find peace, forgiveness for me, and love for Noah. This will be hardest on Claire. She will need you all. While I only have deep regrets that I cannot spend the rest of my life with you, Xavier, Samantha, and Claire, I have tried to make up for my failures by leaving you in good hands.

With all my love forever into eternity,

Lucas

Chapter 29

Noah

I was caught in a veil of fog that seemed to lift, hover, but lift again, getting lighter over time. The air felt unnaturally chilly and smelled of antiseptic. Finally, I was able to open my eyes and discern my surroundings. I am not dead. I know this because of the flood people dressed in blue who were removing tubes out of my arms and the torpedo. I never figured heaven to have a television overhead with CNN broadcasting President Barack Obama cracking jokes at the Nerd Prom.

My eyes focused on a small shadow in the corner of the room. I blink, trying to focus. I know that figure. Claire. Claire is sitting in a chair reading a book on Chess Openings. She smiled, rising to move towards my bedside, adjusting the pillow under my head. I caught a whiff of the scent of bubblegum as she pressed her warm hand against the back of my head.

"Thank you."

She smiled happily, blowing a pink bubble that popped in my ear. Nope, I'm not dead.

"The doctors said you would be waking up soon."

"Why am I here?" I asked, my throat feeling as if it were on fire.

I noticed the yellow band on my wrist with my name on it. I place my other hand on it, fingering it in my nervousness.

"What happened?"

"You want the short or the long version?"

"The short version will do fine thank you."

"I'm not sure you want to hear it."

"Try me."

I inhale a shaky breath.

"Well . . . four months ago in June, you arrived in Pennsylvania to meet me, my brother, and my sister. You were spending time here in order to get to know us. You love my mother."

Four months . . . Did she say four months? Ah yes. Love . . . Riley . . . Picnics . . . Losing at chess.

"One night you and Mommy were out together at Aunt Zoe's birthday party. You guys got back home late. When you arrived, my brother Xavier was having a fight with his then girlfriend Nena."

Claire paused, I supposed to give me time to catch up with what she had said so far. But my mind was keeping up. I listened intently, working to put her words with the pieces of my memory back together so as to explain how I landed in this place surrounded by tubes, beeping monitors, fresh cups of jello, and people dressed in blue.

"It was raining pretty hard. Xavier took off on his motorcycle to chase Nena and you jumped on the back to stop him."

Good Lord I can't believe I've been on my back four fucking months. What the fuuuuuuck.

"There was an accident. You and Xavier were seriously injured."

"What month is this?"

"It's September. September 13th."

Claire paused yet again as if she's unsure whether to continue, but she does.

"Your brother. How is he?" I asked, my voice hoarse and sore.

Claire handed me a cup of water off the side tray and held the straw to my lips. I took a huge gulp. I was so thirsty. My throat felt like it had been stuffed with cotton. I worried that bad news may be coming next. I felt myself shifting on the bed a bit out of my own discomfort.

"Xavier was released two months ago. He's better. Doin' physical therapy."

Oh thank God, Xavier is okay. I would never forgive myself if Lucas's son had been killed.

"He had on a helmet. You didn't. Lucky for you, you landed in a huge pile of sand on a construction site. But you were still hurt pretty badly."

"Thank God he's okay," I said, feeling my voice crack.

I closed my eyes and sipped more water. Claire grabbed the pitcher. She filled my cup again.

"The police determined Mr. Warren was the cause of the accident. He was killed."

Go Figure. Warren was involved. Was he alone. Was Leah Chen with him?

"He was alone in his car," Claire said, practically reading my thoughts.

I nodded.

This was not the short version. I was afraid of what else would come next.

"Then Dr. Nathan came. She's mommy's friend. Ms. Lily's husband. You know her but I'm not sure if you know him."

Ahh, Lily DeLuca. Her husband's a big time cardiologist. I slowly raised my hand to my chest. I hope my heart is okay. My arm was sure sore.

"You needed blood. A lot of it. Everyone donated."

Did she say donated blood? Nobody has my blood.

"Dr. Nathan said only I was a blood match. That I was your daughter."

"Stop right there. Give me a minute," I said, taking a deep breath.

I closed my eyes feeling the wealth of emotion rising within me. I cleared my throat.

Lucas and my secret is out. I wanted to be the one to tell Riley. And now Claire is telling me. This is not the way I planned this to go down.

"So I hear you are my father."

I couldn't tell if she was making a statement or asking me to confirm what we both knew she knew.

I don't have the words. No. I need to find my words.

"Lucas is your father. I am your father too, in a biological kind of way. But I hope to one day be the same kind of father Lucas was to you, if you'll have me. If your mother will have me . . ."

I felt the emotion welling back up in me again as I tried to process this moment of recognition with Claire as to who I am to her.

God I hated the way this information came out. Lucas was probably turning over in his grave. Odds are Riley must hate me now. Somebody kill me now.

Claire nodded her head silently as if she agreed? Understood? I don't know.

"Okay, go on."

"Well, then Mommy and Aunt Zoe had words. Aunt Zoe gave Mommy a letter from Daddy." She stopped as if she's being cautious with her words again. "Sorry, my other Daddy. Anyway, Mommy ran out the hospital upset and in tears. She left the hospital, drove to the cemetery where Daddy's buried, armed with a sledgehammer and cracked Daddy's tombstone in half."

Now I wished I were dead for real. No way did I want to be responsible for hurting Riley like this. Lucas was lucky he's dead. She's going to kill me over this. Maybe that's a good thing. Put me out of my misery.

"Excuse me," Claire said, pulling me out of my thoughts.

"My other Dad. You're my dad too," she said.

"Wow," I moaned, unable to believe my own ears just hearing about Riley running loose through a cemetery with a sledgehammer.

I knew this day would come but I sure didn't want this information to come out like this.

"I guess Lucas and I have really made a mess of things."

"I'm glad you're gonna pull through," Claire said casually, not addressing my comment.

"Is she done with me, Claire?"

"Hard to say. After she finished beating the mess out of Daddy's tombstone, I mean my other Dad, she pretty much stopped talking about you. She cries a lot too."

"I see," I said, hearing the anguish in my own voice.

"Daddy left a letter for Mommy with Aunt Zoe. She wouldn't read it. She finally broke down. Read it on her birthday."

"God I missed her birthday."

"She got your birthday gift but she refused to celebrate."

This is so messed up. I had such big plans for Riley's birthday.

"What did Lucas say in the letter?" I sighed.

"The truth."

"Claire, listen to me closely dear."

Claire's gaze lifted cautiously to mine.

"Lucas loved you more than anything," I said, reaching for her hand, squeezing it tightly.

"He and your Mother wanted you very much. He wanted you so much that he asked me to help him get you here. I wanted you here. I agreed to help him get you here. We both wanted and

268

needed you to be here, but for different reasons. You were our bridge over troubled waters."

"But he left us," Claire said softly.

"He knew he had to go. I knew I had to stay."

Claire placed her other hand on top of mine. She reminded me so much of her mother. Beautiful. Tender. Caring.

"I want to tell you a story Claire."

"Okay," Claire said softly.

"When Lucas and I were working, on those dangerous missions, sometimes he went out on alone. Before leaving, he used to say to me "Take good care of her." I'd answer back, "I know because she's hard to replace." And when I'd go out on flights alone without him, I'd say to him "Take good care of her." He'd respond, "I know because she's hard to replace." It was our ritual of signing off with each other. The "her" was you."

Claire's eyes lit up with interest. She was a sharp kid. Her calculating mind was putting two and two together. I could see her thoughts registering on her face. She realized in that moment how special she was to Lucas and me.

"The shirt he gave you every year on your birthday was a reflection of both of our love and care for you."

Claire stared at me as if in deep thought. She wasn't using her words. I was unsure if this conversation was going well or not. But I needed Claire to understand that she was conceived in love. Lucas's love. Riley's love. My love. I didn't intend to lose Claire after all of this.

"Claire, Lucas wanted your mother to be happy. He would do anything for her. I wanted them to be happy too. I've always loved you. I've known in my heart that the day would come when I would have you in my life as well. We all three love you."

There was a long pause between us. My heart was hurting. I couldn't lose Claire. Not like this. Finally Claire spoke.

"I believe you," Claire said with conviction.

There is a God.

"No daughter could be any more loved. I want you to believe this. Whatever happens between me and your mother, I will love you. I will be here for you. Always."

Claire nodded her head silently in agreement. I supposed my conversation was getting too heavy for her. Claire switched gears, changing the conversation with talk about flowers. But that was okay. I was getting too heavy for myself, so I didn't blame her.

"Aunt Zoe sends flowers regularly every other day from the road. Those are hers," she said pointing to a fresh bouquet of pink lilies. "The money roses came today."

I glanced across the room at the window ledge where she had pointed, noticing what look like a bouquet of flowers made out of hundred dollar bills. I shuddered to think how many hundreds were in that bouquet that looked like real roses. It took a minute before I put two and two together. Claire must have read my thoughts.

"They're from Mr. Becker. The card says you're to get your butt—well that's not the word he used. Ahem," she said, clearing her throat, "you are to get your ass out of bed and look after his investment."

Claire nodded her head firmly punctuating the sentence, affirming Nicky's thoughts as if she were in agreement. I smiled gently, blinking my eyes to fight back my own tears that were threatening to shed. I knew Nicky was pulling for me, but Claire was pulling for me too. It made my heart swell.

"How long have I been here?"

"Four months, remember."

Claire turned the planter of pink lilies towards the sunlight, catching the few rays that were peeking through the window.

"I come every day."

My facial muscles tense, revealing my surprise. Shock.

"She knows. She drops me off and picks me up, but not before going next door to the Monastery of the Poor St. Clare's to pray. You can see it outside your window over there," Claire pointed her finger to something outside the window.

"It's near the hospital across that field."

"What does she say when you leave here?" I asked.

"Mostly, is he dead yet?"

"I understand."

"I don't."

It's what I deserve frankly.

"Don't try to, honey. It's complicated."

Claire shrugged her shoulders. Frustrated. I knew she didn't understand.

"I suppose I'll have to get myself well and get to fixing this mess," I mumbled.

"I have to go now. She'll be expecting me. I'll be back

tomorrow."

I nodded, closing my eyes, half ashamed to look at her.

"By the way, I graduated up a rank now in my martial arts class. I want to be a black belt like my dad. Here's something I made for you," she said, sliding a spiral book on top of my stomach. "It's a scrapbook filled with all the fun family photos we took in the month of June. I'll be back tomorrow."

"Take the money pot with you Claire. Keep it in a safe place until I blow this coop, okay?"

Claire reached across my mid-section and kissed me on the cheek. She nodded her head.

I grabbed my one good arm and hugged her. I held her tight. Painfully, I let her go. I nodded, acknowledging the fact she was leaving. She walked to the window, tucking the money pot under her arm. Claire turned back my direction.

"What took you so long to get here? Twelve years is a long time."

"I've had my reasons. But I've always been on my way. I'm here now."

My daughter waved good-bye. I couldn't decide which pain was the greatest. My physical pain or the emotional pain I was having over the unconditional love of Claire coupled with the loss of Riley.

I ran my fingers across the top of the scrapbook but I couldn't open it. The emotional pain was too great. I was starting to remember it all now. I wondered how long it would take me to be able to walk to that window and look out. Maybe I could catch a glimpse of Riley going into the monastery. All I could see from the bed were that the leaves on the trees were turning orange. I broke down and cried.

CHAPTER 30

RILEY

"Claire, get out of that Halloween candy," Samantha yelled. "It's for the neighborhood kids. Halloween is still days away. You're gonna break your braces, and then Mommy's gonna want me to drive you to the orthodontist again."

"Mind your beeswax Sammi. You're mad because you're on that stupid Weight Watcher's diet again and can't eat any yourself."

"Yo, Shorty, when those wires start popping out of your mouth, cutting your gums, you'll be begging me to take you to the orthodontist then."

"Yes, and you'll drive me, all while begging me for my Reece's Pieces too."

"You got that right," Samantha bellowed.

She and Claire busted out laughing at themselves.

"Shut up the both of you," Xavier interjected. "You two need to be figuring out a way to help mother. She's in emotional pain. She's crying still. She's doting on me now like I'm ten."

Samantha and Claire were silent.

"I've tried to cut her some slack with the accident and all, but mother needs to get her life back with Noah. She was happy with him," Xavier grumbled.

I could hear the conversation my kids were having from the next room over. I wasn't up to engaging, so I listened passively. That was about all I had the energy for anyway. I felt stuck in some kind of time zone. It was as if the universe was punishing me for something I didn't deserve. First the loss of Lucas. Then the broken engagement with that slug Warren. Then Noah comes along. I finally learn to love and trust again. Warren re-appears, sabotaging my business, my relationship, and then tries to kill my son. Warren dies. And the icing on the cake is this news that

Noah is Claire's biological father. My world has been shattered with lies and betrayals by every man I've chosen to love. Even Zoe knew things and kept it to herself. What happened to trust? Who could I trust? This is what happens when you step out on those waters of trust and try to love again. You drown.

This deep seated feeling of betrayal is right up there with the days and nights I wasted crying on Warren Shaw's lying, cheating ass. I thought that was all behind me. Perhaps love's not going to be for me. I seem to attract complicated relationships. Why can't life and love just be easy and simple?. I feel like I've been left on an island with no boat or way to get back to shore.

I have loved myself through losses before and I will love myself now through this loss as well. I will let this go and move on with my life. I can do this.

Maybe Noah didn't love me at all. Maybe he loved Lucas more. Maybe he was only fulfilling a promise and our relationship was more about his sense of honor and obligation. Less about his love for me. After all, these military men live for their honor and duty to each other. Perhaps this was never ever about me.

My mind drifted back to listening to my kids argue over me. Except now they were arguing over Noah.

"Xavier, why don't you get your butt up and help Noah recuperate quicker. You're Mr. LA Fitness. You could help him to heal. You're a trainer. This is supposed to be what you do, isn't it? Why don't you help my dad?"

"Daddy is your Dad," Samantha snapped. "Just stop it Claire."

"Shut up Sammi," Xavier demanded. "Noah is her Dad too."

"Both of you shut up. You both can just shut up," Claire repeated. "I never got to have a relationship with dad. I was too young to have a chance to know him the way you did. You guys had more of a dad than I did. I have a chance now to have a dad, and I won't let either of you take that from me," Claire retorted sharply.

Neither Xavier nor Samantha said a word. I could only imagine the look on their faces.

"Xavier, Noah was Dad's best friend. That almost makes him like an Uncle to you. So shut up and deal with it. Besides, you may gain a stepfather out of the deal."

"Now you wait one minute Claire Cook," Xavier said before she cut him off.

This can't be good, Xavier calling Claire out by her full name. He was starting to become me.

"And, Sammi you're always saying you won't have a dad to walk you down the aisle if you ever get married. Well maybe Noah can be that," Claire said apparently ignoring Xavier.

As I eavesdropped from the other room, I realized how out of control this whole matter had become.

Look how you screwed this all up, Lucas. Our family is officially dysfunctional now. Even my children have been affected by all of this. Look at what you and Noah have done to my happy home. Look at this mess, Lucas.

I was crying even harder now. My heart felt like it had been cracked in two.

"Sammi, you need to talk to mother," Xavier sighed. "You know she loves Noah. She just needs a little reminder to help her to see it."

"Kiss my ass X," Samantha pushed back. "This is not my job to interfere in Mom's love life."

"Dad is dead!" Xavier shouted. "We are all still alive. We have lives to fucking live. We can't live in the past."

"Listen to you. Xavier Cook the big shot. You're the one that can't commit to a woman. Now you're walking around here like you walk on water when it comes to relationships? Seriously? Is that the card you're going to play?" Samantha yelled back at him.

"Frankly, coming from a place of having almost losing my own life, I'm not gonna walk around this earth in tears doing anything I don't want to do. I'm gonna live. I've been given a second chance," Xavier shouted back.

"What makes you think I can help her? I can barely help myself. I need Mother to help me half the time. Not the other way around. It's not that kind of party, X."

"You need to help mother. Get your fingers out your ears and your head out your ass Samantha. You're a smart girl. Convince her to see she needs to stop punishing Noah. He didn't do this shit. Dad did," Xavier exclaimed.

"Oh and let me get this straight. All of a sudden you and Claire are the voice of reason here? Cut me a break," Samantha said. "Mom won't even go and see him for Christ sakes. And Noah went along with Dad's scheme. As far as I am concerned, that makes him equally as guilty," Samantha responded, holding her ground, driving a stake in it.

I wondered how long I should let this stupid conversation between them go own. I hardly had the energy for my kids big brain ideas on how to run my own love life. But then again, I wasn't the smartest player on the playground. So I took my marbles and came home.

"Samantha let me tell your little sheltered pea brain something while you got your head stuck up your 'hip hop think you know everything' ass. Baby, true love doesn't come around that often. If you're lucky enough to find it, you should grab hold of it and not let go. Mom had that in her relationship with Noah," Xavier said, almost pleading now with Samantha.

"Says, who?" Samantha replied.

"What is your problem, Sammi? Do you freaking have blinders on or something? Or are you so pre-occupied with that magazine blog that you can't see pass your own ass?" Xavier continued, not giving an inch.

"Now you wait one minute X," Samantha said.

Right about now if I had to place a bet on the odds, my money was riding on Samantha. She rarely lost those debates she chose to engage in, but Xavier was not willing to let go of the reins either. They both needed to move on from their discussion. Nothing good was going to come out it, because at the end of the day, it would be my decision as to what would happen in my relationship. They were wasting their time.

"Mom's man and you wouldn't be in this position if it weren't for you getting your dick caught in Sophia's vee jay jay while pissing off your relationship with Nena."

Well that was a low blow Xavier couldn't have seen coming.

"It was you who was flying off in the rain on the Ducati like an emotional nutcase. Noah came after you to stop you from behaving like a mad man on that bike in a freaking rain storm. Don't go getting this twisted, you lockless shit-head. You did this!" Sammi shouted wildly.

"Stop it the both of you!" Claire urged. "Who would believe the two of you were the grownups in the room. You both act like sixth graders all the time. Focus on the problem," Claire said.

It sounded like silence from Xavier and Samantha. I suspected they were both pouting, licking their wounds.

"Xavier, you need to help Noah. Samantha you need to work on mom. The sooner those two get back together the better all our lives will be. Have either of you jokes noticed that mom hasn't baked any bread in months? What does that tell you?"

"Jesus, Claire," Samantha sputtered. "This is not about mom baking bread."

"Sure it is, green eyes. Mom bakes bread when she's happy," Claire retorted.

"Who you calling green eyes?" Samantha said.

Xavier must have picked up Claire.

"Let me down Xavier or you'll be sorry," Claire demanded.

"Whatcha gonna do Claire? Put some of that martial arts stuff on me, sister?"

That was the wrong dare to make with Claire. She apparently punched Xavier in the groin, because I heard him groan when he dropped her to the floor.

"I warned you," Claire said.

"Mother!" I heard Xavier shout out to me.

"That's what you get for trying to be Mr. Big," Samantha said. "Who made you daddy?" Samantha laughed. "High five sister."

I shut my door and ignored them all, shaking my head. *Why me Lord?*

Chapter 31

Noah

"So how's your physical therapy going? Claire asked.

"It's slow but sure," I said a bit too grumpily, but couldn't take it back.

"What are they feeding you?"

"What kind of question is that? Hospital food, Claire."

"Yeah, well it's time to make a break from tradition," Claire said with a devilish smirk on her face.

"What do you mean?" I asked, giving her a look one gives to a conspirator.

"Well you know X is Mr. Fitness himself. He eats, sleeps, and drinks that whole fitness and vegan stuff," she said, all while moving towards the closet, packing my things. "He's practically well himself now. You know he majored in physiology in college."

"I do know that yes," I said watching her throw the few things I had in a Georgetown University weekender bag. "What's your point?"

"He's coming to get you any minute now. Gonna help you break these hospital chains. Time for you to make a break for it, Dad."

Man. She called me Dad. I did not know what to do with that. I was fighting back the tears. I felt so inferior, so ill equipped. I need to man up. It was necessary to be strong in the presence of this petite powerhouse because she was being strong for me. She was everything I could ever want in a daughter, and then some. I silently thanked the universe for her. *She's definitely the good that came out of all of this, Lucas. Besides all this mess we got ourselves into, we did good with Claire. If she is the single most thing that comes out of all this heartbreak then we did good.*

"It's time to blow this coop. Time for you to kiss St. Mary's Hospital and their team of do-gooders good bye."

"I don't get it," I mumbled, sitting more upright in the chair I'd been resting in earlier.

"Are you not keeping up here?" Claire snapped. "We're checking out."

"And we're going where exactly, El Captain?" I joked.

"You let me worry about that," Claire said, glancing down at the time on her cell phone. She was moving more hurriedly now.

"I packed your wife beaters and your skivvies. This party is over."

Things were starting to get pretty wild quick. I've got a daughter telling me what to do now. Damn, I'm getting old. Riley's left me. Her kids are kidnapping me to do God knows what with me. I'm screwed for sure. *Fucking Lucas Cook, you stupid shit-head. We really got ourselves in a mess man. Tag I'm it. Gotta pull us out of our mess again.* This was right up there with the time we stole all the officer's reserved parking signs at the Naval Academy and hid them in the janitor's closet. We must have scrubbed toilets for days behind that stunt. But on some level my heart was uplifted. Riley's kids to the rescue. Maybe there's a good ending to this story after all. Miracles do happen, don't they? Because that's what it was going to take. A goddamn miracle. I wondered where Samantha stood in the mix of all of this.

"Hey man," Xavier said warmly as he walked into the room. "I owe you a bit of thanks. I know you tried to help me that night. My mind was clouded by my emotions that evening.

"You shouldn't blame yourself. It was an accident," I said, standing up with the help of my cane in order to embrace him.

"I acted foolishly. I almost got the both of us killed. I'm sorry man. Please forgive me," he said, holding the embrace, patting me on my back.

"No, Warren almost got us killed."

"I just need your forgiveness dude."

"No problem wingman. Deuces. I'd do it all over again the same way if I had to, son. I did it for you. I did it for Riley."

Xavier put his head in my chest and sobbed. I patted him on the back with my one free hand.

"I'm so sorry, man," he wailed through his sobs.

The last thing I wanted was for Xavier to feel guilty about what happen that night. I didn't want him to carry the burden of this on his shoulders. If the wheels were reversed, Lucas would have done the same thing for me and my son.

"Listen, man. We're all in this together. Your father would have done the same thing had it been my son if the tables were turned. I did what any loving father would do, yours included."

Xavier stepped back, nodding his head, wiping the tears from his eyes with the back of his hand.

"We're in this together. Me, you, and Lucas. I want you to put this behind you. Your body may have healed, but I need you to heal your soul too. No guilt on your part. The fact that we were on that Ducati together was borne out of love. Me. You. Lucas."

"I got it," Xavier said, shaking his head in understanding.

"I got it too," Claire said, rushing things along. "Now, C'mon X. Let's go before we have to explain ourselves to these nurses who will call Dr. Nathan down here and we find our butts in a sling."

No sooner had Claire spoken, Samantha came from around the corner into the room.

"Let's blow this spot, roadies, before MRSA gets Noah's ass," she said.

Oh my god, a band of young folks are kidnapping me. Half of me was feeling like 'what the fuck.' The other half of was inspired by Riley's kids who had conspired like a band of navy seals gone rogue. The latter part of me prevailed. I was motivated and on board to get the hell out of this sterile environment. I needed to get my shit together, stop feeling sorry for myself, and get my woman back.

Riley's kids and I checked out of the hospital. They drove me to their Aunt Zoe and Uncle Julian's house in Holland, Pennsylvania. Zoe and Julian lived in a nice home in Holland Estates not far from Washington's Crossing. I limped to the door feeling like half a man.

Zoe opened her huge doors. I could see the love and excitement in her eyes. It was comforting.

"Come in Noah. Welcome. It's so good to see you. I'm so sorry about all of this," she said. "Julian and I love you. Now we want you to take your time to heal. Make yourself comfortable. Consider this home for a while." Zoe put her arms around me. "We are all here for you."

Tears filled Zoe's eyes. I gave her my best one arm hug her back, using my other arm to steady myself with the cane.

"We're coming through, Aunt Zoe," Claire said as she pushed passed Zoe and I who were still embraced in the foyer. "Xavier's got work to do."

"Yeah, we're on a mission, Aunt Zoe," Samantha clamored. "There's work to be done. We're parking Noah in the guest bedroom."

"Sure thing," Zoe said.

"Does Riley know about this yet?" Zoe questioned them.

"Not yet. TMI," Xavier said, walking pass me.

"TMI? And that's English for what?" Zoe asked.

"Too much information," three voices said in unison.

"Comprende?" Samantha spoke next.

"I think I do," Zoe laughed. "Should I be worried?"

"When the time is right we'll tell her," Xavier said firmly. "Until now, let sleeping dogs lie. Not to worry. I got this."

"That's what scares me," Zoe said, guiding me into her living area so I could sit.

For the next several weeks I ate better than I had in weeks. I rested and I healed. Xavier came daily like clockwork, putting me through the paces. He planned a physical therapy regimen that felt like he was working me to my near death. He bossed me around like a crazed drill sergeant. I hated every minute of his routine, but I could feel my own strength improving every day.

Samantha drove me to my doctor's appointments and Claire made sure my mind stayed sharp, beating me at chess, and forcing me to eat peanut butter and jelly sandwiches with her while watching old Nick At Night episodes. Claire was still snapping photos on her mission to create a new scrapbook for Riley, all while insisting that I participate in her martial arts drills. Zoe's husband Julian included me on his music sessions in his home studio, letting me watch him and his band work, frequently asking my opinion on some of his lyric changes.

Zoe and I took long walks together down the bike paths that surrounded her development. It was late October. The trees were showing the earthy signs of fall, turning orange and red adding a touch of beauty to our long walks together. We spent most weekends talking about either Lucas or Riley. Some of our talks were about fond memories. Some of it painful. Zoe and I grew closer as she came to understand the true depth and nature of Lucas and my friendship. On one of our walks she opened up with her own feelings as well.

"You and Lucas were always doing some cockamamie things Noah, but this sperm swap thing was the icing on the cake. You two rose to new heights with that bullshit move," she said, grabbing a branch off a tree, plucking the leaves off one by one.

"It seemed like a good move at the time. Who would have guessed Riley would have impregnated herself before Lucas got back," I said, thinking back on the shock Lucas and I went through over that act.

I remember I got major drunk the night I heard the news.

"Riley still loves you Noah. Before the accident, I'd never seen her so happy in a long while. Don't give up on your relationship with her."

"It's been close to six months since she and I have spoken. She didn't even come to see me in the hospital."

"No, but she went to the monastery every day and prayed for you."

"I really had planned to tell her, Zoe. It was never my plan for her to find out about Claire this way."

"I held on to Lucas's letter out of loyalty to my brother. I had no idea I was holding on to a dark secret that had to do with Claire's parentage. The news came as a shock to me as well. I can only imagine how Riley must feel."

"Looking back, it was a good idea that Lucas left the information about Claire out. It gave you space to be a part of the kids' lives, without feeling like you were betraying Riley," I said.

Zoe smiled, but I could tell she was in deep thought again.

"Lucas would never hurt you Zoe. None of us could have

283

foreseen he would be killed in a plane crash, unable to steer his personal life to a safe landing. Try to make peace with it," I pleaded.

"In retrospect, I get that now. Lucas always lived by the philosophy that what you didn't know couldn't hurt you," Zoe said, grabbing my hand, challenging me again like she did on every walk to turn the last mile of our walk into a run.

I still hadn't beat her yet, but I was happy to oblige. Being able to run these days was a blessing.

I owed my new-found wellness to everyone in Riley's family. While every day I was feeling physically healthier and emotionally stronger, my heart still hurt. I had lost Riley. I was on a medical leave of absence so I hadn't yet thought about returning to Virginia. I kicked the idea around with myself that maybe I could stick around for the balance of the year. I could work with Quentin on building a new home on the land I'd purchased here before the accident. Claire was a good enough reason alone for me to stay in the area. It would give me a chance to be close to her at least. I saw myself living here. I wanted to have a role in my daughter's life. Nothing about that was going to change.

The kids didn't talk about Riley much around me. I figured they didn't want to upset me further with the news that their mother had been hurt so badly by Lucas and me. I couldn't have felt any more guilty and ashamed about the whole mess. But I hadn't regretted my decision to do what I did for Lucas. I did, however, deeply regret that Riley had to find out about Claire the way she did.

I knew Riley wouldn't take my calls. It wasn't lost on me that she wanted me dead. So every night before retiring, I tried to sit down to write her. It wasn't unusual to find the corner desk in Zoe's guest room filled with crumpled starts to letters I'd begin but could never quite finish. Many evenings I stared at Nicky's money pot trying to find the right words to get my woman back. But the words never seemed to be quite perfect enough to express my love, my sadness, and my guilt for not having told Riley myself about Claire, despite the fact it had been plan to do so. It wasn't what I desired nor intended.

Riley was all I could think about. I would have to try to find a way to win her back. The alternative was I was going to be pretty miserable. I knew that. That single fact alone kept me motivated to continue to try to write her and beg for her forgiveness.

By Halloween eve I would later come to learn that Claire was up to more tricks than treats. While on one of her daily visits, Claire picked up one of my crumpled letters and had given it to Riley. Thank God for Claire. She was Halloween's favorite Fairy Godmother. Everybody needs one of those.

CHAPTER 32

RILEY

"You did what?!" I shouted, looking at the loads of Hugo Boss shopping bags filled with new clothes piled in the corner of Xavier's room.

"Samantha, Claire, and I agreed to shelter Noah at Aunt Zoe's," Xavier answered in a tone I'd not heard him use before.

It was if he thought he was in charge. He sounded like a . . . like a husband. And hell I didn't have one of those.

"Noah lost weight since the accident. Samantha, Claire and Zoe took his credit card. They went on a shopping spree to buy him new clothes."

"How the hell did he get out of the hospital?" I quizzed.

"Oh that. Ms. Lily told Aunt Zoe that Dr. Nate was pretty pissed about our checking Noah out of the hospital, and . . . "

"You checked him out of the hospital? When?"

"I did. Well we did. Four weeks ago."

"Four weeks ago? It's Halloween."

"Yes, mother, I know what day it is," Xavier sighed.

He actually sounded frustrated. But he was not half as frustrated as I was that my family kept yet another thing from me. When were they going to learn to stop keeping secrets?

"Actually it turned out okay. Dr. Nate spoke with Noah's doctor, and they agreed that a change in environment would do him good. Most of what medical care he still needed could be done on an outpatient basis," Xavier said, still confident that he was taking ownership for Noah's move to Zoe's. Xavier wasn't backing down from me on this one. It was hard not to see that he was coming into his manhood.

"Fine!" I yelled back at him. "This whole family is one big freaking secret. Everybody's got secrets!" I shouted again, slamming his bedroom door behind me.

I headed down the staircase to my home office, taking deep breaths along the way to clear my head and tamp down my emotions. I had to admit, that on the few days I felt my anger, disappointment, and sadness subsiding, I was glad Noah had survived. I prayed every day that God would put him on the road to recovery. Lord knows he would have never been on that motorcycle had it not been for me. It was because of me he was hurt. That made me sad. But I was sadder that I still hadn't been able to reconcile that Noah was Claire's biological father and he hadn't shared that information with me. I felt so betrayed by both he and Lucas. What a secret to hold all those years. But I didn't want to think about that. I needed to embrace my own healing so I could move forward. So I forced myself not to think about it anymore today and to return to my work.

Throwing myself into my work was a good distraction. I had obligations to Nicholas Becker, my angel investor. I couldn't let Nicholas down. Noah went out on a limb for me to facilitate *Milk Money's* large cash infusion into my business. I needed to not screw up my business relationships. Just because Noah and I no longer had a romantic relationship didn't mean we couldn't network together in a business relationship at some point in the future. I needed to still be a good business investment.

I worked for several hours before deciding to take a coffee break to chat with Zoe.

"Hey Zoe, it's me, Riley."

"Hey Riley, everything okay?"

"I've been working this afternoon and decided to pause for a latte. Interested in meeting me at Starbucks?"

"Sure thing. I can be there in ten. I'm working on some new lyrics with Julian and he's getting on my last nerve right about now. A break sounds good."

Ten minutes later, Zoe and I were taking our much needed coffee break.

"I thought it was a good time for us to have a heart to heart about Lucas. About Noah," I said a bit too somberly.

"I guess you know he's been staying with Julian and me these last several weeks. I told the kids to tell you Riley. I wanted to stay out of it until you were ready to talk yourself. I know how hard it's been on you these last few months."

"Yeah Xavier finally got around to telling me. I'm okay with it, really. I'm glad you and Julian opened up your home to Noah."

Zoe squeezed my hand gently. I put mine on hers.

"I've missed you Riley."

"I've missed you too Zoe."

"He misses you too."

I could feel the lump forming in my throat. I didn't want to cry. I was tired of crying.

"I want you to know that you did the right thing by not betraying Lucas's confidences. Blood is thicker than water."

"I'm not so sure I would have, had I known Noah was Claire's father. Lucas didn't share that part with me Riley. He only asked me to hold his letter. That was all I knew," she said, tears now starting to form in her eyes.

"You stuck by me like a sister when Lucas died, Zoe. I am truly grateful for you. I know how close you and Lucas were. I would have done the same thing for my brother had I been forced to walk in your shoes."

"I've thought about the whole matter a lot Riley. I figured Lucas couldn't bear to share with you the news about his sterility. He always did have that whole machismo thing going on."

"Yeah, I suppose he wanted to be around for me when he told it, in case there was emotional fallout. He couldn't have predicted in a million years that I would impregnate myself without him."

"You were like an unguided missile back then," Zoe laughed. "Nothing was going to stop your mission to have another baby."

I laughed along with Zoe. It was good to have a laugh. I hadn't done that in God knows when.

"Truthfully Zoe, it was a period in my life that I was feeling insecure about my marriage, about myself, about my business. I thought another baby was the answer. And surprisingly it was. Lucas and I grew closer when Claire arrived."

"He loved Claire so much," Zoe said in deep thought.

"Maybe because he knew she was his."

Zoe and I had a pregnant pause. I suspect we both were thinking the same thing.

"Who knows. I don't know anything anymore," I sighed heavily taking a swig of my latte.

"Yeah, who knows," Zoe said. "It's the past right? It's not like we have a crystal ball to look back into the past. Gotta move forward, right?"

"Right," I said, my voice much stronger.

"We need cupcakes," Zoe said, eyeing the glass case filled with pastries.

"Cupcakes it is," I said, colluding with Zoe to add a sugar rush to our coffee break.

Zoe went on to share with me her weekend walks with Noah, as we devoured our cupcakes. She reminded me that while the kids were seeing to Noah's physical health needs, only Noah and I could address the matters of our hearts. Zoe had a front row seat to see how much both of us were grieving the loss of our relationship. She tiptoed around the idea that Noah and I should talk, letting the suggestion float in the air in hopes the idea would somehow take root. I listened, but made no pronouncements either way. Still it was good that Zoe and I got to have our heart-to-heart to clear the air.

I was taking small steps to get my life back on track.

Days later I noticed Xavier and Samantha were starting to drop hints that Noah was getting significantly better. Apparently he was having meetings with Quentin on his plans to build a new home here. Even Madison was stirring the pot, withholding sex from Quentin in hopes she could manipulate him into spitting out tidbits about the plans for the new home Noah was building.

Madison was good about that kind of stuff. If there was information to be had, she was going to get it. From what she learned so far, his new home sounded spectacular. Quentin was pulling out all the stops architecturally and Noah was sparing no expense.

Whatever martial arts drills Noah was practicing with Claire, she was improving daily. Xavier was starting to mumble about training with them in order to protect himself from Claire. He claimed if Claire got any more lethal he wasn't going to have a groin left.

Xavier and Nena's relationship hadn't survived the accident, but the flood of women that rushed to fill the void left Xavier more flirtatious than ever. He was getting a ton of attention at the gym. The women were loving the fact that Xavier was back on the market. Samantha swore those gals had declared open season on my son.

But Xavier managed to maintain his focus on Noah's well-being. The two them were starting to have their own boy's night out, going to the gym, catching action movies, and playing *Call of Duty* together. Xavier had even picked up Noah's habitual early morning pushup routine. He and Noah were apparently trading many of Lucas's "man up" stories. Xavier was even starting to dip his toothbrush and gargle in vodka thing that both Lucas and Noah each did. Whenever I gave Xavier my best 'what the hell are you doing' look, he would say "Mother I am a grown man, so let me be one."

I glanced out the window looking at Xavier completing his pushup regimen on the back deck in the fall morning sun. Every time I'd looked at the tattoo on his arm, I reflected on the times Noah had wrapped his arms around me watching me kiss his tattoo. All three of my men, branded the same way. Strange on every level, but it was our strange.

I shook my head as if I could shake the memories out of my head. I went back to kneading dough, when Claire came in the kitchen.

"Mommy I have something that I think you should read."

"What is Claire? I'm busy right now, dear. Can it wait?"

"Sure, Mom. I'll set it on the chair over here. I'm going out back to shoot some pictures of Cleo and Stogie with Xavier."

"No problem baby."

"I'm making a calendar. I plan to upload it on the Apple website. I'm going to dress Stogie and Cleo up like Thanksgiving turkeys. Maybe I'll get Xavier to be the pilgrim."

"Fine. Leave whatever it is there on the chair."

Xavier as a pilgrim. Never happening.

"You know my Dad really does love you. Sometimes the words come hard for him," she said, as the back screen door closed behind her.

I momentarily stopped kneading the dough.

My Dad. Those two words seemed so surreal. Noah and I have a child together. I sometimes had to catch myself now when looking at Claire. I didn't want her to think I was physically studying her now. She looked so much like me, I guess I never thought about how much Lucas was or was not in her. I assumed she was taking on the physical attributes of my side of the family.

I kneaded the dough some more, turning it a few more times, and then stopped. I wiped my flour-laced hands on my apron and focused on the seat of the chair behind me. A crumpled up piece of paper rested in the chair. I moved slowly to pick up the crumpled piece of paper. I un-crumpled it. It was a letter. A letter written in Noah's handwriting. I felt the quickening of my heart elevating as my anxiety rose.

Dearest Riley,

I'm writing this letter to you in hopes that you will not turn your heart lights out on me. From the first time I laid eyes on you with that sparkle in your eyes, I knew that you were a special woman and that any man was lucky to have you. I could not have been more thrilled that Lucas and you were able to build a beautiful life together, creating a beautiful loving family. Truly, I have loved you right along with Lucas.

Riley, when Lucas first came to me to disclose his sterility, I hurt for him. But I knew he had you. It wasn't the end of his world. When he disclosed your marital plans to have another baby through artificial insemination I listened as his friend. When he asked me to donate my sperm in his place, we fought. I thought it was a stupid idea given the difference in our racial makeup. The fact that you were bi-racial gave him hope that he could pull this off. I tried my best to kick his ass for even conjuring up the idea of considering using me that way. We indeed fought physically. After we exchanged several blows we cried in each other's arms like two hurt siblings. Lucas knew how much I cared for you. He knew how much I disliked everything he was saying to me. He begged me to help him by being his sperm donor, promising to talk you out of the idea prior to any artificial inseminations procedures getting underway. Never in a million years did he nor I contemplate that you might proceed without him as a surprise made in love. A love which yielded the birth of Claire.

I loved Lucas as much as you. I would have done anything for him. I couldn't say no. I didn't say no. You see, Lucas saved my life once on a mission in which we came under deadly attack. I have him to thank for my life. I would have done the same thing for him had our situations been reversed. Saying no to Lucas was not an option. I swore to him on my life that I would look after you and the kids if anything ever happened to him. He in turn promised to love and father the baby as his own.

Some years after Lucas passed I came to town to introduce myself to you. I came for the sole purpose of letting you and Zoe know about Claire. The night I flew into Philadelphia International Airport to meet you and to share this information, you coincidentally happened to be at the airport. What were the odds of that? You were at the baggage claim area the same time as me. It was merely coincidental.

Riley, I was coming for you then. What I wasn't expecting was to catch a glimpse of you. You smiled at me sweetly in the late night hour on what was an extremely cold night. Watching you in the warmth of another man's arms completely unraveled me. To my surprise, I would later learn from Zoe, you were picking up what was your then fiancé, Warren Shaw. I decided my news would be particularly untimely, the outcome of which would not be in my favor. I was so pissed with myself, feeling as if I had come in your life way too late. I agonized deeply for months over how I felt about another man, possibly loving you, marrying you, and raising Claire. I hated the idea of it all. Nonetheless, rather than telling you then, I instead briefly visited Zoe and Julian, cut my trip short, and got back on the plane intending to figure something else out with the full intentions of interceding. I went further by having Warren Shaw investigated. I knew from the outcome of that investigation that he was not the man for you. He was a compulsive liar and a habitual cheat. He represented as a man everything that Lucas and I stood against. I couldn't bear the thought of you marrying Warren Shaw. I would have rather you been alone than with Warren Shaw. As luck would have it and being the smart woman that you are, you ended the relationship with him. That part of my dilemma was quickly solved. I'm glad because I would have never stood by and let you marry him. I also knew you would need time to heal, yet again, so I kept my distance. I kept up with you and the children from afar, checking constantly on your well-being and the children's growth and development. I knew in my heart that fate had prevailed and that the stars were aligning to work in our favor.

The timing couldn't have been better last Christmas when we finally did meet. Again, for a second time, and as our relationship progressed, I was prepared to tell you truth about Claire. This time I had intended to raise the discussion during our family visit time this past June. I wanted to be able to discuss the news with you sensibly and be available to share the information with Claire and the kids personally. I never intended even now to keep this information from you. My timing seems to always be so poor.

Riley, if you were to look in my luggage that still remains at your home I urge you to look in the side pocket. You will find two items. One item is a letter from Lucas to me, thanking me for helping him, and giving me permission upon his death to pursue whatever relationship with you that both you and I would desire. It wasn't a given that you were going to like me or love me, but he and I both so wanted it to turn out that way.

The second document is an official recordation of me as sperm donor for Claire along with Lucas's power of attorney. I intended to have this discussion with you in a manner in which we both could hear each other and process the information together with the family. Unfortunately, I could not foresee that the accident would happen nor foresee that you would find out this challenging news while I was in an unconscious state. That was not the way I intended for you to learn this very difficult news as I have only had your best interests and deep love for you at heart.

Riley, I am deeply sorry. I ask for your forgiveness. I have never wanted to hurt you. I would move heaven and earth for you. I know that you are afraid. Lucas and I have managed to shake your world and rock the very foundation we thought we were helping to build. For my part, I only ask that you forgive me. I know right now that you must seriously doubt all my motives and my intentions. All that I can say is that I love you for you.

Riley, life is better with you at my side. The sun shines three times as bright when we're together. I pray each day that you might try to find a way in your heart to love me again, to give me another chance. I want nothing more in my life than for you to try to open the door of your heart for me. I will forever give you my heart if only you would let me start all over again. Loving you is . . .

The words ended. The letter was incomplete. I ran upstairs to the guest room. I pulled Noah's bag off the top shelf of the guest room closet. I tore opened the side pocket. Sure enough both documents were there. I could taste the salt of my tears that were streaming down my face. I reached for my phone to call Madison. My call went into her voicemail.

"Madison, you need to come over. I need you, Maddy." I sent Maddy a text message. *911, call me.* That was our code for urgent. Shortly thereafter my phone rang.

"Riley, what's going on? Is everything okay?" Madison asked, sounding worried.

"Claire gave me a half written letter that Noah was writing to me. There are documents here too," I said tearfully between my sobs.

"Slow down Riley. I have no idea what you're talking about. I'm on my way."

Within minutes Madison arrived, reading everything that I had read from Noah, including the documents I found in his bag.

"Well damn. Dude had big plans to discuss this up front. Maybe you should give him another chance Riley. After all he is your baby daddy."

"Stop it Madison. This is serious. I don't know what to do."

"Well, do you love him, Riley?"

"Of course I love him."

"Then you should let him in, Riley. Your feelings are your feelings Riley. You can't change who you love."

"I know, but . . . "

"But nothing Riley. We all are human. We all make mistakes. The man made a mistake. Most women would love to have a man love them the way Noah loves you."

"I'm scared Madison. How do I know if this is real? I'm so confused."

"You are not confused Riley Cook. That man has rocked your world. You're angry, yes. But you're a romantic at heart, and that man crawled straight into those cold cracks of your heart, set them on fire, and lived there. You were tripping on your happy for months. But, none of us could see that baby daddy curve ball coming."

"Maybe what Noah thinks is love, is really his sense of obligation and promise to Lucas. Maybe this isn't love at all."

"If it were me Riley, this is not the man I'd be throwing back in the pond. He knows what love is and so do you. If I thought he wasn't right for you I would tell you."

"*Hmphf,* I don't recall you telling me to dump Warren back in the pond back in the day," I said wiping my tears with a tissue. "As I recall all you ever said was "we can't tell people who to love"," I mocked. "Or did you forget?"

"You know what Riley, if we knew better we'd do better. We both were young and stupid then. The fact still remains, you're Noah's queen, Riley. Perhaps you should let him, be king. And for the record, that king is over there building your ass a castle."

I flipped my eyes up in my head.

"Whatever."

"Girl you know the deal," Madison giggled.

She looked at the mound of dough on my marble cutting board and shook her head.

"Good God woman, you're back to baking bread. Things are looking up."

"I've been under a lot of stress Madison."

"No damn way you're going to start plowing the pounds back on me, Riley, because you're all stressed out at getting your groove back on."

"Girl you need to be writing a romance instead of this food stuff, because you've got some real stories here to tell about your relationships," she laughed.

"To hell with you Madison."

We both started laughing.

"Riley, face it. You need to go get your man, girl. What's done is done and cannot be undone. But you can move forward."

"Easier said than done," I said.

"We already know where Zoe stands. Let's call Lily. She can weigh in for kicks cause we already know how this story is gonna end."

"No you don't."

"Yes we do. Siri, call Lily."

CHAPTER 33

RILEY

It had been a month since Madison and I had called Lily about Noah's half-written letter that Claire had smuggled. Still, I'd not received a letter or a phone call directly from him. But I waited. I worked, and I waited. Work had become my coping mechanism the last several weeks. Noah was still living at Zoe's awaiting the completion of his new home.

I read and re-read his letter every night before going to bed, realizing he hadn't intended for me to see it. Who could fault Claire for conspiring to get our relationship back on track. The more I read Noah's half completed letter, the more the cold places in my heart began to thaw. I could feel his love igniting my soul, coursing through my veins like a soothing balm as my mind absorbed the power of his words. I couldn't deny that I missed him. My doorbell rang playing "Have Yourself A Merry Christmas", announcing Lily's arrival.

"It's Lily!" Samantha yelled through the house loudly.

"Tell her to come on in!" I shouted back. "I'm almost dressed."

The year had gone by way too fast. It was that time again for the Memorial Gala Fundraiser for the Navy Tots. Lily had flown in for the event. But everything about the event was different this year. I was only going because I'd promised Lily and Madison that I would get out of the house. They insisted I needed to take a break from business. The good news was, this year they weren't bending my ear about how much I needed to find a man. My gals were scared to mention m.a.n. around me unless his name was Noah, and even then they tiptoed.

Tonight's gala was going to be hard enough as it was. It was going to be a difficult reminder of how my love story with Noah began. I needed to get through this night. I'd chosen to have

Black Sequinned Bows and Champagne Nights opt out the event planning this year. I didn't need the unnecessary pressure this year nor did I have the energy for it. I was making it okay to give myself a much needed a break from taking on extra projects beyond those my business required. Since the accident I made it a point to be more mindful of not taking on too much. It was good for me to spend more time with my children. My plate was full enough as it was.

Lily had even decided to let another committee person be in charge of this year's overall event planning. She said Noah had declined the invitation to be Masters of Ceremonies for the first time in years. I doubted I would be seeing him tonight. I loved Noah, but I was so overwhelmed with all that had happened, I hadn't known where to begin. After tonight's gala, I promised myself I would be the one to break the ice, drive over to Zoe's in the morning, and hope like hell he had not forgotten me and how much I love him. I wanted my man back.

I came down my staircase ready to endure tonight's gala, only to find my son fawning over Lily yet again.

"Hey Ms. Lily," Xavier swooned, as he twirled Lily around with one hand. "You make me wanna do things a man only dreams about," he said, kissing her on both cheeks.

"My goodness X, you look so handsome with your hair cut close. And the mustache . . . you look so much like Lucas."

"Doesn't he, now?" Samantha agreed. "If only we can work on the big mouth that opens and foot goes inside. Every time he sees a beautiful female, he starts drooling like some overgrown frat boy."

"Yeah," Xavier said, ignoring Samantha's remark. "Noah tells me that too."

"How is Noah?" Lily asked, silently watching me taking my lipstick and mascara out of my tote and into my clutch.

"He's good," Xavier said. "He's pretty much healed. We both are. He's building a new home."

"Madison calls it the castle," I added casually.

Lily shot me a glance. Yeah I admitted I was keeping up.

"All he needs now is his queen," Xavier said, coughing twice, peering at me to take the hint. "He's in tip top physical shape, willing and ready to move forward with his life. The rest is up to . . . " Xavier paused, choosing his words carefully. "Up to the powers that be," he said, feeling proud he came up with that line of bullshit.

"I see," Lily said softly, her brow raised. "The powers that be, eh? You know what they say, don't fight the power."

"Yeah Ms. Lily, don't fight the power," Xavier said, twirling her around a second time.

"That's not what or who I meant," Lily said, blushing from embarrassment.

I hugged and kissed Lily on the cheek.

"You look beautiful as always," I said, hoping to change the subject off Noah.

Lily was her usual beautiful self. She was wearing vintage Chanel in red tonight. I'd chosen to wear black single sleeve off-the-shoulder full length Elie Tahari gown that I thought was quite elegant. I wasn't up to having to bat off any suitors tonight. I called myself toning it down by covering most of myself up.

Xavier had me lifting hand weights all month, doing a slew of repetitions to tone my arms. He claimed my arms were looking better than Michelle Obama's. I was glad to be getting some use out of that expensive Georgetown University education of his that I'd paid an enormous amount of money. Xavier had been promoted to Regional Manager of all of the gym's trainers for the northeast franchise, so he was pretty proud of himself. So was I. He'd recently received a call to come interview with the New York Jets training staff after the first of the year. His Uncle Reese was more than thrilled that he might be joining him in New York next year. We all were keeping our fingers crossed. I was so proud of how far Xavier had come.

I put my La Perla black wrist garter on my bare arm that tied around my wrist and between two fingers. I wore Noah's gold charm bracelet on my sleeved arm, thinking it had a festive flair about it. A part of me wanted to take Noah with me this evening. I missed him. I missed our marathon phone chats. I missed our lovemaking. I missed watching him with the kids. I was glad Claire had given me his draft of a letter. It helped to explain things a bit more for me. I realized Noah wasn't the kind of man that had ever intended to conceal the truth about Claire from me. I realized he had attempted on more than one occasion to get that story out, due to no fault of his own.

Prior to my reading his letter, not only was I questioning his character, but I was questioning my own judgment in men as well. The disclosure of Claire's parentage felt like such a huge emotional setback. I had done an incredible amount of work on myself since my breakup with Warren. I believed I was much smarter, a better judge of character than to end up loving a deliberately deceitful man yet again. But I better understood now why Noah had done what he did. I knew that what Noah had done, he did out of his love for Lucas and for my happiness.

"Nathan is back in D.C. working on some white paper for the American College of Cardiologists. I left him behind," Lily said, nudging me out of my thoughts.

"You guys seem to be in a strange state of existence I don't fully understand. Are you co-existing?"

"We're not moving towards divorce or separation, but not really working on the marriage either," Lily answered, fluffing up her hair, applying a fresh coat of fuchsia lipstick to her pouty lips.

"I kinda get that," I said, closing my clutch and opening it back up again. I was overstuffing it again.

I wondered if Lily and Nathan's state of marriage had anything to do with Gabriel or if they were in some state of denial or avoidance. But far be it from me to try to mentally take on the affairs of someone else's relationship. It was enough for me to get through my own these days and nights.

"I guess I'm going to be your plus one tonight, Lily. Madison and Quentin are going to meet us there. Reese is taking a rain check."

"Wow, you mean we have the night to ourselves without Mr. Overprotective Reese around," Lily chuckled.

"We do," I said. "That should make for a decent night, huh? Lucky us," I laughed.

"Where's Claire?" Lily asked looking around.

"She's over to Zoe's. Zoe and Julian are still sheltering Noah. Claire spends a ton of time over there now. She even spends the nights some weekends, soaking up as much quality time as she can get with Noah. They're playing their own game of father daughter catch up."

"It's kind of nice they're getting close. Claire did get the short end of the stick not really having a Dad around."

"Yeah, and she hated Warren with a passion. He spanked her once as a little girl when I ran out one day on an errand. She never forgave him. I hated he had put his hands on my child."

"Well he's dead for real this time. She has Noah now," Lily said, grabbing her coat.

"Noah tells her lots of stories about Lucas and how the two of them used to sign off their flights with each other by talking about Claire. Zoe says he tells her that story over and over again, as if he's reflecting back on that moment in time as if it were yesterday."

"Sounds almost poignant," Lily said. "Who knew."

"I don't want to interfere in her relationship with Noah, so I let her spend time with him whenever she pretty much wants at this point. They've gotten close, so I stay out of it."

"Sounds like the right move. We all need a father figure."

"Actually Noah's pretty much won Xavier and Samantha over as well," I added, grabbing my black ranch mink. "You know when Lucas died, Xavier saw himself stepping in as the man of the family. I wondered when Noah came along, how Xavier was going to react."

"Yeah like whether the presence of a new man in your life would feel threatening to him in his role as the man of the house."

"Yeah, I think the fact they almost lost their lives together, and then later leaning on each other for their own physical and mental healing, has helped them to bond closer. It's an experience they both will forever share together. By the way, Zoe and Julian aren't doing tonight's entertainment. They are going to meet us there. The wanted to take their time and drive over separately."

"What's up with those two?"

"Nothing much beyond doing whatever they do helping Noah, along with the rest of these Cooks whose claim to fame has been helping him get his life back on track."

"You okay with that Riley? You're not jealous he's getting all the attention are you?" Lily chuckled.

We both climbed in the back of the limousine that was waiting. I adjusted my gown, smoothing out the surfaces so as to avoid any wrinkles.

"No, I've adjusted to the idea. I do have some heart left you know. Trust that I haven't gone completely mad. You know how it goes, Lily."

"Yes I do," Lily laughed, grabbing the bottle of chilled champagne, pouring us both a glass.

"Mending hearts and breaking hearts," we both said in unison.

Lily and I gave each other a high five.

"Geez, all of us have no real role in tonight's event. Do you think we'll be able to suffer through it?" she said.

"I have no idea," I answered, taking another huge swig of my champagne.

Madison, Quentin, Zoe, Julian, Lily, and I were delighted some smart planner put us all at the same table again. I doubt it was merely a stroke of good luck. I suspected Lily had something to do with it, but she rarely shared all her little secrets.

Madison was wearing a lovely Emilio Pucci gown, looking totally stunning this evening. Quentin must have thought so too, because he hadn't taken his eyes off of her all evening. I leaned into Madison.

"What's up with Quentin, girl? He hasn't taken his eyes off you all evening."

Madison leaned into my ear, "He's in love. That's a good thing, right?"

"Of course it is Madison. Why are you questioning it? Is it mutual?"

"I'm all about the companionship," Madison winked.

"You know, I don't even know why I talk to you. Forget about it," I laughed.

Madison has had difficulty expressing the L word since the beginning of time. If she was in love, I'd have to see it with my own eyes, because trying to get her to admit it was like pulling teeth.

Diane Sawyer was this year's guest speaker so the room was all a buzz. I had managed to suffer through long reading of the names of the Fallen. It pained me that we had lost so many men in their service to their country. But this year there were no awards to accept on behalf of Lucas.

Much of my anger toward Lucas had subsided since Xavier had pulled through. I'd like to think he had that chat with the big man upstairs, because I'm pretty sure if I had lost Xavier, Lucas likely believed I was going to dig him up out of his grave and kill him again. I wanted my son here with me in this life. The fact that he was, I figured Lucas had held up his end.

After the reading of the Fallen, the official part of the evening was complete. I was glad we were getting to the party portion of the Gala. The bar was opened, the band was playing music, and the guests were starting to dance. The air in the room took on a more festive tone. As my lips touched the rim of my champagne flute, I pondered if I was going to do this to myself again next year. Probably, likely.

Surprisingly, Zoe and Julian had been called to the microphone to sing a duet. Oh habits die hard.

"Oh how nice is that," I said to Madison.

"Very nice," Madison replied.

"Excuse me, Riley. Madison, come with me for a minute, I'd like to introduce you to some friends of mine across the room," Quentin interrupted. "Will you excuse us Riley."

"No problem. I'll just sit here alone Quentin, and hope you didn't just put a target on my back," I teased.

"Of course I did Riley," Quentin playfully teased me back.

I was the only one left at our table. I shifted in my seat, noticing a man to my left at a nearby table that was beginning to make eyes at me. *Jesus, I hope he does not come over to ask me to dance; I am so not interested.* The possibility of dancing with a man here tonight only reminded me of Noah. This was where we began. I was not going to do that to myself. If he comes over, I'll politely say no, and head to the bar.

Thank goodness the lights in the room were being dimmed. The man at the other table could no longer make eye contact with me. The lights in the room dimmed further. A spotlight appeared, focusing on Julian at the baby grand piano. Zoe stood near the piano, microphone in hand, looking angelic in a sheer white gown with hints of sparkle that dazzled under the lights. The noise in the ballroom from the servers moving about seem to still as a more hushed mood filled the air.

"Ladies and gentlemen we have a special treat for you tonight."

Oh, good, Zoe's going to sing. Perhaps she and Julian are going to test drive the new song they'd been working on for weeks. They weren't originally supposed to perform tonight. This should be fun.

"There's a special person here tonight for which we dedicate this song. Her name is Riley Cook."

What? I raised my chin up, not believing my own ears. Riley Cook? Why is Zoe up there talking about me? Julian was playing softly in the background as she spoke.

"This is special number, a song called *"All The Way,"* sung by our favorite Masters of Ceremonies, Captain Noah Dunham."

The room broke out in spontaneous applause. Oh my God. This can't be. Did she say Noah? What was he doing here? He's going to sing? Julian began playing the melody on the piano. Before I knew it, Noah's voice rang through the microphone in song, as he walked across the cleared dance floor from the opposite side of the room, now standing under the same spotlight where Zoe previously stood. He was dressed differently this year. He was no longer wearing his traditional military dress attire, but was outfitted in a black tuxedo. Noah began singing melodically, walking slowly towards me. A slow hot cadence of passion was building inside me as he bellowed out the words.

"When somebody loves you, it's no good unless he loves you, all the way. Happy to be near you when you need someone to cheer you all the way. Taller than the tallest trees, that's how it's got to feel, and deeper than the deep blue sea , that's how deep it goes when it's real."

I could taste the salt of my tears as they streamed down my face. Noah's eyes traveled up my body, locking me in love's merciless grip. I placed my hand over my mouth, the other across my chest, my heart caught in a sweet collision with his. When he reached my table, he place the microphone down, extending his hand.

"Dance with me Riley."

I never got a chance to answer. He pulled me to my feet, pressing my body towards his, my own feet falling into step with his. Julian continued playing on the piano while Noah led me to the middle of the ballroom floor where we slow danced alone, moving in a small circle in each other's arms. Zoe picked up the singing where Noah's melody left off. I was trembling, my heart beating wildly. Noah placed a tender kiss on my lips as Julian and Zoe played and sang our song, my heart exploding with each beat.

"Let me love you Riley," Noah whispered.

I was rendered speechless. I put my arms around his neck, kissing him back passionately, speaking softly between my own tears.

"I love you too, Noah. I don't want to live my life without you anymore. I'm sure of it."

My voice and my body was trembling. I wanted my man back.

"I'm a lucky bastard. What are you doing the rest of your life Riley Cook? Marry me baby?"

Oh my god, he didn't propose did he? I felt my knees weakening. Noah held me securely in his arms sending a silent message that he wasn't going to let me go anywhere.

"Marry me Riley," he repeated.

Noah dropped down on one knee, pulling out a small black velvet box tied with a black sequinned bow. I carefully untied the bow, lifting the lid. Harry Winston.

I nodded my head up and down in agreement, still unable to form words.

"Is that a yes, baby?" Noah said, rising to his feet.

I nodded again, tears flowing uncontrollably. The audience was clapping loudly, as Zoe and Julian moved to another song, singing and playing 'No Ordinary Love.'

"Oh hell Riley," Noah laughed as I stood looking at the most beautiful ring, like I was awestruck. He placed the cushion-cut micro-pave five carat diamond engagement ring set brightly in platinum on my left finger. The crowd was still applauding.

My head was still nodding nervously in agreement before I could hear myself mouth the words.

"Yes, Noah. Yes I will marry you. Yes," I said again, hardly succeeding at choking back the tears that were running down my face.

He kissed each tear gently and slowly on the side of my face.

"Riley, I'm so sorry I hurt you. I promise I'll never ever hurt you again," he whispered in my ear.

We continued to hold each other in the middle of the ballroom floor. The lights came up a bit. Zoe and Julian turned the microphone and piano back over to the band, who began playing Lauren Wood's *Fallen*. The guests crowded on the dance floor, many of whom expressed their congratulations. Noah's slow sexy smile was my undoing, as he shook hands with some of the men who were extending congratulatory remarks, still not letting me out of his arms. Madison and Quentin joined us on the dance floor to our right, while Lily and one of the admirals danced next to us on our left, our closest friends surrounding us in love.

"Go on with your bad self," Madison grinned.

"Congratulations Riley. Captain," Lily winked.

"Yeah man, you did good," Quentin added.

"You two need to get a room," Madison said jokingly.

Noah and I continued to slow dance, still kissing each other passionately. We never let go of each other, hardly noticing anyone else in the room.

"Did you notice they were playing our song?" he said, in between kisses.

"Yes. And I noticed you were singing our song," I laughed in glee, grinning like a school girl.

"I will sing it to you every day and night Riley, if need be. Just in case you forget," he said, before kissing me on the top of my forehead, then again on my lips.

CHAPTER 34

NOAH

"Claire finally told me she gave you my half written letter of attempted forgiveness. I never felt I'd gotten it right, but I'm glad she gave it you."

Riley paused, glanced up from her laptop, looking over the top of her glasses at me. She smiled at me with that same smile that unleashed uncontrollable desire throughout me. Surely she knew the effect her smile had on me. I loved the look of happiness on her face.

We were working together in her home office today. She had a wonderful workspace that struck me as being conducive to creativity. I needed to remember to incorporate and re-create the feel in the office space I was building for her in our new home. She liked soothing colors, clean lines, with a touch of whimsical sprinkled about.

Riley was working on an updated business forecast deliverable for Nicholas, and I was supposed to be signing off on architectural changes for Quentin. She was likely getting more down than I was. It was too hard for me to focus around her. She was a beautiful distraction and she knew it.

"Claire said I needed to read it to get closure so I could act on how I really felt. She claimed she realized how sad I was when I stopped baking bread. She knew I was miserable without you, that I needed you back in my life."

"Not as bad as I needed you baby," I said, raising myself up out of the leather ottoman, reaching for Riley's chin, kissing her on the lips softly, catching a fresh whiff of her scent of lavender and vanilla body wash.

A hot blush swept across her face. I loved it when I could get that kind of reaction out of her.

"I used to think that out of all of my children, Claire was

most like me," she said, tapping her pen on top of her mousepad. "But now, I see your genetic encoding in her. She's wise, insightful, and hates to lose at most anything competitive."

"Her quest to be a photojournalist has taught her how to look into the souls of people. She can discern what others can't, spending so much time behind that lens of hers."

"Umm," Riley hummed, giving my words more thought.

"I'm proud of Claire. Most of all I'm happy she's been willing to embrace me as her father. Things could have turned out differently you know, could have gone either way. One thing for sure, I was never going to give up on her . . . on you . . . on us."

"Xavier and Samantha are happy their plan to get you back in my life has prevailed. You're the new found basketball buddy whose giving him free advice on women, even opening up the old playbook I hear," Riley said slyly.

"I don't know baby. My "playbook" might be too far out of date for X. I used to pride myself on thinking I knew women, but I sure as hell almost lost you."

"No need to cry over spilled milk. We're together now, That's all that matters," she said, blowing a kiss my way, her fingers still working the keyboard. I reached my hand up in the air, and caught her kiss.

"Not letting those get away," I grinned.

Riley laughed. I loved hearing her laugh again.

"Xavier wants a new Ducati."

The sound of her fingernails tapping like rapid fire on the keyboard came to a sudden halt.

"He needs to forget about it."

"No doubt he will respect your wishes babe. But he's a man now. He's gonna do what he wants to do when he wants to do it."

"I never wanted my son on that damn bike to begin with," Riley said, leaning back in her chair, crossing her arms across her breast. "I swear if you don't talk him down off that stupid idea I'm going to cut the torpedo off."

I glanced up from Quentin's architectural plans to look into her eyes. Dead serious that one. I ran my hand swiftly up my thigh and over the torpedo in an act of self-protection, before I poked that bear again.

"Baby he's a grown man."

"Uh huh," she answered. "And I'm a grown woman with knife skills."

Color that topic dead for now. No new Ducati was coming through these doors anytime soon. Xavier was on his own. She had threatened the torpedo.

"Hey family," Samantha said, her appearance timely. I wanted off this subject. "Ya'll still boo lovin'," Samantha grumbled, Cleo and Stogie walking on her heels. "Madison and Aunt Zoe are starting to ring my phone, asking *me* of all people when you two were coming up for air. Nobody's seen you guys."

"Excuse me?" Riley said to Samantha, not letting that crack go by. "Last I checked, you had your own life to worry about, daughter."

Cleo jumped in my lap. I patted her head gently. No one noticed I'd been feeding her doggie biscuits on the side before the accident. Stogie barked at me, wanting attention from me. Stogie was an easy sell. Stogie loved everybody, but Cleo required a bit of coaxing. Cautious. Just like the rest of the women in this house. I reached in my jeans pocket, handing both of them a fresh biscuit.

"And I intend to live it," Samantha quipped back at Riley. "I gotta hot date tonight Momma Dukes. You can't be the only woman around here getting their freak on," she said, calling both the dogs and heading out the back door.

"Freak on?"

I stared at Riley waiting for her to respond. Good lord, is this what life is gonna be like having daughters around? I chuckled to myself at the thought of how much my life had changed in the last year. But I was loving every minute it. We had all gone through the fire, making it to the other side, grabbing the pot of gold at the end of the rainbow. Family life was its own reward.

"Do you think Cleo's getting fat?" Riley asked quizzically.

"Nope," I said, not looking back up at her, afraid my guilty face would give me away.

Thankfully Riley's messenger on her computer made a loud ding. Lady luck was on my side today, having managed to sidestep some of the afternoon's conversation.

"It's Nicholas," she said. "He wants to know if we've set a wedding date yet. He claims I need to build wedding and honeymoon time off into next year's business plan forecast. This man is relentless," Riley said, reading his message, her head cocked to the side, her facial expression skewed. "Really?"

"Welcome to the world of all things Nicholas Becker," I grinned.

"Who builds a wedding into a business plan?" Riley asked.

"A die hard type A workaholic making a gazillion dollars a year man, that's who."

Riley shook her head in exasperation, typing something back.

"I forgot to mention babe, I asked Nicky to be my Best Man."

"Really?" Riley said. "Nothing like mixing business with pleasure," she said sarcastically.

"Is that a problem?"

"Nope. Madison will be my Maid of Honor, Nicholas will be your Best Man. Sounds like a lot of fireworks will be had whenever we get married."

Riley continued to peck on her laptop. She paused.

"Nicky wants to give us a wedding planner. He's hoping to delegate the task of a wedding planner to Lucia. He claims Lucia knows all he best wedding planners in New York."

"Wow, that's a total surprise seeing how Nicky is the penultimate bachelor."

"I'm thanking him," she said, typing back. "Wedding planner accepted. I don't want to wait another year," she said, leaning away from the screen, looking at me for confirmation.

"Good, because I told Nicky we might want to get married on New Year's Eve."

"New Year's Eve?" Riley gasped. "That hardly gives us time to plan a wedding! You do want a wedding don't you?"

"I want whatever you want gorgeous."

"Then, New Year's Eve it is," Riley said, texting Nicholas back to confirm. "But I have no idea how we pull this off in such a short period of time."

"The wedding planner will pull out all the stops on the strength of the Nicholas Becker name alone. Four weeks might not seem like a lot of time to plan a wedding, but once Nicholas's name gets kicked around, the wheels will start turning incredibly fast. Put your seatbelt on baby."

Riley's computer dinged yet again. She stared at the text message.

"Well I don't know about that," she exclaimed out loud.

"What now?" I ask.

"He claims he's gonna call "your boys," and tell them how to throw you a hot bachelor party. Says he won't be able to make it because he's business in France, but he'll see to it you'll have a good time, "Navy style?""

Riley looked at me as if to ask what the hell did that mean, Navy style. I knew exactly what it meant, but I wasn't about to educate her. So I changed the subject, stepping to the left again today.

"The torpedo misses you baby," I said, shuffling the architectural plans off my lap. "I think we should go dark for a while . . . in the dark . . . for a couple of days. If wedding plans are imminent, I might not see you for a while."

"You do have a point there, Captain," Riley said, getting up from the computer, sitting on my lap, wrapping her hands around my neck. I kissed her nose and then her sweet lips. She grabbed my hand, leading us upstairs to the bedroom.

I basked in the view of that beautiful ass as she climbed the stairs ahead of me.

"I'm all for giving that posse of yours something to talk about," I moaned.

I smacked her ass as we both fell onto the bed together, stripping our clothes off, tossing them across the room like two teenagers afraid of getting caught.

"I don't know what kind of protein shakes Xavier's been feeding you, but the torpedo never wears out."

"A wingman never tells," I groaned, as Riley shed her pink lace bra and panties, giving me full view of every inch of what was mine.

CHAPTER 35

NOAH

I could hear the noise a mile away as I pulled the Commander up to Quentin's house. It hardly mattered though. Quentin's home sat on so many acres you'd have to walk a mile before you would get to the next neighbor, let alone any signs of life.

Quentin, Julian, Xavier, and Nathan had all agreed on Nicholas's orders to hook up and throw me a rockin' bachelor party. They didn't know Nicholas like I did. Nicholas was Mr. Hollywood Lights, Miami Nights. If Nicky was involved in the party plans, everybody here was in trouble. I knew before I walked inside I was getting too old for this shit.

I told Nicky not to go too far over the top, getting the fellas pumped up. Xavier somehow ended up being Nicky's point man here in Pennsylvania. I reminded Nicky that Xavier was Lucas's son, young with tendencies that leaned toward the wild side. I wasn't sure what to expect tonight.

I heard several of Xavier's posse friends from the Kids of Navy Vets Motorcycle Club were going to be here. Xavier still didn't have a new bike, and I hoped to keep it that way. No way was I letting Riley cut the torpedo off.

I rang the doorbell twice. The music was so loud, I wasn't sure if these guys could hear a doorbell.

Quentin answered.

"Oh shit man, the guest of honor has arrived."

Quentin gave me a bear hug as I came through the door.

"Hey Q. You guys went all out," I said, looking around and taking in the view.

Quentin's house was set up like a huge casino.

"Am I in the right place Q?"

Quentin starting laughing out loud.

"Compliments of your good friend, Nicholas Becker," Q said, with his arms spread out. "You needed to warn me about your friend, Noah. You should see the "grown and sexy" he sent to your party. All tens baby."

I made my way through the game room. I better understood Q's level of excitement. He had no idea what he was getting into conspiring with best man Nicholas. This bachelor party was no joke.

The oversized game room was set up with poker tables, crap tables, pool tables, card tables, and a couple of roulette tables. A trio of spicy looking blue-eyed blonde twenty-something triplets were dressed in scanty cocktail dresses, their heads adorned with dealer's hats.

Beyond the casino area, another room was set up as a cigar and a cocktail bar, both manned by female bartenders. A small stage rotated in the middle of the room. A stripper pole was center stage, a couple of strippers dangling upside down off the side of the pole, their bodies tangled up closely together. Red velvet couches were neatly placed around the stage giving whoever sat there full view.

I took my eyes off those beauties, perusing the room. Xavier was across the room in the corner with some brunette packing a pair of double D's giving him a lap dance, teasing him, juggling those ginormous breasts in his mouth. Nikki Minaj's *Truffle Butter* was playing loudly throughout the entire house over the intercom system. Note to self: Didn't know Quentin liked rap music. A couple of hot gal servers were working the smoked-filled room taking drink orders. It was hard to tell whether this was Quentin's home, a gentlemen's club, or Dante's Inferno.

"Yo, everybody, the guest of honor has arrived!" Q shouted out to everyone in the room, shoving a cigar in my mouth, handing me a chilled vodka martini. Quentin gave me another bear hug and patted me on the back, clinking my glass.

"Congratulations, man."

Xavier raised the bottle of Corona planted in his hand, looking a bit tilted, but signaling his acknowledgement of my arrival. I nodded at him, smiling, thinking Riley's gonna kick my ass for bringing her son home wasted tonight. I kind of hated the fact Reese couldn't make it. He was in the middle of some major audit. I was hoping to be able to bond with him some more now that I was marrying his sister. It had been almost a year since I had seen him, though I heard he had come to the hospital several times when he was in town visiting the family.

There was a large fishbowl at the end of the bar for car keys. I surrendered, throwing mine in the mix, knowing it was highly unlikely I was going to be driving myself anywhere tonight. With the looks of this party, it going to be a long crazy night. Xavier caught a glimpse of me dropping my keys in the bowl. He busted out laughing, throwing his keys at me from far across the room.

I caught them and nodded a silent thank you at him.

"Yep, you know the deal," I mouthed under my breath. His mother will not be killing me tonight. No sirree. Not if I expected to get married. I dropped his keys in the bowl next to mine.

A huge home theatre screen was playing a porn flick. Six Degrees of Penetration flashed across the screen. A couple of Xavier's motorcycle friends were dressed in biker leather, throwing back tequila shots with a couple of twins licking in their ears. My eyes scanned the room looking for the safest place to be in this smoke-filled bedrock of trouble. My gaze landed on Julian and Dr. Nathan at the poker table. I unbuttoned my shirt, loosened my tie, and moving their direction to join them.

"Hey Captain. Looks like your friend Nicholas and Xavier really know how to throw a bachelor party. I wish I could get married all over again," Julian said, wide eyed and laughing.

"Yeah man, who knew Xavier had it in him," Dr. Nathan seconded. "And Quentin is living large. He's obviously not letting all that family money go to waste," he said, pulling his cigar to his mouth, sipping on large glass of brandy.

"Quentin and Xavier had help," I said, rolling my eyes, looking peripherally to catch a glimpse of Xavier motor-boating those double D's.

"Yeah I heard it on the grapevine," Julian said, throwing a flush down. "I can't wait to meet your friend Nicholas at the wedding, if this party is any indicator of what's to come," he laughed.

"I'm outta touch with the grapevine," Dr. Nathan said. "Lily

315

ignores me most of the time. I'm living my marriage in the margins."

"What's that mean, in the margins?" Julian asked.

"Means we're not on the same page," Dr. Nathan answered.

A blonde busty server approached Nathan, sporting her boobs in his face, asking him if could she get him something.

"Yeah, I'll take whatever he's having," Julian said, acknowledging that Nathan was the chick magnet at the table. Julian fell out laughing, cigar hanging out of his mouth, re-dealing the cards.

"Yeah man," I said to Julian, slapping him five and laughing.

"Fine with me. As long as none of you mutherfuckers don't have a heart attack in here tonight, it's all good.," Dr. Nathan responded.

We fell out laughing and I doubled down on my hundred dollar chips.

"Oh hell no," Julian said. "You're my man and all Noah, and I know you're getting married, but don't think you're gonna be beating me at poker tonight."

"Fuck you man. You know I'm getting married. If I lose tonight, I'm still coming out the winner, dude."

"Don't mess with the Chocolate Thunder," Julian said. That's right, BMW in the house. Beautiful Mister Wonderful," Nathan squealed, disguising his voice like a high shrill girl.

"What the fuck are you two talking about?" I frowned.

"The grapevine baby," Julian said, both of them laughing together, slapping each other high fives.

"Fuck you guys. You assholes are jealous."

"What man wouldn't be. That Riley is a real keeper," Dr. Nathan said, dragging a long pull on his cigar.

"Man, I'm only here because of you, Nate. Thank you man, for pulling me through. I will be forever grateful to you."

"Just doing my job, Noah."

"I heard what you did. How you watched over me, giving me special treatment and all. I appreciate you saving my life. I'm only able to get married, because of you."

I threw a couple of my cards down, asking for two more.

"Forget it man. I had no choice but to save you," Nathan laughed. "Lily's one step away from cutting my dick off. Man, if I didn't get you to pull through I'd be walking around dickless, with one ball right about now."

Nathan turned his head towards the server who was coming back to the poker table with another round of drinks, his eyes squinting from the smoke of his cigar that was curling above his head. He waved the smoke from out in front of his face.

"Oh baby. Oh baby, shake that money maker, baby," Julian said, as he tucked bucks between her beautiful set of breasts as she set our drinks down, grinning ear to ear, her eyes locked on Dr. Nathan.

"Ah you big pimpin tonight," Dr. Nathan said to Julian.

Where did these guys come from? I had not seen this side of them. But then again, I'd been unconscious half the summer.

The woman swung her long blonde hair around, and Julian shook his head.

"Lord help me Jesus. My heart can't take it Dr. Nathan," he said loudly, as he slapped his cards down.

I looked across the room to check on Xavier. He was dancing, sandwiched in between two sweet fine sweet young women. One was in front of him, twerking. The other was in back of him shaking her booty to the music, both hotties grinding on him at the same time. Xavier had a Corona in each hand, one for him, and one he was pouring in the mouths of those two hotties.

I heard a loud whistle blow. Before I knew it, Quentin swept in the room with a couple of new blondes, and two black girls built like brick houses, all wearing gold thongs. A couple of red-headed smoking hot tens dressed in police officer shirts with fuck me heels were handcuffed to Quentin, yelling "lock all these playa's and pimps up bitches."

God this night was testing my resilience. Scanty tops were popping off again. I was getting horny, but not for any woman in this room. I wanted Riley. Quentin had a cigar in his hand, shaking his hips, laughing like a wild man as the women swerved their asses in front of him. A couple of Quentin's company's sales brokers were slinging Benjamin's at the girls on the poles. The girls on the poles were working them like they were holding the keys to a brinks truck. This party had turned into a high roller den of inequity.

"Damnnnnn Quentin," Julian said, peering so hard at the girl cops he fell off the back of the chair, hitting the floor. I swore Zoe must keep Julian on lock down for a reason. The red-headed twins had little police caps on that were cocked to the side. Quentin was dragging them by their navy blue ties. Mystikal's *Bouncin'* was playing throughout the room when the girly cops made their entrance.

"Julian man, are you okay? I said staring down at him on the floor, helping to pick him up.

"Noah man, your bachelor party is off the chain."

"Hold it together man." Julian gave me a fist bump from the floor. "Nathan's got to keep his balls tonight," I said, bumping his fist back.

"I told you idiots, I'm not working tonight," Dr. Nathan, said, grabbing server girl and pulling her on his lap for a kiss, whispering something in her ears. This party had ratcheted up a yet another notch as everyone got even more drunk, sex crazed, in a room full of beautiful gold-diggers making bank, getting their hustle on.

I eyeballed Xavier. He no longer had a shirt on. He was showing off his six pack. Those young girls were still all over him. One of them was licking her tongue, squeezing lime juice all over his wingman tattoo. The other one was grinding on him so hard, you would thought she was making a baby.

God damn, torpedo! I'm going to declare war on your ass motherfucker if you even so much as think about getting aroused, bitch. The torpedo had declared all-out war against me tonight. The little muthafucking head was not in charge tonight. bachelor party or no bachelor party. This shit belongs to Riley. *Do not get it twisted up in here with all this pussy being slung in your face. Forget about it.* I took another puff on my cigar, asked Julian for another card once he got back upright in his chair. The scantily clad red-headed police woman did a booty shake of her ass in front of me with whip cream hanging off her breasts. She started speaking with a French accent. I didn't speak French.

"Est-ce votre entorrage?"

Apparently Nathan did.

"Hell yeah, we're his entourage," Nathan clamored, his speech slightly slurred.

"I have orders tonight from Monsieur Becker to put the

groom-to-be on lock down. Looking for Mico."

Damn Nicholas. My head snapped up as my eyes registered surprise. Before I knew it, the police women spun my chair around, riding their asses in my lap. My brow broke out in sweat. Those women were smokin' hot. No doubt they were getting ready to jump the torpedo. It was getting far too hot up in here.

"Sorry Mommy, you've got the wrong man, the groom's over there in that corner with his shirt off. The one with those sweeties licking tequila off his arm."

I pointed my finger at Xavier. I was getting too old to be corrupted like this. My life in the fast lane was over. By now Julian and Nathan were rolling out of their chairs. Those hot momma's eyeballed Xavier across the room, grinning as they closed in on their mark. They glided their way over to Xavier, kissing each other along the way. Fucking Nicholas. I couldn't believe he was trying my patience all the way from France.

"Man you know you are wrong, motherfucker," Julian grumbled.

"Yeah man you should have told them I was the groom," Nathan pleaded

"Shit man. We are all are getting entirely too old for this young pussy. Nathan, dude, you know that's a heart attack waiting to happen."

"Hell Noah, you killing me anyway, sending those beauties over to Xavier. Old playa's need lovin' too," Nathan laughed heartily.

"You have a wife Nathan."

"Life in the margins baby."

I shook my head in frustration.

"I'll be back," I said, throwing my cards down on the table.

I stood, headed to the head to empty my bladder and get the torpedo back under control. God damn, it's hot in here. I glanced outside towards the deck, thinking I might take a minute to cool myself off. I pulled the sliding doors to the deck back, not realizing Quentin was there. Quentin was sprawled out on his lounge chair getting a blow job by one of those pretty pole dancers.

"Hey man, come on outside. Cool off," he said, pushing the girl off him.

She looked at me with a raised eyebrow, as to ask if I was interested.

I shook my head no. She shrugged her shoulders and headed back inside.

"Nah, man, I need to take a leak."

I found my way to the bathroom, at the same time a couple of the scantily clad dolls exited the bathroom sporting a couple guys licking lines off their chest. I looked at my Rolex. It was close to five in the morning. and I needed to take care of my business, shake some of this vodka off and keep an eye on Xavier. There was more free pussy running around at this bachelor party than the law allowed. The guys really pulled out all the stops on this bachelor party with a little help from my friend. Madison's really got something on her hands. I would forever look at Mr. Squeaky Clean a whole lot differently going forward. To think I pegged Quentin as shy and reserved. Motherfucker is not only the life of the party, HE IS THE PARTY. I was starting to feel like I was in a movie scene from the Hangover. Note to self: Make sure Nicholas and Quentin never bond. No way would I ever be able to rein those two in at the same time.

As soon as I entered the bathroom, I locked the door behind me, making sure none of those women made their way in here to try to get a hold of my ass. The torpedo was under extreme pressure. Naughty thoughts had gone wild around here. I kept the big head working overtime to stay in control, lest that little head got out the silo trying to take off on its own. I needed a moment to cool down.

I calmed myself down, slapping cold water on my face. When I exited the bathroom, I could see one of Quentin's friends give one of those pole dancers a shotgun with a blunt. Alcohol overflowing, drugs, sexy women. This was a prescription for trouble. I headed back into the game room, stuck my stogie in my mouth, chug-a-lugged my chilled vodka, and ordered another. Xavier looked to be near to passing out. It was time I rescued the poor boy. Still not ready for the big leagues, but he gave it a good crack at bat, that was for sure.

I managed to locate Quentin in this maze of madness.

"Thanks Q for the party. I had a blast. It's time for me to rock and roll. Need to get Xavier home."

"No problem man. You know the young bloods can't hang like us old heads. Give me a minute and I'll have my driver come around to take you guys home."

"C'mon Julian, help me with Xavier. Grab Nathan," I ordered.

Nathan still had a couple of those police women swinging on his arm. I grabbed Xavier's and my keys out the bowl. The four of us headed for the limousine Quentin made available to take us home. I threw Xavier in the side seat of the limousine. The rest of us followed.

"Quentin, I'll come back tomorrow to pick up the Commander and Xavier's ride."

"Commander? You call your ride the Commander? You trippin' bitch," Quentin laughed.

The pretty redheads slipped themselves under his armpit.

"Safe travels my brother."

Q waved us off, heading back inside to the party.

Nathan and Julian were gonna thank me tomorrow for dragging their asses out of my party. I was just thankful my own ass had survived. In the past I'd live my life in the fast lane, but my bachelor party was on warp speed by anybody's standards. I instructed the driver to take both of them to Julian and Zoe's where Lily and Nathan were camping out this trip.

When I arrived back at Riley's home, I was carrying Xavier over my shoulder. I still had a cigar hanging out of my mouth. I was pretty sure Xavier and I smelled like a distillery. Riley opened her door wearing nothing but a sexy little black lace baby doll nightie. The torpedo shot to attention.

"What in the world happened to my son?" Riley said, a look of worry passing across her face.

"Not to worry baby. The question is not what happened, but what didn't happen," I answered.

Riley followed on my heels closely as if she were watching over her cub. I felt like the prey. The last thing I needed was her to pounce on me if she didn't feel comfortable her son was okay.

I carried Xavier to his room, tossing him across the bed. I pulled his shoes off, kicking them into the corner. He was mumbling words I didn't understand. I prayed he wouldn't puke.

Riley was still talking twenty miles an hour, bending my ear over Xavier's state of being. I got that. She was my baby, but

Xavier was hers.

"What did you guys do to him, Noah?" she said, her brow frowning.

"We can talk about it in the morning, love. Right now it's about what I'm going to do to you."

I closed the doubled doors to her bedroom behind me. I picked Riley up, cuddling her in my arms, carrying her to the bed.

I scrambled to pull my pants off. I tore off my shirt, practically ripping the buttons like I was Rambo. I wanted my woman. Riley peered at me with those big sexy brown eyes.

"Were you and the torpedo on your best behavior tonight?" she said all soft and innocent, her soft skin reminding me of honey mustard that I wanted to lick.

I grabbed Riley's ass, pulling her on top of me, right on top of the torpedo.

"Bringing him home safe and sound to you Mommy."

CHAPTER 36

RILEY

"Riley, you ready?" Madison asked.

"Yes, I'm ready, Maddy."

"Okay then let's do the damn thing," Samantha said.

"Xavier get the door," Lily said.

"I'm right behind you," Zoe responded. "Let's go Claire."

We each piled out of the white limousine. Nicholas's wedding planner was standing outside the limousine with a headpiece in her ear, directing us as if she were managing traffic on a busy morning.

"Xavier help me please," I pleaded, as the doors of the limousine opened. "What time is it son?"

"It's 11:30p.m. mother," Xavier said, straightening his tie, adjusting his Ray Bans.

I didn't understand why Xavier wore Ray Bans at night. But this was not the time for me to challenge his choices. Far be it for me to rock the cool factor tonight.

Tonight was New Year's Eve. I was marrying Captain Noah Dunham. I exited the limousine. I was standing on the steps of Saint Patrick's Cathedral in Manhattan, New York. Noah, Nicholas, Quentin, Nathan, and my brother Reese would be at the end of the long walk I was preparing to take. Both our families and the who's who of east coast political wannabes had arrived to see us tie the knot.

Madison, Zoe, and Lily were standing at my side. They were dressed in full length cream colored Ralph Lauren gowns tied at the breast with my signature black sequinned bow. Claire and Samantha opted for tea length black silk dresses, with cream colored bows tied at the bodice.

I chose a beautiful Calvin Klein off-white satin gown. A soft short white veil covered my face. Elegant and simple. I carried a simple bouquet of white calla lilies tied with long black sequinned ribbons. I'd slipped a black sequinned garter under my gown with Noah's name monogramed on it. My surprise. I could hear Julian playing the church organ softly as we entered the cathedral.

"Mother, are you ready?" Xavier asked. "I'm honored to give you away today."

"I wouldn't have anyone else by my side tonight."

"You look beautiful, mother."

"Thank you son. You're looking pretty handsome yourself."

Xavier adjusted the tie on his tuxedo.

"He's a good man. My father would be pleased. As am I. This is going to be a fun ride Mother. You wait and see. You deserve happiness. And Noah makes you happy."

I smiled a huge grin, squeezing my son's hand.

"Xavier, this man is not getting thrown back in the pond, trust me."

"You and that damn pond," Xavier said, shaking his head and laughing.

My son looked so sexy in his tuxedo and Ray Bans. I fully understood why the women flocked to him like bees to honey. My son was handsome like his father, and my new husband-to-be. Noah and I were surrounded by the people we loved the most in our life. No big fanfare. Just those we loved.

At midnight, the ball would drop at Times Square, signaling a new year. Fireworks would go off tonight in the sky. The fireworks in my heart would ablaze as well. Noah had given me a 18k gold tiffany Hershey kiss for my charm bracelet as his wedding present. I'd given him a Cartier watch. I gave both he and Xavier a half a heart on a David Yurman dog tag. Samantha and Claire each got Tiffany heart tags reminding all my family daily that they each had a piece of my heart. A new life would begin for Noah, the kids, and I tonight. We would all bring in the new year together.

It would take several months before Quentin would finish with our new home. I was pleased there was a delay. It would give me time to add my own personal touches to our new home while the new construction was still underway.

This would be the first time that Madison and I would be living more than a couple of houses away. The thought made me sad. It felt like an adjustment. Quentin and Noah joked that one of them was going to have to move the other into the other side of the "castle." Madison would say to their teasing saying "there can only be one queen in the castle." Perhaps Quentin needed to build another castle next door.

Claire was coming with Noah and me, but Xavier and Samantha were going to stay in the home Lucas and I built. They both needed some experience in paying rent. They couldn't afford the mortgage by themselves. Noah and I would help them, but this would be a good opportunity for them to learn some financial responsibility. It was time to clip their wings. Claire would get the benefit of both worlds. Noah promised to teach her to drive this year. She was motivated by the idea of being able to shuttle back and forth between both homes.

After the marriage ceremony, the wedding party would head over to the Marriott Marquis View Restaurant for the reception, dinner, and dessert. Noah and I were flying to the South of France for our honeymoon, compliments of Nicholas. Nicholas had loaned us one of the *Milk Money* jets. Our wedding present.

"Do you, Riley Nelson Cook, take Noah Michael Dunham for your lawfully wedded husband?"

"I do."

I hardly heard a word the priest was saying in my own level of excitement. I did remember hearing Noah say "I do" loudly and proudly.

"I now pronounce you husband and wife," the priest said loudly, his voice ringing throughout the cathedral.

Everyone was smiling as we excited the church. Confetti was being thrown on top of our heads. I heard Madison tell Quentin,

"Thank God. It's about time."

Lily was behind us taking credit with everyone for putting us together. Noah was beyond happy.

Noah helped me back into the limousine, as the rest of the bridal party entered their limousines behind ours. We were all headed to the Marriott Marquis next for our wedding reception. Nicholas's wedding planner did an awesome job. Everything went off as planned without a hitch.

"I swore Nicholas was crying real tears," I said to my husband as he opened the door to the white limousine.

"There's only one person that could bring tears to Nicholas Becker's eyes and it isn't me, trust me babe."

I was certain there was a story there in his words. I just

happened not to know it. As we settled into the limousine headed to our reception, Noah kissed me hard, reaching under my gown fingering my black sequinned bowed garter.

"Behave, honey."

"Baby, you know I can't keep my hands off you. I love you Riley. The torpedo loves you too."

I felt a hot blush rush across my face.

"What do you have planned for us this evening, my love?" I asked as I kissed him softly.

"Better than you could ever dream my love."

"Is it going to be better than I'm expecting?"

"More than you could imagine my dear."

Oh he was such a tease. I doubt he was going to tell me what he had planned for our honeymoon.

"Really? I can't imagine." I play along.

"Baby, it's going to be a champagne night, wrapped in black sequinned bows."

I grinned widely. My heart melted. I loved this man.

THE END

A WORD ABOUT THE AUTHOR

I am Jude E. McNamara. Virtual adventurer. Keyboard ninja. Guardian of sassy romantic encounters. I am the alter ego of that other woman, Jude. You know, the one that loves snowy nights, is in a relationship with love, and looking for her own hero. While by day she's off being the disciplined scrappy businesswoman with the mind of a shark, I gallivant her keyboard by night, running wild and free on the down-low. I figure she'll have to catch up to me. Because once that blue power button turns on, I'm far too busy breathing life into those colorful characters that run around in her head, incessantly telling me their stories even if it's at the break of dawn.

You can find me and my merry band of jet-setting girlfriends running from the paparazzi at the high-end cocktail bars in Manhattan, drinking Patron Silver. I'm the flashy one wearing the sparkly tiara on my head. Like clockwork, when she faithfully dons her track shoes to catch up with me, I usually have to listen to her lecture me about my behavior over a glass of champagne. She loves champagne. Actually I love champagne too—except I like mine with a side of tall, handsome hunk begging me to stop at the intersection of heartbreak hotel and romantic encounter road, demanding a happily ever after.

It's an arduous race to "The End" before her blue button goes dark and I cease to exist. But once the blue light appears, the race is on, right up to the point when we two Judes meet on the same page, often in a book like this one.

For more about the author, visit: www.judeemcnamara.com

Two Judes Publishing
668 Stony Hill Road Suite 339
Yardley, Pa 19067

STAY CONNECTED WITH JUDE

Thank you again for your readership and support. If you enjoyed this book, please leave a review on Amazon, Barnes and Noble, and Goodreads. If you would like to learn more about my other books, below is an excerpt of my next soon to be released novel. Also, you may wish to sign up for my Newsletter to be notified when my new novels are released.

Visit me online at www.judeemcnamara.com where you can learn more about me, find book trailers, my blog posts and other new upcoming work.

Best Regards

Jude E. McNamara
www.judeemcnamara.com
Email Jude: jude@judeemcnamara.com

Follow me on Twitter @judeemcnamara
Follow me on Instagram: iamtwojudes
Follow me on Facebook: Jude.E. McNamara

AN EXCERPT FROM *MILK MONEY*

For more about Nicholas and Harper, read Milk Money *from Jude E. McNamara.*

CHAPTER 1

NICHOLAS

"The second best thing about this New Year's Eve night, next to my getting married, is the fact that you're my best man, Nicky. Thank you for standing up for me," Mico said, giving me a bear hug.

I tapped the rooftop of the limousine, waving my hand to let my driver Silas and my security chief Stephen Parks know that we were ready to head to Saint Patrick's Cathedral. Stephen was following behind us in the black armored Chevy Suburban. His security team were positioned ahead of us in another Suburban. Tonight's wedding celebration was a huge affair. My good friend Noah "Mico" Dunham was marrying Riley Nelson Cook. This time last year, my friend and his new bride's son had both almost lost their lives in a serious motorcycle accident.

"Silas, get us to the church on time!" I yelled. "If we're late, Mico will put me in one of those famous headlocks he was known for at the Naval Academy."

"Yeah man, how's our time? Riley will have my ass if I'm late."

"It's 10:15pm. Don't worry. Silas will have us there on time. Your bride is scheduled to arrive at 11:30pm."

"I take my vows at midnight, Nicky."

"Don't worry about it Mico. I've got the ring. We're on schedule."

Tonight was a big deal for my good friend. It was a bigger deal for me because I was standing up for him. Best Man. I wanted this night to go without a hitch.

"Here, take a shot to calm your nerves," I said, grabbing the crystal decanter off the limousine bar, pouring Mico and myself a shot of vodka.

"Thanks for the wedding present, Nicky. Loaning us the Milk Money jet so we can spend our honeymoon in the South of France is beyond wonderful," Mico said.

I could tell by his huge grin my gift had made him happy.

"Not a problem Mico. Riley's company was a great investment decision. I'll get it back from you one way or the other," I laughed heartily.

"Thanks Nicky. I earned major cool points with her when Milk Money took her company on as a client. That was a really good decision."

"Nah man. I should be thanking you for bringing Riley's business to my attention. Of the ten companies Milk Money has provided angel investment funds to this past year, hers has been one of the more profitable businesses on my leader board."

"Riley's worked really hard to make her business a success."

"Well it shows. That investment is showing lots of promise right off the bat. Even Lucia is happy," I said proudly.

"Well if Lucia is happy, then life is pretty good. Lucia is one badass woman. She is not to be messed with, Nicky."

"You're telling me? Dude, you're preaching to the choir."

"Does she ever chill, or does she always work herself into oblivion?"

"Rarely chills," I said, shaking my head back and forth.

What Mico didn't realize, was that "badass" didn't even begin to appropriately describe my business partner Lucia Falco's talents.

Lucia had been with me from the early days eight years ago, when I formed *Milk Money*. Together, she and I nurtured the firm, having started it on a shoestring budget. Today Milk Money was one of *the* most premiere angel investment firms on Wall Street. And Lucia Falco was central to the company's success. She was a beautiful, smart, no nonsense workaholic. When it came to business, we were a lot alike.

"Mico, I have nothing but good things to say about Lucia. She's a wonderful business partner. She keeps me on the straight and narrow. Lucia is the Yin to my Yang. I could not survive without her."

"Yeah, Beauty and the Beast," Mico grunted.

"Just like the POTUS needs a body man, Lucia is my body woman."

"Well somebody needs to keep you in line, Nicky. I suppose it might as well be Lucia," he said casually. "Everywhere I turn, you're in the gossip columns with this heiress or that model."

"Oh, don't believe everything you hear Mico."

"I don't. But I know you. No doubt, most of the gossip is true. You even give the foreign press a workout. Nicky, don't you think it's time to slow your roll?"

"Why should I?" I said, glancing at Mico quizzically.

"Look, I know you've got this whole "I'm not going to commit to any woman" thing going on, but dude, you're forty-one."

"Give it a break, Mico."

"No Nicky, I think it's time you retire that 'playa' card of yours. Get on with it. Settle down. Tie the knot. Make some babies."

"Babies?" I said, choking on my drink. "Good Lord."

"You're Big Willie now. You are on Forbes' list of the top one hundred richest men. You are *the* most eligible bachelor in Manhattan. Quit the shenanigans, man, and settle down," Mico pleaded.

"Jesus man, you're starting to sound like Big Daddy."

The mere thought of my kingpin father brought memories of his recent communication today.

"How so?" Mico said, glancing at his own watch, clearly getting more nervous the closer we got to the cathedral.

"I received a very lengthy voicemail earlier today from Big Daddy. He was dribbling on and on about why I needed a wife and kids. He claimed I need to focus on the family legacy."

"See Nicky, even Big Daddy and I are on the same page."

"Mico, please. You know there has only been one woman that has ever meant anything to me. And, she has managed to walk away with my heart. Matter of fact, she stomped on it, crushed it into a thousand pieces, and beat the heel of her pricey stiletto into it." I sighed and took a big swig of my drink, wondering how the hell things got so messed up between me and her. "And as far as Big Daddy is concerned, he wants me to do what he wants me to do, when he wants it," I babbled. "You know how he is."

"So?" Mico said sharply, shifting nervously in his seat.

"Sooooo, some people respect him, some people fear him. Big Daddy doesn't care which you choose, as long as you stay out of his way and give him what he wants. He forgets that *I'm* not other people. *I* don't have to give into his demands."

"Not the wisest move for you to be getting on the bad side of Big Daddy Blake Ross Becker II," Mico chuckled, putting full emphasis on my father's full name.

"Yeah yeah yeah," I said, waving my hand wildly in the air.

I was ready for this conversation to end. I could hardly deny that my father was starting to put his foot on my neck over my state of singleness.

"Man, you best to get with the program with Big Daddy. I'm not really sure you should be poking that bear, if you know what I mean. How hard can it be Nicky, for you to find a woman and settle down?"

"After Harper, I don't give my heart away anymore. She feels like unfinished business," I said solemnly.

"You've got to start somewhere Nicky."

www.ingramcontent.com/pod-product-compliance
Lightning Source LLC
Chambersburg PA
CBHW061327170626
46817CB00001B/343